The door was not locked, and opened easily. He switched on the light, and Richard followed him into the room.

Nella lay on the bed. She had on the nightdress she had been lent, but the bedclothes had been pulled halfway down. Her head was twisted back grotesquely. There was blood all over her, and one glance showed that she was dead. Black marks on her throat showed that she had been strangled. Her mouth gaped open and her tongue had been cut out. It had been carefully placed in the valley between her naked breasts.

D1122919

BY DENNIS WHEATLEY

NOVELS

The Launching of Roger Brook
The Shadow of Tyburn Tree
The Rising Storm
The Man Who Killed the King
The Dark Secret of Josephine
The Rape of Venice
The Sultan's Daughter
The Wanton Princess
Evil in a Mask
The Ravishing of Lady
   Mary Ware

The Irish Witch
Desperate Measures
The Scarlet Impostor
Faked Passports
The Black Baroness
V for Vengeance
Come Into My Parlour
Traitors' Gate
They Used Dark Forces

The Prisoner in the Mask
The Second Seal
Vendetta in Spain
Three Inquisitive People
The Forbidden Territory
The Devil Rides Out
The Golden Spaniard
Strange Conflict

Codeword—Golden Fleece
Dangerous Inheritance
Gateway to Hell
The Quest of Julian Day
The Sword of Fate
Bill for the Use of a Body

Black August
Contraband
The Island Where Time Stands Still
The White Witch of the South Seas

To the Devil—a Daughter
The Satanist

The Eunuch of Stamboul
The Secret War
The Fabulous Valley
Sixty Days to Live
Such Power is Dangerous
Uncharted Seas
The Man Who Missed the War
The Haunting of Toby Jugg
Star of Ill-Omen
They Found Atlantis
The Ka of Gifford Hillary
Curtain of Fear
Mayhem in Greece
Unholy Crusade
The Strange Story of Linda Lee

SHORT STORIES
Mediterranean Nights
Gunmen, Gallants and Ghosts

HISTORICAL
A Private Life of Charles II (*Illustrated by Frank C. Papé*)
Red Eagle (*The Story of the Russian Revolution*)

AUTOBIOGRAPHICAL
Stranger than Fiction (*War Papers for the Joint Planning Staff*)
Saturdays with Bricks

SATANISM
The Devil and all his Works (*Illustrated in colour*)

Dennis Wheatley

GATEWAY TO
HELL

ARROW BOOKS

Arrow Books Ltd
3 Fitzroy Square, London W1

An imprint of the Hutchinson Publishing Group

London Melbourne Sydney Auckland
Wellington Johannesburg and agencies
throughout the world

First published by
Hutchinson & Co (Publishers) Ltd 1970
Arrow edition June 1972
Second impression August 1972
Third impression June 1974
Fourth impression September 1974
Fifth impression 1975
Sixth impression 1976

© Dennis Wheatley Limited 1970

CONDITIONS OF SALE: This book shall not, by way
of trade or otherwise, be lent, re-sold, hired out or
otherwise circulated without the publisher's prior
consent in any form of binding or cover other than that
in which it is published and without a similar con-
dition being imposed on the subsequent purchaser.
This book is published at a net price and is supplied
subject to the Publishers Association Standard
Conditions of Sale registered under the Restrictive
Trade Practices Act, 1956.

Made and printed in Great Britain
by The Anchor Press Ltd
Tiptree, Essex
ISBN 0 09 905860 X

For those to whom my wife and I owed many years of
happiness and comfort
at
GROVE PLACE, LYMINGTON
Our housekeeper Betty Pigache, her
husband Captain George, and young George
My secretary Kay Turi
Mrs. Shaw and Mrs. Colby
and in the garden
Bob Smith and Joy Ibbetson

Contents

1

No Cause for Celebration

It was New Year's Eve, 1953. Normally the Duke de Richleau would have been occupying a suite at the *Reserve* at Beaulieu; for it was his custom to leave England shortly after Christmas and spend a month or so in the South of France. But this year he had other plans that had temporarily delayed his departure.

Usually, too, Richard Eaton would have been playing host to a carefree party of neighbours down at his ancient and gracious home in Worcestershire, Cardinal's Folly. But his wife—that enchanting pocket Venus, the Princess Marie-Lou, whom he and his friends had brought out of Russia* some years before the war—had had to have an hysterectomy. So, after the Christmas festivities, they had come to London, and Marie-Lou was in King Edward VII Nursing Home, having had the operation four days earlier. Their daughter, Fleur, was about to enter London University, so had been installed in a flat she was to share with two other girl students, and Richard was staying with his friend, Simon Aron.

It was at a pleasant little Georgian house in Pond Street, Hampstead, which Simon had bought shortly after the war, that the three of them had dined that night, and they were still sitting round the table.

Simon and de Richleau delighted in producing for each other epicurean meals and fine wines. The dinner had consisted of smoked cods' roe, beaten up with cream and served hot on toast, after being put under the grill, followed by a *Bisque d'Homard* fortified with sherry, a partridge apiece, stuffed with *foie-gras*, and an iced orange salad laced with crème de menthe. With the roes they had had a glass of very old Madeira, with the soup a Marco-brunner Kabinet '33, with the partridge a Château Latour '28, and with the orange salad a small cup of cold China tea. Now, having cleared their palates with the tea, and as they lit up the eight-inch-long Hoyo de Monter-

* *The Forbidden Territory.*

9

reys which were the Duke's favourite cigars, Simon was giving them an Imperial Tokay of 1908.

Sitting there, they made a very diverse trio who, to a casual observer, would have appeared to have little in common.

De Richleau was in his seventies: a Frenchman who had long since made his home in England and acquired British nationality.* He was of medium height and spare figure. The exercises he did each morning, learned from a Japanese, had kept him in excellent trim and, for his age, his muscles still concealed surprising strength. His lean features were those of a born aristocrat: a broad forehead beneath neatly brushed white hair; a haughty, aquiline nose; firm mouth and chin; grey eyes flecked with yellow which, at times, could flash with piercing brilliance and, above them, upward-slanting 'devil's' eyebrows.

Simon was also slim, with a frailer body and narrow shoulders. His sloping forehead, great beak of a nose and slightly receding chin would have called to mind the head of a bird of prey had it not been for his gentle and often smiling expression. When young he had been afflicted with adenoids, and his parents had neglected to have them removed until his early teens. By then the growth had caused him to keep his full-lipped mouth always a little open, and it was a habit he had never lost. His hair was black, his eyes dark and short-sighted, so that he tended to peer at people, unless he was wearing his spectacles. He was descended from Spanish Jews; but his family had lived in England for many generations and had a high reputation as merchant bankers.

Richard was a typical English country gentleman. In re cent years he had put on weight; but hunting and shooting saved him from a middle-aged spread, and the worst weather never shook his nerve when flying his private aircraft. His eyes were brown, as was his hair which came down to his forehead in a 'widow's peak' with attractive wings of grey above the ears. He had a good, straight nose, a mouth with laughter lines on either side of it, and a chin that suggested that, on occasion, he could be very aggressive.

It was de Richleau who picked up the Tokay bottle, looked at the label and raised an eyebrow. 'By Jove! 1908 *Essence*; the last vintage that old Franz-Joseph thought good enough to have bottled at the Hofberg. What a treat you are giving us, Simon.'

* *The Prisoner in the Mask; Vendetta; The Second Seal.*

'Must have cost you a packet,' added Richard. 'Where did you get it?'

'Justerini's,' Simon replied in his jerky fashion. 'You're right about the stuff costing a packet these days. Still, what's the good of "mun", except for what it'll buy you? Like to give you a toast. Here's luck to all of us in 1953 and—er—specially to old Rex. 'Fraid he needs it.'

His words carried the thoughts of the others to Rex Van Ryn, the great, hulking American with the enormous sense of fun. Before the war he had been the most popular playboy between Paradise Beach in the Bahamas and Juan les Pins, and a record-breaking airman. During the war he had been one of the pilots who, in 1939, had volunteered to fight for Britain, formed the Eagle Squadron and had covered themselves with glory. He was the fourth of that gallant little company, christened by him 'we Modern Musketeers'. In Russia, Spain, the Balkans, the West Indies and many other places, they had adventured together and survived many perils.*

As Simon sipped the thick, richly-scented, honey-coloured wine, his companions followed suit; but his reference to Rex had taken their minds off the wine. De Richleau was recalling Rex's gay dictum about cocktails, 'Never give a guy a large one; make 'em small and drink 'em quick. It takes a fourth to get an appetite.' He looked a question at his host. Richard anxiously voiced it.

'What's this, Simon? You imply that Rex is in trouble. Have you just heard from him?'

'Ner.' Simon shook his bird-like head as he used the negative peculiar to him owing to his failing to close his mouth. 'Not from, but about. Old Rex must be in a muddle—a really nasty muddle. He's embezzled a million dollars.'

'What!' exclaimed Richard. 'I don't believe it. This is some absurd rumour you've picked up in the City. It's the most utter nonsense.'

De Richleau had raised his 'devil's' eyebrows in amazement, and said more slowly, 'It is almost impossible to credit. As we all know, apart from the *nouveau riche* Texan oil kings, the Van Ryns are one of the richest families in the United States. Rex inherited several million from his father, and is one of the biggest stockholders in the Chesapeake Banking and Trust Corporation. What possible reason could he have had for doing such a thing?'

* *The Golden Spaniard; Strange Conflict; Codeword—Golden fleece.*

'Don't know,' Simon shrugged. 'Could have gone haywire and tried to beat the market.'

'No,' de Richleau declared firmly. 'Rex has risked his neck a score of times in making long-distance flights, in battle, and in private ventures when he has been with us. But he has never been a gambler where money is concerned.'

Simon nodded vigorously. 'You're right there. Can only tell you what I've heard. Family is keeping it dark, of course. They'd never prosecute. But we bankers have our special sources—better very often than those of the "cloak and dagger" boys in M.I.6. A fortnight or so ago Rex disappeared, and he made off with a million.'

'He's been in Buenos Aires for the past year or so, hasn't he?' Richard asked. 'Was it from there that he absconded?'

'Umm. The Chesapeake have big interests in South America. You'll recall that, when the old man died, Rex's cousin, Nelson Van Ryn, became President. It was after the war that Rex decided to cease being a playboy and take an active part in the family business. In the autumn of '49, Nelson asked him to take over their South American interests. Good man for the job, Rex. Gets on with everybody. The Latin tycoons were soon eating out of his hand. He made his H.Q. in Buenos Aires, but did a round of Brazil, Chile, Bolivia and the rest. Made excellent connections. Now this. But why? God alone knows.'

Richard took another sip of the Tokay, then said with a worried frown, 'It's past belief. Simply incredible. But I know your intelligence on this sort of thing can be graded A1. And one thing sticks out like a sore thumb. To have chucked everything and made off into the blue with a wad of his bank's funds, Rex must be in very serious trouble.'

'There can be no doubt of that,' de Richleau agreed. 'And I won't be happy until I know that he is out of it.'

Simon's dark eyes flickered from one to the other. Covering his mouth with the hand that held the long cigar, he gave a little titter. 'Yes, Rex must be in a muddle—a really nasty muddle. Felt sure that when I told you about it, you'd agree that it's up to us to get him out. We'll have to take a little trip to South America.'

2

The Search Begins

On January 2nd, Simon and Richard left for New York. Changing aircraft there, they flew down to Rio, changed again and arrived in Buenos Aires on the morning of the 4th. Richard had been reluctant to leave Marie-Lou, but she was sufficiently recovered from her operation to be out of all danger, and had insisted that he should accompany Simon, because it would have seriously upset de Richleau's plans to do so. Now that he was ageing, he found the winter months in England trying, even with a break on the Riviera after Christmas; so he was thinking of making his future home on the sunny island of Corfu. He had been invited out there to stay in the lovely villa of an old friend of his, with a view to buying it, and was loath to forgo this opportunity. He had told the others that he would be back in London by the beginning of February and that, should they by then still have failed to solve the mystery about Rex, he would fly out to help them.

Simon had met Rex's cousin, Nelson Van Ryn, on several occasions and, before leaving England, had had a long conversation with him over the transatlantic telephone. As soon as the President of the Chesapeake Banking and Trust Corporation was made aware that news of Rex's disappearance had reached his English friends, he spoke of that most worrying matter fully, but in guarded terms.

Apart from the mammoth embezzlement, Rex's affairs appeared to be in perfect order. He was, as Simon had believed, very rich and, in recent months, had made no inroads into his fortune. While living in Buenos Aires, his life had been the normal one of a wealthy man moving in the highest circles of American and Argentine society. His health was as robust as ever, and everyone questioned had declared that he had shown no indication that he was a prey to any kind of worry. The loss to the bank had promptly been made good from the family's private funds and, in no circumstances, were the Press to be allowed to know what had occurred. But Nelson had instructed the Pinkerton Agency that, while preserving the strictest secrecy, they were to do everything possible to trace his cousin. So far, half a dozen of that famous firm's 'private eyes' had failed to produce a single clue to Rex's disappearance.

When Simon said that he and Richard were so worried about their old friend that they had decided to fly out to Buenos Aires, on the chance that they might be able to help in the search, Nelson willingly agreed to inform his top man there —a Mr. Harold B. Haag—of their intention, and tell him that he was to withhold nothing from them.

The friends' long, two-day flight was without incident and the last lap ended by landing them at the Buenos Aires airport, at a little after ten o'clock on the morning of the 4th. When they left the Customs hall, they were approached by a tall, fair-haired young man who introduced himself as Silas Wingfield, and said he had been sent by his chief, Mr. Haag, to meet them. He dealt efficiently with the shouting porters and drove his charges away in a huge car, the chromium radiator of which bore a resemblance to the mouth of a grinning Japanese General.

Although not yet mid-morning, it was already very hot and, to the east, a blazing sun was mounting rapidly in a brassy sky. On either side of the broad motorway spread what appeared to be an endless park of undulating grassland, planted here and there with groups of specimen trees. When Richard commented that the city had an unusually beautiful approach, Wingfield replied, 'The quickest route from the airport to the city is real tatty, mainly through slums and shanty towns. This is a few miles longer, but a sight more pleasant.'

After a twenty-minute drive, the park-like land merged into a real park, with palm-lined avenues, playgrounds for children, flower-beds, fountains and benches. At the far end, the park was overlooked by big blocks of luxury flats, behind which was massed the city.

By that time the three occupants of the car were perspiring freely, but they had to endure another twenty minutes' grilling, while being driven right through the great metropolis. At length they reached the far side, where the broad, park-like Plaza San Martin led down to the waterfront. At the landward end, among gnarled, ancient trees, stood the statue of José San Martin, the liberator of the Argentine and, opposite it, the Plaza Hotel. The car drove into a covered courtyard and, gasping with relief, its occupants got out.

The Plaza had the atmosphere of an ancient Ritz. Upon the floor above the street level, a broad, immensely long corridor stretched away from the reception area and, opening off it, there was a whole series of lounges and banqueting rooms of varying sizes. It was strangely silent and almost deserted. Having made certain that their booking was in order, young Wingfield left Richard and Simon to be taken up in a slow but spacious lift to their suite on the sixth floor.

As the comfortable first-class seats in the several aircraft in which they had travelled had enabled them to doze for a good part of their long journey, they were not particularly tired; so they decided that, after refreshing themselves with a bath and changing into lighter clothes, they would lose no time in calling on Mr. Haag.

Shortly before midday, having learned that the bank was only a few blocks away, they decided to walk there; but, before they had covered a hundred yards, regretted it. Not only was it high summer in Buenos Aires but, as they were shortly informed, for some days the city had been afflicted with a heat wave. The sun blazed down with such intensity that, each time they had to step out from the narrow band of shelter on the shady side of the street to let someone pass, or cross the road, the heat hit them like a blast from a furnace.

The marble-pillared hall of the bank was impressive, and beyond it the better part of forty people were working behind a long counter. Although the ceiling was lofty and had slowly-revolving fans, all the men were in shirtsleeves, the women in thin cotton blouses, and the garments of all of them were stained with perspiration.

After a short wait they were taken through to Mr. Harold B. Haag's office. He was a middle-aged, semi-bald, paunchy man and, as his surname implied, of Dutch descent. While shaking hands he said he had received instructions from his President to render them all possible assistance, which he would willingly do. But, when it came to the point, he did little more than shake his head and murmur at frequent intervals, 'A sad business. A very sad business.'

From him they secured only the following basic information. On the morning of Saturday, 16th December, Rex had told Haag that he was negotiating to buy a small ranch from a once-wealthy man who had been nearly ruined by Dictator

Peron's taxation, and was collecting as much cash as he could before leaving the country clandestinely. The price he asked for the ranch was seventy thousand dollars. Rex had said that he was going up-country for the week-end, as he had an appointment to meet this man and conclude the deal on Sunday. That morning he had brought a suitcase with him to the bank. Having cashed a cheque for the seventy thousand, he had opened the suitcase in front of Haag, and put the money into it with his week-end things. He had then said that it would be foolish to risk losing such a considerable sum by leaving the suitcase in the cloakroom of the restaurant where he was lunching, so he would put it in the bank vault and call for it later.

Although overlord of all the Corporation's branches in South America, Rex did not hold the keys to the vaults of any individual bank. They were in the custody of managers and chief cashiers; but it had not even occurred to Haag to refuse the loan of his keys to his chief, who had promised to put them in an envelope, then into the wall safe in his office, to which both of them had the combination.

No irregularity had been suspected until the Monday morning when the vault was opened. Inside, the contents of Rex's week-end suitcase had been found in a heap on the floor. When questioned, the watchman stated that Rex had returned to the bank a little after four o'clock on the Saturday afternoon, spent about twenty minutes in the vault, then relocked it, come upstairs and calmly handed the suitcase to the man to carry out to his Jaguar for him. As Rex was exceptionally large and strong, while he was holding the suitcase it had not appeared to be particularly heavy; but, as the watchman took it from him, its weight had almost wrenched out the poor man's arm. The reason was not far to seek. It must have been packed solidly with banknotes in several currencies. Apart from the seventy thousand for which Rex had given his cheque, it emerged that he had practically cleared out the bank, and had made off with the equivalent of one million one hundred and fifty-two thousand dollars.

To that Haag had nothing to add, and he could suggest no line of enquiry. Moreover, he did not seek to disguise the fact that, as the matter had been put into the hands of professionals, he considered it most unlikely that amateurs would succeed where they had failed; and that Richard and Simon were not only wasting their time but, by poking about, would increase

16

the likelihood of this unsavoury scandal concerning a member of the Van Ryn family becoming common knowledge.

Haag went on to say that he would have liked to offer them lunch; but, unfortunately, was already committed to entertain an important client. However, he hoped that they would give him the pleasure of their company one evening during their stay. While thanking that solid but uninspiring citizen for his invitation, they made mental reservations that only in some unforeseen circumstance would they accept his hospitality. They then secured the address of the apartment Rex had occupied, cashed a considerable sum in travellers' cheques, and took their departure.

Out in the blinding glare of the street, Richard murmured, 'Not a propitious start. D'you think the feller's holding out on us?'

'Ner.' Simon shook his head. 'Typical Dutch-American middle-class mentality. No imagination and puts everyone into categories. You are an effete English "cheque-writer", as they call people with money and no obvious occupation. I'm a Jew. Both of us got an axe to grind. Trying in some way to cash in on old Rex's disappearance.'

Sweating profusely, they returned to the Plaza and found their way to a not very attractive downstairs bar. A surly bar-man could produce no list of drinks and refused to make up Planter's Punches to Richard's specification; so they settled for Rum and fresh limejuice on the rocks. With their drinks there was brought a dish containing a dozen, spoon-shaped pieces of Cheddar cheese, evidently dug out as one does with a Stilton. The flavour of the cheese was delicious, and they soon found that to serve it with all aperitifs was an Argentinian custom.

As they carried their drinks to a leather-covered settee, Simon said in a low voice, 'British not popular here—any-how, not with the lower classes. During the war they made a packet by supplying us with their meat, but since Lease-Lend ceased, we've been in a spot financially, and had to limit our purchases very strictly. Peron is squeezing the rich so unmerci-fully, too, that the big cattle-raisers can no longer afford to maintain herds of the size they used to; so the beef is not on the hoof for other people to buy it, even if we can't. But as for generations we were their best customer, they put the blame for the slump on us.'

'Peron is a disaster,' Richard agreed, having given a cautious

17

look round the nearly empty bar, to make certain no one was close enough to overhear their conversation. 'Before his time, the Argentine was wonderfully prosperous. She was in a fair way to becoming a minor United States, and her chances of doing so were immensely strengthened by Britain having to sell all her assets here during the early years of the war, in order to buy arms from the U.S. Instead, Peron's greed and extravagance is ruining the country. Do you know, I was told by an Argentinian friend of mine that in a basement cold store under his palace Peron keeps over a thousand fur coats, available as hand-outs to any young woman he may fancy. And that was before Eva's death last year.'

Simon tittered. 'Wonder that she stood for that.'

'Oh, come! That type of woman feels no resentment at her husband indulging himself with others. She was interested only in power and endeavouring to raise the masses from the abject poverty which she herself once endured. For that she has my admiration. The tragedy is that she pushed Peron into going the wrong way about it.'

'She was quite a girl,' Simon conceded. 'Even got votes for women, and that can't have been easy in a Latin country. Always thought our people blotted it pretty badly when the Perons were on a visit to London, and the Foreign Office advised against their being received at Buckingham Palace. That slap in the face was one of the high spots in setting the Argentine against us. Whole population resented it intensely.'

By this time it was two o'clock, but South Americans keep Spanish hours, so people were only beginning to filter into the grillroom that was adjacent to the bar. When Richard and Simon went in to lunch, they found the head-waiter much more polite and helpful than the barman; and, advised by him, they enjoyed a very pleasant meal.

Afterwards they began to feel the strain of their two-day journey, so they went up to their rooms, undressed and spent several hours dozing on their beds. At six o'clock they went out again. It was still very hot, but they were relieved to find that a light evening breeze was blowing from the river. A taxi took them to Rex's apartment, which was on the eighth floor of one of the luxury blocks overlooking the park.

The door was opened by a short, thick-set manservant with a swarthy complexion. Simon, who spoke passable Spanish, told him that they were friends of Rex's, and had come to make some inquiries about him.

The man gave him a sullen look and said, '*Señor*, I am tired of answering questions about my master. I have nothing to say that I have not already said to officials from the bank and the American detectives they sent here.'

Simon took out his pocket book, extracted a fifty-*escudo* note and said with a smile, 'Perhaps this will compensate you for your time in repeating to my friend and me what you have said to others.'

Unsmiling, but with a polite little bow, the man took the note and showed them into a large, well-furnished dining room, with a fine view over the park. As they sat down, he closed the door behind him, remained standing near it, and began in a toneless voice to recite what, by this time, must have become a familiar piece to him:

'On the morning of December 16th, my master told me that he was going up-country for the week-end. Contrary to custom, he packed several suitcases. He had me take only one of them down to the car, and drove off to the bank as usual. At about one o'clock he returned. I made for him as usual his Martinis, which he drank out on the balcony while reading *Time* magazine. He then had lunch, eating, as was his custom, a substantial meal. At about half past three he left the apartment. In a little over an hour he returned and collected his other suitcases. I have not seen him since.'

'Thanks,' said Simon. 'Had your master recently been in good health, and his usual cheerful self,'

'Yes, *Señor*. I have never known him ill; and he showed no sign of worry.'

'Had he many visitors during the weeks before his departure?'

'Not more than usual, *Señor*. Once or twice a week he had friends to drinks or dinner. Most evenings he was out being entertained by other people.'

Simon produced another fifty-*escudo* note and laid it on a small table beside him. 'No doubt you could give me the names of your master's closest friends who came here regularly?' The man nodded and, pausing now and then, mentioned a dozen people. Most of them were Americans and only three were women, all of whom had come with their husbands. Simon had taken a slender note pad from his pocket and took down the names. 'Now,' he went on, 'during the first fortnight in December, did any stranger call upon your master?'

'No, *Señor*. No-one.'

'Can you recall any unusual happening whatever, which might account for his disappearance?'

'*Señor*, there is positively nothing more that I can tell you.'

'What staff are there here besides yourself?'

'My wife, who is cook-housekeeper, and a woman who comes in the morning to do the cleaning.'

'Did your master make arrangements for you to receive your wages during his absence?'

'I do not know, *Señor*. They have since been paid by the *Señorita* Miranda.'

Simon's dark eyes gave a sudden flicker of interest, as he repeated, 'The *Señorita* Miranda. Who is she? *Señor* Van Ryn's secretary?'

'No, no, *Señor*. She is his niece, and has been staying here with him since early in November.'

After a moment's silence, Simon remarked, 'I assume that the *Señorita* is not at home, or you would have mentioned it when I told you that we were friends of your master's.'

'She is at home, *Señor*; but she is an invalid and I did not wish her to be bothered unnecessarily.'

Taking a visiting card from his wallet, Simon gave it and the second fifty-*escudo* note to the man and said, 'Please give my card to the *Señorita* and tell her that I am very anxious to see her. I will telephone tomorrow morning to ask if she will receive me.'

There being no more to be said, the two friends left the apartment and went down to the taxi they had hired to take them out there.

As they were driving back to the hotel, Simon gave Richard the gist of the conversation with the servant. When he had done, the latter asked, 'D'you think he was telling the truth?'

'Umm,' Simon nodded. 'I gave him a good sight of the wad of notes I was carrying. If he had had anything really worthwhile to tell, odds are he would have attempted to barter it for money. And it's very unlikely that his wife or the woman who comes in to clean knows anything he doesn't. That's why I didn't bother to ask him to produce his wife. This niece business is puzzling, though. Didn't know Rex had one, did you?'

'I've never heard him speak of one, although I've a vague idea that Nelson has children. On the other hand, it may be a euphemism. It wouldn't be the first time that a well-heeled widower has passed a young mistress off as his niece.'

Simon put his hand to his mouth as he tittered. 'Maybe

you're right. Old Rex has always enjoyed his fun and games. Queer, though, for him to pick on an invalid for his mistress. But my Spanish isn't all that good. It's possible the word I took for invalid really meant ill, or laid up. Woman might be, if she was very fond of Rex, and he's taken a run-out powder on her.'

'Anyhow, he made a jolly neat job of flitting, I must say.'

'He certainly did. And how typical of his sense of humour suddenly to hand the watchman that suitcase stuffed with half a hundredweight of notes, to carry out to his car for him.'

Back at the hotel, Simon telephoned Pinkerton's office in Buenos Aires. He made no mention of Rex, and had no intention of raising the matter of his disappearance with them, since he felt sure they would tell him nothing. He simply gave his name, then read off the list that he had taken of Rex's most frequent guests, and asked that dossiers on them should be furnished him as soon as possible.

Reluctant to have drinks in the uncongenial bar again, they enquired if there was another. The reception clerk told them that, adjacent to it, there was the ladies' bar, which was much frequented by Buenos Aires society, and that they could also have drinks sent up to the roof garden.

Electing for the latter, they went up to the eighth floor in the lift, then walked up two flights of stairs, to emerge on what was euphemistically called the roof garden. It consisted only of three small roofs connected by narrow walkways, a few tubs of sadly-wilted flowering shrubs, a large, ugly water tank which partially blocked the view, and eight or ten garden chairs —a strange adjunct to such a palatial hotel.

Only one couple was sitting on the most distant square of roof, and no waiter was in attendance; but, on the wall in which was the door by which they had come out, there was a telephone and a small service lift. Optimistically, Simon telephoned down for two rums and limejuice, and they sat down to take stock of their surroundings.

On either side of the big water tank, over lower roofs, they could see a number of ships berthed along the docks, and lying off. Beyond them spread the estuary of the mighty River Plate; but it was so broad there that they could not see the further shore and, instead of offering a pleasant seascape, the water was an ugly, muddy yellow.

After a while the lift rattled and the two drinks appeared. A waiter then emerged from the door, to serve them. The great heat of the day was long past, and a gentle breeze from the river now made it pleasant there; so they lingered until the sun began to go down. Then, tired after their active day, they decided to dine in the grillroom and go early to bed.

Before they drifted off to sleep, both of them pondered the mystery they had set out to solve, and both felt a sense of disappointment. They had been confident that, either through Rex's bank or his servants, they would at least learn the reason for his disappearance, if not secure a possible clue to his whereabouts. But they had drawn a complete blank. There was not a single thing to indicate why a rich, sane, healthy banker should suddenly have disappeared with a million dollars.

3

Enter the Crooked Baron

Next morning, when they met in the sitting room of their suite for breakfast, Simon said, 'Can't expect Pinkerton's report on Rex's friends for a while yet, and it's very much on the cards that when it does come in it will tell us nothing. In any case, Rex must have had acquaintances other than the socialites he entertained at his apartment. So we must explore other avenues. Some place where gossip can be picked up would be our best bet; but where such a place would be, I don't know.'

'His club,' suggested Richard. 'It's certain that a man like Rex would belong to the most exclusive club here, and I can find out what that is from a friend of mine. He is an Argentinian diplomat named Carlos Escalente and was for some time *en poste* in London. Of course, he may have been posted elsewhere since his recall; but I think that's unlikely, because he sent me a Christmas card from here. Anyhow, I'll make enquiries at the Foreign Office. If Escalente is still in Buenos Aires, I feel sure he'll help us, should his club be the one to which Rex belonged, by getting me made a temporary member.'

'Good. You do that, then, while I go out and call on the *Señorita* Miranda—that is, if she'll see me. Close on ten o'clock now, so I'll ring up.' As he spoke, Simon went over to the telephone and put through a call. After a brief conversation, he hung up and grinned across at Richard. 'It's O.K. That was the chap we talked to yesterday. The *Señorita* will receive me at twelve o'clock.'

Soon after half past eleven, clad as lightly as decency permitted, Simon again had himself driven in the sizzling heat out to Rex's apartment. The manservant showed him straight into a spacious drawing room, in which the blinds were drawn, shutting out the sun. As his eyes adjusted themselves to the

23

dim light, he found himself facing two women who were sitting side by side on a sofa.

Simon judged one of them to be in her fifties. She was plain, grey-haired, flat-chested and his idea of a typical spinster. The other was at least twenty years younger. She had lustrous, short, dark, curly hair and an excellent figure, but it was obvious that at some time her face had been very badly burned. In spite of plastic surgery, it was a pale mask with the skin drawn tight, and the features slightly distorted in several places. Her eyes were large and blue, but they had a fixed stare that was disconcerting.

It was the younger woman who stood up as Simon entered the room. Taking a couple of paces forward, she extended her hand rather uncertainly and said, 'You must forgive me, Mr. Aron. My sight is so poor that I can hardly see you. But please come in and sit down.'

As Simon took her hand she went on in a low, musical voice, 'I have often heard Uncle Rex speak of you and Mr. Eaton, and if only Pedro had let me know yesterday evening that you were both here, I should have been delighted to see you then.'

'It wasn't exactly his fault,' Simon smiled, 'because, not knowing that you had been staying with Rex, we didn't ask for you. And when that did emerge, we got the impression you were—er—not very well, so could not be disturbed.'

She returned his smile. 'I'm not ill, only rather badly handicapped as a result of a fire several years ago, in which I nearly lost my life; and everyone insists that I must be protected from tiring myself.' Turning her head towards the older woman, she added, 'Dear Pinney, here, is a treasure as a companion, but a positive dragon when she thinks I'm about to overdo things.'

Simon gave a jerky bow to Miss Pinney, to which she responded with a curt nod. Then Miranda said to her, 'Pinney dear, I'm sure you have lots to do, so you can leave me to entertain Mr. Aron.'

With ill-concealed reluctance, the companion left the room. As the door closed behind her, Miranda said, 'You have come, of course, to talk about Uncle Rex's disappearance. How much of the story do you know?'

'Nelson—that's your father, I presume?' She nodded, and Simon went on. 'Nelson instructed the bank manager, Mr. Haag, to keep nothing back from Richard Eaton and me. We saw him yesterday morning and he told us all he could.'

'You do know about the money then?'

24

'Umm. As a matter of fact, being a banker myself, I learned of it through confidential channels in London. That's why Richard and I came out here. Obvious that Rex had got himself into some sort of nasty muddle, and we hoped we might be able to help.'

Miranda's blue eyes remained expressionless, but she smiled. 'That was good of you; yet, after all I've heard from Uncle Rex of his great friendship with you both and the Duke de Richleau, I'm not surprised.'

'Greyeyes, as we all call him, is in Corfu at the moment. He has some rather important business to settle there, otherwise he'd have come with us.'

'I see. Anyway, you do know about the embezzlement. I thought you might. That's why I sent Pinney out of the room. She and the servants know only that Uncle Rex has gone away without leaving an address. I was told by Mr. Haag on my father's instructions, in case I could throw any light on the affair. Unfortunately, I couldn't. But naturally we're anxious that as few people as possible should get to know that Uncle Rex has robbed his own bank.'

'Of course. It's disappointing, though, that you can't put us on to some new line of inquiry. Is there nothing you can think of to do with your uncle's private life that might give us a lead?'

'Not a thing. I arrived here early in November. I suffer from the cold and Uncle Rex suggested that I should spend the winter months with him here, where it is summer. Since I have been here, he's been his perfectly normal, cheerful self. The whole business is an extraordinary mystery. He has masses of money. For him to have become a thief and made off with a suitcase full of notes just does not make sense. At first I refused to believe it; but there's no denying now that that is what he did.'

'Er . . .' Simon hesitated. 'Forgive my asking, but do you know if he was having a love affair, or—er—had a mistress?'

Miranda laughed. 'I don't know for certain, but I'd take a bet that he had. I don't sleep well and on the evenings that he went out I often heard him come in at three or four o'clock in the morning.'

'From his behaviour towards the women who came here to parties and so on, did you suspect that any one of those might be the lady in question?'

'No, I didn't have the opportunity. You see, owing to my—

my disability, I'm not allowed to go to parties. Exposing my eyes to bright light could rob me of the little sight I have left. The small library here has been turned into a sitting room for me and, when Uncle Rex entertained, Pinney and I had our dinner served there.'

'What awful luck you've had. Life must be terribly dull for you.'

She shrugged. 'Things might be worse. At least I have every comfort and distraction that money can buy for me. The first few months were the hardest to bear. There was not only the pain after many operations to make my face a little less revolting . . .'

'It's not revolting,' Simon broke in quickly. 'You're jolly good-looking. Nothing wrong at all, except that the skin is stretched a bit tight here and there. And your eyes are lovely.'

'Thank you. You're very kind. As I was saying, apart from the pain, there were so many things I missed dreadfully. I'd loved dancing, and ski-ing and, of course, I'd had lots of boyfriends. But, after a time, I gradually became resigned. Classical music had been a closed book to me before, but I've come to enjoy it enormously and I have a splendid collection of records for my hi-fi. I can write without effort by touch-typing, and I've become very good at making lace without using my eyes. Pinney reads the newspaper to me every morning, and a lot of books. I thoroughly enjoy my food, too, and fine wine. But that reminds me. I'm being most remiss as a hostess. After the heat outside, you must be dying of thirst. What would you like to drink?'

'Oh . . . thanks. Pretty well anything.'

'I know!' Miranda exclaimed. 'I so seldom have a visitor. We must celebrate. We'll have a bottle of champagne.'

'Suits me,' said Simon with a grin. 'Nothing to beat it at this time of day.'

When the wine was brought, they sat over it for the best part of an hour, talking, laughing and telling each other about their lives. As Simon was about to take his leave, she asked hesitantly, 'Have you an engagement for this evening?'

'Ner,' he shook his head. 'Why?'

'I—I was wondering if you would come and dine with me. I mean, if you wouldn't find it too depressing having to eat in semi-darkness.'

'But I'd love to,' he said quickly. 'It's awfully kind of you to ask me.'

She smiled. 'On the contrary. It's you who will be doing me a favour. Eight o'clock then, and we'll share one or two of Uncle Rex's best bottles.'

When Simon got back to the Plaza, Richard said to him cheerfully, 'Our luck is in. I succeeded in getting hold of Don Carlos Escalente. As I thought might be the case, he is doing a spell at the Foreign Office. The top club here is the Jockey. He is a member, of course, and so is Rex. They are only nodding acquaintances, and he didn't even know that Rex has left Buenos Aires. But he is going to put me up as a temporary member, and introduce me to several men he's seen Rex lunching with. I'm afraid I'll have to desert you tonight, though, because I'm dining at the Jockey with him.'

Simon tittered behind his hand. 'Glad of that, old chap. Otherwise I would be deserting you.' He then told Richard about his visit to Miranda Van Ryn.

After a late lunch and an hour's siesta they decided, as there was nothing more they could do for the time being, to take a stroll and see something of the city. The hall porter told them that the street with the best shops was the *Floredor*, and that it lay only just round the corner.

It proved to be as long and narrow as Bond Street. By a wise decree, no traffic was allowed down it, which was just as well, as the pavements were uneven and wide enough to take only two people abreast. Apart from a few good jewellers', the shops were unimpressive and, in view of the Latin ladies' love of sweet things, it was surprising to find only one good *pâtisserie*. They went into Harrods, which in the old days was said to be famous, but found it to be a very ordinary store in the middle of one of the blocks, and bearing no resemblance to its great parent in London.

On two occasions they turned down side streets, to find, almost immediately, that these nearby narrow ways were shoddy almost to the point of being slums. The shops offered only poor quality goods behind dusty windows, and were interspersed every hundred yards or so by open stalls, carrying piles of fly-blown fruit, cheap *pâtisserie* and glass containers holding highly-coloured, dangerous-looking drinks. Lounging about these stalls, or sitting on the broken pavements, were silent, ill-clad men and bedraggled women, watching with lack-lustre eyes the half-naked children playing in the gutters.

As they made their way back to the hotel, Richard remarked, 'What a tragedy. Old Greyeyes was here for a while round about 1908. I've heard him speak of it as wonderfully prosperous, and the Paris of South America. But now, it's plain to see that, apart from the very rich, the people have barely enough money to support themselves. That greedy devil, Peron, has a lot to answer for.'

That evening he saw the other side of the picture in the luxuriously-furnished Jockey Club. When he arrived, it was already half-full of men whose clothes suggested Savile Row, and elegant women. None of them was in evening dress, but the jewels of the women proclaimed their wealth.

Don Carlos was a jovial, middle-aged man. He came of a long line of aristocrats. One of his ancestors had been sent out by the King of Spain to govern a vast, newly-discovered territory in the Americas. Over drinks he was soon asking Richard a score of questions about their mutual acquaintances in London.

When he enquired the reason for Richard's visit to Buenos Aires and why he was anxious to get in touch with Rex Van Ryn, Richard replied, 'I came on this jaunt partly for pleasure, but also on business. I am travelling with a friend of mine named Simon Aron. He is a banker and had a proposition to put up to Van Ryn, which might have proved most profitable to them both; and, if they do come to an agreement, I'm to be cut in on the deal.'

With a nod, Don Carlos said, 'As I told you over the telephone this morning, Van Ryn is a member here, but only a casual acquaintance of mine, and I have not seen him for some time.'

'That is not surprising. His people tell me that he left Buenos Aires in mid-December, but gave no indication where he was going, and neglected to leave an address to which letters could be forwarded. Presumably he did not want to be troubled with business. It occurred to me, though, that he would be sure to have friends here, and might have mentioned his plans to one of them.'

'It will be a pleasure to help you in any way I can,' Don Carlos smiled. 'For how long do you wish to be a temporary member here?'

'A few days should be ample. If, by the end of that time, I have drawn a blank and Van Ryn has not returned, Aron and I will have to shelve our proposition, as it needs to be acted on with some urgency.'

Don Carlos stood up. 'Come along then. Five days is the

usual period for which temporary membership is granted, but it can be extended. I will take you to our Secretary, and we'll go through the formalities.'

These were soon completed, after which they dined. The largest and most delicious Avocados Richard had ever eaten were followed by the famous Argentine 'baby' beef, then cheese balls of a fairy-like lightness. When they had finished dinner, Don Carlos took his guests up to see the club library. It filled five large rooms on an upper floor, and was said to be the finest in South America.

It was while they were admiring the serried rows of ancient, calf-bound volumes that Richard made the acquaintance of Don Salvador Marino. He was a tall, strikingly-handsome man, who appeared to be in his middle thirties. His hair was dead black and slightly wavy. He wore it full at the sides and, below his ears, it tapered off in close-cut curved whiskers that stood out against his dead-white skin. His eyes, below a pair of haughtily-arched eyebrows, were large and luminous; his nose prominent but delicately shaped, and his mouth must have been envied by many a woman, for the lips were firmly moulded, an almost startlingly natural red and, when open, disclosed two rows of gleaming, white teeth.

As he came into the room, Don Carlos exclaimed, 'Ah! Here is a man I have seen frequently with Van Ryn. Perhaps he can tell us something.'

Introductions followed, and the handsome Don Salvador could not have behaved with greater charm. After hesitating only a second, he readily agreed that he knew Rex well, and expressed his liking for him; but he had not seen him for the best part of a month and could tell Richard nothing about his recent movements.

The three of them went down together in the lift. Over coffee and liqueurs they speculated on why Rex should have left without leaving a forwarding address, and where he might have gone; but none of them could produce a plausible suggestion.

As they were about to part, Don Salvador said to Richard, 'It has just occurred to me that I know one man who might be able to help you locate Van Ryn. He is the Baron von Thumm. During the war he was a high-up Nazi—a *Gruppenführer* in the S.S. I believe—and one of those who succeeded in escaping to South America. Now, of course, he protests that he was always averse to Hitler's policies, and only narrowly escaped

29

arrest for complicity in the Generals' abortive conspiracy to assassinate the Führer. Evidently Van Ryn believed him. In any case, they see a lot of each other, so Van Ryn may well have told him where he intended to go for a holiday.'

'Could you put me in touch with the Baron?' Richard asked.

'Why, yes.' Don Salvador gave his charming smile. 'As you no doubt know, the Jockey has its Country Club a few miles outside Buenos Aires. The Baron is a very keen golfer. As it is Sunday tomorrow, it is almost certain that he will be out there, playing a round or two. I should be delighted if you will both lunch there with me and, with luck, the Baron will be able to give you the information you are seeking.'

Don Carlos had a previous engagement, but Richard eagerly accepted.

Next morning, over breakfast, Simon and Richard gave each other accounts of their previous evenings. Simon had had a most enjoyable dinner with Miranda, and afterwards had spent the best part of two hours listening to recordings of Brahms, Liszt and Beethoven. When Richard told Simon about the Baron von Thumm, his dark eyes showed swift suspicion.

'Queer friend for Rex to make,' he said. 'He's too old a bird to fall for stories about Nazis who at heart were all the time little white lambs and hated Hitler's guts. We may be on to something here.'

A little before midday Richard set off for the Country Club. The drive proved no light ordeal. Thousands of cars were streaming out of the city to the wonderful bathing beaches at Tigre, or inland to shady glades suitable for picnics. For the first few miles the procession moved at a snail's pace. Meanwhile the sun struck down unmercifully on the roof of the car, so that all its metalwork became red-hot to the touch. Fuming with impatience, Richard sweltered in the traffic blocks. At length, the congestion lessened; although not the heat. Dripping with sweat, he was eventually set down in front of the three-block, timbered building of the Jockey Country Club.

Don Salvador gave him a smiling welcome and, apparently impervious to the heat, took him for a short tour of the grounds which far outdid those of similar clubs in Europe. There were four swimming pools, one of which, some way apart from the others, was for the use of the servants. As it was a Sunday, the whole great playground was sprinkled with family parties seated under a sea of gaily-coloured umbrellas,

30

while the children of Buenos Aires' richest citizens chased one another, gave vent to shrill laughter and splashed in the pools.

To Richard's relief, the tour soon ended at the back of the clubhouse, on a shady verandah and, shortly afterwards, he was enjoying a long, cool drink. The verandah gave immediately on to the golf course, and it would have been difficult to find a more beautiful vista. The greensward, undulating away into the distance, had been planted here and there with a wonderful variety of now well-grown specimen trees.

Richard soon found that his host was not only strikingly handsome, but highly intelligent. He had travelled widely, particularly in the United States, having, at one time or another, stayed in every principal city there. He was also well acquainted with every country in Central and South America. Frequently showing his splendid teeth in a flashing smile, he talked with great fluency. Yet, despite his charm, there was something Richard did not like about him. What this something was he found hard to determine, but he decided that it might be the man's arrogance and a certain, undefinable aura of ruthless power.

They were on their second round of drinks when Don Salvador spotted the Baron coming in from his morning round, and called to him to come over.

Von Thumm made a far from attractive figure, owing to serious injuries he had sustained as a result of an aircraft in which he was travelling, towards the end of the war, having been shot down. He was short, broad, ungainly and walked with a limp which caused his left shoulder to stand up permanently higher than his right. In addition, his face was twisted as though he had been the victim of an attack of apoplexy. His right eye and the corner of his mouth below it were both drawn down.

Nevertheless, his misfortune had not lessened his amiability, although he greeted them in a deep, harsh voice. As soon as a drink had been ordered for him, Don Salvador asked if he knew of Rex's whereabouts.

The Baron gave a crooked smile, and replied in very heavily accented English. 'No. Our good friend Van Ryn left Buenos Aires about three weeks ago. For me his departure quite unexpected was. Also for me this causes annoyance. For a good time now, many weeks, he has been a member of the Saturday evening school of poker that I haf. That he fail to turn up leave us one short.'

Don Salvador then explained that Rex's English friends were particularly anxious to get in touch with him about an urgent financial matter, and asked the Baron if he could suggest anyone who might know of Rex's whereabouts.

After a moment, von Thumm said, 'One person only I know that for certain Van Ryn would where he was going haf told. That is Silvia Sinegiest. But she is no longer in Buenos Aires. If to question her you wish, you will haf to make a journey to the end of the world.'

4

Where There's a Will There's a Way

'Silvia Sinegiest?' Richard repeated. 'Wasn't she a film star in the thirties?'

'In two big films she starred, then found it less hard work to marry her producer,' von Thumm gave his crooked smile. 'That was three marriages ago. The name under which she starred she still uses. Since then she makes two marriages and is much talked about. Her last two husbands haf been million-aires. If she married yet again, I think it all odds it would not be a man who had less than a million. Those of only modest fortune—well-known actors, authors and big-game hunters—haf to be content with being her lovers.'

'From what you said, I gather that Van Ryn is a close friend of this woman's?'

With a twisted grin, the Baron nodded. 'Most close. He was crazy about her, and judging by her past record I should be much surprised if his mistress she had not become.'

'In that case, there is certainly a good chance that she knows where he is to be found. But what on earth do you mean by saying that to see her I'll have to go down to the end of the world?'

Don Salvador smiled. 'Von Thumm means Punta Arenas. It is known here as the End of the World, because it is at the extreme tip of Chile, and further south than any other large town. Beautiful women who are free to go where they will, rarely remain in Buenos Aires during December and January. They find the heat-waves such as we are now experiencing too great a tax on their vitality and looks; so they can go down to one of the watering places in the south.'

Richard looked across at the Baron. 'Are you certain that Madame Sinegiest is in Punta Arenas?'

'I make a big bet on it. She is fond of gardening. At present season the flowers there are beautiful. A few years ago she lease a house just outside the town. Since then she spend about six week down there every winter.'

'I thought that part of the world was quite god-forsaken—perpetual ice and snow.'

'So it is during our winter,' said Don Salvador, 'but at this time of the year it can be quite pleasant. Personally I would prefer Rio Gallegos, which is on the Atlantic coast, or Puerto Montt, just over the border in Chile. Those places are somewhat warmer, and there is much more to do in them.'

The Baron nodded agreement. 'Truly so; but, as I haf told you, Silvia Sinegiest has the lease of this house at Punta Arenas. Down to it she went a few days after from Buenos Aires Van Ryn disappeared.'

'Could you give me an introduction to Madame Sinegiest?' Richard enquired.

'With much pleasure. Where do you stay?'

'The Plaza.'

'Very good.' The Baron stood up. 'Tomorrow morning I will send a line round to your hotel. Now you excuse please. I lunch with a friend.'

When he had clicked his heels in the approved German fashion and bowed himself away, Richard thanked Don Salvador for the introduction, then he added, 'I find it surprising that Van Ryn should have made such a close friend of von Thumm. Ever since the war he has displayed a rooted dislike of all Germans.'

'I, too, am surprised that they became intimates,' Don Salvador agreed. 'But they must have had some interest in common. Perhaps it was the Baron's poker school, or Silvia Sinegiest may have acted as a bridge between them.'

After a pleasant lunch, Richard returned to the Plaza, stripped and—an unusual thing for him as he infinitely preferred a proper bath—had a cold shower. He then lay naked on his bed for the siesta hour. When he roused, Simon was still absent and did not appear until close on six o'clock. When he did, Richard asked:

'Where have you been? I was getting quite worried about you.'

Simon replied airily. 'Oh, out to Rex's place. After last night, thought I ought to take his niece a few flowers. She asked me to stay to lunch; so, with you off on your own, I naturally accepted.'

'Visiting the sick, eh?' Richard commented. 'Jolly decent of you. And you didn't run out on the girl after the meal either, or was it that you didn't reach the coffee stage until five o'clock?'

'Owing to her near blindness and poor, scarred face, Miranda leads a lousy life,' Simon countered. 'But I didn't spend the afternoon with her out of charity. Stayed on because I was enjoying myself. She's a fine person. Brave, intelligent and fun to be with. You don't deserve it, but I'm taking you to lunch with her tomorrow. She doesn't normally entertain at all, but she wants to meet you because you're such an old friend of her uncle's.'

'I'll be delighted to meet her,' Richard replied. 'That is, if we are still in Buenos Aires. But if transport is available, we'll be on our way to Punta Arenas.' He then told Simon about the lead he had been given by von Thumm.

Simon agreed that no time must be lost in their endeavours to trace Rex; so they went down to make enquiries about travel facilities to the far south. It soon emerged that they were minimal. Punta Arenas was fourteen hundred miles from Buenos Aires and the railway ran only a quarter of that distance. The last thousand miles had to be covered on horseback, as in many places the tracks through the mountains were too dangerous for cars. The alternative, adopted by the majority of people going there, was a three-day voyage by ship down to the Straits of Magellan. However, it transpired that, during the past year, an intermittent air service had been started, and a small 'plane left each Wednesday, if enough passengers to justify it had booked seats.

Time being important, Simon asked the hall porter to get on to Argentine Airways, book seats for Richard and himself, and say that he would also pay for any seats that might be left vacant, in order to ensure that the 'plane would fly on Wednesday next, the 9th.

That evening they dined at a restaurant where there was a cabaret show. The dancing proved excellent, and there was an amusing mock bull-fight, where two men played the part of the bull and, as a finale, a pretty girl dressed as a matador leapt on the dying bull's back, jabbed it into new life and rode it off the stage. But the show was strictly decorous, owing to Eva Peron's ordinances aimed at eliminating vice spots.

On the Monday morning, as Punta Arenas was just over the Chilean border, they went to the Chilean Consulate to get their passports visaed. On returning to the hotel, they found both

35

von Thumm's promised letter of introduction to Silvia Sine-giest, and Pinkerton's report on Rex's friends. As Simon had feared, the latter proved of no value. All the people Rex had entertained with any frequency were highly respectable, and had no known idiosyncrasies. They then drove out to lunch with Miranda.

On the two previous occasions when Simon had had a meal with her, they had enjoyed it *tête-à-tête*; but that day Miss Pinney was present, to make a fourth, so they kept off the subject of Rex's disappearance. Apart from Miranda's beauti-ful blank eyes, Richard thought her scarred face worse than the description Simon had given of it; but he formed an immediate liking for her, and was filled with admiration at the way she made light of her disability.

As they were leaving, she said to Simon, 'Your coming to Buenos Aires has proved a wonderful tonic for me, and I do want to see as much as I can of you before you fly down to Punta Arenas on Wednesday. Will you come to dinner with me again tonight?'

He shook his head. 'Ner, I'm terribly sorry. I'd love to but I've accepted an invitation to meet Richard's friend, Don Carlos Escalente, and dine with him.'

'Lunch tomorrow then?' she suggested.

He hesitated a moment, then smiled. 'Yes; but on one con-dition. That in the evening you let me take you out to dinner.'

'That is quite impossible,' Miss Pinney broke in. 'It would be most distressing for Miranda to show herself in a restaurant. Besides, the light would be very harmful to her eyes.'

'Nothing's impossible,' Simon retorted firmly, 'and I give my solemn word that she shall neither be embarrassed nor her sight harmed. I've thought of a way to overcome that. Miranda, what do you say?'

She smiled at him. 'How can I not trust you? Yes, I will if you like.'

The party that evening, for which they changed into dinner jackets, proved most enjoyable. It was given by Don Carlos in his own apartment. Like that of Rex, it overlooked the park and was even more luxurious. Being situated on a corner of another of the great blocks, it had two balconies, and it con-tained a fine collection of paintings. *Donna* Escalente was a dark, lovely woman; well read, amusing and vivacious. Richard had known her in London and she showed great delight in seeing him again. The party consisted mainly of diplomats and their wives. A dozen of them sat down to dinner at a table sparkling with crystal glasses and gay with a great centre-piece of tropical flowers. Each delectable course was washed down with wines from the best European vineyards and, out of consideration for Richard, mainly English was spoken throughout the meal.

Afterwards, tactful enquiries by him revealed that several of those present knew Rex, but none of them showed any inkling that there was anything unusual about his absence from Buenos Aires, and supposed that he had gone off on a holiday.

On the Tuesday morning, the two friends woke to the sound of teeming rain. The weather had at last broken, and it was pouring in torrents. Soon after breakfast, Simon said that, in spite of the rain, he must go out, as he had to make certain preparations which would ensure Miranda's having a happy evening. Half an hour later, Richard finished the paperback he was reading; and, although he could have bought another down in the hotel lobby, it occurred to him that he had so far seen very little of South America's largest city, and he might never have another opportunity of exploring it. So he too donned his mackintosh and went out.

A map provided by the hall porter showed him that Buenos Aires consisted of several hundred blocks, divided by parallel streets, so a stranger could not get lost. Two great boulevards, each the best part of a mile in length and about two hundred yards in width, formed a cross in the centre of the city. One was the *Avenida del Mayo* and the other the *Avenida 9th de Julio*.

As the former ran right down to the waterfront, Richard first made his way there, to find, at its end, the handsome Presidential Palace, which was Peron's residence and, on one side of the Plaza on which it faced, a cathedral that looked like a great temple.

Turning about, Richard splashed his way up the wide, tree-lined thoroughfare until he reached the other great boulevard that crossed it. Between the belts of trees lining a huge square, there reared up the tall Radio Tower, and a lofty obelisk. Having made the round of the vast open space along the sides of which there were many cafés and passable shops, he entered the upper section of the *Avenida del Mayo*. At the far end stood the imposing Congress building. From there he walked down several side streets to the *Palais de Justice*, on the corner of the *Plaza Lavalle*: a square made particularly attractive by its great palm trees and huge magnolias. From there he found no difficulty in threading his way back to the Plaza.

He reckoned that he must have walked a good seven miles, and all the time the downpour had never ceased; but the atmosphere was so warm that the rain was almost tepid and he felt no discomfort from it. Having made this tour of the principal streets and squares, he had no desire to stay longer in Buenos Aires, or to return there. Apart from the few fine buildings and blocks of luxury flats that overlooked the park, he had found the city to be shoddy and populated by gloomy-looking, down-at-heel people, which made it depressing.

On his return it occurred to him to make some enquiries about Silvia Sinegiest, so he telephoned Pinkerton's office and got on to the man there who had sent Simon the report about Rex's friends. She was so well known in Buenos Aires that the following information was sent round in less than an hour.

Her age was uncertain; but, as she had made her two films in the mid-nineteen-thirties, it could be assumed that she was at least forty. She had been born an American but was of Swedish extraction. Hers was no case of 'Poor girl makes good'. Her father had been an engineer, and sufficiently well-off to send her to a college of good standing. She had then gone to New York and swiftly became the top model in a leading fashion house. This had given her the entrée to wealthy 'Café Society'. She had not gone to Hollywood; it had come to her, in the person of Gabriele Carriano, the film producer. He had met her in New York, decided that she was star material, taken her back to California with him and groomed her for her new role. For the trouble he had taken he had been well rewarded by her success and, after her second film, he had married her. But evidently life in Hollywood had not appealed to Silvia, as she had parted from her husband a year later, and left the 'Coast', never to return.

Her second husband had been Sir Walter Willersley, the millionaire chairman of one of Britain's largest shipping lines. She had travelled extensively with him and, as his wife, been accepted into English society. The war had put an end to that, presumably pleasant, period of her life. During the greater part of the war she had remained in London, and had been decorated for bravery while driving an ambulance in the blitz. In 1943 she had had an affaire with a Swedish diplomat, which led to her being divorced by Sir Walter.

For some years after the war she had led an unsettled life in

Europe, the United States, Mexico and the Caribbean. Contemptuous of public opinion she had, during that time, lived more or less openly with the pianist Ladoloski, the author Brian Stores and the playwright François Debré. In 1948 she had married again. This time it was the Argentine meat-packing king, Edouardo Varodero. But the marriage had been dissolved eighteen months later and, while remaining based on Buenos Aires, she had resumed her restless existence.

When Simon returned from his lunch with Miranda, Richard told him all this, upon which Simon grinned and remarked, 'This Silvia must be quite a girl.'

'Hardly a girl,' responded Richard. 'She cannot now be far off fifty, but she is undoubtedly a personality. Her wartime record shows that she has guts, and the fact that she does not seek to hide her illicit amours, moral courage. Moreover, while millionaires quite frequently fall for women whose only assets are their looks, for her to have captured men like Stores, Debré and Rex required a considerable degree of intelligence.'

'You're right there,' Simon nodded. 'Rex is certainly not the sort of chap to get all steamed up about a glamour-puss. Wonder if he's making a bid to marry her? Seems her price for getting hitched up is seven figures plus; d'you think he could have pinched that million as part of a campaign to make her Mrs Van Ryn?'

'No, Simon. That doesn't make sense. The money Rex made off with is stolen. Unless he takes a new identity he would be called to account for it, and a woman like Silvia Sinegiest would never be willing to live in secret under a false name. What use would a million be in such circumstances? To enjoy it, they'd have to come out into the open; and that would be impossible as long as Rex is wanted for embezzlement.'

'He's not. Not by the police, anyway. If he does reappear, what could his family do, except grin and bear it? They'd never prosecute.'

'But Rex must have much more than a million dollars of his own.'

'Maybe he has some reason for not wanting to draw on it for the time being, and the lady was impatient. She may have demanded that he settle a million on her before she agreed to become hitched up. If Rex was really bats about her, he could have taken this way to clinch matters, while intending to repay the bank later.'

'That seems a bit far-fetched. Still, I agree that it is a possibility. Anyhow, it looks as though Madame Sinegiest holds the key to our riddle. With luck, we'll get it out of her in a few days' time.'

When Simon was driven out to Rex's apartment that evening, he took with him a jeweller's leather case which, at one time, had contained a necklace supporting a large central pendant. Assuming that Miranda would have no evening dresses, he had not put on a black tie, but he found her in a black cocktail frock, trimmed with beautiful lace that she told him she had made herself. Miss Pinney was with her, radiating intense disapproval; but it was clear that she had failed to persuade Miranda to alter her decision to dine out.

Simon opened the leather case he had brought, and showed them the result of his efforts during the day. He had first gone to a costumier's which stocked every kind of item for hire during the annual carnival, and had bought there a black satin mask with a heavy fringe, and ornamented with diamanté. Next, he had gone to an optician's and bought two glass eyes with blue irises. Taking his purchases to a jeweller, he had asked for the eyes to be cut in half, so that their backs would be flat; that they should then be fitted behind the slits in the mask, and the backs covered with soft material. The result was a blindfold, with eyes in it that no-one would suspect were false, except on close inspection, and with a fringe that would hide the worst of Miranda's scars.

She could see Simon's ingenious present only through the perpetual mist in which she lived; but, when it was explained to her, she was delighted. Not only would her eyes be fully protected and her disfigurement not be apparent, but she would have the fun of knowing that everyone in the restaurant would be wondering who the mysterious masked lady was.

They dined at the *Avenida*. Simon was careful to suggest dishes for her that did not need cutting up, and long practice had made her adept at feeding and drinking without using her eyes. When they finished dinner, he insisted that she should dance with him and, as he was a good dancer, she found no difficulty in following him.

It was close on two in the morning before he saw Miranda home. As he said good night to her in the hall of the apartment, she exclaimed, 'It's been a wonderful evening, absolutely wonderful! I can never thank you enough.'

Smiling, he said, 'For me, too.' Then he put a hand behind her back, drew her quickly to him and kissed her on the lips.

40

She made no effort to resist him, so he pressed his mouth to hers more firmly, and gave her a real lovers' kiss.

Suddenly she broke away, gave a little gulp and burst into a passion of tears.

For a moment he stared at her blind blue eyes from which the tears were running down her scarred cheeks, then he stammered:

'I ... I'm terribly sorry. It was rotten of me to take advantage of you.'

'You haven't,' she sobbed. 'Oh, Simon, dear Simon! It's such ... such a very long time since I've been kissed like that.'

5

The Lady in the Case

Soon after eight o'clock next morning, Richard and Simon drove out to the airport and, at nine o'clock, took off for Punta Arenas. It was an eight-seater, and all but two of the seats were occupied. For most of the journey they flew at about two thousand feet. The first lap down to Bahia Blanca was across the great cattle country: flattish land of an almost uniform colour, on which they occasionally saw a great herd grazing far below. After refuelling, they flew down the coast, at times over it, at others over the sea, with land to be seen only in the distance. When they passed within a few miles of the port of Trelew, they saw that inland from it mountains rose steeply with, in the distance, lofty, snow-covered peaks. Further south they crossed the great Golfo San Jorge, then came down for the second time at Deseado. From there on they flew overland again and, even at the height at which they were flying, they could see that it was wild, hostile country. But, as they approached Punta Arenas, instead of the grandeur of great, rugged mountains falling precipitately to deep green fiords—as they had expected would be the case—the landscape flattened out into barren, undulating plains which stretched as far as the eye could see. Beyond them lay the grey Straits of Magellan, a few miles in width, and the equally unimpressive coast of the great island of Tierra del Fuego.

The airport, like those at which they had come down to refuel, consisted of a few low hangars, grouped round a watch tower and waiting room, manned only when an aircraft was expected. Two aged hire cars carried the passengers and crew along a coast road to the town, which proved to be as disappointing as the landscape. The majority of the buildings had been erected at the turn of the century and were only two storeys high. The long main street, leading to a central square, boasted only the sort of shops to be found in a suburb in which the population was far from wealthy; and the place had the unnatural appearance of a Scandinavian town inhabited by Spaniards. Simon had telegraphed for rooms at the best hotel. It was called the *Cabo de Hornos,* and lay on the seaward side of the square.

To their surprise, they found it, in contrast to the town, not only modern and cheerful, but with a restaurant that was really excellent. Their flight had taken a little over nine hours; so, after freshening themselves up, they had a cocktail, then went in to dinner. As their main course, they selected freshly-caught *bonito* and found it delicious. Now, too, that they were across the border into Chile, they were able to wash it down with a wine greatly superior to those grown in any other South American country.

After they had dined, Richard had the telephone operator put him through to Silvia Sinegiest's house. Having got on to her, he said that he had a letter of introduction from Baron von Thumm, and asked when he might present it.

'If you have made no plans, why not drive out here tomorrow morning?' she replied. 'Say about midday. You will find me in my garden, a much more pleasant place to be in than that dreary town.'

Next morning they learned that her house was some way along the coast, so they hired a car to take them there. As they went out to the car, a blustering wind made them grab their hats. The previous evening it had been blowing hard, but they had thought that to be the after-effects of a storm.

The road ran eastward within sight of the cliff, through bare, inhospitable country unfit for growing crops. Dotted about there were a few small factories and, here and there, barns which were the winter quarters for the flocks of sheep that are almost the only means of support available to the inhabitants of Patagonia.

Although it was high summer, the sky was only a pale blue and the green waters of the Straits were made choppy by the strong, gusty wind. When Simon remarked on it, their driver laughed and said:

'You should come here in winter, *Señor.* A tempest rages almost constantly, for here the currents of both water and air from the Atlantic and the Pacific meet and clash. Even in our best months, the sea is rarely calm, and the wind is always with us.'

After a few miles the car turned up a side road towards a belt of trees on the edge of the cliff. They were not tall, and

43

no roof of a house stood out above them; but, having passed through a gate in an iron fence that enclosed this patch of woodland, a drive descended steeply, revealing an utterly different scene. On the landward side, the trees protected a cove between two headlands that sheltered it from east and west. In the centre stood the house. It was entirely surrounded by a succession of terraces that ran down to the beach, and the whole area was a kaleidoscopic mass of flowers.

As the car pulled up in front of a wooden porch, a woman emerged from a path on its far side, carrying a gardening basket. She was tall, broad-shouldered and carried herself very upright, walking towards them with unstudied grace. Her hair, above a broad forehead, came down in a 'widow's peak', from which it rose in a strawberry-blonde halo several inches deep. She had a regal air and was beautiful in an unusual way. Her mouth was perfectly modelled; her cheeks full, below high cheek bones; her eyebrows well-marked and her eyes bright with the joy of life. She gave them a ravishing smile, that displayed two rows of even teeth, and said in a lilting voice with only a slight American accent:

'Hello! I'm Silvia.'

As she spoke, a small shaggy dog that was pattering along beside her suddenly began a furious barking. 'Be quiet, Booboo!' she chid him. 'Stop it now! D'you hear me?' But evidently inured to such mild reproofs he ignored her and continued his excited yapping.

When, at last, his barks subsided Richard took the hand his mistress extended, bent over it with an old-world courtesy that would have done credit to the Duke, and murmured, 'Madame, my congratulations on having created in this bleak land a small paradise that forms a perfect setting for yourself.'

She gave a ready laugh. 'How nice of you to say that. But I cannot really take the credit for the garden. I only lease this house. It belongs to one of the Grau-Miraflores, whose family practically own Punta Arenas. But I enjoy keeping it in good order.'

As she shook hands with Simon, he said, 'Never seen such lupins. What a riot of colour. Pleasant change, too, to find all the old English flowers here, instead of the exotics one sees everywhere in Buenos Aires.'

Again she gave her dazzling smile as she replied, 'It's that which attracts me to the place. One of my husbands was an Englishman, and I became very fond of England. We had a

44

house in the Cotswolds and, before the war, I had a lovely garden there.'

Her words came as a sharp reminder of the fact that she must be nearly fifty; yet neither of her visitors could believe that. With her bright hair, not even the suggestion of a wrinkle, and tall, sylph-like figure, no-one would have taken her for a day over thirty.

She went on, 'I love people and adore parties, but one can have too much of anything. After burning the candle at both ends during the winter season, I enjoy coming here to vegetate for a few weeks: sleeping a great deal, reading quite a lot and, during the daytime, pottering in the garden.'

Richard smiled. 'Few women are so sensible. They want to be the centre of attraction all the time. But I think you have discovered the secret of perpetual youth.'

Throwing back her head, with its crown of strawberry-blonde hair, she gave a happy laugh. 'Nonsense. I'm an old woman, or at least getting on that way. Anyhow, I'm old enough to have grown-up children. But you must need a drink, so come into the house.'

It was not a large place and far from pretentious. The furniture was mostly good, solid oak, of the type favoured by people of moderate fortune in late Victorian times. As a background for Silvia, it struck Simon as incongruous. Even in the simple clothes she was wearing, she had an air of great elegance, and her height gave her a commanding presence. He felt sure whenever she entered a strange restaurant, the head-waiter would at once single her out for special attention.

They followed her through a dining room to another, larger room which had a big bay window overlooking the cove. Over her shoulder she said, 'I am going to make myself a dry Martini. Would you care to join me?'

Richard shook his head. 'You must forgive me if I refuse. Martinis always give me indigestion.'

'Champagne then?' she suggested, as she opened a corner cupboard that contained a fine array of glasses and assorted drinks. 'I always keep a bottle on the ice.'

'You are very kind. I should enjoy that.'

Simon nodded. 'Me, too, if I may.'

She pressed a bell and a Spanish manservant appeared. to whom she gave the order. While the wine was being brought, she mixed herself an outsize cocktail with professional efficiency. Watching her long, slender hands move with swift precision, Simon grinned and said, 'In the unlikely circumstance of your ever needing a job, you'd make good money as a bartender.'

Her spontaneous laugh came again. 'I was one once for a few weeks, and in a luxury joint that was a very shady spot. But I made it clear that the couch was not in the contract. I've never got into the sack with anyone I didn't care about.'

Richard found her frankness refreshing, and said with a smile, 'Were I not happily married, I should endeavour to make myself one of the men you did care about.'

She gave him a steady, appraising look. 'So, Mr Eaton, you are the faithful kind. That is rather a waste of good material in a man who is so good-looking. We must go into that some time. But not for now. How long do you intend to stay in Punta Arenas, and what do you plan to do?'

'We don't expect to be here for long, as our only purpose in coming to Punta Arenas was to talk to you.' As he spoke, Richard handed her the Baron's letter.

Raising her well-marked eyebrows, she took it. While her man poured the champagne, she glanced at the few lines of writing, then said: 'This is only a formal introduction. Why has Kurt von Thumm sent you to me?'

'Because you are the only person he could think of who might be able to help us.' Richard gestured towards Simon. 'Mr Aron and I are very anxious to get in touch with an old friend of ours. It seems that he has gone off on a holiday, and he's left no address. Von Thumm told us that, before our friend left Buenos Aires, he was seeing a lot of you, so we thought you might be able to tell us where he has gone. His name is Rex Van Ryn.'

'I see.' Silvia's voice had taken on a sharp note. 'And I suppose that ugly little gossip led you to believe that I am Rex's mistress?'

'Were that so,' replied Richard smoothly, 'I should count Rex an extremely lucky fellow, and you a lucky woman.'

She smiled then. 'You are right on both counts. And I am— or, rather, was. I've never seen any reason why a woman should conceal the fact that she has taken a lover—unless it is going to harm the man. To be open about it makes things far easier, and the only people who show disapproval are women who, through circumstances or lack of attraction, are prevented from taking a lover themselves. If they don't want to know me, I couldn't care less. In fact, I'm rather sorry for the poor things.

46

About Rex, though, I don't know what to say. He had a very good reason for going off on his own, and I'm certain that he does not want his whereabouts known.'

'Thought as much,' Simon put in quickly. 'But he told you where he was going?'

'I did not say so.'

'But you implied it. And we've got to find him.'

'I'm sure he would rather that you didn't.'

'Don't want to seem rude, but you're wrong about that. Richard Eaton and I are Rex's best friends. Rex is in a muddle. We're certain of it, and we've come all the way from England to help him out. Now, please tell us where he's got to.'

She shook her head. 'What proof have I that you are his friends? Even if I were sure of that, and did know where Rex is, I wouldn't tell you, because you might lead others to him. And, as you are right about his being in trouble, I could not risk making his situation worse than it is.'

'Do you know what sort of trouble Rex is in?' asked Richard.

She looked away from him, and lit a cigarette. 'Yes, I know. But I'm not prepared to discuss it.'

'It's clear that Rex has gone into hiding, and one of the things that worries us is that he may have had to leave in a hurry. If so, it is possible that he is leading a grim life somewhere up-country and is desperately short of money.'

This subtle approach by Richard proved abortive. Either she was unaware that Rex had absconded with a million; or, if she knew it, did not mean to give away the fact. With a shrug of her shoulders, she replied: 'I don't think you need worry about that. Rex is a rich man, and he would not have been such a fool as to take off without having cashed a fat cheque.'

'Perhaps,' Richard hazarded, 'you will at least tell us when you last saw him?'

'On the night before he left Buenos Aires. As a matter of fact, we had quarrelled. He was very upset by what had happened, and so anxious to make it up before leaving that he came to see me at three in the morning. Of course, my servants were used to his coming and going at all hours, so they thought nothing of it. He stayed for only twenty minutes. I forgave him for . . . well, that is no concern of yours . . . and that's the last I saw of him.'

She had been sitting in a low chair, with one knee crossed over the other, and the thought drifted through Simon's mind that he had never seen a more perfect pair of legs. His glance

47

was inoffensive, but she evidently became aware of it, for she pulled down her skirt and came to her feet. Picking up the bottle of champagne, she refilled their glasses and said:

'I do understand how worried you must be about your friend. But I really don't feel that I would be justified in telling you any more than I have. At least, not until I've thought it over very carefully.'

'It's good of you to go that far,' Richard said quickly. 'When may we hope to learn your decision?'

For a moment she remained thoughtful, then she replied, 'There's not a thing for you to do in Punta Arenas, so come and dine with me tonight. When I'm down here I rarely entertain. It's an opportunity for me to slim and catch up on my sleep; but it would be a pleasant change to have a little dinner party. Presently I'll ring up a few people I know. But don't order your car to pick you up until half past eleven. By then the others will have gone and, if I decide to talk, we'll be on our own.'

Her two visitors gladly accepted. When they had finished their wine, she took them for a walk round the upper part of the garden. Only Alpine flowers were growing there, but there was an amazing variety of sub-Arctic shrubs and trees. Then she gaily waved them away in their car.

As it carried them towards the town, Richard said, 'I wouldn't mind betting that she knows about Rex's having robbed his bank, what led him to do so and where he is at the moment.'

'Don't wonder he fell for her,' Simon remarked.

'Yes; she's a quite exceptional woman and, on the face of it, a very nice one. I had expected her to be completely different: vain, spoilt from having too much money, and hard as nails.'

After a late lunch, they put on their overcoats and went for a walk round the town. Having driven through the eastern side, they turned west and, at the end of the roughly-paved streets that led seaward, they caught glimpses of the dock. It was no more than a wharf, with piers projecting from it and lying off there were a few rusty steamers. The wind had never ceased blowing hard enough to make the skirts of their overcoats flap and force their trousers hard against their legs; so they gave up and hurried back to the warm comfort of the hotel.

So far south it was still broad daylight when they drove out again to Silvia Sinegiest's retreat. Booboo was with her and again barked furiously, but evidently without animosity. His

48

small black eyes gleaming between the hair of his long fringe, he ran round them in circles to work off his excitement.

Besides themselves, the party consisted only of the American Consul and his wife, and a member of the Grau-Miraflores' family. They were not surprised to find that, in such a distant outpost, where commercial activities were limited, the Consul was no ball of fire, and that his wife's conversation consisted largely of nostalgic references to the much pleasanter life she had led in her own small home town. But *Señor* Pepe Grau-Miraflores proved interesting.

His family was a large one. For several generations they had owned a good part of Punta Arenas and vast sheep farms in Patagonia. They had also developed many other interests in the Argentine and Chile. He was a cheerful man and showed no pessimism about the future prospects of his own family, who were in a position to increase their wealth from industry; but he spoke with deep concern of the smaller sheep farmers, for whom he foresaw a time when, although few of them yet realised it, the new synthetic fabrics, such as nylon, would make wool a drug on the market.

Silvia proved an admirable hostess. She drew her American compatriots out to talk about their children and hopes of a more congenial post, surprised Simon by showing a shrewd knowledge of stocks and shares, reminisced with Richard about Ascot and Goodwood, exchanged witticisms with Grau-Miraflores, laughed a lot and saw to it that their glasses were never empty.

At about a quarter to eleven, the party began to break up and Grau-Miraflores offered Richard and Simon a lift back into Punta Arenas; but they told him that they had a car coming for them.

When the others had gone, Silvia ordered her houseman to bring another bottle of champagne. While he was fetching it, she said, 'I hope you weren't too bored with the Consul and his dreary wife; but I've deliberately discouraged the advances of the majority of the locals and they were the best I could produce at such short notice.'

Her guests politely murmured their understanding, while both of them waited with concealed impatience to learn whether she had decided to tell them about Rex. She had been chain-smoking all the evening. As the houseman left the room, she lit another cigarette and said:

'Well, I've thought things over and it has occurred to me

49

that if I don't tell you why Rex left Buenos Aires, you will continue your efforts to find him; and that could bring him into grave danger. In a way I am responsible for the trouble he is in, so I feel badly about it; although, of course, I had no idea that our quarrel would have the results it did.'

She paused and sat staring down into her glass for so long that Richard decided to prompt her, and asked gently, 'What was the cause of your quarrel?'

Still looking down she replied, 'I found out that he was having an affair with another woman. I wouldn't have minded in the ordinary way, provided I remained first in his affections. After all, men are made like that. It's quite natural that they should want to get in the sack with any pretty girl who shows willing and, thank God, I've never been cursed with jealousy. But this woman was a Negress, and the idea of having him in my bed after he had been in hers revolted me. I told him that either he must give her up, or I'd have no more to do with him.'

'How did he react to that?'

'He swore he loved only me, and promised not to see her again. But he didn't keep his promise. She must have had some hold over him. What it was, I have no idea, but he freed himself of it in the most terrible fashion.'

'In what way terrible?' Richard enquired anxiously.

'He murdered her.'

Simon's eyes widened, and he clapped a hand over his mouth to suppress an exclamation of horror. Richard caught his breath; then, with an effort, keeping his voice to the same low tone, he asked: 'Are you sure?'

'Yes. He told me so on that Friday night, the last time I saw him. He said he could not bear to give me up, so he had gone to see her and told her that he had finished with her. She threatened him. They had a most ghastly row. He hit her. You know how strong he is. His fist caught her beneath the chin and jerked her head back so violently that it broke her neck.'

'So that is why he left Buenos Aires. Are the police after him? Did they come and question you?'

'No. But they may. I have reason to believe that I am being watched. It is quite possible that they are hoping that I will lead them to him.'

'I see. And that is why you are anxious that Aron and I should not try to find him?'

'Yes. Since you have been making enquiries about him in B.A., they may have learned of that. If so, they will have put a tail on you too.'

'If they know that he killed this woman, or suspect him of having done so, it's strange that they've not set on foot a public enquiry, published his photograph in the papers and that sort of thing.'

'Their line may be to lure him into a false sense of security, hoping that he will return and that they can then pounce on him.'

'That's possible. Do you think anyone other than you knows that he committed this crime—members of the woman's family, for instance?'

'I have no idea.'

'If they do, that could account for Rex's having taken such a huge sum from his bank. He could dole instalments to them, to buy their continued silence.'

'Before he left me, I asked him if he had any money, and offered him my jewels. He said he could get all the money he needed; but I did not know that he meant to take a specially large sum. Perhaps he felt that his only chance of remaining free permanently would be to change his identity. If he did that to live in any comfort he would need capital.'

'I hope that is the explanation, and not that he expected to have to pay blackmailers.'

As Richard was speaking, a telephone began to shrill somewhere in the house. After a moment he said to Silvia, 'We can only pray that by this time Rex is out of the country. Is it really true that you have no idea where he meant to head for?'

She nodded. 'Our talk on that awful night was very hurried, and he told me only that he must get out as soon as he had collected some money.'

At that moment there came a quick knock at the door, and it was opened by the manservant, who said, 'I am sorry to disturb you, *Señora*. You are wanted on the telephone. It is the Baron von Thumm calling you from Buenos Aires.'

Coming to her feet, Silvia stubbed out her cigarette, looked first at Richard then at Simon and said, 'I'm sorry. This is a private call. Please excuse me if I take it up in my bedroom.'

As the door closed behind her, Simon said in a low voice, 'Don't believe it. Don't believe a word of it. Never known Rex to lose his head. He's well aware of his great strength. If he did hit that Negress, he'd never have bashed her with a

51

pile-driver like that. Not in his character either to go off the deep end and commit unpremeditated murder.'

Richard nodded. 'I agree. Of course, like us, he has killed before, when it has been a matter of necessity. But even if he was berserk about our charming hostess he would not have done in the other woman. However big her price, he could have afforded to buy her off. And there is more to it than that. Rex's family come from the deep South. In the old days his ancestors would have taken Negresses as their concubines; but not in these days. Like most Southern whites, he'd have a prejudice against coloured women.'

These exchanges had taken no more than a minute. Smiling at Richard, Simon said, 'Now going to behave like a cad. But where helping one's friends is concerned, end justifies the means.' Walking over to the telephone, he picked up the receiver.

Silvia and the Baron had just greeted each other, and the Baron asked her, 'How go things with you down there?'

'Couldn't be better,' she replied. 'But I wish you hadn't called me until tomorrow. Both of them are still here. They came this morning before lunch. I led them to suppose that I knew where Van Ryn was, but refused to tell, then invited them to dinner with the bait that I might be persuaded to change my mind.' She gave a quick laugh and went on, 'I had no trouble selling them our story, that Van Ryn was on the run because he committed murder. I made it very clear, too, that, if they continued to try to find him and succeeded, it was likely they would lead the police to him, and so put him on the spot. They'll not dare risk doing that, so we've no need to fear they will give us any further trouble.'

'Well done,' the Baron chuckled. 'Well done. The Prince, he will be most pleased with you.'

'Will he attend the barbecue at Santiago?' she asked.

'I think not,' came the reply. 'If not, for him I shall deputise. I look forward to see you there, this night next week.'

They said good-bye, then Silvia rang off. Simon replaced his receiver, looked across at Richard and said earnestly:

'Whole affair now stinks of conspiracy. Our charming hostess lied in her lovely teeth. Von Thumm concocted with her a pretty little plot. Could have pulled the wool over our eyes. But now we've found them out, advantage lies with us. They know where Rex is. Bet my shirt on that. And she's going to lead us to him.'

6

The Search for the Barbecue

When Silvia returned to the room, she again apologised for leaving them. 'I'm so sorry. That was von Thumm. He was ringing up to know whether you had been here and if I had been able to tell you anything about Rex; because, apparently, he too would like to get in touch with him. I could quite well have taken the call here, but I just didn't think. I'm so used to nattering over the 'phone up in my bedroom.'

Richard and Simon had both stood up as she came in. The former said, 'Oh, don't mention it. But while you were on the telephone, I heard our car drive up; so I think we ought to be going.'

Her perfect teeth flashed in a smile, and she held out her hand. 'It was a pleasure to have you both. You must come again.'

'We should love to, if we were held up for a few days before we can get a flight back to Buenos Aires. But you were our last chance of tracing Rex. After what you've told us, it seems that there is no alternative to abandoning our quest. Apart from your delightful retreat here, I can't say I find this part of the world attractive. Such time as Aron and I can continue to give away from England I feel we should devote to visiting some of the Argentine's real beauty spots.'

'Then don't miss the Iguazu Falls,' she advised them. 'They are the biggest in the world, and in the middle of a jungle that abounds in wild life, orchids and birds with the most lovely plumage.'

Having thanked her for a most pleasant evening, they took their leave. While their car drove off, they turned to wave to her as she stood framed in the lighted doorway of the house, a tall, elegant figure, crowned by a mass of bright hair.

On the way back, as their driver understood a little English, they refrained from discussing what had transpired. Shortly before midnight they reached the *Cabo de Hornos*, to find that, in keeping with Spanish hours, a number of people were still sitting about the lounge, chatting and drinking. Ordering brandies and soda, they sat down in a quiet corner.

'Now,' said Richard, 'I can't wait to hear what you found out about the tie-up between Silvia and the Baron.'

Simon told him what they had said to each other over the telephone, and added, 'What a break, eh? Knew she was lying; but what a lovely liar. Don't wonder old Rex fell for her.'

'Nor I,' Richard agreed. 'Apart from that marvellous figure, she's not a beauty; but she has tremendous personality and no-one would credit that she is a day over thirty. It would be difficult to imagine a more delightful companion to spend care-free hours with.'

'She's on the other side, though, and covering up for some-one. What d'you make of it?'

'Your guess is as good as mine. This story that Rex has disappeared because he was afraid that he might be arrested for murder is no more real than a red herring designed to induce us to give up the search for him.'

'Ummm. It's clear that they're anxious to put an end to our snooping. But not so certain that Rex hasn't done someone in. Story about his having an affaire with a Negress is a phoney. I'd take a big gamble on that. Couldn't have a better reason for quitting B.A. in a hurry than having committed murder, though.'

'True. And if there are people who could fix it on him, that would account for his having absconded with so much money.'

'Doesn't quite add up,' Simon remarked thoughtfully. 'As he was rich enough to silence blackmailers, why shouldn't he have stayed put in Buenos Aires?'

'He might not have been able to buy off the police if they were after him, and he may have believed they were.'

'D'you believe that?'

'No, I don't. If they were, it's certain that Pinkerton's people would have known. They would have reported it to that bank manager feller, Haag; and he had received orders to conceal nothing from us. So, cagey as he was, he would not have dared keep us in the dark about Rex's being suspected of murder.'

'Exactly.' Simon gave a quick nod. 'So there's no fear of our leading the police to him.'

'To my mind, not the least. So in the morning I think we should make enquiries about an aircraft to get us up to Santiago. God knows what sort of service, if any, there is from this benighted spot. But, fortunately, Silvia's date with the Baron is not for another seven days. So, if the worst comes to the worst, there should still be time for us to fly back to B. A., then across the Andes to Santiago. There must be a regular service between the two capitals.'

On the Wednesday morning, Simon made enquiries at the hotel desk. He learned that, as was the case between Buenos Aires and Punta Arenas, there was, given sufficient bookings, a weekly service up to Santiago, but it flew only on Mondays. The information perturbed him considerably, since it not only meant that they would have to kick their heels in bleak Punta Arenas for another five days, but it would give them only a single day in Santiago to try to find out where the barbecue was that Silvia and the Baron were to attend. He was just wondering if it would be possible to hire a private aircraft to take them up, when a voice behind him said:

'Good morning, Mr Aron. I gather you are going up to Santiago. Have you urgent business there?'

Turning, Simon found Pepe Grau-Miraflores at his elbow. Giving a mock shiver, he replied, 'Ner, constant wind here makes this a place to stay in no longer than one has to, though. Richard Eaton and I want to leave for the north as soon as we can, to get some sunshine.'

Grau-Miraflores smiled. 'Then, may I suggest that you fly up with me in my private aircraft? It would take a couple of days, as I have an engagement in Puerto Montt tomorrow, and intend to spend the following night at my *fonda* on the river Laja. But at least I'll get you to Santiago by Friday; three days before you could get there by the weekly service.'

Simon eagerly accepted this kind offer and agreed to be ready to leave the hotel by eleven o'clock. But when he told Richard of the arrangement, his friend said with a slight frown:

'I wonder if this is altogether wise? Grau-Miraflores is a close friend of the Sinegiest woman, and she is an enemy. Our going with him could keep her informed of our movements. There is also just a chance that if we spend a night at this *fonda* of his, he might stage an "accident" that would put us out of the game for good.'

'Ummm. You're right. Hadn't thought of that. Best perhaps to back out.'

'No. I don't think we'll do that. Such situations cut both ways, and he can't know that we are wise to the lady's having attempted to double-cross us. If he is in cahoots with her, we may be able to jolly him into unwittingly giving us some useful information. In any case, we're going to have our work cut out to learn whereabouts in Santiago this barbecue is to be held. We'll need more than a day to do that; so we'd better risk it.'

Simon then endeavoured to telephone Miranda; but, on learning that there would be a delay of at least three hours in getting through to Buenos Aires, he sent her a telegram, letting her know that he and Richard were going to Santiago, where they would be staying at the new Carrera Hilton Hotel. He sent another telegram to the Hilton, booking a suite as from the coming Friday.

On their drive out to the airstrip, they learned considerably more about their host. His family was one of the richest in southern South America. Not only were they the potentates of Punta Arenas, but they owned great estates on both coasts, and the interior of the peninsular, which they had acquired before the boundary between Argentina and Chile had been settled.

The aircraft, an ex-fighter bomber from the war, had been converted into a comfortable four-seater, and its German pilot was an ex-officer of the Luftwaffe. At midday they started on their flight up the lower part of Chile, a country made unique by its geographical situation and isolation from the rest of the world.

Chile is as long as from northern Norway to southern Spain. Yet, in one place it is only twenty miles in breadth. The Andes— that vast range of eternally snow-crowned mountains with, apart from the Himalayas, some of the loftiest peaks in the world—cut the country off from its neighbours to the east. Trackless, and still largely unexplored, few men and no commerce could possibly cross the barrier and reach Chile from Europe or Africa until the coming of the recent age of air travel. For many centuries, Chile's ports on the Pacific formed almost her sole contact with civilisation.

Yet Chile, alone of all the countries of the world, has everything that is both bad and good. In the far south the land is broken up into innumerable islands, snow-covered for the greater part of the year: barren, inhospitable, a prey to terrible storms and a thousand swift, dangerous currents. In the far north, there are vast areas of uninhabitable desert, bitterly cold at night and scorched by unbearable heat during the day. But the greater part of central Chile provides everything men could wish for. From the mild climate and green fields of an

English spring, it progresses through warmer regions with Mediterranean beaches and sunny vineyards to a land of palms and tropical fruit, an abundance of flowers and trees garlanded with orchids. The many lakes and rivers abound in fish, fine herds of cattle graze on the undulating downs, birds with gorgeous plumage flit through the twilit forests and, from every township, the mountains with their snow-covered slopes offering the pleasures of winter sports could be seen in the distance against a bright blue sky.

That day they flew for several hours at only a few miles' distance from the great chain of lofty, forest-covered mountains that ran down to an archipelago consisting of many hundred islands great and small. Only the larger ones showed any sign of habitation: little clusters of primitive buildings nestling beneath the lee of cliffs that sheltered a few fishing smacks. In many places where the channels were narrow, conflicting currents churned the sea into a mass of boiling foam, and great waves broke furiously on the jagged rocks, tossing the white spray high into the air. From time to time, Grau-Miraflores pointed out to his passengers places, the names of which indicated the almost incredible grimness of this stretch of coast: Gulf of Sorrows, Ice-water Valley, Hill of Anguish, Last Hope Sound.

Well on in the afternoon they landed at Puerto Montt and, on driving into the town, found it very different from Punta Arenas. Here, six hundred miles further north, the air had the balminess of spring, and the strolling crowds on the esplanade showed it to be a popular holiday resort. Actually, it was some distance from the Pacific, but it gave the impression of looking out on an ocean, dotted in the distance with islands.

The hotel to which Grau-Miraflores had telephoned for rooms had a gay, modern décor and, in the evening, the dance floor was crowded with young people. For dinner their host gave them *Cazuela de Ave,* a delicious soup, conger-eel and, as a savoury, cheese pies. They washed down the meal with an excellent white wine called *Savereo.*

Over the meal, Grau-Miraflores talked to them about Chile and how, owing to its isolation, it differed greatly from all other South American countries. Its earliest inhabitants had been the Araucanian Indians, the most fierce and brave of all the races in the southern continent. Even the splendidly-trained armies of the mighty Inca Empire had proved no match for them, and penetrated only the northern part of the country.

57

Then, early in the sixteenth century, had come the Spanish Conquistadores. But, as the land had no gold or silver, they had scorned it. Pizzaro, the brutal conqueror of Peru, had given Chile as a sop to his partner, Diego de Almagro, whom he had consistently cheated.

For many years Spanish settlements had been few and far between; so, although Spain's law and language had been generally accepted by the white and half-caste population, a very high proportion of the Europeans who had colonised Chile in the eighteenth and nineteenth centuries had been Italians, Irish, Germans, Scots, English, French and Dutch, with the result that inter-marriage had produced a people more broad-minded, vigorous and business-like than in the countries shackled more closely to Spain.

Next morning, while Grau-Miraflores went about his business, Richard and Simon strolled round the town. At the eastern end of the waterfront there was a large street market with, below it on the beach, a fish market the like of which they had never seen. The stalls were actually in the sea. Rowing boats brought their catch right up to them. The fishermen un-loaded the still-flapping fish and wriggling squids directly on to the counters, behind which the colourfully-dressed fishwives stood up to their knees in water. There could be no better guar-antee that the fish they sold were fresh. Some customers waded out in gum boots to take their pick of the best, while others waited ashore until the tide went down sufficiently for them to make their purchases dryshod.

Simon eyed the fresh-caught lobsters with a gourmet's delight, hoping that he might enjoy one for lunch. He was not disappointed, although he did not eat it in Puerto Montt. At midday, after they had rejoined Grau-Miraflores, the latter took them in a car to the airport. As they boarded his 'plane, he said:

'I am taking you for lunch to the island of Chiloe. You can see it over there to the south-west. It is Chile's largest island, over a hundred miles long, and the best lobsters in the world are caught off its shores.'

A quarter of an hour later, they landed at the little town of Castro and, after a most succulent feast, flew north once more, heading for their host's *fonda* on the river Laja.

This second stage of their journey was even more fascinating than the first, as they flew low over Chile's two largest lakes, Villarrica and Llanquihue. The mountains on their right.

many of which retained their snow caps all the year round, made the scene reminiscent of Switzerland, and here the country broadened out, with many rivers running towards the now distant sea. As they progressed, villages and towns became more frequent, and the land green with crops between easily discernible roads. They were entering Chile's fertile seven-hundred-mile-long central valley, in which grazed herds of cattle; and, at five o'clock, put down on their host's private landing strip.

They were met by the manager of the *fonda*, a young Australian, who took them to the house in a jeep. The country, with its fields, flourishing vegetation and mild climate, might have been England, but the *fonda* itself bore no resemblance to an English country house. The garden was gay with daisies, geraniums, cannas and roses, partially shaded by magnolia and chestnut trees; but it had not been laid out to any plan. The house stood a hundred yards or so from the picturesque, rock-strewn river, but had no view of it or the country on the landward side. It was not a large building, and was sparsely furnished, but there was an air of cheerful activity about the place, and they all enjoyed a plain, well-cooked dinner.

Soon after they had gone up to bed, Simon went to Richard's room, sat himself down and asked, 'What do you make of Grau-Miraflores?'

'A charming and intelligent man,' replied Richard.

'I mean, d'you think he's mixed up in this muddle about Rex?'

'No. I asked him casually whether he knew a club in Santiago called the "Barbecue", and he said he'd never heard of it.'

'That doesn't mean a thing. If there's anything fishy about the place, he wouldn't admit to knowing it anyway.'

'Not if he was in this racket and had been given the job of bear-leading us. But I don't believe that to be the case.'

'It was your idea that he'd suggested taking us in his aircraft in order to keep tabs on us.'

'I agree I thought that a possibility. But on closer acquaintance, I think I was wrong. I've laid little traps for him several times and he's not fallen into one of them. I'm convinced now that the beautiful Silvia is no more than an acquaintance of his, and that he knows nothing about Rex. He is simply a cultured and generous South American who delights in showing visitors the beauties of his part of the world.'

Simon nodded. 'Hope you're right. Still worries me that

we've so little to go on in our hunt for Rex. Wonder if we're correct in assuming that our lady friend's mention of a barbecue did refer to a club?'

'You told me she said "The" barbecue, and that sounds like a club. But quite possibly it is a meeting in a private house.'

''Damn' difficult to locate if that is the case.'

'True. Remember, though, that our glamorous strawberry-blonde is coming to Santiago for the party. She did not strike me as a lady given to hiding her light under a bushel. With a little luck we should be able to find out where she is staying, and have her kept under observation.'

'Or make her talk,' Simon said thoughtfully. 'Never been much good at that sort of thing myself. But you and old Greyeyes didn't give a second thought to sticking a knife into anyone's ribs until he decides that if he wants to live he'd better do what you tell him.'

Richard laughed. 'Simon, Simon; what ogres you make de Richleau and me out to be. Personally I've always found it most distasteful to inflict physical suffering on people. But, if the interests of one's country or a friend's safety are at stake, one can't afford to be squeamish.'

Their host spent the greater part of the next day riding round the estate with his manager. Richard accompanied them; but Simon never mounted a horse unless he positively had to, so he stayed behind and, with an Indian to pole him some way up stream in a punt, spent several hours fishing. In consequence, it was late in the afternoon when they again boarded the aircraft.

The evening light gave a new beauty to the landscape as the shadows lengthened and, twice during their flight, their pilot made detours to fly them down to within a hundred feet of and right round the craters of active volcanoes. Dusk was falling by the time they were over Santiago airport, so on coming in to land, they saw the myriad lights of the city. Half an hour's drive took them into it and Grau-Miraflores set them down at the Carrera Hilton.

He refused their invitation to dine with them, because he already had a dinner engagement with one of his brothers, in whose house he was staying the night. He was then flying on to Buenos Aires the following afternoon. With hopes that they would meet again, they thanked him warmly for having enabled them to see so much of Chile; then, smiling and waving, he was driven away.

They had been given a suite on the tenth floor of the hotel and, on a table in the sitting room, stood a big bowl of tuber-roses.

'Very generous of the management, I must say,' Richard remarked; but Simon had spotted an envelope attached to the stem of one of the flowers. It was addressed to himself. On opening it he found it contained a note from Miranda. She said that, on receiving his telegram, she had decided to join him in Santiago and, accompanied by Pinney, she had flown in that day. The few lines ended, *Only the blindfold mask you gave me has made this possible. It has opened a new life for me. Bless you, dear Simon.* It then gave the number of her suite.

Simon's dark eyes flickered towards Richard, and he came as near to blushing as his sallow skin would permit, as he said awkwardly, 'They're from Miranda. Er—jolly decent of her, isn't it? She's here. Flown across from B.A.'

'Well! Well!' Richard roared with laughter. 'When girls start sending men flowers, wonders will never cease.' But Simon had already picked up the telephone and was asking for Miranda's number. She and Pinney were just about to go down to dinner, so she said they would wait in the cocktail lounge until Simon and Richard had freshened themselves up, then they could all dine together.

At this hour they found the Elizabethan cocktail lounge on the ground floor of the Hilton crowded; but the intriguing appearance of the masked lady had led to a waiter securing a table for Miranda and her companion. They had ordered the drink of the country, Pisco sour, a weak spirit made from grapes, and fresh limejuice. When the men joined them, they followed suit and declared the drink made a delicious aperitif.

Although the prim Miss Pinney was unaware that Rex had made off with a million dollars, she knew that he had disappeared without warning and that his friends were anxious to find him; so Simon was at once able to give Miranda an edited account of what had occurred in Punta Arenas, and their hopes of tracing Rex in Santiago.

When Simon thanked her for the flowers, Miranda said, 'It was nothing. Only a tiny gesture to show my appreciation of what you have done for me. Before, I had to live the life of a recluse. Now I need do so no longer. I can go anywhere, wearing my blindfold mask. Pinney tells me that everyone stares at me; but it is not with repulsion or pity, only curiosity; and that is rather fun.'

After half an hour, they went up to the restaurant and, over dinner, talked of the respective flights they had made. Even Pinney thawed out and said how fascinating it had been to fly over the Andes—that strange, primitive world of hundreds of miles of mountains alternating with deep, lifeless valleys through which rushed foaming rivers. There was now a daily service between Buenos Aires and Santiago, and the aircraft had been much larger than the one in which Richard and Simon had flown down to Punta Arenas.

When Simon and Richard awoke next morning, they found that their rooms looked out on to the *Plaza Constitucion*, the principal square of the city, and that the view from their windows was positively breathtaking.

Santiago lies in a bowl which is almost entirely surrounded by mountains. To the west, behind the hotel, ran the coastal range; to the east the far higher, massed peaks of the Andes, their white caps standing out sharply against a bright blue sky. In the foreground, the irregular roofs of the city were broken in one place by a four-hundred-foot-high wooded hill, crowned by a ruined castle. Further off, to the north-east, the buildings gave way to a great expanse of tree-covered slopes rising to a thousand feet, and surmounted by several buildings, above which towered an enormous statue of the Virgin.

As a waiter wheeled a breakfast trolley into the friends' sitting room, they caught the sounds of martial music, and went to the window again. From a lower and much older, domed building on the right hand side of the plaza, a band, followed by a company of troops, was emerging to form up in the square. The waiter told them that the building, *La Monada*, had once been the Mint of Chile, but was now the President's Palace, and that the guard was changed in the square at that hour every morning.

Over breakfast they discussed what their next move should be. It had been on Tuesday the 10th that von Thumm had said he would see Silvia 'this night next week', at the barbecue. This being Saturday morning, they still had four days to go before the meeting. That Rex was mixed up with these people there could be no doubt at all; so it was possible that he might attend this party they were holding, and already be in Santiago. If so, owing to his build and character, assuming that he was still a free man, it was just possible that enquiries might enable them to find out where he was staying. But his having made off with a million dollars put it beyond question that he was in some very serious trouble; so all the odds were that he was in hiding.

On the other hand, Silvia, the Baron, or both, might arrive at any time in the Chilean capital and, if either of them could be located, a watch could be kept on him or her. There was the possibility that they might stay in private houses, but an equal chance that they might go to an hotel; so it was agreed that Simon should make the round of all the best hotels in the city and give their hall porters handsome bribes to let him know if Silvia or von Thumm booked in.

However, the meeting at 'the barbecue' was the only firm line they had to follow. That it was not a recognised club Richard had already satisfied himself, by enquiries of the head porter on their arrival at the Hilton the previous evening. But it might be a small, private club that a limited number of people would know about. Having considered the matter, he said to Simon:

'The best informed people in any city are the reporters on the largest newspapers. I know a chap who frequently comes to England and stays with neighbours of mine. His name is Don Caesar Albert, and he is probably the wealthiest man in Chile. The family are immensely rich, and among their many interests they own one of the leading dailies.'

'Ummm.' Simon lit a cigarette. 'I've heard of the Alberts. They got in early on nitrate, when it was first discovered here. The Germans gave it a nasty knock when their supplies were cut off during the First World War. Their chemists invented a substitute. But by then the Alberts had become incredibly rich, and they are very highly respected.'

Richard nodded. 'Anyhow, I feel that Don Caesar might be able to help us.' Going over to the telephone, he asked the operator to get him Don Caesar's number. He was duly put through and, after he had had a few words with a secretary, Don Caesar came on the line. He at once recalled Richard, welcomed him warmly to Chile, and asked him to lunch.

Simon rang Miranda and arranged to give her and Pinney lunch, then the two friends went out to see something of the city. Santiago being on nearly the same latitude as Buenos Aires, it was very hot; but not with the scorching heat they had experienced in the Argentinian capital, and the people in the streets displayed much more vitality. Like the majority of comparatively modern cities, its centre consists of scores of square blocks and long, straight vistas with, in this case, the snow-capped mountains in the distance. The goods in the shops were, as in Buenos Aires, of second-rate quality, but the streets were cleaner and there was much less evidence of poverty.

Don Caesar asked Richard to meet him at the Crillon; so at one o'clock Simon left him in Augustines Street. On entering the hotel, Richard immediately appreciated its atmosphere. It was a building of the last century, with all the spacious elegance and décor that is found in hotels of that period in France. In the lounge there were a few Americans, but it was clearly a resort of the Chilean aristocracy. The clothes of many of the men in the lounge suggested Anderson and Sheppard and those of the women Dior or Fath.

As Richard walked in, Don Caesar, a tall, dark-haired man of about thirty, rose from a chair and smilingly extended his hand. In an ice bucket beside his table there was already a bottle of French champagne. When their glasses had been filled, they talked of mutual friends in England, and good days' hunting in the Shires. It transpired that the Chilean Millionaire had never met Rex Van Ryn, but knew of him through mutual banking interests.

Richard used the same story as he had with Don Carlos Escalente and Don Salvador Marino in Buenos Aires: that he and his friend Simon Aron were anxious to discuss an interesting business proposition with Rex but, on arriving in Buenos Aires, they had learned that he had gone off on a holiday, without leaving an address. He added that there seemed just a possibility that Rex had come to Santiago. But Don Caesar said that he had heard nothing of Van Ryn's being on holiday in Chile.

In hot weather the restaurant at the Crillon was little used, and they lunched in a delightful courtyard that ran alongside it. An awning protected them from the sun, flowering shrubs in big pots stood among the tables, and the trellised walls were covered with bougainvillaea. As a pleasant change from still wine, they drank, with an excellent meal, a really good peach *bola*.

It emerged that Don Caesar knew the Escalentes and several members of the Grau-Miraflores family. He had never heard of the Baron von Thumm, but had met Silvia Sinegiest twice at parties. If she had recently arrived at Santiago, he felt certain that a mention of her would have appeared in the social column of his paper, unless she was staying with friends and, for some reason of her own, not appearing in public.

Richard then asked if his host knew of a club called the 'Barbecue'. Don Caesar shook his dark head. 'No. Are you certain that there is such a club in Santiago?'

'I have reason to suppose so, because Van Ryn mentioned it to me once,' Richard prevaricated. 'And, if he is here, I hoped I might trace him through it.'

'It may be a new place, or quite a small one. Anyway, my people are used to making every sort of enquiry, so I'll get them to find out and let you know.' After a moment, Don Caesar added, 'Have you made any plans for tomorrow? If not, my wife and I are driving down to Viña del Mar, and you and your friend might like to come with us.'

Anxious as Richard was to get on with his quest, there was nothing more that he could do for the time being, so he accepted for himself, and said he would pass on the invitation to Simon.

Having walked the few blocks back down the shady side of the street to the Hilton, he lay down for a siesta. Simon did not reappear in their suite until six o'clock. He had given Miranda and Pinney lunch in the roof restaurant on the seventeenth storey of the hotel. Outside it there was a sun-bathing terrace and a swimming pool and, before lunch, he had gone in for a swim. But, to his surprise and annoyance, when he came out he had been told that drinks could be served to people in bathing wraps only at four umbrella-shaded tables on the far side of the pool. At the tables on the other sides, gentlemen must wear coats and trousers, and in the restaurant itself, ties were insisted on.

After lunching, he had gone out and made the rounds of the best hotels. None of their reception clerks could give him any news of Rex, Silvia or von Thumm, but the hall porters had eagerly accepted the *escudo* notes he offered them, taken down his address and promised to let him know should any of his friends book in at their hotels.

During his tour of the city he had two pleasant surprises. He found that the taxi drivers all refused tips, and outside one of the hotels there had been a man with a barrow piled high with the largest nectarines he had ever seen. He had bought a dozen and had eaten four of these luscious fruit on the way back to the Hilton. As he offered the bag containing the others to Richard, his friend shook his head, and said uneasily:

'Really, Simon. You should know better than to eat rindless fruit in a tropical country, without first washing it in disinfectant.'

'Why?' Simon rubbed his arc of nose with his forefinger. 'They look perfectly clean.'

'Perhaps. But God alone knows by what filthy fingers they have been handled. You had better take several Enterovioform pills right away.'

That evening Richard took them all out to dine at the *Jacaranda* a restaurant that Don Caesar had recommended to him as one of the best in the city. The night air was delightfully warm and softly-lit tables were set outside the restaurant in a broad alley that was closed to traffic. Their thoughts were never far from Rex and, although they could not mention the missing million dollars, as Pinney was present, they again speculated fruitlessly on what had become of him.

On their way back to the Hilton, Simon fell silent. Then, breaking out into a sweat, he confessed that he felt very ill. Richard's foreboding about the unwashed nectarines had proved only too well founded. Miranda was greatly perturbed and wanted to call in a doctor, but Pinney briskly declared that all he needed was dosing, and shortly after they got back, she came to their suite with appropriate medicine.

On the Sunday morning Simon still had an upset stomach and, in any case, he had already refused Don Caesar's invitation, in order to spend the day with Miranda; so, when the Alberts arrived at ten o'clock to pick Richard up, he set off alone with them to Viña del Mar.

Richard had already met *Donna* Albert in England. She was young, gay and spoke English as well as her husband, so they made a merry party. The large, comfortable car took the road to Valparaiso, and was soon running through a valley, the lower slopes of which were sparsely wooded, mainly with a silvery blue gum, above which towered holly oaks and firs of various species.

Fifteen miles outside Santiago, they began to cross a lofty region known as the 'Mountains of the Coast'. There were many hairpin bends, but the road was exceptionally wide for a highway through such terrain. In most places it had, on either side, sandy verges of ten feet or more; so, even in a collision, there was little danger of a car going over a precipice.

On the far side of the ridge there were more broad valleys and, as they approached the coast, the scenery became very picturesque. Areas of forest, consisting mainly of acacias and mimosa, were broken here and there by lakes, or fields in which grew water melons, pumpkins, wheat and, occasionally, sunflowers.

After crossing a last deep valley, they mounted to high downland; then, quite suddenly, saw the Pacific several hundred feet below them. Speeding down, they completed their ninety-mile run to the coast by entering Valparaiso, Chile's largest port: a dreary, dirty city, retaining no trace of the romance associated with it in the days of Spain's glory, when many a treasure galleon had called to revictual and take on water there.

Turning north, they ran round the huge bay and into Viña del Mar, a lovely watering place, with numerous fine hotels and a splendid Casino, of which the Chileans are justly proud. Continuing along the coast for some miles, they passed through several villages set in rocky bays, and fine beaches with white sand on which hundreds of holiday-makers were enjoying themselves. The last of these was called Concon. A little way beyond it, Don Caesar pulled up and, leaving the car, they walked out along a rocky promontory, perched on the end of which was a rustic restaurant. He told Richard that he had brought him there because the place was famous for its crabs; and, later, Richard agreed that he had never eaten better.

Afterwards, on the way back, they stopped in Viña del Mar, to spend twenty minutes strolling round the lovely park; then took the road to Santiago. On arriving at the Hilton, Richard asked the Alberts to come in and have a drink with him. To his surprise and pleasure he found that Simon was not in their suite, so he must obviously have felt much better before he would have left it.

Half an hour later Simon came in and was introduced to the Alberts. They were just about to leave, and had already asked Richard to dine with them the following night. Now, they included Simon in the invitation and when he asked, a little hesitantly, if he might bring Miranda with him, explaining about her blindness and saying that it would be a treat for her, they agreed at once. When they had gone, he told Richard that he had stayed in bed for the morning, had a light lunch, then spent the afternoon up beside the swimming pool with Miranda.

On Monday morning, at about half past ten, Don Caesar telephoned. He said that one of his reporters had picked up some information that might interest them. He was lunching at the Union Club with a friend with whom he had to discuss business; but he suggested that they might join him there at midday for a drink.

When they arrived at the Union Club, they found that Don Caesar had with him a tall, youngish man with hooded eyes and an exceptionally long nose, whom he introduced as Philo McTavish. He added, 'Mr McTavish is a Chilean, and he was born here; but his mother was Greek and his father a Scot, and they sent him to Scotland to be educated, so he speaks good English. That's why I chose him to try to find out about this barbecue place. You see, my wife and I are leaving for England on Wednesday morning, and McTavish will be able to report to you in your own language.'

They were soon settled in a quiet corner of the club smoking room, with drinks before them. Don Caesar nodded to McTavish. 'Now let's hear what you have to tell us so far.'

The tall Greco-Scot-Chilean leaned forward and, looking at Richard and Simon, spoke in fluent English, but with a strong Glasgow accent, 'There's not a club called the "Barbecue" here in Santiago, *Señor*. Of that I'm now certain. But many barbecues are given by folk here. In our summer the climate lends itself to that form of entertaining. Most folk who're wealthy enough to own a house wi' a garden of any size have one in it. Ye'll see then the only line o' investigation I could pursue was to enquire for any barbecue parties that were held regular an' might have some special feature.

' 'Tis customary fer the hostess's cook to buy the food an' prepare the dishes; but, in cases where the party be a large one, caterers or hotels are called on to supply the victuals. I drew a number o' blanks, then visited the *Danubio Azul*, a restaurant renowned for its Chinese food. There I got on to it that once a month the proprietor receives an order for food enough for a hundred people, everything to be of the very best, an' no expense barred. Aboot this order there are several unusual circumstances. Fer such large parties, 'tis common practice fer waiters to be provided by the restaurateur. In this case, they're not; although, as far as I ken, the staff of the house consists only of an elderly couple. Also, in spite o' that, the restaurateur's delivery men are not permitted ter carry anything into the house. The food, dishes, linen an' all are received by the two servants at the gate of quite a long drive, an' the dirty things collected from there the following morning.'

'Whereabouts is this house?' enquired Don Caesar.

'Tis on the south-east outskirts o' the city, beyond the best residential district, *Señor*. You could reach it by going on past the far end of the *Avenida Amerigo Vespucci*, where you live. The property is a very extensive one, two or more hectares maybe; an' the house is screened from observation on all sides by belts o' trees.'

'Can you tell us anything more about it?'

'Nay, very little, *Señor*. I went out there an' tried to get the servants talkin', but it were not possible. Believe it or not, they were both dumb, or pretendin' to be. I then tried some of the servants at properties nearby. They could tell me nowt, except that these parties usually go on till sunup, an' are real rowdy affairs. There's drummin' goes on and, faint from the distance, strange cries: the like of animals or persons gone mad wi' excitement. Folks round about are of the opinion that these monthly barbecues are orgies. Aye, for a' that, those who attend them come an' go quiet as can be. They cause noo inconvenience, so gi' noo ground for complaints to the police. An' there's noo law against men making merry wi' lasses in private, provided the lasses be willing.'

'Who is the owner of this property?'

''Tis a rich Negro, *Señor*; by name Lincoln B. Glasshill.'

'A Negro!' Richard repeated. 'There aren't many in Chile are there? I mean, there were no great sugar plantations here for which they would have been brought in to labour as slaves during the Spanish occupation.'

'No,' Don Caesar replied. 'We have very few. However, I know of this man. He is not a Chilean, but a distinguished American lawyer. He settled here some six or eight years ago. He is reputed to be a very able man, and has built up a fine connection.'

McTavish nodded. 'Aye, *Señor*. The couple he employs are also Negroes, an' act mainly as caretakers. They keep the place habitable for him. During the week, he lives in an apartment near the Law Courts. He goes out to his place only fer week-ends an' fer these monthly parties.'

'Does he always give them on the same day of the month?' Richard enquired.

'Nay, *Señor*. I asked one o' the men at the restaurant tha' does the catering aboot that. He told me these skeedoos are always held at the full o' the moon.'

7

The Barbecue

At the words 'full o' the moon', Simon's eyes flickered towards Richard, who raised an eyebrow then asked, 'Is there anything else you can tell us, Mr. McTavish?'

The tall Chilean shook his sandy, close-cropped head. 'Naught else, *Señor*; except that I have it from the restaurateur that a barbecue is to be held there tomorrow night.'

Again Simon and Richard's eyes met, now conveying their excitement.

Don Caesar glanced at his watch and said, 'You'll forgive me if I now break up this little party, but my luncheon guest should be arriving in a few minutes.'

The others stood up and Richard smiled. 'Of course. Very good of you to let *Señor* McTavish spend his time helping us to trace our friend. I think this monthly barbecue given by the Negro lawyer must be what Van Ryn referred to. Anyhow, Aron and I will go out there and see what we can discover. In the meantime, we'll see you this evening.' He then thanked McTavish for the work he had put in, and the party broke up.

As Simon and Richard walked back to the Hilton, the former asked, 'What d'you make of it?' This full of the moon business sounds like a Witches' Sabbat to me.'

'Could be. I find it difficult to believe, though, that Rex would have got himself mixed up in that sort of thing, knowing as he does, from your clash with Satanism* way back in the thirties, how damnably dangerous it can be.'

Up in the roof restaurant of the Hilton, they found Miranda and Miss Pinney waiting to lunch with them. Eagerly, Miranda asked if the meeting had thrown any light on the possible whereabouts of her uncle. Simon told her about the barbecue regularly held by the American Negro lawyer, and ended, 'All this secrecy and the rest of it sound pretty fishy. Could well be Satanism.'

* *The Devil Rides Out.*

'Oh, come, Simon!' Miranda laughed. 'What nonsense. Uncle Rex has his feet on the ground as firmly as any man I know. He is the very last person to start dabbling in devil-worship.'

Miss Pinney gave a disapproving sniff and added, 'The practice of Black Magic went out with the Dark Ages. Of course, natives in Africa and some other places still perform revolting rites; but that an American gentleman like Mr Van Ryn should do so is unthinkable.'

Simon did not pursue the matter. After they had lunched, they all went down to a car that he had hired for the afternoon. Going for drives, while wearing a heavy veil, had been one of the few pleasures that Miranda had been able to enjoy before Simon had enabled her to go about in public free from embarrassment and without harming her eyes.

They drove out to the Carro San Cristobal, the wooded mountain to the north-east of the city, and up the winding road to the wide terrace from which rose the huge statue of the Virgin. The whole area, several miles in extent, was one vast park. On a lower slope there was a Zoo, on the higher ones large public swimming baths, tennis courts, cafés and restaurants. There was ample room for thousands of people to picnic there on Sundays and national holidays; for innumerable glades, hollows and rambling paths provided so many secluded spots that no part of this fine retreat for dwellers in the close, hot streets of the city would have been crowded.

Although, unlike her companions, Miranda could not see the magnificent view, she enjoyed the cool, clean air as they sat at a table on the top terrace, eating *casata* ices.

That evening she accompanied Simon and Richard out to Don Caesar's home. As Simon gave the driver of the car the address, she asked, 'Do you know about the man after whom the *Avenida Amerigo Vespucci* was named?'

Both of them murmured that they did not, so she went on, 'As we all know, Christopher Columbus was the first discoverer actually to land in the new world, but Amerigo Vespucci was the first to write a book about it. That's why it became known as America.'

The Alberts' house proved to be a spacious, airy building, furnished with many beautiful objects, and set in a three-acre garden. Ten people sat down to dinner, and it proved a jolly party. Afterwards they went out into the garden, which a nearly full moon made as light as day. It was redolent with the

71

scent of moonflowers, and they drank their coffee and liqueurs at the side of an artistically-designed swimming pool. After a while, Richard got Don Caesar to take him for a stroll round the garden, and when they were out of earshot of the others, he asked, 'Does much black magic go on in Chile?'

Don Caesar shook his head. 'Not as far as I know. You see, Chile is rather different from the other South American countries. Of course, in the interior the native Indians still practise their magic, but it is of a very primitive kind, and you certainly could not call it Satanism. It was the Negroes who brought voodoo to South America; but, as Chile was not particularly suitable for sugar plantations and, apparently, lacking in natural wealth, comparatively few Spaniards settled here, so only a very small part of our population consists of the descendants of Negro slaves.'

'That's interesting, as from what I have heard most of the other Latin-American countries are riddled with diabolic cults.'

'You're right. That's particularly true of Brazil. Naturally, Brazil differs from the rest of South America, because it was colonised by the Portuguese. There has never been any colour bar there, and a high proportion of the Portuguese settlers not only took Negresses for mistresses, but married them. Such women made a show of accepting Christianity, but they were too strongly imbued with a belief in their own dark gods to give up worshipping them. As wives, they acquired a much greater influence over their husbands than mistresses would have had; and, on the principle that it is better to be safe than sorry, many of the husbands were persuaded by their wives to placate the African gods by attending midnight blood sacrifices. The wives' influence over the children of such marriages was, obviously, even greater, so although they were baptised as Christians and regularly attended Mass, they in fact became devotees of voodoo, or *Macumba*, as it is called in Brazil. Even today, in spite of modern education, a large part of the upper classes pay only lip service to Christianity, and pin their faith on attending pagan rites.'

'It's your opinion, though, that this Negro lawyer's parties are not that sort of thing?'

'I doubt it. Much more likely to be sexual jamborees. But as you and Aron are going out there tomorrow night, you ought to be able to satisfy yourselves about what actually does go on. As you might have difficulty in finding the place, I've already told Philo McTavish to take you out there in his car. You had better telephone him at the office in the morning and let him know what time you want him to pick you up. As I'm off to Europe the day after tomorrow, I've also told him that he is to place himself at your disposal as long as you remain in Santiago, and that, whatever you may find out about Lincoln B. Glasshill, in no circumstances is anything to be printed in the paper.'

'That's awfully good of you, and I couldn't be more grateful,' Richard said. They then rejoined the others by the swimming pool.

The following morning Simon, Richard, Miranda and Pinney went for another drive; this time round the centre of the city and up its broadest boulevard—named after Bernardo O'Higgins—the Chilean hero who had led the war against the Spanish, which had gained Chile her independence—then along the river Mapocho, the banks of which were carefully tended lawns, gay with beds of flowers and flowering shrubs.

On the way back, Richard asked to be dropped off at the Carro Santa Lucia. It was a four-hundred-foot-high hill, which had once been the citadel of Santiago, but was now a most picturesque public park. Innumerable winding paths led up to the ancient ruin that crowned it, and Richard was interested to see that, on the benches in the many shady nooks along the paths, there were quite a number of teenage couples who were obviously courting; but all of them were behaving most decorously, just sitting silently, and holding hands.

He got back to the Hilton in time for a swim in the roof-top pool, then he and his friends lunched together and afterwards spent a good part of the afternoon dozing on their beds. In due course, they all dined together; but the meal was rather a silent one, as Richard and Simon were secretly speculating on what they might find out within the next few hours.

At half past ten, Philo McTavish picked them up. Neither Richard nor Simon had taken a very good view of McTavish. No doubt, his long nose was excellent for sniffing out news; but the sandy hair he had inherited from his father's side of his family seemed the only thing Scottish about him. His black eyes had a slightly shifty look, and his handshake was clammy. Nevertheless, they were grateful to Don Caesar for having placed him and his car at their disposal; as, to get a sight of the barbecue, they might have to leave the car for some time; and to do that from a hired car out in the country in the middle of the night would have been difficult to explain to their driver.

As the journalist drove them through the streets of the city, Richard asked him:

'While doing your job, have you ever come across any evidence that there are Satanist gatherings in Santiago?'

The Scottish-educated Chilean laughed. 'Good gracious, no, Mr Eaton. As in every city, there are a few old crones who are credited with practising witchcraft, but I've never heard of their getting together to hold a Sabbat. What with their radios, motor-cycles and self-service stores, most of the people who live in Santiago are much too modern-minded to believe in that sort of thing.'

'That applies to most other countries now,' Richard replied. 'But the fact remains that Satanism is still practised in them.'

'If you say so, *Señor*, I will take your word for it. But any educated person would now look on believing in the Devil as nonsense.'

'Of course they would, if they think of the Devil as people did in the Middle Ages: a terrifying apparition with horns, hooves and a spiked tail. But that was only a form his emissaries took as suitable to the beliefs of the period. Now that people have so many things, other than religion, to occupy their minds, they naturally give little thought to the powers of good and evil. That is because they are not tuned in to such influences. But it does not mean that the Devil no longer exists.'

To Richard's surprise McTavish replied, 'If not by nationality, by heredity and education I'm a down-to-earth Scot. I can accept that the Devil is still stooging round tempting people with this an' that in exchange for their immortal souls.'

'May I ask if you are a Christian?'

'Aye, I'm certainly that.'

'Then, if you believe in God, you cannot logically disbelieve in the Devil, because he was part of the original Creation. What is more, when Lucifer was cast out of Heaven, God gave him this world as his province. That is made abundantly clear in the New Testament, in the passage where Satan took Jesus Christ up into a high place, showed him all the cities and the fertile valleys and said, "All this will I give to Thee if Thou wilt bow down to me." He couldn't have offered something that wasn't his to give.'

'I suppose that is so.'

'It certainly is. And it's a great mistake to imagine that the Devil went out of business with the coming of the scientific age. He simply went underground, and adapted his methods to modern conditions. One of his names is "Lord of Misrule", and his object is to destroy all law and order among mankind. What could do that more effectively than the creation of wars, in which countless thousands of people legally murder one another, and there follows widespread arson, pillage, rape and anarchy? In the present century, the Devil has brought about two world wars and a score of minor ones, by bemusing the minds of statesmen and about the best interests of their peoples; so it seems to me that he has surpassed himself.'

'Am I right, *Señor*, in thinking you have formed the idea that these parties given by Glasshill are some form of Sabbat?'

Suddenly it struck Richard that, should that prove the case, it would be just as well to keep McTavish in ignorance of the fact. Although Don Caesar had banned any account of what they found out being published, McTavish might, if the story had the making of a juicy scandal, sell it to a friend for publication in another paper. After a moment, he replied, 'It's just possible; but I doubt it. Otherwise, surely you or one of your colleagues would have picked up some rumour about Satanic rites being practised in Santiago.'

At a little before eleven o'clock, the car was running over a country road that led towards the lower slopes of the Andes. McTavish pointed to a group of trees a few hundred yards ahead on the right, and said, 'That is the place, *Señor*. Just before we reach it there is a track leading off. Would you have me take it so that I dinna' have to wait for you in the main road an' perhaps be noticed by people in other cars driving up to the entrance?'

'Yes,' Richard agreed. 'But pull up somewhere wide enough to reverse the car so that, if necessary, we can make a quick getaway.'

Two hundred yards down a curving lane, that followed the belt of trees surrounding the grounds of the house, McTavish halted the car. As Richard got out, he said, 'I'm afraid you may have a long wait: an hour at least, perhaps a bit more.'

McTavish shrugged. 'Don't worry, *Señor*. Wi' me I've a book to read, an' a flask wi' a drop in it.'

Simon followed Richard out of the car. He was carrying an attaché case which contained certain items he had procured earlier in the day, and which they might need in an emergency. The moonlight enabled them to see their way without trouble between the trees and patches of undergrowth. After they

75

had penetrated the screen for some twenty feet, they came upon the tall wire fence that McTavish had said surrounded the property, when he had described it at the Union Club. Against the possibility that it might be electrified, Simon had brought rubber gloves. Getting them out, he put them on and held two of the strands wide apart, so that Richard could get through without touching them. Then Richard took the gloves and held the wires apart so that Simon could follow him. Cautiously they advanced through the belt of trees. On the far side of the fence it was some sixty feet in depth. When they reached its further edge, they were able to look out across a wide expanse of lawn to the house, which was about two hundred yards distant. It was a long, low building, with turrets at each corner, suggesting that it had been built in Victorian times. All the ground-floor windows were lit, and a few in the upper storey. Only light curtains had been drawn across them, and through these moving shadows could be seen here and there, showing that considerable activity was going on inside the rooms. Outside the back of the house trestle tables had been erected below a long verandah. On the far side was an ornamental lake. In the centre of the row of tables, two had been put side by side to form a broader platform, and upon it were two large elbow chairs.

As Simon surveyed the scene, he said in a low voice, 'Queer sort of dinner party, for two people to sit on top of the table.'

'They may be thrones,' Richard whispered back. 'Anyhow, if it is to be a Sabbat, the setting is right. That lake serves the purpose of the traditional pond near which such ceremonies must be held.'

After about ten minutes, four men came out of the house. They wore sombreros and the breeches and jack-boots of herdsmen; but each of them carried a Sten gun. Separating, they walked off in different directions towards the screen of trees.

'Come on,' said Richard quickly. 'They're about to search the grounds in case some curious neighbour is snooping, to find out what goes on here. We must hide, or we'll be for it.'

Here and there among the trees there were groups of bushes and tangled undergrowth. Simon had already turned and was tiptoeing his way back towards the fence. Just inside it they chose two patches of thick bramble-covered saplings, and wriggled down behind them. Presently they caught the sound of heavy footfalls snapping fallen twigs and rustling dry leaves.

Slowly the footsteps grew nearer. Now and again they stopped. Evidently the man was halting every ten yards or so, to peer from side to side as he advanced.

Simon could hear his own heart pounding. Neither he nor Richard was armed. If they were caught they would be at the gunman's mercy. Anything could happen to them then. South America was not like Europe. Many people habitually went about armed, and nearly everyone kept a pistol in his car as a precaution against a hold-up in a sparsely-populated district. Shootings were everyday occurrences, and the police took scant notice of them, unless someone important was involved.

Holding their breath, they lay absolutely still. Fortunately, the clumps of undergrowth were so numerous that the searcher could not make a close examination of them all, and the trees prevented the moonlight from coming through except here and there in irregular patches.

After what seemed an age, the guard passed their hiding places and his footsteps faded into the distance. With sighs of relief they came gingerly to their feet. Having listened intently for a long moment, they crept back to the place from which they had retreated; but now they lay down there, in case their silhouettes should be spotted among the trees.

While they had been crouching behind their cover, they had caught the intermittent beat of drums. As they looked towards the house again, they saw that eight Negroes had emerged from it and were seated in a group on the verandah. It was difficult to see them clearly, as they were partially in the shadow cast by the verandah roof, but they appeared to be a band, mainly of drummers and some with other instruments, who were tuning up. The sounds they made gradually merged into a steady rhythm.

Other figures began to come out from the house; but at first sight they did not appear to be human beings. All of them were wearing costumes that made them look like animals, reptiles or enormous insects. There were leopards, wolves, jackals, pigs, cats, dogs of various kinds, a bull, a frog, a ram, several huge blue-bottles and mosquitoes. Many of them were wearing head-dresses in keeping with their costumes, all the others were masked. They came out of the house carrying dishes piled high with food, and dozens of bottles of wine, with which they proceeded to furnish the long tables.

'Going to be a Sabbat,' Simon whispered. 'Give you a hundred to one on that.'

'Not taking you,' Richard replied promptly. 'But how Rex got himself mixed up in this devilish business beats me. It's not as though he were ignorant of such matters. He was with us on that awful night, years ago, when, as near as damn it, Satan broke through the pentacle in which we were all cowering in the library of Cardinal's Folly.'

'Ummm. We've no proof yet, though, that Rex is involved.'

'Can you doubt it? He was the Sinegiest woman's lover. She must be up to the neck in this. It's a sure thing now that this must be the "barbecue" at which she and von Thumm are to meet tonight. It's clear, too, that when we asked him if he knew what had happened to Rex, he took alarm, sent us down to the Sinegiest, then concocted a yarn for her to spin that would cause us to call off our search for Rex. Somehow they've got hold of him. It's quite on the cards that he is here tonight, and one of that crowd of creatures laying the tables.'

'What do we do if we spot him? We just might, as he's a head and shoulders taller than most people.'

Richard gave a heavy sigh. 'What the hell can we do? Unarmed, we wouldn't stand an earthly if we went in against that mob. If we could get McTavish's car through the fence, we might charge them in it, as Greyeyes did when we pulled you out of that Sabbat on Salisbury Plain. But there's no possible way of getting the car in here. Even if we could, the odds are that those boys with the Sten guns would riddle us with bullets before we could get away.'

As Richard finished speaking, he turned, crawled back a few yards into the trees, then stood up. Glancing over his shoulder, Simon whispered, 'Where are you off to?'

'Speaking of those gunmen brought to my mind that one of them may come on us unexpectedly, so it would be as well to have to hand something with which we could at least defend ourselves.'

After some minutes he returned, carrying two pieces of fallen branch that would serve as rough clubs, and gave one to Simon. By then the drums were being beaten with a steady rhythm that was gradually increasing in tempo. Also, a glow that they had noticed on the far side of the house had increased to a lurid glare, and it could be assumed that food was being cooked there. Meanwhile, the men and women in fantastic disguises had taken their places round the table.

With a final crash of drums, the band suddenly ceased playing. Complete silence fell. There was a stir on the veran-

dah. Two figures emerged from it and walked down the steps.
One was evidently a man clad as a goat, with a head-dress
from which rose four instead of two, great, curved horns. The
other was a tall, fair-haired woman stark naked.

Simultaneously Richard and Simon recognised the woman
as Silvia Sinegiest. Nude, her broad shoulders and superb figure
were displayed to the best possible advantage.

'My God, she's beautiful!' Richard muttered. 'She must be
pretty chilly, though, in spite of the warm night.'

'She doesn't need clothes for this,' Simon murmured back.
'Surely you remember? The Devil's people can create a warm
atmosphere or a mist that will envelop them whenever they
wish. Look at the man playing the Goat of Mendes. From his
height and lopsided walk, one would know him anywhere as
von Thumm.'

The two figures, holding hands, advanced to the centre table
and mounted by some concealed steps on to it. When they
reached the two big elbow chairs, they halted in front of them
and a great shout of salutation went up from the assembled
company. Silvia remained standing there, but the goat turned
about and bent down to rest his forelegs on the seat of the
chair, revealing that the back of his costume had been cut
away to expose his posterior. The other participants then filed
past, in turn performing the revolting *Osculum inflâme* by kissing the man-goat's fundamental orifice.

Meanwhile, Simon had been fumbling in his attaché case,
and took from it two necklaces made of small roots strung
together. Passing one to Richard, he said, 'Now we're certain
what we're in for, we'd better put these on.' The roots were
garlic, and Richard loathed both its taste and smell; but he
knew that it was a most powerful protection against evil
forces, so he slipped the necklace over his head without protest.

When the procession past the goat was over and all the
beast-clad men and women were back in their original places
at the tables, the band started up again. But this time the drums
were only subsidiary to a weird, tuneless cacophony of notes
from a lyre, a trumpet and Pan pipes. It was the signal for the
feast to begin. There were already many cold dishes on the
table. To these there were now added steaming tureens of hot
food brought from round the far corner of the house. No
knives, forks, spoons or plates were used, and the company
fell upon the edibles as though they were starving: grabbing
up handfuls of food and cramming it into the mouths of them-

selves or their neighbours, then seizing the bottles and drinking from them.

This disgusting exhibition of gluttony continued for the best part of half an hour; then, at a signal from the goat, the band stopped playing. A tall man clad as a black panther rose from one end of the long table, drew a basket from beneath it and held it aloft. A great shout went up, then complete silence fell. At the same moment a hugely fat woman, wearing a cloak of feathers and the mask of a vulture, came to her feet at the other end of the table, and held on high a silver vessel shaped like a phallus. From opposite ends of the table the two advanced, until they met in front of the naked Silvia, and the goatskin-clad von Thumm, who both rose from their thrones. The vulture-woman handed up to Silvia the big silver vessel modelled on a male organ, and the panther-man handed up to her companion something which he took from the basket. For a moment Richard and Simon could not see what it was that the panther-man had presented. Then, as he bowed and moved aside, they saw that it was a black infant.

'Oh God!' gasped Simon. 'They're going to sacrifice it! We've got to stop them! We must!' He started to scramble to his feet.

Richard grabbed him by the arm and pulled him back. 'Stay where you are, you bloody fool!' he hissed into Simon's ear. 'We haven't a hope in hell of saving the child. We'd only be murdered ourselves, and to no purpose. Those gunmen are lurking somewhere among these trees. They'd shoot us down before we were halfway across the lawn.'

With a groan, Simon sank back and shut his eyes.

The baby made no sound. Evidently it had been doped before the party started, and had since lain in a drugged sleep in the basket under the table. Von Thumm held the offering to Satan aloft. Before he did so it had been difficult to see it clearly. Now, Richard suddenly realised that it was not a piccaninny, but a young ape.

Von Thumm began a long incantation in Latin. At intervals the evil congregation shouted a loud response. These shouts roused the ape, and it began to chatter. His incantation finished, the Baron lowered the ape into the crook of his right fore-leg. At one side of the silver phallus there hung a glittering, curved black-hilted knife. He took it in his hoof-covered left hand. Silvia held the phallus out by its two great testicles. Von Thumm drew the knife sharply across the ape's throat.

80

Its one wailing cry was cut short, and its blood poured into the vessel that Silvia was holding ready to receive it.

A great cry went up from the congregation. When all but a few drops of the ape's blood had drained from its body, the Priest of Evil threw it from him. The nearest members of the congregation seized upon it and tore it limb from limb. Meanwhile, the Baron had transferred the knife to his right hand, and plunged his hoof-covered left hand into the hollow phallus Withdrawing it, dripping with blood, he made the sign of the Left-Hand Swastika on Silvia's stomach. Again the members of this unholy crew formed a procession and filed past the throne. As they did so, the goat sprinkled each of them with a few drops of the sacrificial blood.

All this time, Simon had been lying with his face buried in his hands, praying fervently for the Lords of Light to destroy these gruesome followers of the Left-Hand Path. Richard had witnessed everything, because he had been half hoping, half fearing, to identify Rex among the assembled Satanists. But none of the grotesque, animal-like figures was tall enough to be his friend. When the last in the procession had been anointed with the ape's blood, he said gently:

'It wasn't a child but an ape, Simon. And even though we've failed to find Rex, we can thank God he is not among that awful crew.'

As Simon looked up, the Satanic anointing with blood had just finished, but the procession did not break up. Instead, with the black panther-man heading them, the others, each clutching the one before him, entered on a strange, follow-my-leader dance, copying the leader's lewd gestures and contortions and winding about like a huge centipede. The drums had begun to beat again. As the tempo increased into a throbbing, compulsive rhythm, the procession broke up and the people began to dance singly or in couples: a big, spotted dog with a hyena, a jaguar with a baboon, a wolf with a bear, and many other unnatural combinations. For a few minutes they jigged about, then merged into circles, each of thirteen, on the broad lawn, facing outward and back to back as they pranced round and round, some of them staggering drunkenly.

Another ten minutes passed; then the circles dissolved. Most of the assembly appeared to have already selected partners for this new phase of the Sabbat. Avidly they seized upon one another, ripping down the zip fasteners that held their animal costumes in place in front. Beneath the costumes most of them were naked. Their arms were clasped round their partners, who either subsided willingly or were thrown to the ground. A babel of shouts, grunts and cries ensued as two score of fiercely-embraced couples began to copulate. From the positions that several of them took up, with one man discarding his garment altogether, it could be seen that a number of them were sodomites; in other cases the form of lust displayed was obviously lesbian.

After a while, Richard said, 'There's no point in our staying longer. We now know what we came to find out, and Rex isn't here. But now we can have Silvia and von Thumm kept under observation and I'm sure one of them will lead us to him.'

'Yes,' Simon agreed. 'Sight of all this makes me want to vomit. Let's get back to the car.'

It was at that moment that a woman dressed as a black cat, who had just staggered to her feet after being bestrode by a man dressed as a bull, was seized upon by another wearing a cobra head-dress. But she broke away from him and ran, screaming, towards the place where Richard and Simon were hiding.

Von Thumm and Sylvia had not participated in the orgy. For the past ten minutes, while it had been in progress, they had remained seated on their thrones, the living representatives of Satanic power, calling out to applaud acts of special obscenity and encouraging to new efforts those whose lechery seemed to be weakening.

On seeing the cat-woman detach herself from the writhing mob and go racing across the open lawn, the Baron jumped to his cloven-hoof-covered feet and yelled in Spanish, 'Guards! Guards! Stop that cat! She must not be allowed to get away.'

8

The Victim

Richard and Simon had come to their feet just inside the screen of trees. The cat-woman could not see them. Her head-dress had fallen back, revealing her face. It was that of a girl in her twenties, and disordered by terror. Her eyes were bulging, her mouth gaped open and her dark hair streamed out behind her. With all the speed she could muster, she was blindly heading for the nearest cover.

That happened to be within fifteen feet of where Simon was standing. Swiftly he moved sideways towards the spot where she would enter the trees. Richard followed him. As he did so, he glanced over his shoulder. In all but a few cases the violent writhing among the tangle of bodies had ceased. Most of them had released their partners, or broken away from the lascivious groups of which they had formed members. More than half of them now nude, they were staring in consternation at the running woman. Their animal cries and screams provoked by sadistic acts no longer made the night hideous. A tense, stunned silence was broken only by von Thumm's continuing to shout for the guards.

They had not been slow to answer his summons. Richard saw that two of them had emerged from the trees on the far side of the lawn. With their Sten guns at the ready, they were giving chase.

As the cat-woman dashed in among the trees, Simon grabbed her arm, intending to guide her to the place in the wire fence beyond which the car was waiting. Scratching at his face with her free hand, she resisted furiously, and gasped in English:

'No more! Let . . . let me go! I won't submit again. I won't. I won't!'

Simon gave her a quick shake. As her teeth snapped together, he said hurriedly, 'For God's sake don't struggle. Trust me! We'll help you to escape.'

Doubtless it was because he had spoken to her in English

83

that she relaxed, and allowed him to pull her, still panting for breath, in the direction of the spot from which he and Richard had been watching the orgy. Seeing that Simon had the girl, Richard ran on ahead, pulled on the rubber gloves and held the strands of wire apart, so that they could get her through the fence. The two gunmen had just reached the place where their quarry had entered the belt of trees, a third could be heard crashing through the trees to the right. They were not far off. Richard feared that, at any moment, they would hear the sounds made by himself and his companions. To hold the wires apart, he had to drop his cudgel, so he had not even that with which to attempt to defend himself.

The thought of the gunmen made the hairs on the back of his neck prickle. They were somewhere behind him. The Sten guns they were carrying would not be only to scare people. He had not a doubt that their orders were to shoot at anyone they found spying on the doings of their employer and his guests. They certainly would at anyone helping an unwilling participant to escape. Simon, too, was seized by the awful fear that, at any moment, bullets would come smashing into his back and that, choking up blood, he would die there.

Somehow they got the girl through the fence. As Simon followed her, she slumped to the ground and lay there inert. She had fainted. Richard swore under his breath. The odds against their getting away were now a hundred to one, unless they abandoned the woman. Before they could carry her, unconscious, to the car, it seemed certain that the gunmen would be upon them.

In desperate haste Richard tore off the rubber gloves and thrust them at Simon. It took only a moment for him to pull them on, grab two wires and hold them wide apart so that his friend could get through, but every second was precious. The sound of trampling feet was now loud. One of the gunmen, if not two, must be within a dozen yards of them; and they were screened from sight only by the trunks of the trees and the tall patches of undergrowth.

Stooping over the woman, Richard saw that the cat costume she was wearing zipped down the front. The two sides had fallen open. Beneath it she had on only underclothes that were torn and bloodstained. It was imperative to bring her out of her faint, so that she could take at least part of her weight on her own feet. Without compunction he slapped her hard across the face. She moaned and opened her eyes. Between them, they dragged her to her feet. To their utter consternation, not yet having fully regained consciousness, she failed to realise that they were trying to save her. Desperately she endeavoured to break away and again began to shout: 'Let me go! Let me go! I won't let you! I won't! I won't!'

Answering shouts came through the trees. The woman's pursuers were no longer in doubt about the direction she had taken. To silence her, Richard jabbed his elbow hard in her ribs. Grasping her arms, they thrust her forward. Another minute and the three of them were out in the lane. But they had misjudged the place where the car had put them down. In the bright moonlight they could see it clearly; it was a good fifty yards away in the direction of the main road. Puzzled by the shouts, Philo McTavish had just got out of the car and was standing beside it.

The girl had now realised that they were helping her to get away. She no longer resisted, nor used her weight to hamper them. Fear of capture lent her new strength. With the two men still holding her arms, she began to run with them towards the car.

Richard threw a glance over his shoulder. The sound of their feet pounding on the earth could not fail to be heard by their pursuers. It needed only one of the two, or perhaps by now any of the four they had seen earlier, to reach the road, and the game would be up. The fence would prove no obstacle to them, because it would cause them no concern if they set alarm bells ringing.

Simon was not used to exerting himself. He had broken out into a sweat and was gasping for breath. As he ran he shut his eyes in an agony of apprehension. He felt certain that before they were halfway to the car they would all be riddled with bullets.

They would have been, had not the Lords of Light intervened to save them. Unnoticed by them during the past few minutes of intense activity and excitement, a dense black cloud had been approaching the moon. Almost as suddenly as though an electric light switch had been pressed down, the cloud blotted out the moon. At one minute the light was so bright that one could easily have read by it. The next they were plunged in stygian blackness.

Philo had switched out the lights of the car, to save the batteries. Now he switched them on again. The glow of the rear lights made two red spots ahead in the all-pervading gloom. It was at once a beacon of hope and a new danger: a perfect target for the gunmen to aim at. Richard yelled:

'Put out those lights! For God's sake, switch your lights off!'

It was at that moment there came a blinding flash behind them. It was followed by a scream of agony. The wires of the fence had been electrified, but not, as they had thought, only to operate an alarm bell if they were cut. They were fully charged, to inflict grievous injury on anyone who, without being insulated, touched them. In the darkness, one of the gunmen had blundered into the fence; and, as he would have been holding his Sten gun in front of him, the metal coming into contact with the wire must have caused the explosion.

Their lungs nearly bursting from the strain put upon them, the three fugitives reached the car. Philo had ignored Richard's shout, but opened all four doors. As he slipped into the driver's seat, the other two men pushed the girl into the back of the car, and Simon scrambled in after her. Richard ran round to the front. The second he slammed the door, Philo pressed the starter of the engine. He let it rev up for a moment, then threw in the clutch. The car moved forward along the bumpy track. At that moment, one of the gunmen opened fire.

All other sounds were drowned by the furious clatter of his Sten gun. Then came the thud and clang of bullets as they smashed into the metal of the boot. The rear lights were shot out. But again the Lords of Light gave their protection. No bullet hit a tyre, and the car was within yards of a bend in the lane. Only seconds later, they were round it and out of danger.

As they turned into the main road, Philo asked angrily, 'What the heck has been going on? I didna' bargain to get meself shot at.'

It was Richard, having got his breath back quicker than Simon, who answered him. 'As we thought possible, it was a wild party. So wild that Lincoln B. Glasshill thinks it worth while to employ gunmen as a protection against snoopers. We were darned lucky to get away.'

'You certainly were. How come the dame?'

'She wasn't enjoying the party. I suppose it was wilder than she had expected. Anyhow, she broke away and made a bolt for it. We could hardly sit tight in the bushes and watch her being dragged back to be raped again.'

Simon spoke from behind him. 'What are we going to do with her?'

'We'll drop her off wherever she is living.' Philo volunteered.

'No, we can't do that,' said Richard promptly. 'Those people would get hold of her again. God alone knows what they might do to stop her talking.'

'Take her to some small hotel, then.'

'How can we, dressed in this fur cat's thing?' Simon protested. 'And if she takes it off, she's next to naked.'

'Yes,' Richard agreed. 'Somehow we've got to get her some clothes.' After a moment, he added, 'There's only one thing for it. We must take her to Don Caesar's.'

'The boss *will* be pleased,' Philo observed sarcastically. 'I'd not like to haul him an' his lady oot o' bed at gettin' on fer one in the morning. Aye, and them off to Europe first thing tomorrow.'

'It can't be helped. That is, unless you've got a wife or mother who would lend the young woman some clothes.'

Philo shook his head. 'Nay, *Señor*. Taking Don Caesar's orders is ma bread an' butter. But I don't like the smell of this party at all, at all. The less I ha' to do with it, the better I'll be pleased.'

Ten minutes later, he pulled the car up before the front door of the house in the *Avenida Amerigo Vespucci*. It was in darkness. Richard said to Simon, 'We don't want any of the servants to see her. You'd better get out and take her into the shrubbery until I've had a talk with Don Caesar.'

'Ummm,' Simon agreed. 'Tell you what. If you remember, there's a summer house behind the shrubbery. We'll wait in it till you join us.'

The girl, evidently exhausted after her ordeal, had not spoken since they had got her into the car, but had lain back with closed eyes. Now she took the hand Simon extended to help her out, and obediently accompanied him along a path leading to the back garden.

Philo had also got out, and was ruefully regarding the line of holes made by the bullets from the Sten gun in the boot of his car.

'Don't worry,' Richard told him. 'I'll pay for the damage, and the hire of a car for you while yours is being repaired.'

Then, Simon and the girl now being out of sight along the path through the shrubbery, he walked up to the front door of the house and rang the bell. He had to ring a second time, and some minutes elapsed before a sleepy manservant in a dressing gown answered the door. Recognising Richard from having seen him the night before at the dinner party, he went up to get Don Caesar.

Meanwhile, Simon had escorted his charge to the summer house and settled her on the verandah, in a wicker chair with comfortable cushions. Some while back the moon had come out again from behind the big, black cloud and for the first time he had a chance to take a really good look at her. Being short-sighted, he had not before realised that she was a Jewess. Patting her on the arm, he said kindly:

'Now listen. You've nothing to be afraid of. We want to help you. To do that, we must know a bit about you. What's your name?'

'Nella Nathan,' she replied in a low voice.

'D'you live here in Santiago?'

'No. I'm here . . . here on a holiday.'

'Umm. Where do you live, then? You're an American, aren't you?'

'Yes. I come from Beaufort, South Carolina. But it's four months since I left there. I've been living up on the Sala de Uyuni.'

'Where in the world's that?'

'It's a vast plateau high up in the Andes, just over the border from Chile, in Bolivia.'

'And what were you doing there?'

'Working . . . working for . . . for the Cause.'

Simon stared at her, then said angrily, 'For the Devil's cause. Then you weren't drawn into this hellish business through some stupidity of your own. You willingly became a Satanist.'

'No!' she protested quickly. 'No. I mean the cause of Equal Rights.'

'Equal rights for whom?'

'Why, coloured people, of course.' To explain herself, she suddenly burst into a torrent of words. 'I'm a school-teacher. At least I was. I became a Freedom Marcher. The suffering that white people have inflicted on their coloured brothers is terrible—just terrible. You are a Jew, aren't you? The sufferings of our people were simply nothing to theirs. When they were brought over to America as slaves, they were treated worse than cattle. They died in agony by the tens of thousands, from thirst, disease and the most brutal flogging. It should be on the conscience of every white person to do what he can to make it up to them. Although technically they've been free for a long time now, they're still despised and rejected. Not one per cent

88

of them are given the chance of a good education. Not one in ten thousand succeeds in fighting the prejudice which bars them from getting top jobs. The vast majority still live in squalor and misery, deprived of everything that makes life worth living. They're just made use of to do all the dirtiest, meanest jobs for a bare subsistence. Even justice is denied them if their case is opposed in the courts by a white man.'

'I know, I know,' said Simon soothingly. 'But all this is beside the point.'

'It's not,' she retorted furiously. 'It is the reason why I'm here. As I've told you, I became a Freedom Marcher campaigning for Equal Rights. I wrote articles, but the paper in my rotten little home town refused to publish them. I went on protest marches and spoke on street corners. I got the pay-off I might have expected. The School Board decided that I was a bad influence on children, so I lost my job. My parents are dead, and I lived alone. After I'd been sacked, I was hard put to earn a living. In the South no-one wanted to employ a girl who was pro-Negro. I suppose I could have become a whore, but I was a virgin and wanted to remain that way until I met a man whom I liked enough to marry. To get enough to eat I had to take dimes they could ill afford from my Negro friends, for giving private tuition to their children.'

Nella paused a moment to get her breath, then hurried on. 'A month or two after I'd been jeered out of my school by rotten little white children, I was approached by one of the leaders in the campaign for Equal Rights. He told me that they were determined to win through, but could hope to do so only if their efforts were properly co-ordinated. To have established a headquarters in the States was out of the question. The F.B.I. would have got wind of it and, on some filthy excuse, had the police raid the place, beat up everybody there and throw them into prison. So they had established a bureau in South America, at a place where there wasn't a Federal agent within five hundred miles and there they were planning a world-wide campaign aimed at achieving Black Power.'

'Black Power,' Simon repeated. 'That's a new one on me.'

'It was on me, too. But for them to secure a real say in how the countries they lived in are run seemed to me a very worthwhile project. This man told me that, at their secret headquarters, they were terribly short of people who were competent to draft manifestos, or knew anything about India, Pakistan and North Africa, as well as the problems we were faced with in the States. He offered me a job there. I took it and was flown out to La Paz. then down to Sala de Uyuni.'

'What did you find there?' Simon interjected.

'A town of hutments, where two or three hundred people were all working for the same end. They were of many races, but there were comparatively few whites. To begin with, I enjoyed it enormously. It was wonderful to meet people from so many countries and discuss with them how the white tyranny could be overthrown, so that everyone in the world had the same chances, rights and share in God's blessings. Of course, we all knew that it was a long-term project. We could not hope for big results until the sixties, or perhaps even the seventies. But in every continent we were building up cells and chains of command; so that, when the time was ripe, Black Power would be really formidable.'

'You say that, to begin with, you enjoyed it enormously. What went wrong later?'

'It was the man I was working under. His name is El Aziz and he is a Moroccan. He persistently endeavoured to seduce me, and I wouldn't play.'

'So you do draw the line about colour when it comes to going to bed with a man?'

'No. Oh no; it wasn't that. For a husband I'd prefer a coloured man. They're nearly always kinder to their wives. It was . . . well, although I'm twenty-seven, as I told you I was still a virgin. The fact is I . . . I suppose I'm just naturally frigid. I've always found the thought of sex repulsive.'

Simon nodded understandingly. 'I see. Ummm. Some women seem to be born that way. What happened then?'

'It is far from healthy up on the Sala. There are many marshes and swamps that breed fevers. That is why even the Andean Indians shun the place, and it was such a good choice to carry on secret activities. Most of the coloured folk seem to be immune. But whites and Eurasians need regular medication and, every few months, they are sent away for a change of air.

'My turn came soon after Christmas, and a party of us were flown down to Viña del Mar. We spent ten days there, having a lovely time, then we were brought up to Santiago so that we could see something of the capital before returning to our jobs. A Jamaican mulatto named Harry Benito was in charge of us. He made all the arrangements and paid the bills. Yesterday afternoon he told me he was going to give me a special treat and take me to a party. The other women were quite jealous, because he had singled me out. He had told me it was to be a late party; so I wasn't surprised that we didn't leave the little hotel where we were staying until after ten o'clock.

'He drove me out to that big house. When we got there I was told it was to be a fancy-dress affair, and taken to a room where there were a lot of animal costumes, and other women changing into them. I've always loved cats, so I chose this one. Then we joined the men and had a few drinks. I'm sure Benito put something into mine, because for some while afterwards I didn't properly take in what was going on. It wasn't until I was out in the garden that my mind began to clear. Everyone was gathered round a long table, and to my amazement a lovely woman who hadn't got a stitch of clothing on came out of the house, accompanied by a man dressed as a goat. The two of them mounted the table and sat down on sort of thrones. But, if you were watching from among those trees, you must have seen them, and what went on.'

'Ummm,' murmured Simon. 'My friend and I were there from the beginning.'

'Well, the next thing I realised was that I had Benito on one side of me and El Aziz on the other. It wasn't until much later that it struck me that the two of them must have hatched a plot to get me there. I was still terribly muzzy when they all formed a long line. Automatically I moved forward between the two men; then I found myself staring at the naked bottom of the man who was dressed as a goat. Before I could stop him, El Aziz suddenly put a hand behind my head and pushed it down, so that my face was pressed for a moment against the warm flesh. I was utterly revolted and almost sick. As I gave a gasp and jerked my face away, El Aziz whispered in my ear, "If you make a scene, we'll cut your throat."

'From that moment I was petrified with fear. I would have given anything, anything, to get away; but I simply didn't dare attempt to. The drumming began to make my heart beat faster, and my head began to ache. When the feast started, they tried to make me eat, stuffing food into my mouth. But I couldn't swallow anything solid, and spat it out. I did gulp down some wine, though. I thought it might give the courage to try to escape. There must have been something in the wine, because I felt a queer sensation and became . . . well, you know what happened, so I may as well say it . . . all moist and itching between the thighs. I've no doubt that El Aziz had given me

91

an aphrodisiac. If it hadn't been for that, I'm sure that when the orgy started I should have resisted, whatever they had threatened to do to me. I did resist to some extent. Yet, in a way, I felt an urge to let it happen and be for good free of my inhibition. Then, when I did, I suffered absolute hell. The pain was simply terrible.'

At that point, Nella burst into a flood of tears. Patting her shoulder, Simon endeavoured to comfort her. 'There, there, my dear. Must have been ghastly for you. Don't wonder you went berserk when this chap El Aziz pushed you into the arms of a second man. But don't worry. You've nothing more to fear. We'll look after you. I promise we will.'

For all the good his words did, they might have fallen on deaf ears. Ignoring them, Nella continued to sob as though she would never stop. She was still crying bitterly when Richard appeared. He was carrying a small suitcase and over his other arm had a blue cloak. To Simon he said:

'At first, Don Caesar practically refused to believe my account of tonight's doings, and he was anything but pleased about our having brought the woman here. But I offered to take him out and show him the bullet holes in the boot of Philo's car. After that he agreed that, in the circumstances, as we are strangers in Santiago, the only course open to us was to come here and ask his help. He went upstairs then, and came down with this old suitcase. It's got some of his wife's things in, including a nightie, a toothbrush, comb and so on. Anyway, all that's needed to make our renegade witch respectable enough for us to get a room for her at an hotel.'

The three of them were on the verandah outside the summer house. Taking a pace forward, Richard thrust the suitcase at the still weeping Nella with one hand and, grasping her shoulder with the other, gave her a quick shake.

'Now then, young woman. You brought this on yourself, and no good will come of snivelling over it. Take this inside and get yourself dressed. We can't hang about here all night.'

Coming unsteadily to her feet, Nella took the case and obediently walked through the door into the semi-darkness while the two men turned their backs.

During the few minutes she took to change, Simon gave Richard a condensed account of what she had told him, and ended by saying, 'So you see, the poor girl isn't really to blame for getting mixed up with this unholy crew; and we must be gentle with her.'

'I've not suggested that we should actually apply the thumb-screws,' Richard replied testily. 'But you're a sight too soft-hearted, Simon. The silly bitch has brought this on herself. From what you tell me, she is a typical do-gooder, and it's those people who run round carrying torches for this and that who stir up half the trouble in the world. It's interesting about this Black Power thing, though. Such a movement might cause endless trouble. We must get out of her everything she knows about it.'

Nella rejoined them, wearing the blue cloak over a dark dress and carrying the suitcase and the cat costume. Richard took the latter from her, and said, 'We'll jettison this on the way to the city. Then we'll get our driver to drop you at a small hotel where you can spend the rest of the night.'

'Ner,' countered Simon. 'We'll take her to the Hilton. Promised to look after her. Mean to see she's all right.'

'As you wish,' Richard shrugged, then turned to Nella. 'Our driver knows nothing about what went on in the grounds of that place, and I don't want him to; so please refrain from talking until we get to the hotel.'

Walking round to the front of the house, they got into the car. When it had covered half a mile, Richard threw the cat robe out of the window. Ten minutes later, Philo set them down outside the Hilton and, with evident relief, drove away.

With the calm assurance natural to him, Richard asked the night clerk for a room for the lady. While she filled in the usual form, he took a few paces back from the desk and said in a low voice to Simon, 'We'll take her up to our suite first, and get what we can out of her.'

'Why not wait till the morning?' Simon demurred. 'It's after two o'clock. Poor child needs some sleep.'

'Poor child, my foot,' retorted Richard. 'I'm not wasting a moment until I find out if she can tell us anything about Rex.'

'O.K. then.' Simon was already carrying Nella's case. Walking up to the desk, he collected the key to the room she had been given, and the three of them went up in the lift.

As soon as they were in their sitting room, Richard went over to the drinks table and mixed for them all badly-needed brandies and soda. Handing one to Nella, he said:

'Now, young lady. Mr Aron has passed on to me what you told him about yourself. You've been through a very bad time tonight and, naturally, we are sorry for you. But we were not talking among those trees out of idle curiosity or for the good

93

of our health. We have reason to believe that through your—er—friends, we may be able to trace a friend of ours who has been missing for some weeks. While you were up at this place Sala-something, did you happen to meet, or hear anything of, a compatriot of yours named Rex Van Ryn?'

Nella hesitated for a moment, then she replied, 'The name rings a bell. Yes, I remember now. Isn't he a very big man with an ugly, attractive face?'

Simon gave a jerky nod. 'That's Rex. What d'you know about him?'

She shook her head. 'Nothing really. I saw him only once; he was with a man they call "The Prince", who is the head of the movement. I asked the person I was standing beside your friend's name, only out of curiosity, because he was such a splendid specimen of manhood.'

'So Rex *is* up there!' Richard's brown eyes lit up. 'And hob-nobbing with the top brass. How extraordinary. It's almost unbelievable. What could possibly have led him to get himself mixed up in this?'

'Maybe he's not there of his own free will,' Simon suggested. 'This place sounds so isolated that escape from it may be next to impossible. If so, he could be a prisoner, but allowed to walk about.'

'That must be it.' Richard turned again to Nella. 'Tell us now what you know about this movement.'

Her face took on a sullen look. 'Why should I? What has it got to do with you? I can see you're not in sympathy with it.'

'By God, I'm not! It sounds about as dangerous as anything could be.'

'I don't agree,' Nella protested angrily. 'Its aim is to bring equality to all the coloured people in the world, to secure for them a fair share of all the good things of which they have been deprived all too long.'

With difficulty Richard retained his temper. After a moment he said, 'Now listen, my girl. You're talking through your hat. You can't possibly have grasped the significance of this thing you've got yourself involved in. I've nothing against coloured people, any more than I have against poor whites. We'll all like to see the slums abolished, every child given a decent education and a fair chance to lead a prosperous, happy life. But this Black Power idea, which woolly-minded Liberals like you have fallen for, and are abetting, is something utterly different. Surely you can see that, after what happened to you tonight?'

'No, I can't. The two things have nothing to do with one another. El Aziz and Harry Benito happened to belong to this awful sect—Devil-worshippers, I suppose you'd call them. And they tricked me into going to that house. But none of the others in the party I was with was present. They could have had no idea what would take place, otherwise they wouldn't have said how lucky I was to be chosen by Benito as his guest. They are all decent, respectable people. So are those up at Sala de Uyuni. Nothing of that kind takes place up there.'

'Maybe it doesn't; that is, as far as you know.'

'If it did, El Aziz would have fixed it for me to be taken to a meeting of that kind, weeks ago. I tell you, the people I have been working with are some of the finest I've ever met. Many of them have given up good positions to travel to the Sala and serve the cause for nothing but their keep. We're dedicated to securing equal rights for coloured people, and I'm not going to give you any information about the movement that might enable you to sabotage it.'

Richard shook his head wearily. 'I don't doubt that you're right about most of these people, but I'm convinced that you're not about the leaders. They are obviously trading on the sympathies of idealists and making use of them. The fact is that you have fallen into the hands of the enemy. By that I do not mean coloured people. They have the same sort of bodies and urges to kindness or cruelty as whites. In both cases, the majority are good and only the minority bad. And surely you can see that the men who started this Black Power idea must be evil?

'Just think what will happen if they succeed in their plans. In a few years' time this organisation you are helping to build will be given the word to begin operating. There will be increased agitation everywhere. That will lead to riots and clashes with the police. No city with a coloured population will be immune. By the sixties, there will develop a sort of sporadic civil war in the United States, and by the seventies it will have spread to Europe. There will be bloody street battles, rape, arson, murder, the lot. Nothing could be better calculated to destroy civilisation. Law and order will go by the board, and your coloured people are going to suffer even worse than the whites; because you can be sure that the whites will fight back. They won't pull any punches, either. When their shops are looted, their houses burned and their women raped, they'll take the law into their own hands and go out to kill. And, believe you me, white men are tougher than blacks. Thousands of innocent people whose lot you are trying to better will be massacred. That is the situation that you and your friends are working to bring about.'

Nella's eyes distended with horror at the picture Richard had painted. She stared at him and murmured, 'Do . . . do you really believe that?'

'I do,' he replied firmly. 'I'm certain of it. Without realising it, you have been fighting on the Devil's side. His one object ever since the Creation has been to bring about disruption. One of his names is "The Lord of Misrule". And what could possibly be better calculated to bring about disruption than this Black Power movement? It is Satan's most powerful weapon in his remorseless fight to dominate mankind. Now, you really must tell us all you have learned about it.'

'Ner,' Simon intervened. 'Nella's been through a terrible time, and she's about all in. Tomorrow, or rather in a few hours' time, when we've all had a bit of shut-eye.'

'Tomorrow,' she repeated miserably. 'Oh, what am I going to do? I can't go back to the Sala now, even if I wanted to. I've no money, not even clothes, and nowhere to go.'

'Don't worry, my dear,' said Simon. 'We'll look after you. Have you no family at all?'

'I've an aunt and uncle who live up in Connecticut.'

'Couldn't you go to them?'

'Yes, I suppose I could. Up there in New England, there is not the prejudice against sympathisers with the Equal Rights movement that there is in the South. I've got quite good qualifications, so up there I could probably get another job as a teacher.'

Simon nodded vigorously. 'That's the idea then. When we've had some shut-eye, we'll go shopping and get you an outfit, then buy you a seat on an aircraft to take you north. You needn't worry about mun, either. I've plenty in New York. I'll give you a draft on my bank there for five hundred dollars. That should keep you going until you get a job.'

Tears came into her eyes. 'You're very, very kind.'

'Not really.' He looked a little embarrassed. 'Enjoy helping people out, that's all.'

'May I take it that you'll tell us all you can?' Richard asked. As she stood up, she nodded. 'Yes. I'm only just beginning to realise how stupid I've been. And thank you both. Thank you for everything.'

Picking up the suitcase, Simon said, 'You're on the fourth floor, aren't you? I'll see you down to your room.'

Ten minutes later, when he returned, Richard had already gone into his bedroom. Calling out 'Good night', Simon put out the light and went into his. He now felt terribly tired and, contrary to his custom, simply got out of his clothes and flung them higgledy-piggledy on the armchair. Crawling into bed, he stretched out luxuriously, gave a great yawn, switched off the light and, within five minutes, was sound asleep.

But he was not destined to sleep as long as he would have wished. A little over three hours later he was twisting, turning and moaning, in the grip of a nightmare. He was standing naked on the edge of a smoking pit. Nella was with him, and with his right hand he was grasping her wrist. Beyond her, rearing up from the depths of the pit, there was a great serpent. Its head lay pressed against Nella's terrified face, its upper part was twisted round her neck and body. It was striving to drag her from him, down into the unseen depths of the pit.

Simon awoke, his body drenched in sweat. For a moment he lay weak and spellbound. With an effort he sat up and switched on the light. He saw from his bedside clock that it was just on six o'clock. Picking up the telephone he dialled the number of Nella's room 421. He could hear the 'phone ringing, but there was no reply. Thinking it possible that he might have fumbled the dial and rung the wrong number, he put the receiver down, then dialled again. There was still no answer.

Slipping out of bed, he pulled on his dressing gown and shuffled into his slippers, then hurried through the sitting room to Richard's bedroom. Richard was lying on his side, snoring gently. Simon put a hand on his shoulder and shook him awake. Richard raised himself on one elbow, stared with sleepy eyes at his friend, and muttered:

'What the hell? Not time to get up yet, is it? I haven't over-slept, have I?'

'Ner, but you've got to get up and come with me,' Simon said in an urgent voice. 'Nella's in danger.'

'Nella? Oh, the little schoolmarm do-gooder who got herself taken for a ride.'

'Yes. The girl we rescued last night. Just had a dream about her. In colour. It was a true dream, I'm sure. I must have been up on the astral. She's threatened in some way. I rang her room, but could get no reply. Only pray to God she was in too deep a sleep for it to rouse her. But we've got to find out.'

Still half asleep, Richard slid from his bed and wriggled into the dressing gown that Simon held out for him. Together they left the suite and hurried along the corridor to the lift. When they reached the fourth floor, Simon led the way to the room at the door of which he had left Nella some three hours earlier. He knocked, but there was no reply. He knocked much louder: still no response. Grasping the handle of the door, he tried it. The door was not locked, and opened easily. He switched on the light, and Richard followed him into the room.

Nella lay on the bed. She had on the nightdress she had been lent, but the bedclothes had been pulled halfway down. Her head was twisted back grotesquely. There was blood all over her, and one glance showed that she was dead. Black marks on her throat showed that she had been strangled. Her mouth gaped open and her tongue had been cut out. It had been carefully placed in the valley between her naked breasts.

9

The Great Gamble

'Oh God, how awful!' His birdlike head thrust forward, Simon peered at the figure on the blood-soaked bed.

'Poor little devil,' murmured Richard. 'But we are partly to blame. We should have foreseen this.'

'How could we?'

'You should know well enough, after your past experience of the occult. People with power have no difficulty in over-looking others, by means of a crystal or dark glass. After we got Nella away, the first thing von Thumm and Co. would have done would be to find out where we took her. Then, an hour or two later, one or more of them got into her room somehow and did her in. Look at that bootlace laid across her neck. She wasn't strangled with it. Greyeyes told me once that Satanists always leave that symbol when they've bumped off someone who's betrayed them.'

'That's about it. Ought to have kept her with us.' As Simon spoke, he took a step towards the bed

Richard's hand shot out and caught his arm. 'Stay where you are! You mustn't touch her!'

'Why not? Can't bear the sight of the poor girl's face. Only going to cover it with the bedclothes.'

'You bloody fool! Don't you realise that murder has been done? Within a few hours the police will be here. They mustn't find our fingerprints.'

'Suppose you're right. But oughtn't we to tell the manage-ment and ask them to send for the police?'

For a moment Richard did not reply, then he said, 'I don't think so. Heaven knows, the fact that we brought this woman here is going to be difficult enough to explain. If they know it was us who discovered her body, we'll be in it right up to our necks. The sooner we get out of here, the better.'

As he moved towards the door, he lifted the skirt of his silk dressing gown and put it over the light switch, as he turned out the light. When they were both out in the corridor, he again used the silk to shut the door, then gave the handle a good rub to remove the fingerprints Simon had left there when he opened it.

Side by side, they walked quietly along the passage. As they turned the corner into the broad main corridor, both of them halted, and drew back. They had seen a cleaner, a woman carrying a bucket, walking towards the lift. Although she had been facing their way, they did not think she had caught sight of them; but they could not be certain. Tense and silent, they waited for a good two minutes, then Richard took a quick look round the corner.

'She's gone,' he whispered. 'Come on. But we'd better take the stairs. Less likely to run into anyone than coming out of the lift.'

It was a long haul from the fourth floor up to their suite. They reached it without incident, but very short of breath. As Simon closed the door behind him, he burst out:

'The bastards! How can men perpetrate such horrifying deeds? God knows, murder is bad enough. But to have mutilated the poor girl like that after she was dead, by cutting out her tongue.'

Richard was at the drink table, pouring neat brandy into a glass. Over his shoulder, he said, 'The reason they did that is clear enough. They'd know that even if we didn't see what they'd done, we were certain to be told about it. Nella's tongue was a message to us. "If you want to stay alive, you'd better not talk." '

'Damned if I'll let them get away with this. Best not to let anyone know we found Nella's body. I agree about that. But when someone else finds it, we're certain to be questioned. Nothing to stop us giving the police a full account of what happened tonight, and why we brought Nella here.'

'No good, old chap. They'd never believe us. You can bet your bottom dollar that, within minutes of Nella's getting away, those filthy swine would have scrapped all thought of further fun and games. They would have been frantically clearing up, getting into their ordinary clothes and disappearing. If the police went out to Glasshill's place, even at this moment, I doubt if they'd find a scrap of evidence to show that a Sabbat had been held there. No. Later we may find some way of getting back at them. At the moment, our first concern is to think of some plausible reason to explain why we brought Nella here.'

100

'It's important if we're going to let ourselves be questioned by the police; but if we're not going to come clean with them, hadn't we better try to get out?'

'That would start a hue and cry after us.'

'Doesn't follow that they'd catch us. Not if we acted quickly.'

'There's something in the idea,' Richard said thoughtfully. After taking a second swig of brandy, he went on, 'Having brought Nella here in the middle of the night has got us in damn' deep. It's pretty certain that it will mean our being detained here for questioning, perhaps for weeks.'

'Ummm. And put a stopper on our hunt for Rex.'

'Yes. I'm afraid recent events had made me forget that for the moment. But the one good thing that has come out of this night's work is that we now know where he is. Or, at least, where he was a fortnight or so ago, before Nella left the Sala. In the normal course of events, today would see us on our way up there.'

'Then why shouldn't we skip while the going is good? Don't suppose a chambermaid will get sufficiently impatient to do Nella's room to barge in there before eleven o'clock. By that time we could be on an aircraft. Nella said the Sala is just over the border in Bolivia. With luck, there may be a 'plane flying up to the capital, La Paz.'

Richard nodded. 'If only there is, we'd be out of trouble. It's hardly likely that the Chilean Government could secure an extradition order just to get us back and ask us what we knew about Nella. Even if they could, by the time the Bolivian police started to look for us, we'd have left La Paz days before. There's one thing, though. We ought to make our leaving look as natural as possible. We could say we've been invited to stay up-country for a few days, so we're keeping on the suite; and leave most of our baggage here.'

'We'll need to do a bit of play-acting then. Carry on as usual till we actually leave the hotel.' Simon glanced at the clock. 'It's getting on for seven. Bit early for breakfast, but if we were catching a 'plane the odds are we'd be getting up by now. Shall I ring down for breakfast?'

'Yes. But don't order our usual Continental. People who are about to travel generally fortify themselves with something more solid. I'll have ham and eggs with mushrooms, and a "fruit plate" to follow.'

'Feel too sick to eat anything, but I'll try to manage an omelette,' Simon muttered unhappily.

Breakfast having been ordered, they went to their respective rooms and began to sort out the things they could cram into overnight bags. Richard had just switched on the radio when the floorwaiter wheeled in the trolley. Raising a cheerful grin, he told the man that they were leaving that morning, but would be returning in a few days, then gave him an extra large tip. Their attempts at conversation during the meal lapsed into silence. Neither could keep his mind off Nella's blood-soaked body in the bedroom down on the fourth floor, and wondering how soon it would be discovered. When they had finished, Richard rang the reception desk, asked for their bill to be ready by nine o'clock, and told an under-manager that, although they would be leaving that morning, he wished to keep on the suite.

After they had bathed, shaved and dressed, Richard said, 'It's a quarter to nine. L.A.N., the Chilean Airlines office, is only just round the corner. I expect it opens at nine o'clock. I'll go there now and see if there's any chance of getting up to La Paz.'

'While you're out, I'll go along and see Miranda.' Simon paused, then added, 'How much d'you think I ought to tell her?'

'As little as possible. The less she knows, the better, as there is a chance that the hotel people will tell the police that they've seen her up in the restaurant with us; then they'd question her. You told her only that we thought the party we were going to investigate last night might be a Sabbat, so there is no need to admit that it was.'

'True. And she brushed the idea of Satanism aside. The odds are she'll accept that it was simply a wild party, and be hoping that it gave us a line on Rex.'

'Good. Then you can tell her that it did, and we're losing no time in following it up. It would only worry her to know that her uncle is mixed up with a bunch of Satanists.'

Although Miranda could not see the sights or scenery, she enjoyed the fresh air when being driven in a car, and Simon had promised to take her for a drive that morning. When he told her that he couldn't, after all, she was very disappointed and, when he went on to say that he and Richard were leaving Santiago within an hour or two, she did not seek to hide her distress. But she cheered up when she learned that they now had a clue to Rex's whereabouts, and resigned herself to Simon's leaving her.

During the past few days they had had little chance to be alone together, because Pinney was nearly always with her. But they had made the most of the few occasions when Pinney had not been present; and now Miranda temporarily got rid of her by sending her down to the lobby to buy a magazine.

No sooner had the door closed behind the companion, than Simon moved over to the sofa on which Miranda was sitting, and took her in his arms. For some minutes they kissed passionately. Simon could not tell her that it would be impossible for him to return to Santiago in the foreseeable future, or give her an address where she could get in touch with him; so he told her that, as soon as he possibly could, he would write to her and they would then make arrangements that would bring them together again. On Pinney's return, they parted with great reluctance.

Back in his own room, Simon finished his packing, then waited with as much patience as he could muster for Richard's return. When Richard did get back, he was looking far from cheerful. There was a flight up to La Paz only once a week, leaving on Saturday, and no other aircraft by which they could leave the country until the following day.

To have remained in Santiago overnight meant that, for certain, they would be questioned by the police; and the possibility of being detained for a considerable time as material witnesses. In consequence, he had booked two seats on the flight to Valparaiso, which left daily at midday. That, at least, would get them out of the capital and, with luck, before the police caught up with them, they might find, in the big harbour, a ship about to sail for Callao, or some other port further north.

'Might be worse,' Simon commented. 'Must drive out to the airport. Can't prevent the police from learning we've gone there, and the name of the place for which we've taken off. If it was La Paz, they'd tumble to it at once that we were skipping. Perhaps they'd even have the aircraft radioed to return. As it's Valparaiso, they'll probably think that we've only gone off to spend a few nights at Viña del Mar, and not burst their guts coming after us.'

'That's true. It will certainly look less as though we had something to hide. As you say, it will need only a 'phone call to the airport for them to find out where we are heading; so we might give our departure an even greater air of innocence by telling the hotel people that we're going to get a breath of sea air at Viña del Mar. We'll do that when we pay the bill.'

For the next twenty minutes they hung about uneasily, fearful of appearing to be in too great a hurry to get to the airport; but it was a forty-minute drive so, at half past ten, they had their overnight bags taken down. While Simon was settling the account, the hall porter came up to Richard and asked him for a forwarding address for letters. Momentarily taken aback, Richard stared at the man and then said, 'We'll be back here on Friday, so there's no point in forwarding anything.'

At last they were in the car. When it had reached the outskirts of the city, Simon glanced at his watch. It was exactly eleven o'clock, the deadline after which they could expect a chambermaid to enter Nella's room at any moment, and come upon her dead body.

With luck, at the horrid sight of that gaping, tongueless mouth, the woman might faint, gaining them ten minutes before she revived or, in turn, was found and the management informed. Another ten minutes, or perhaps twenty, would elapse before the police arrived on the scene. Porters, floor waiters and other employees would be questioned. Of these the night clerk was the key man, because it was he who had seen Nella arrive with Richard and Simon, and go up with them in the lift. But the odds were that he was now in bed, and asleep. If so and, better still, he did not live in the hotel, well over an hour might pass between the discovery of Nella's body and a connection between her and them established. But those delays would bring their zero hour to midday, and none of them could be counted on.

It was eleven-twenty-five when they checked in at the airport. They spent half an hour of almost unbearable suspense, walking up and down the hall. Then, when they joined the little queue at the exit gate, a loudspeaker blared in Spanish. Simon swallowed hard, then said to Richard, 'Something wrong with the bloody 'plane. That announcement. Slight delay before take-off.'

Richard gave a sigh. 'I'm afraid it's not the 'plane. More likely that the police have just telephoned from the Hilton, ordering it to be held until they come out and pick us up.'

Grimly, they continued waiting in the queue, their eyes anxiously roving about the hall. Whenever they spotted a policeman in the crowd, coming in their direction, they felt certain that he was looking for them. But the minutes ticked by. At ten past twelve the flight was called again. They went out to the 'plane. The next five minutes seemed to them an eternity. Every moment they expected an official to come aboard and call out their names. But the brief routine of the captain's announcement and fastening safety belts passed without interruption. At twelve-fifteen the aircraft took off for Valparaiso.

Yet their ordeal was far from over. The flight would take the best part of half an hour. By this time it seemed certain that Nella's body would have been found, and the police have begun their enquiries. At any moment they might telephone the Santiago airport, to ask the destination of the 'plane by which Richard and Simon had left, then they would only have to telephone Valparaiso for them to be arrested on landing.

In an agony of apprehension they sat through the brief journey, refusing the coffee and biscuits that the air hostess offered tnem, but accepting American magazines and toying with, but not reading, them.

At what seemed a dangerously low altitude the little aircraft skimmed over the Mountains of the Coast, then came down out of a cloudless sky, to make a smooth landing. Tense and alert, they left the 'plane and walked across the tarmac to the airport building. As they had come in on an internal flight, there were no passport or Customs formalities, and no dreaded policeman was waiting there to accost them. Carrying their grips, they walked straight through to the taxi rank. Simon asked the driver of a cab to take them to a travel agency near the docks. The man drove them into the city and set them down outside an office in the window of which there were a number of fly-blown posters; but, by then, it was past one o'clock and the place had been closed for the siesta.

Paying off the cab, they crossed the street to a café. It was a gloomy place, with a solitary, surly waiter. They did not feel like eating anything, so ordered only pisco sours and, when they had drunk them, they repeated the order at intervals until they had whiled away the next two hours. Eventually the travel agency was reopened by a short, plump young woman whose blonde hair was obviously dyed. Simon told her that they wanted to make their way to the United States by easy stages, and asked her what ships carrying passengers were about to sail for the north. After much shuffling through papers, and two telephone calls, she told them that she could get them accommodation on a Dutch cargo ship that was sailing the next day. The ship had cabins for twelve passengers, and was bound for Curaçao in the West Indies, which was her home port; but on the way there would call at Callao in Peru, Guayaquil in Ecuador and at Panama on going through the Canal.

Simon never ventured abroad without taking a considerable sum in U.S. dollars, to supplement the travel allowance to which he was entitled as a business man. So he had ample funds to pay the fare for the two of them up to Callao, the port of Lima. The Peruvian capital being much nearer La Paz than Santiago, there was a good hope that they would reach it perhaps as soon as the Saturday 'plane would have got them there.

Outside the agency, they debated where to spend the night. Richard's view was that if the police made up their minds that it was worth going after them, at whatever hotel they stayed they would be picked up, so they might as well go to a good one in Viña del Mar. Simon disagreed, on the grounds that, if the police believed the story that they had gone to the coast only for a couple of nights, they would naturally make enquiries for them at the best places first. Whereas it would take many hours for them to check up at the scores of hotels in both the big watering place and the great port; so they would evade a police search for a few hours longer if they took a room at a small hostelry down near the docks.

Richard felt there was something to be said for that; and, after a quarter of an hour spent hunting for a suitable place, they found an inn that looked as though it might be patronised by the officers of merchant ships. There they were given adjacent rooms and, having unpacked their few belongings, went out to while away the rest of the day as best they could. By evening they were so tired of wandering aimlessly about and sitting over drinks in cafés, that they took a taxi into Viña del Mar, dined at the Casino and afterwards played roulette. Richard won the equivalent of three pounds and Simon over twenty, which cheered them up considerably as it seemed an omen that their lucky stars were in the ascendant.

Next morning Simon rang up the ship on which they had booked passages and was told that she was not sailing until the evening, but they could come aboard at any time. Having nothing else to do, they walked along to the dock at ten-thirty. A solitary Customs man lowered a newspaper he was reading, glanced at their bags and nodded to them to go through. Getting out their passports, they walked over to the Immigration desk.

A policeman was lolling against it, smoking a cheroot and carrying on a desultory conversation with the Immigration official. Richard put his passport on the desk. The official opened it, laid it down and said to the policeman:

'These are the two you want.'

The policeman suddenly became alert. Putting his right hand on the holster of the revolver at his side, he said politely, '*Señors*, I regret the necessity of preventing you from going on board a ship; but police headquarters in Santiago have issued an order that, wherever found, you are to be sent there for questioning. Be pleased to walk in front of me to the exit.'

They had no option but to obey. Their careful planning, the periods of acute anxiety and dreary boredom they had suffered during the past twenty-four hours, had all been for nothing. After making a futile protest, seething with suppressed bitterness while endeavouring to appear no more than annoyed that their lawful intentions had been interfered with, they made their way back through the Customs hall, and through an archway to the street.

There, their captor spoke to another policeman, who then went into a telephone box. For the best part of a quarter of an hour they stood on the pavement, pretending to take their arrest light-heartedly, but in fact now filled with gloomy apprehension. A police car then arrived and took them to the airport. There a police inspector took charge of them and locked them in a small, bare room. For the first time they were able to talk, in low voices, of their unhappy situation. But they were not left there for long. The daily service between Santiago and Valparaiso consisted of flights each way, both of which left at twelve noon. The prisoners were put aboard with an escort and, after the short flight, taken in another police car into the city. At a little before half past one, they arrived at police headquarters.

A sergeant took charge of their bags and, when they had been searched, the contents of their pockets. Again Simon protested. He pointed out indignantly that they were not criminals, but law-abiding citizens who had every intention of aiding the police in their inquiries, to the best of their ability. It was of no avail. They were marched off to separate cells and locked in.

Had they been treated in such a way in Britain, they would have taken a very pessimistic view of their prospects; but, as they sat on the wooden benches in their cells, both of them

107

tried to cheer themselves up with the thought that police procedure in most Latin American countries was very elastic, and on lines which differed considerably between rich and poor. Therefore, as wealthy tourists, it seemed unlikely that, after having been questioned, they would be permanently detained.

It was not until four o'clock that they were taken from their cells to a large room on the first floor of the building. There, behind an impressive desk, a much-beribboned police officer was sitting. Just behind him stood a short, plump, dark civilian; and, at a smaller desk to one side of the room, sat a uniformed man with pens and paper.

The officer did not invite them to sit down, but stared at them for a full minute; then he asked, 'Does either of you speak Spanish?'

'I do,' replied Simon.

'That is good. But if there are any questions I ask that you do not understand, I have here an interpreter who will make them clear to you.' He jerked his thumb over his shoulder towards the short, dark man, and went on, 'What was the name of the woman you took to the Carrera Hilton, the night before last?'

Simon pretended to rack his memory. 'Nathan, I think. Yes, that's it, the *Señorita* Nathan.'

'How well did you know her?'

'Hardly at all. We met her only that night.'

'She was, then, a prostitute, and you picked her up?'

'Oh, no; she was not a prostitute; at least, not as far as I know. But I suppose you could say we picked her up.'

'Anyway, you took her back to the hotel with you for immoral purposes.'

'We did nothing of the kind,' Simon declared firmly.

'Why, then, did you take her to the hotel?'

Soon after arriving in Valparaiso, Richard and Simon had agreed on the account they would give if they were caught and questioned. Now, Simon gave it:

'My friend and I are fond of exercise, but we find it too hot here to take much in the daytime; so, after a late dinner that night, we decided to go for a long walk. I don't know how far we walked, but it was right out past the suburbs, and must have been five or six miles. On our way back, when we reached that wooded hill—the St Lucia Park I think it's called—we decided to go up to the top. Our idea was that, from the ruin

108

up there, we'd get a wonderful view of the city in the moonlight. But we never got to the top. A little way up we came upon this woman. She was sitting on a bench, crying. I asked her what was the matter. She said she had had a terrible quarrel with her husband and had walked out on him. To calm herself down, before looking for a small hotel in which to spend the night, she had sat for a while in a café and had a couple of drinks. Five minutes after leaving it, she found that she had left her handbag behind. When she went back, it wasn't on the chair where she had left it. In her absence the waiter, or one of the other customers, must have stolen it. The bag had all her money and a few pieces of jewellery in it. Having lost it, she was penniless; she couldn't pay for a room and had nowhere to spend the night.'

'So you fell for her story that she was a respectable woman? It did not even occur to you that she might be a prostitute, hoping that you would offer to take her to your own bed?'

'I had no reason to disbelieve her. She was quietly dressed and had a small suitcase with her. That supported what she had said about having left her home.'

'Did you try to persuade her to go back to her husband?'

'Yes. But she wouldn't hear of doing that. She said she would rather starve.'

'Was there nowhere else she could have gone?'

'Apparently not, or we wouldn't have found her sitting weeping on a park bench.'

'What was her nationality?'

This was a question that had not occurred to Richard or Simon they might be asked. After hesitating a moment, thinking it hardly likely that they would have come upon a foreigner in such a situation, Simon replied, 'Chilean.'

'In that case it seems very strange that, in a great city like Santiago, she had not a single relative or friend whom she could have asked to give her shelter for the night.'

Simon shrugged. 'She may be a stranger here. Perhaps she had come up from the country with her husband and had the row with him in an hotel.'

'Did she ask you for money?'

'No.'

'Did you offer her any?'

'No.'

'I see,' commented the officer sarcastically. 'So, instead of giving her the price of a room for the night in a modest pension, you took her off to the most luxurious hotel in the capital.'

'By then, Mr Eaton and I were tired, so . . .'

'Really! Yet a few minutes earlier you had decided that, before returning to your hotel, you would walk another kilometre up steep paths, for no better reason than to see the city in moonlight.'

Simon swallowed hard. 'I meant we were anxious to get the matter settled and, as we had ample money, it seemed simplest to take the poor woman with us to the Hilton.'

'And when you got there you asked for a room for her, and she went straight up to it.'

Simon had been ready for that one. 'Not right away. She was about all in; so first we took her up to our suite and gave her a brandy and soda.'

'How long did she remain there with you?'

'Ten minutes, perhaps a quarter of an hour.'

'What then?'

'I took her down to the room she had been given on the fourth floor.'

'How long did you stay there?'

'I didn't. I didn't even go in. I gave her her case and left her at the door. Then I went back upstairs and Mr Eaton and I went to bed.'

'How long was it before one or both of you went down to her room again?'

'Neither of us did. We had already planned to go down to Viña del Mar for a couple of nights; so next morning we paid our bill and hers, and left for the airport.'

'Without even seeing her?'

'Yes. She wasn't our responsibility. We felt that, after a night's sleep, she should be able to sort out her own problems.'

'Then you did not know that she had been murdered?'

Simon had known that, sooner or later, he would be confronted with that fact. Letting his mouth gape, he exclaimed:

'What d'you say? Murdered?'

'Yes. That is what I said.'

Turning to Richard, Simon said in English, 'That poor woman. She's been murdered!'

Richard pretended equal astonishment and swiftly came out with, 'Good God! How terrible!'

Simon's dark eyes flickered back to the officer and, reverting to Spanish, he asked, 'When was this? And who murdered her?'

'The crime was committed between three and six in the morning. By whom, we have yet to find out. Tell me now. When you and your friend reached Valparaiso, instead of going to an hotel in Viña del Mar, as you say you had intended to, you booked passage in a ship that was leaving for Callao the following day. Why did you do that?'

'Just an idea,' Simon shrugged. 'Mr Eaton and I are travelling in South America for pleasure, and we've plenty of money. We have already visited Buenos Aires, Punta Arenas and Santiago. When we got down to Valparaiso, it suddenly occurred to us that a few days at sea would make a pleasant change from air travel, and the obvious place to go was Callao, as then we'd be able to see something of the nearby Peruvian capital.'

'Indeed? It had occurred to me that your sudden change of plan was due to an urgent desire to leave this country for good.'

'Why should we want to do that?' Simon asked, with an air of innocence. 'We hadn't the least intention of doing so. If you ask the people at the Hilton, you'll find that we left most of our belongings there, and arranged to retain our suite.'

'That I already know. But there are occasions when it is well worth while to abandon even valuable property. For instance, if one had reason to fear arrest.' Picking up a gold-braided cap from his desk, the officer put it on, stood up and said, 'For today, *Señors*, that will be all. I am detaining you for further questioning.'

'One moment!' Simon said quickly. 'With what are we charged?'

'Nothing, as yet. I am holding you as material witnesses in a case of murder.'

'I see, but I imagine we shall not be refused bail?'

'Perhaps bail will be granted. It all depends on how the matter develops.'

'In any case, we shall require the services of a lawyer. I formally request that the British Ambassador be informed of our situation and asked to arrange for us to have suitable legal aid.'

The officer nodded. 'That shall be done.' Then he signed to the escort, and the prisoners were marched back to their separate cells.

Later, it transpired that as they were able to pay for a dinner of their choice and bottles of wine, they were allowed to send out for them. On hard beds both of them spent a far from

111

happy night. But they felt that, although the police obviously suspected them of not having told the whole truth about their relations with Nella, Simon's story was quite plausible and had been received reasonably well.

At a little after ten o'clock on the Friday morning, they were taken from their cells to a bleak room furnished only with a table and a few chairs. Standing there was a tall, fair-haired, youngish man. He introduced himself as Ernest Phillips, one of the secretaries at the British Embassy.

Sitting down at the table, Simon and Richard gave him their own account of their brief association with Nella, then discussed the situation. When the question of bail arose, they had reason to regret Don Caesar's departure for Europe, as they knew no other solid citizen in Santiago. Neither of them made any mention of Philo McTavish, as they would have been most reluctant to bring him into the affair. Moreover, they felt that, even had he been willing, it was unlikely that he would be able, at short notice, to produce the considerable sum required.

However, Richard stoutly maintained that, as they had not been charged with any crime, the police had no right to confine them in separate cells. Phillips agreed to do what he could to have that matter rectified, said he would arrange for the Embassy lawyer, a *Señor* Fidel Cunliffe, to come to see them that afternoon, and took his departure.

His representations proved effective. Twenty minutes after he had left them, they were taken from their cells and put together in a larger one. So, for the first time since their arrest, they were able to talk over their prospects.

Richard was inclined to be pessimistic, because of their having been arrested when about to go aboard a ship at Valparaiso. That they should have attempted to leave the country within a few hours of Nella's murder could have been a coincidence; but nothing could have suggested more strongly that either they were her murderers or in some way involved in the crime. He now felt that it had been a cardinal mistake to try to escape being questioned by the police. But he did not press the point, because it had been Simon's idea.

However, Simon argued that, although the police would continue to believe that Nella was a prostitute, and that they had brought her to the hotel for immoral purposes, it could not possibly be proved that they had had anything to do with her death. So, with the aid of a capable lawyer, they would soon be released.

Señor Fidel Cunliffe did not arrive until eight o'clock. He was a bulky, red-faced man, with grey hair, prominent blue eyes and a forceful manner. It transpired that he had lived in Chile all his life, but his father had been English and he spoke that language perfectly. Between them they gave him the same account of their brief association with Nella as Simon had given the police. Having made some notes, he then asked them a series of very searching questions. As by then they had their story pat, they did not falter in their replies, and he appeared satisfied. Before he left, Simon tactfully assured him that they had ample funds to pay for the best advice, so he need not be worried about money for expenses. The lawyer replied that, in that case, it would be worth while to instruct a private detective agency to endeavour to find out who, in fact, had murdered the *Señorita* Nathan.

Although Simon had small hope of such an enquiry proving successful, he readily agreed. *Señor* Cunliffe then said that his relations with the police were excellent, so he was confident that he could find out if they knew anything about the murder that his clients did not, and that he would come to see them again the next day.

On Saturday, the hours seemed to them to crawl by. The warders in charge of them proved well disposed. In addition to bringing them good meals and drinks, one of them went out and bought Richard some American magazines, and Simon two packs of patience cards. But, even with these aids for killing time, every few minutes their minds reverted to the promised visit from their lawyer and learning what he had found out from the police.

They had practically given him up when, at half past ten that night, they were taken from their cell to the interviewing room. Cunliffe was standing beside the table, looking very grave. When they had all sat down, he said:

'I fear you have not fully confided in me. For your own sakes I must advise you very earnestly to do so. Now, what else have you to tell me about Miss Nathan?'

It seemed to Richard that it was a question of telling all, or nothing. Although both he and Simon were convinced that Nella had been murdered by Satanists, to prevent her revealing what she knew about the Black Power movement, he could not believe for one moment that, if they gave an account of the Sabbat and of how they had carried Nella off from it, they would be believed; so he replied:

113

'I am sorry you distrust us, *Señor*; but we have already told you everything we know about this terrible affair.'

Simon backed him up by nodding vigorously.

Cunliffe stuck out his jaw aggressively. 'I cannot accept that. When interrogated, Mr Aron lied to the police. You do not appear to have noticed that when, just now, I referred to the murdered woman, I did not use the prefix "*Señorita*", but "Miss". Mr Aron said she was a Chilean; but she was not. She was an American.'

'What leads them to think that?'

'The shoes she was wearing had inside them the address of a shop in Beaufort, South Carolina. Her dress carried the label of an expensive Paris couturier. Her blue cloak, that of Sax, Fifth Avenue. The little suitcase also came from New York. Such items may occasionally be imported, or find their way into Chile; but, for all four of them to be the property of a Chilean woman of the middle classes, is most unlikely. There is then the matter of your deciding to go on a short sea trip which, incidentally, would take you out of the country. In Mr Aron's disposition, it is stated that this idea did not occur to you until *after* you arrived in Valparaiso. Is that correct?'

Simon nodded.

'In that case why, earlier that morning, did you, Mr Eaton, go to the office of L.A.N., make enquiries for flights leaving that day for La Paz, Lima and places further north; and, only when you learned that there was none, take tickets for Valparaiso?'

As Richard did not answer, Cunliffe went on, 'The police suggested to you that you took the woman to your hotel for immoral purposes. You denied that. But medical examination of the body disclosed that she had been raped by a man, or men, within a few hours of her death. Her vagina was terribly lacerated and semen found in it.'

'We had nothing to do with that,' Richard declared swiftly. 'I swear to you that neither of us touched her.'

'Then what were you doing for the best part of three hours in the room to which you took her?'

'Three hours? What nonsense. After we had given her a drink up in our suite, Mr Aron took her down to her room. He rejoined me within ten minutes, then we both went to bed.'

'That you gave her a drink in your suite is accepted. There were three used tumblers there. Then you took her down to her room and remained there with her. At about six o'clock, a cleaning woman saw you both coming out of it.'

'She couldn't have!' Simon burst out. 'She was in the main corridor and Nella's . . .' He had been going to add, 'room was round the corner in a side passage'. Too late, he realised that he had given himself away.

The lawyer gave a grim little smile. 'You see? I was right. Both of you have been lying to me. And, *Señors*, I must warn you that your situation is now extremely grave. You are both about to be charged with murder.'

10

A Desperate Situation

The eyes of Richard and Simon met. Without words, those of each told the other how fully they realised the desperateness of their situation. It was Richard who spoke first. Turning to Fidel Cunliffe, he said:

'It's useless to deny that we have not told you the truth—at least, not the whole of it. The devil of it is that if we did I greatly doubt if you, or anyone else, would believe us. The police are right about Nella—that was the woman's name— Nella Nathan's having been an American. They are right, too, that it was because we knew of her death and feared that we would become involved in it, that we attempted to leave the country. The reason we have given for bringing her to the Hilton in the middle of the night is a complete fabrication. None the less, neither of us was in any way responsible for her murder. Upon that I give you my solemn word.'

Simon nodded. 'That's the truth. Ready to swear to that on the Torah.'

The lawyer looked from one to the other. His expression had softened, and no longer held a veiled dislike. After a moment he said in a more gentle voice, '*Señors*, I find your earnestness convincing. I will now admit that only my obligations to the British Embassy would have overcome my reluctance to defend men I believed guilty of such a heinous crime. But, if you are truly innocent, I will do my utmost for you. For your part, though, however improbable-sounding it may be, you must withhold nothing from me.'

During the next quarter of an hour, the two friends gave him a full account of all that had occurred on the night of the previous Tuesday, withholding only Rex's name as that of the friend they had hoped to trace through the Satanists.

When they had done, Cunliffe said, 'No-one is ever going to believe that, by the use of spells, these Satanists had the power to conjure up an evil force capable of committing a physical act such as this murder. But that a clairvoyant could have over-looked the woman and located her at the Hilton would be regarded as plausible. Given that, one or more people could have been despatched to the hotel to kill her. There cannot have been many arrivals at the hotel in the middle hours of the night; so it should be possible to trace those who did, and an investigation into their backgrounds might provide us with valuable material for the defence.'

'Ner,' Simon murmured unhappily. ' 'Fraid we'll get nowhere along those lines. Hotel people have been got at. Just a chance that cleaning woman did spot us as we were about to come round the corner into the main corridor. But I doubt it. Any-how, she definitely could not have seen us come out of Nella's room. It's clear now that those clever swine had a double motive for killing Nella. First, to silence her. Second, to pin her murder on Eatoh and me, to get us out of the way. They must have either terrified or bribed the cleaning woman into saying she saw us; and I think you'll find the night clerk very unhelpful. Besides, Nella's killers may not have actually booked in at the hotel, but got in through one of the service entrances.'

'I fear you are right, Mr Aron. However, there is the house at which the "barbecue" was held. If we can produce evidence that it was actually a Sabbat, we shall have gone a long way to shake the prosecution.'

It was now Richard who struck a pessimistic note. 'It will surprise me if you succeed in that. Of course, the owner of the place, the American Negro lawyer Lincoln B. Glasshill, will not deny that he gave a party there last Tuesday night. We could produce the caterers who delivered the food, and there was so much noise that some of the nearest neighbours must have heard it. But that was four nights ago. They have had more than enough time to remove every trace that Satanic rites are practised out there.'

'That still leaves us Philo McTavish.'

'You may find him a little difficult. After we had rescued Nella, he showed great reluctance to becoming involved further in the affair. And we deliberately refrained from letting him in on the fact that the "barbecue" was actually a witches' Sabbat.'

'As things have turned out, that was a pity,' Cunliffe com-mented. 'But, no matter. We shall, of course, subpoena him, and he will have no option other than to give an account of what occurred during the time he was acting as your driver.

117

That, at least, will establish the fact that you did go out to Glasshill's estate and brought back Nella Nathan from there, wearing the costume of a cat and in a state bordering on collapse. Besides, there are the bullet holes in the boot of his car. Your having been fired on will provide ample proof that those people were, even then, prepared to murder the woman and yourselves, who were protecting her. That will make it illogical for the prosecution to maintain that it was you who killed her an hour or so later. Provided we can shake the cleaning woman and other false witnesses they may produce, I feel there is a very good chance of my securing your acquittal.'

The prisoners were greatly cheered by this, and Richard asked, 'When are we to be brought before a magistrate?'

'As the police completed their investigation today, you would normally be charged tomorrow. But, as tomorrow is Sunday, you will not appear in court until Monday. That is just as well. It gives me an additional day in which to work. I will instruct the detective agency to find out all they can about Glasshill and his house, and I will see McTavish myself.'

When they had thanked him, Simon said, 'Be grateful if you'd do me a favour. This case is certain to make an awful stink in the papers. To learn of it that way would be a terrible shock to a friend of mine. She's staying at the Hilton. I'd like to let her know in advance that Eaton and I are being charged with murder, and beg her not to worry too much. If I wrote a note, would you drop it in at the hotel for me?'

'By all means. I pass the Hilton on my way home. I'll get the warder to bring you a pen and paper.'

When these had been produced, Simon wrote a brief letter to Miranda. He told her only that he and Richard had fallen foul of a group of Satanists who were attempting to fix a murder on them; but that the British Embassy had sent them an excellent lawyer, whom they hoped would secure their release on Monday.

The following morning, shortly before midday, a warder again beckoned them out of the cell, and took them to the interviewing room. They naturally expected to find Cunliffe there, having come back either to ask more questions or to bring them some piece of special news. But their visitor was Miranda, accompanied by Miss Pinney.

As soon as Miranda realised that Simon was in the room, she cried, 'I had to come! I simply had to come. I couldn't bear not knowing everything about this terrible trouble you are in.'

Simon beamed at her, 'But it's lovely to see you. Sweet of you to think of coming here to cheer us up. 'Fraid we're in a muddle, a really nasty muddle. But I think our lawyer chap will get us out of it.'

'Oh, I pray to God he does.' Sitting down at the table, Miranda added quickly, 'Now please tell me what has been happening to you. Right from the beginning, when you left the Hilton, after letting me know that you had learned something that might lead us to Uncle Rex.'

Between them Simon and Richard put her fully in the picture; then, with Pinney a silent listener, they discussed with her the pros and cons of their case. Miranda showed a very clear grasp of the situation, and suggested that the only certain way out for them was to produce an alibi, but there seemed no way in which they could do that. A warder then looked in to say that, in another two minutes, the visitors' time would be up.

For a moment Miranda was silent; then she caught her breath and said quickly, 'There's something . . . something I must tell you. I had to play a trick to be allowed to come here. When I telephoned the authorities, at first they refused me permission to visit you. They were quite adamant about it, and I felt absolutely desperate. So . . . so I went to the British Embassy. A nice young man named Phillips fixed it for me.'

Simon looked puzzled. 'Good idea. But I don't see where playing a trick comes in by your having done that.'

'No . . . no.' Below Miranda's mask, her cheeks had become pink with blushing. Suddenly she burst out, 'But I lied to him. I told him I was your fiancée.'

At her confession, Simon's mouth dropped open. Quickly grasping her hand, he gulped, 'I only wish . . . oh, I wish you were.'

Taking off her blindfold mask, she peered up into his face. 'Do you mean that, Simon? Do you really mean that?'

'My dear, of course I do. I've loved you since that first day in Buenos Aires.'

'But . . . but loving's one thing, and marrying is another. I'm so useless. I'd be a terrible handicap to you as a wife.'

'Nonsense!' He cast a glance at the other two, gave a little giggle, and put his hand up to his mouth. 'Extraordinary place to propose to a girl in, isn't it? Before other people, too. Still . . .'

Easing off the antique gold ring he always wore on his left finger, he put it on the third finger of her left hand, laughed

119

again and said, 'Now you're committed. You're mine, and I'll never let you go.'

She came to her feet and kissed him. At that moment the warder returned. Good-byes had to be said. Dazed with happiness, Simon accompanied Richard back to their cell.

On Monday morning, a most unpleasant surprise awaited them. They had only just finished breakfast when they were taken to the interviewing room. Cunliffe was standing there. As soon as the door was shut, he glowered at them and snapped, 'I accepted the story you told me on Saturday night; but you lied to me again.'

'We did nothing of the kind,' Richard retorted hotly. 'Every word we told you was the truth.'

'Up to a point, perhaps,' the lawyer said angrily. 'But not the whole truth. You said that between approximately three a.m. and six a.m. on the day of the crime you were both in your own beds, asleep.'

'That is perfectly true.'

Cunliffe swung round on Simon. 'Of course, I understand your wish to protect the good name of your fiancée; but one can't afford to make such chivalrous gestures when one is being tried for murder. Yesterday afternoon Miss Van Ryn got my address through the British Embassy, and came to see me with her companion. She made a statement. After you had got rid of the Nathan woman, you went up to Miss Van Ryn's suite and went to bed with her.'

Simon's eyes flickered wildly, while Richard asked, 'And what was I supposed to be doing?'

'You know well enough. You were down in your own suite, playing six-pack bezique with Miss Pinney. She, of course, is entirely dependent on Miss Van Ryn, so reluctantly had to submit to her wishes. Apparently this party was arranged before the two of you went out. It was not expected that it would be so late before you returned. But Miss Van Ryn refused to forgo the—er—pleasure that she expected to enjoy in Mr Aron's company. It seems that Miss Pinney had proved squeamish about remaining in the suite while her young mistress was conducting herself in a manner of which she highly disapproved; so you had stepped into the breach and offered to keep her mind occupied with a game of cards down in your suite, while Mr Aron entertained his fiancée in hers.'

Richard and Simon exchanged a glance. They both realised

that this alibi that Miranda had provided for them at the expense of her reputation would enormously strengthen their chances of obtaining a favourable verdict. Philo McTavish's evidence would show that, far from wanting to murder Nella, they had protected her. That of Miranda would show that they had not even had the opportunity. To deny it would only confuse the issue, and seriously jeopardise the credibility of such other statements as they made.

Simon swallowed hard, and muttered, 'All right. I'm sorry I didn't come clean with you about my having been with Miss Van Ryn, but my reason sticks out a mile. Everything else we told you was the truth.'

The lawyer accepted their apology somewhat coldly, then he said, 'It's just as well that Miss Van Ryn has had the courage to come to your assistance in this way, because I'm far from happy about the evidence McTavish will give.'

'I feared he might prove a bit sticky,' Richard remarked.

Cunliffe scratched his red nose. 'He is prepared to say only that he drove you out to Glasshill's, where you remained for some time; that you then emerged from the trees with a woman, upon which he drove the three of you back to the Hilton. You see, although you told him that the "barbecue" was only an ordinary wild party, from what he heard going on there, the woman you rescued being clad like a cat, then learning about her murder and mutilation, he has tumbled to it that she was the victim of Satanists.'

'Do you think that they have warned him not to talk?'

'They may have. I think it more likely that he is concerned to keep his job. He feels that if, in any way, he allowed Don Caesar Albert's name to be connected with this scandal, he would be out on his ear. He told me that, perjury or no perjury, he'll deny taking you to Don Caesar's house and that it was Don Caesar's wife who supplied the Nathan woman with clothes. He stubbornly refuses to confirm that, when he first saw her, she was dressed as a cat. He will say that the clothes that were found with her are, to the best of his belief, those she was wearing when you bundled her into the car.'

'We could prove that, on the way back, we went to Don Caesar's house. The servant who opened the door to me could be called.'

'He could, but would that get us anywhere, unless he actually saw the girl in her cat get-up, and his mistress' clothes being brought out for her?'

'No; unfortunately he saw neither. It is even more unfortunate that McTavish has dug in his toes. If he would give a full account of the cries and weird sounds he must have heard while the Sabbat was in progress, that would have helped a lot. Anyhow, he can't deny that we were shot at and the boot of his car riddled with holes.'

'Yes, he can. The car cannot be found. He says that it has been stolen. That may be true, or it may be that he has hidden it somewhere, owing to his anxiety to make everyone believe that nothing much out of the ordinary occurred during this trip on which he acted as your driver.'

'I can't understand why he should be so unhelpful.'

The lawyer shrugged. 'I can. Firstly, as I've told you, he believes that he'll get good marks if he can prevent his boss from being connected in any way with black magic, and very bad ones if he fails to do so. Secondly and more important, he can have very little doubt that Nella Nathan was killed by Satanists to keep her from giving them away; and he is scared that if he opens his mouth too wide they will have a crack at him.'

'If we could get Don Caesar back, I feel sure he would give evidence in our favour. He is not the sort of man to stand by and see two friends condemned unjustly, just because a few stupid people might get the wrong end of the stick and think he had some connection with Satanists. After all, he helped us when we were getting the girl away from them.'

'Do you know where he is?'

'No. He was going first to London I think; then on to Switzerland to get some ski-ing. But his office must know.'

'I will get on to it and find out. Then, if matters go badly, we could cable him. That is, if you really feel we should be justified in asking him to abandon his holiday and return. You see, he could only repeat what you told him about having witnessed a Sabbat, and that is not evidence. His giving you some of his wife's clothes proves nothing, and I gather he did not even see the woman. In any case, he knows nothing about what happened later at the Hilton; and that is the crux of the matter.'

'You're right,' Richard admitted gloomily. 'Still, we have our alibis. May God bless Miss Van Ryn.'

An hour later, the two friends were taken into Court. Phillips from the British Embassy was present and with him an interpreter who, for Richard's benefit, translated every stage of the proceedings into English.

The prosecutor made an opening statement, then called a doctor who had carried out an autopsy on Nella's body. He deposed the cause of her death, described her mutilation and affirmed that she had been violently raped a short while before her death.

Next came the cleaning woman who had been in the main passage. She was middle-aged, with a workworn face and humble manner. She gave her evidence clearly, but in a sing-song tone that suggested she was reciting lines she had been taught. Simon thought it probable that she was being controlled from some distance by a powerful hypnotist, but there was no way of testing that. She stated firmly that it was Richard and Simon whom she had seen come out of Nella's room at about six a.m., and that she could not be mistaken.

The desk clerk related how Richard and Simon had brought Nella to the hotel, booked a room for her and taken her up in the lift. No-one else had come in and booked a room that night after they had done so.

A floor waiter testified that, when taking away the breakfast tray from the sitting room of the accused's suite, he had also collected three used glasses.

A policeman from Valparaiso described how he had detained the accused as they were about to board a steamer bound for Callao.

A woman clerk from the office of L.A.N. related how Richard had enquired there, within a few minutes of the office opening on Wednesday the 18th, about flights that day to La Paz and Lima.

Finally, the senior police officer who had interrogated them after they had been brought back to Santiago, read a long statement, showing how the replies to the questions he had asked the accused conflicted with evidence already given.

Cunliffe then made a statement on behalf of his clients. At his first mention of Satanism, a rustle of excited interest ran round the Court, and the pencils of the reporters at the Press table began to fly. As this was not a trial, but only a preliminary hearing before a magistrate to determine whether there was a case against the accused, Cunliffe's statement was no more than a brief résumé of events as described by Richard and Simon, after they had withdrawn the statement they had made to the police.

123

McTavish was then called. He ran true to the form Cunliffe had predicted he would show. He said that his Chief had ordered him to investigate the house of *Señor* Lincoln B. Glasshill and the nature of the parties held there. He had done so, but had no reason to suppose that they had any connection with Satanism. On Tuesday, the 17th, his Chief had ordered him to drive *Señors* Eaton and Aron out to the house late at night. He had done so. They had told him to pull up in a lane behind the house, then had left the car and disappeared into a screen of trees that bordered the estate. They had been absent for the best part of two hours. When they reappeared they were running and, with them, had a young woman. Pushing her into the car, they had ordered him to take them back to the city. When he had asked them what had been going on, they had replied to the effect that a wild party was being held in the garden of the house, and that it had proved too wild for the young lady. They had said nothing about witchcraft or black magic. During the drive the woman had not spoken. He had dropped the three of them at the Hilton Hotel shortly after two o'clock in the morning.

Cunliffe made no attempt to trap McTavish into contradicting himself, neither did the prosecutor cross-examine him. Such questioning to test the veracity of witnesses would be carried out by Counsel if the case was sent to trial.

When Miranda was led to the stand there was a new stir of interest. She gave her evidence in a low, firm voice, frankly stating that Simon was not only her fiancé, but also her lover and that, on the night in question, he had spent the hours between about three o'clock and seven in bed with her. As she stood down, a hush ensued that, in a subtle way, conveyed the sympathy of those present for the blind girl who had publicly declared her frailty to protect the man she loved.

Miss Pinney followed her. Unlike McTavish and Miranda who, although they intended to perjure themselves, had both taken the oath without hesitation, the companion held the Bible by a corner and well away from her, as though she almost expected it to burst into flames. Cunliffe took her through her evidence as quickly as possible; but she faltered several times in her replies, and spoke in such a low voice that twice the magistrate had to ask her, through the interpreter, to speak up.

It was clear to Richard and Simon that her Nonconformist conscience was giving her a very bad time. The latter wondered

124

how Miranda had ever succeeded in persuading her to participate in this deception, and it occurred to him that Pinney had perhaps consented only because, being a Van Ryn, Miranda was very rich and had promised to settle a large enough sum of money on her to ensure her a comfortable old age.

But the fact remained that she had made a far from good impression, and the two accused were not surprised when the magistrate ruled that they should be sent for trial.

Greatly depressed, they were taken back to their cell. Shortly afterwards, Cunliffe came to see them. Angrily, he said, 'After Miss Van Ryn's evidence, I thought we were going to get away with it; but that sanctimonious companion of hers bitched everything up. When she had faltered through her piece, anyone could see they had both been lying, and it must have been obvious to the magistrate that Mr Aron's fiancée had courageously hatched this little plot in the hope of clearing you both.'

Neither Simon nor Richard sought to disabuse him of his belief, and he then proceeded to cheer them up by going on, 'But you must not be despondent. We have plenty of shots in our locker yet. I'll see to it that the Pinney woman makes a much better showing when she next gives evidence; and Counsel will take McTavish to pieces. Now that Lincoln B. Glasshill has been brought into it, we can subpoena him and the couple who look after his house. He'll have to give an account of those parties he holds. Plenty of people can be brought to testify that they take place, so something may come out of that. I'll have that cleaning woman investigated, too. If it is found that she's spending much more money than she normally would, we'll insist on knowing where she got it, and may be able to show that she was bribed to give false evidence.'

When Cunliffe had left them, they held an inquest on the morning's proceedings, and the conclusions they reached were less optimistic than his. Richard summed up the situation by saying:

'What he fails to realise is that the people we are up against have occult power. I'll swear that cleaning woman was under hypnotic control from a distance, and they're much too clever to allow her to be trapped. Counsel won't shake Philo either. They've got him where they want him, and they'll keep him there. Our side can subpoena Lincoln B. Glasshill, but you can be certain we'll get nothing out of him; and Pinney is a hopelessly weak reed. Since her mind is in such a state of

125

doubt and distress, it must be open to the Satanists. They will work on her while she is sleeping, and it would not surprise me if, at our trial, she suddenly breaks down and confesses that she has been lying.'

'Ummm,' Simon agreed. 'How I wish we had Greyeyes with us. I don't mean involved in our muddle, but on hand to help us. By pitting his occult powers against von Thumm and Co., I'm sure he'd turn the tables on them and, somehow, get us off.'

'Yes. The big mistake we made was not cabling him to come out the moment we realised that Rex had become involved in a black magic set-up.'

'I did think of it. But we had no chance. We didn't know for certain that Glasshill's parties were Sabbats until Tuesday night. Everything happened so quickly after that. Wednesday morning we were on the run.'

'D'you think it's too late to send him an S.O.S.?'

' 'Fraid so. Cunliffe's just told us that our trial should come on in a week. Our dear Duke will still be in Corfu, staying with those people whose villa he's thinking of buying. Could send a cable, but it would take the best part of a day to reach him. Shouldn't think for a moment that there's an air service yet to an out-of-the-way place like Corfu. He'd have to go by ship and rail to Rome; and from there it's a three or four day flight out to Santiago.'

Richard sighed. 'No, I'm afraid it's not on. The odds are that even if our trial were not over by the time he got here, at best he'd have very little time to work in.'

During the next few days, both Miranda and Cunliffe paid them several visits. The lawyer reported that he had secured a Court order to search Glasshill's house; but, when it was executed, nothing incriminating was found there. As McTavish reported earlier, the couple who lived there were either deaf and dumb, or acting the part of deaf-mutes. From the descriptions given to them it now occurred to Simon that they might be Zombies. In any case, they were completely useless to the defence. Still worse, the day after the magistrate's hearing, Lincoln B. Glasshill, evidently deciding that whatever course the trial might take, it would do his reputation no good to be interrogated as a witness, had left Santiago for an unknown destination.

Miranda brought the prisoners luxuries to eat and drink and spent every walking hour cudgelling her wits for new ways in which to help them. She had Pinney take her to Philo's lodg-

126

ing, upbraided him furiously for having borne false witness, then offered him a huge bribe to give a true account of what he knew. But he had told her frankly that he believed it to be more than his life was worth to accept it. She had then spent a thousand dollars inserting large advertisements in all the papers, offering ten thousand dollars' reward to anyone who could give information leading to the whereabouts of Philo's bullet-riddled car.

On the morning of Friday the 27th, the prisoners were taken, as so often before, to the interviewing room. They expected to find either Miranda and Pinney or Cunliffe waiting for them there. Instead, to their amazement, it was de Richleau who stood behind the bare table.

With fervour and delight, the three old friends embraced. To the eager questioning of the prisoners about how he came to be in Santiago, the Duke replied:

'I learned that you were in serious trouble through a dream or, rather, when I was up on the third level of the astral plane. Naturally, I left Corfu immediately for Rome, and had myself flown out. I arrived yesterday afternoon, got particulars of the trouble you are in and your lawyer's address from the British Embassy, then went to see him. He gave me all the facts as far as they are known.'

'What do you think of our chances?' Richard asked quickly.

De Richleau frowned. 'Not very good at the moment, I'm afraid. But I may be able to help. I told Cunliffe that I was gifted with clairvoyant powers and that, if he could arrange for me to go into a trance in the room in which this woman was murdered, I might be able to visualise the crime as it took place. If I could succeed in doing that, I would be able to give a description of her murderers, and that could lead to their being traced.'

He broke off for a moment then, a smile lighting up his grey, yellow-flecked eyes, went on, 'It has been arranged with the hotel people and the police that I should make the attempt this afternoon.'

For half an hour he remained with them, while they told him of their endeavours in Buenos Aires, Punta Arenas and Santiago, to trace Rex. Then he left them, infinitely more cheerful than they had been for many days.

That evening Cunliffe came to see them. He said that the Duke had telephoned to say that his session at the hotel had produced results which would justify another hearing by a magistrate, before the case came up for trial. In view of the sensation the case was causing, consent had been given to this new evidence being heard in court the following morning.

On the Saturday, at ten o'clock, the prisoners were again in the dock. Shortly afterwards de Richleau, a calm, impressive figure, took the witness stand. After the formalities were completed, he gave an account of the arrangements made with the management of the hotel, and continued:

'I succeeded in establishing contact with the spirit of the dead woman. She described to me how she had been murdered by two men, one of whom was a Negro and the other, she thought, an Arab. I then asked her about her relations with Mr Aron and Mr Eaton. She related how they had helped her to escape from the Sabbat, spoke of her gratitude to them and directed my attention to the Bible in the drawer of the bedside table. Coming out of my trance, I telephoned down to the manager and he came up with two police officers. They are here, and will inform you of what followed.'

A police lieutenant replaced de Richleau on the stand. He testified to having joined the Duke in the bedroom and having taken the Bible from the drawer. Producing it, he opened the book and held it up, to show some writing in pencil on the inside of the cover, then handed it to the interpreter, who translated into Spanish what had been written there. It read:

'I am terrified. I'll never forget the horror I went through tonight. I would probably have been killed at that ghastly party if the Englishman and the kind little Jew had not got me away. He has promised to pay for me to get back to the States. But I've an awful premonition that I'm fated to die here. Those fiends will come after me, and kill me if they can, to stop me from telling what I know about them. Oh, God help me! Have mercy on me!'

As the interpreter lowered the book there fell a brief, tense silence; then the magistrate dismissed the case.

Half an hour later, Simon, Richard, Miranda and Pinney were with the Duke in the suite he had taken at the Hilton. Unutterably relieved, carefree and laughing, they were toasting one another in champagne. As Simon set down his glass, he grinned at de Richleau and said:

'Lucky it didn't occur to anyone that, as you were left alone in Nella's room, you might have written that piece in the Bible. Don't see how you could have proved you hadn't.'

The Duke threw back his head and laughed. 'With your

128

subtle mind you'd make an excellent detective, Simon. As a matter of fact, you are right. I did succeed in contacting Nella on the astral; but the poor woman was still hopelessly confused and quite unhelpful. As no-one could have produced a specimen of her handwriting; I was able to write that piece in the Bible for her. To risk you and Richard being found guilty was unthinkable.'

His statement was greeted with cries of surprise, admiration and gratitude.

Waving them aside, his face again became grave as he said. 'But now you two are out of the wood, we have other things to think of. Since it has emerged that we are up against Satanists, it has become more urgent than ever to find our dear friend, Rex.'

11

A Perilous Journey

That night, after dinner, the three friends held a conference. While still in prison Simon and Richard had given the Duke the main facts about their hunt for Rex. Now they filled in the details. When they had done, he said:

'Since Nella Nathan actually saw Rex up at this headquarters on the Sala de Uyuni, the obvious course is for us to go there. As the best part of a month has elapsed since she saw him, he may now be somewhere else; but, even should that be so, it is there lies our only chance of picking up his trail.'

'To go there is what Simon and I intended to do, if we had not been arrested when about to leave Valparaiso,' Richard said. 'I can't help wondering, though, whether it really was Rex the Nathan woman saw. It seemed so extraordinary that he should have been up in that place as a free man and, apparently, on excellent terms with the big-shot there.'

Simon turned on him. 'Nella more or less described Rex. On asking the name of the man she was looking at, she was told it was him. That couldn't be coincidence. And we agreed, you remember, that this place Sala being right off the map, it might be possible to detain someone there without locking him up.'

'It was that I had in mind when I said that Rex may now be somewhere else,' put in the Duke. 'They may have thought he couldn't escape; but if he had the free use of those big limbs of his, I'd back him to get away from any place other than a locked cell.'

'How shall we go?' Richard enquired. 'Rail or road? The Sala is well over a thousand miles from here as the crow flies and, of course, very much further by either rail or road. I spent half an hour before dinner going into alternatives. By rail we must go up the coast to Arica, inland for two hundred and fifty miles across the Andes to La Paz, then south. The only town of any size within a hundred miles of the Sala is

Ouoro. After that the railway runs on the eastern side of Lago de Poopo. It's the hell of a long lake and the northern end of the Sala is on its western side; so it might be better to stick to the railway for another eighty miles and get off at a small place called Sevaruyo. By road, we'd have to make an immense detour through the Andes valleys, via Mendoza and Villa Maria to Cordoba; but from there we'd have the Pan-American highway, which runs almost due north, and it would take us within about seventy-five miles of the southern end of the Sala.'

De Richleau smiled. 'I had other ideas. But I shall not be the least surprised if you veto them. It occurred to me that we might hire a private aircraft, if you are willing to fly us up.'

Richard smiled back. 'I wonder if you realise what you would be letting yourself in for? The air currents among those mountains must be about as bad as one could encounter anywhere short of the Himalayas. But if you are both willing to risk your necks, I'll risk mine.'

Simon's eyes flickered wildly. 'Sounds stark crazy. No aspersions on you as a pilot, old chap, but to fly an aircraft between those scores of mountains sounds like juggling with death to me. Crossing the Andes by car, bad enough. On primitive roads subject to frequent blockages by landslides, good chance of ending up over a precipice. Train would be safer. Between Arica and La Paz we'd be reduced to grease spots, but at least we'd arrive.'

'You are right, my son,' the Duke agreed. 'My own enquiries before dinner lead me to suppose that both roads and trains in Central South America are little better than they were when I was in those parts in 1908. But it is not really a question of whether we spend many hours slowly roasting in a stinking, insanitary train, or take the very risky flight. The nub of the matter is how to penetrate the Sala de Uyuni when we arrive in the neighbourhood.'

He took a long pull on his cigar, then went on, 'The Sala is approximately one hundred and fifty miles in length and one hundred miles in breadth—roughly the area of Wales. Whether we make the greater part of the journey by road or rail, we can assume that we shall arrive on the edge of this vast, roadless plateau of salt marshes and near-impenetrable low jungle, in a car. What do we do then?'

'You're right, of course,' Richard nodded. 'Even if there were tracks along which we could drive a car—and it's very doubtful if there are—we wouldn't stand a hope in hell of finding the newly-built town in which Nella worked. The only possibility of doing that would be to fly to and for across the area until we spot it.'

'Hadn't thought of that,' Simon conceded. 'But I get Grey-eyes' point now. Got to have an aircraft to locate the place, and one might as well expect to find a Dodo bird up there. As one's got to be flown up, might as well go in it. O.K. then. I'll swallow a handful of sleepers and you can take me along as baggage.'

'Splendid.' the Duke smiled. 'Then, when we arrive, having had your sleep Richard and I can take a nap, while you prepare and cook a meal for us.'

'Ummm. We'll be landing in a wilderness; so we'll need supplies. Looks as though this is going to be a bit like going on safari.'

'Except that once we leave the aircraft we'll have to be our own porters,' Richard added, making a grimace.

De Richleau shrugged. 'We should be able to find somewhere to land far enough from the town for the people in it not to realise that we have come down, yet not so far off for it to be an easy trek to the place. We shall have to take precautions against being spotted when we enter it, though. Dressed in our usual clothes, we would stand out like sore thumbs, and immediately draw attention to ourselves as strangers. But the Nathan woman told you there are people of all races there, so we should be able to pass unnoticed in that sort of crowd if we wore sombreros and the kind of clothes most commonly seen in Andean towns.'

In consequence, it was decided that on the Monday Richard should go out to the airport and make enquiries for a suitable aircraft that could be hired, and that Simon should purchase both a good stock of supplies and the sort of garments that would make them inconspicuous.

They were well content to spend Sunday in its traditional role as a day of rest. Richard and Simon were still recovering from the awful anxiety to which they had been subjected during their nine days in prison. Miranda, too, had been under a great strain, and had lost both weight and sleep. When they all met for lunch and later in the day by mutual consent they avoided speaking of Rex and Satanism. Nevertheless, the now double mystery of why Rex should have absconded with a million dollars and fallen into the hands of the followers of the Left-Hand Path was never far from their minds.

Pinney alone was not gravely troubled by those unsolved problems, nor greatly concerned about the dangers the three men would soon have to face. De Richleau amused himself by drawing her out, and she fell completely under the spell of his charm; for once, in her somewhat acid way, enlivening the subdued atmosphere by becoming quite amusing.

On the Monday morning, Simon and Richard set off on their respective ploys. De Richleau, as befitted his age, was taking things easy and did not intend to get up until it was time to dress for lunch. At half past ten his bedside telephone rang. It was Miranda. She said she wanted to talk to him privately, and asked if she could come down to his suite.

'By all means,' he told her. 'But I'm still in bed. Give me half an hour to have my bath.'

Normally he always travelled with his manservant, Max; but, on their arrival in Rome, there had been only one seat available on the aircraft, and he had felt it to be of such urgency to join his friends that he had left Max behind. While washing and shaving himself, he ran a bath, poured a generous ration of scent into it and luxuriated there for ten minutes. Another ten went in doing his exercises, then he put the final touch to his toilette by brushing up his white 'devil's' eyebrows. A few minutes before eleven, clad in one of his beautiful silk dressing gowns—of which at home he had a large collection— he was in his sitting room ready to receive Miranda.

Pinney was with her, but had evidently been told that her presence would not be required; as, having said a polite good morning to the Duke, she at once withdrew. As soon as Miranda was comfortably settled in an armchair, the Duke said lightly:

'Now, tell me, dear, what is it you wanted to talk to me about? If it was to ask my opinion of Simon's suitability as a husband, I can assure you at once that I have never known a kinder and more sweet-natured man.'

'Oh, how right you are about him,' she agreed quickly. 'And you can have no idea what his coming into my life has meant to me. I was virtually a prisoner of my disability. For over two years, after the fire in which I so narrowly escaped death, a long series of operations to patch me up rendered me incapable of doing anything. By the time I was able to get about, doing next to nothing had become a habit and everyone treated me as a permanent invalid. Then Simon came and, like a knight in an old romance, rescued me from my prison. He has made me the happiest woman in the world.'

De Richleau smiled. 'I am delighted for you, truly delighted. And for him, too. I'm sure you will both be very, very happy. I suppose, though, it is about him that you wanted to talk?'

'Yes. Greatly as I love him, I wouldn't seek to dissuade him from continuing to take his part in the search for Uncle Rex. But I'm sure you'll understand how worried I am about him —and Richard and you—going up to the Sala. I don't think I'd be quite so scared if you were about to pit yourselves against a gang of ordinary bad men. It's the unknown that frightens me. You see, until a few days ago, I had no idea that there were still people who worshipped the Devil. Can he really give them powers to do serious harm to their enemies?'

'He can. Naturally, I should like to allay your fears; but I would not be honest if I told you the contrary. I'm speaking now of the real thing. Since the war there have been increasingly frequent reports in our newspapers of people desecrating churches, black magic circles and that sort of thing. In ninety-nine cases out of a hundred, I believe that the occult plays no part in them. They are either attributable to unscrupulous men interesting girls in this fascinating subject, with the object of getting them to participate in pseudo rituals at which they can easily be seduced; or run by clever crooks who promise their credulous victims communication with a departed loved one, or foreknowledge by which big money can be made, then photograph them committing some obscene act, and afterwards blackmail them. But there are men and women who have acquired genuine Satanic powers, and they can be very dangerous indeed.'

'Are there many of them?'

'Throughout the world there must be a considerable number, particularly in South America, Africa and the West Indies. Voodoo, of course, developed from the witch-craft practised by primitive African tribes. Haiti is its greatest stronghold, but Brazil bids fair to rival it. The lives of a good eighty per cent of the people in those countries are dominated by witch-doctors, male and female, and several times each year they make sacrifices to the Powers of Darkness. In Europe and the English-speaking world such activities are, naturally, conducted under cover, and comparatively rare. As I have said, most mentions of them in the newspapers refer to the vicious and the criminal

134

cashing in by exploiting people who are superstitious. Nevertheless, in every great city in the States, Europe and Australia there are a limited number of Satan worshippers, vowed to use every means in their power to incite violence against law and order, sow discord between nations and bring about the disruption of civilisation.'

'How do you come to know so much about these things?' Miranda asked.

'As a young officer, I became a thorn in the flesh of the French Government; so my superiors virtually exiled me to garrison duty in Madagascar. I found the boredom of living in that great island unbearable so, after a few months, I made friends with a powerful witch-doctor and, under his guidance, trained to fit myself to acquire occult power. One is initiated into the Mysteries by degrees, of which there are eleven. Having reached the fifth degree and become a Philosopher, one must then decide whether to follow the Right- or Left-Hand Path.'

'Does that mean to use your power for Good or Evil?'

'Yes. Those who follow the Right-Hand Path practise only white magic. That is the use of occult power for unselfish ends, such as curing warts, taking pain from others and so on. It may interest you to know that recently the British Medical Council carried out an investigation, which disclosed that white magic is still practised in every county in the British Isles. The majority of people who practise white magic are, I think, simple souls who do not realise that such powers are given from beyond. But many of the Saints must obviously have believed that their ability to perform miracles was due to a force which they regarded as being bestowed upon them by their god. The followers of the Left-Hand Path are black magicians. Their object is to gratify their own desires with regard to women, money and influence over the lives of others. For this they must pay by worshipping Satan, and carrying on the evil work of the Power of Darkness.

'In every community, whether primitive or civilised, both black and white magic are practised; but, unfortunately, there is far more black than white in the world today. Both in the East and the West the great Faiths have decayed. Few priests, whether Buddhist, Mohammedan or Christian, are any longer aware of the Great Truths and have knowledge of the Logos. They still perform their rituals and pay lip-service to their respective Gods, but during the past half-century more and more people have come to see through them as the empty vessels that they are.

'Even though their Faiths have long become distortions of the Eternal Verities from which all of them originally sprang, they were still forces for good, and those who subscribed to their doctrines were armoured against evil by the discipline they imposed. But we have now entered the age of doubt and rebellion against all controls. All over the world the new generations are rejecting the old Faiths, and have come to despise adherence to convention. It is termed "The New Freedom", but it leaves them rudderless. When in trouble they have nothing to turn to. And, with the taboos abolished, there is no restraint upon them from taking refuge in drugs, drink and promiscuity. Under the influence of these, they become the unconscious pawns of Satan, and an easy prey for recruitment as active participants in a Satanic Circle.'

'You think, then, that comparatively few people in our world have occult power? How does one acquire it?'

'By long periods of contemplation, fasting and undergoing a series of increasingly severe ordeals. After a while, one's spirit is able to leave one's body at will, and travel first on the lower astral planes when we sleep. Our dreams are memories of our experiences on them; but the untrained mind brings back only fragments of dreams, so that these telescoped events are meaningless. The Adept can recall, whether awake or sleeping, everything his ego has seen or done during its absence from his body. While on an astral plane he will meet and talk with other spirits, some whose bodies are thousands of miles away, and others whom you would term dead, but in fact are for the time being out of incarnation.'

'You are a believer in reincarnation, then?'

'I am indeed. It is the original belief held universally when the world was young, and the only logical one. If you believe in survival, it is the only possible explanation for our being here and undergoing the trials we have to face in life. Otherwise that would be pointless. We are sent here to travel the long road from being entirely self-centred, lustful, gluttonous savages, to wise, controlled, benign personalities, ever thinking of the happiness of others, until we are fitted to become one ourselves with the Lords of Light. How could one possibly achieve that tremendous transition in one life on earth? What chance would you have if you were born seriously deformed, or the child of criminal parents? It is that which makes so absurd the Christian heresy of a Last Judgement. To reward one person with unending bliss in Heaven and condemn another to eternal torment in Hell solely on the evidence of a single life on earth would be the greatest conceivable travesty of justice. It makes the present conception of the Christian God a mockery.

'But, of course, that was not the original Christian teaching. The doctrine preached by Jesus Christ was sadly perverted by that ignorant fool, Paul, and others, in the early centuries of our era. Christ knew the truth. There can be no doubt of that. You will recall His words, "The sins of the Fathers shall be visited upon the children even unto the third and fourth generation." Is it conceivable that so enlightened and gentle a man, who showed His love for children, should have threatened infants not yet born with dire punishment because their grandfather had been a murderer or sodomite? To initiates, His meaning has always been transparently clear. He was saying that every man is the father of the person he becomes in his next incarnation, and if he does evil in his present life, he will suffer for it in his future lives, until he has made good the evil that he did.'

Before Miranda had entered the room, de Richleau had pulled down the blinds, so that she would not need to wear her mask. While he was speaking, her big, blue eyes had remained fixed upon him in fascinated wonder at this, to her, new presentation of the meaning of life. As he paused, she said:

'What a tragedy that the Christian Church should for so many centuries have misled Christ's followers. Is there no way in which a new Reformation could be brought about, so that in future people would be taught the truth?'

De Richleau shook his head. 'I fear not. It is decreed by the Lords of Light that the way to enlightenment is for ever open. Those who seek shall find, and to those who are ready to receive it, it shall be given. You, my dear, I now know to be such a one, and I am overjoyed that I should have been chosen to unveil your spiritual eyes, so that henceforth you will never have any fear of death, and realise that leaving your present body is only the casting away of an outworn garment. Each life down here is like a term at school. During it we must learn some new lesson. Each time we leave an earthly body, we go on holiday. Free of the flesh, we are no longer subject to pain, and are infinitely more perceptive. Waiting to make us welcome we

137

find beloved friends who have left their bodies before us and others whom we have loved in previous incarnations. The state of those who are out of incarnation is beautifully expressed in the Koran, by the words, "For them there are gardens beneath which rivers flow."

'But it is useless to endeavour to win converts to these beliefs. Fear and ignorance are the two states by which the Devil befuddles the wits of mankind. The Mau-Mau initiate their young warriors by hideous ceremonies in which the youth couples with a sow. The act has the effect of causing the initiate to commit himself absolutely. He feels that, after that, should he waver in his fanatic devotion to Mau-Mau, the dark gods will seize upon and destroy him utterly.

'At the other end of the scale you have the Christian clergy. They are civilised and kindly men; and they do much good among the poor and afflicted. But spiritually they are empty vessels, bound by centuries of tradition to their way of life. The great majority of them continue to gabble their rituals, although they no longer believe in them. Ask them how the eternal war between Light and Darkness is going, and they would think you a little mad. For them the Devil is a myth of the Middle Ages, and to suggest that he is still active would greatly embarrass them.'

Sadly, Miranda shook her head. Then, after a moment, she asked:

'This expedition on . . . on which you are going. Do you think you will be able to protect yourself and the others?'

'I can only pray that it will be so,' the Duke replied seriously. 'It depends upon the degree of power that can be called down by the Satanist who heads this Black Power movement. I have achieved the ninth degree, and am a Magister Templar, represented in occultism by eight circles and three squares. If my opponent is a Magus or an Ipsissimus, he could prove too much for me. But I beg you not to worry. Instead, every time you tend to do so, pray for us. Prayers often appear to be ignored, but they never go unheeded. At times they conflict with the fate decreed for the person on whose behalf they are offered up; but at others they can be of great help to those we love.'

By lunchtime Richard was able to report that he was in negotiation to buy an aircraft from the executors of a rich Chilean who had recently died. He meant to spend the afternoon going over it with mechanics. If the examination proved satisfactory, he would take it up for a trial next day.

Simon had spent the morning buying stores and, as far as tinned food could make a gourmet's mouth water, the list he produced would certainly have done so.

For that evening they had arranged a dinner party, to which they had asked Fidel Cunliffe and young Mr Phillips from the British Embassy, in order to show their appreciation of the help the lawyer and diplomat had given Richard and Simon during their ordeal.

On the Tuesday, Richard took the aircraft up, first for a few minutes, then for over an hour's flight down to Valparaiso and back. Having satisfied himself that the 'plane was reliably air-worthy, he reported to Simon, who arranged for its purchase through the bankers with whom he was associated in New York.

That evening Simon produced the costumes he had selected for them to take with them, and a lighter note was brought into their preparations as, assembled in de Richleau's suite, they tried on gaudy shirts, leather breeches and other items of Andean attire which normally they would have worn only to a fancy-dress dance. The Duke had also been shopping that day, and he added a sober note to the proceedings by producing three automatic pistols, with a good supply of ammunition, remarking as he did so:

'We cannot hope to win our battle with "down here" weapons, but they may come in handy if we find ourselves up against lesser fry.'

After an early breakfast on the Wednesday morning, Miranda put on a brave face to say good-bye to them, and they were driven, with all their paraphernalia, out to the airport. The 'plane had been filled to her maximum capacity, the stores and baggage were loaded, and at ten o'clock they took off.

Heading west, they flew over the Mountains of the Coast, which presented no difficulties. On their far side, Richard turned the aircraft north and, for nine hundred miles, followed the coastline up to the port of Iquique. There they came down on the landing strip, to refuel and have a meal. On taking off again, Richard set a course due east. For a short while they flew over flat, arid land, on which small patches of cultivation struggled for existence. Ahead of them, clear in the afternoon sunshine, rose the formidable rampart of the Andes. On either side it stretched as far as the eye could see. Immediately in front, it mounted in a succession of ever-loftier highlands to a veritable forest of peaks that appeared to continue indefinitely into the distance. At this point the range was, in fact, nearly four hundred miles in depth.

The great plateau of Sala de Uyuni was situated on the far side of the Cordillero Occidenta and a little to the west of the centre of the main chain. Its nearest edge was only about a hundred and twenty miles from the coast, but the last hundred could be covered only by a continuous succession of twists and turns through valley after valley, many of which were a thousand feet deep.

Had Richard's passengers not been so acutely aware of their peril, they would have marvelled at the grandeur of the scene. The sun glared down on a desolate wilderness of rock, barren slopes and precipices, but the clarity of the atmosphere made them appear terrifyingly near and dangerous. Seeming infinitely far beneath them, turgid rivers foamed over rocky beds as they wound through the gorges towards the sea. Here and there they broadened out into placid lakes that looked as though they were bottomless. Occasionally, the dead-black shadow of a cloud blotted out the colour of an irregular patch of land, moving slowly until it slid from view. One small shadow kept pace with them, that of their aircraft, and the sun now being in the west it was always ahead, as though leading them on through the precipitous, trackless waste, in which there were neither roads nor human habitation.

As Richard had anticipated, flying through the mountains proved extremely hazardous. Although he had seen to it that they had oxygen masks, it was not possible to fly the 'plane over the high crests. He had to steer between them, and the aircraft was constantly subjected to the force of strong air currents. At times it was unexpectedly swept fifty feet higher or, on striking a pocket, dropped like a plummet for a hundred feet.

It was impossible to keep the machine on an even keel for more than a few minutes at a time. Being unheated, it was bitterly cold at that altitude; yet, although the temperature was near zero, Richard was sweating as he battled with the controls. As an adept in Yoga, de Richleau was able both to keep his body warm and render his stomach impervious to the constant bumps and lurches. But poor Simon was terribly airsick. Again and again, as the 'plane slid sideways, his heart seemed to come

140

up into his mouth with fear that the aircraft would be smashed to fragments on the nearest cliff.

At last they passed between two lofty, snow-capped peaks and, ahead of them, they saw a vast expanse of level ground. Another few minutes and their hour-long ordeal was over. The western edge of the Sala de Uyuni lay below them.

Coming down to five hundred feet, they surveyed the uninviting prospect. As far as the eye could see the almost level plateau stretched away, with no sign of either human or animal life. The greater part of it consisted of marshes so white with crystallised salt that they looked like irregular patches of snow. Here and there they were broken by patches of stagnant water, on which the sun glinted. Where there was slightly higher land, it was a reddish colour, and covered with pampas and occasional groups of stunted trees.

Their next concern was to locate the secret headquarters of the Black Power movement. To increase their area of vision, Richard went up to two thousand feet and flew a zigzag course, while de Richleau and Simon scanned the land on either side through binoculars. After a while they realised that to spot a settlement in an area covering over ten thousand square miles was like looking for a needle in a haystack.

But the Duke solved the problem by leaving his body. Mounting to a great height, so that the whole of the Sala de Uyuni was spread below him, he was able, by his spiritual eyes, to identify their goal; then, returning to his body, he directed Richard to it.

The settlement lay some thirty miles inside the south-eastern edge of the Sala. It took a further twenty minutes before they were close enough to see it clearly. It's layout consisted of thirty or more long, low buildings, divided by parallel streets, and one solitary square building upon a piece of higher ground, some distance from the others. Between it and them there stretched an airstrip, upon which were five aircraft and several hangars. There were no roads leading from it in any direction; so, except by air, it was entirely cut off from the outer world, and no more perfect site could have been found for a secret headquarters.

Anxious that no-one down there should suspect that they were being spied upon, but assume that the 'plane was in the neighbourhood only because the pilot had lost direction, Richard flew straight on until the settlement was out of sight. He then banked and began to circle it, low down, at a gradually decreasing distance, as he searched for a place that offered a good chance of making a safe landing.

He chose a spot about four miles from the settlement, where it seemed almost certain that the ground was firm because it was well above the average level and, on three sides, bordered by an irregular screen of trees. The aircraft touched down and he brought it to a halt on the edge of a small coppice. Greatly relieved, they climbed out and set about unloading some of their stores, in preparation for a picnic meal.

By the time they had eaten, the sun was setting and the air had become chilly. Anxious to lose no time in finding out what they could about the settlement, they changed into their picturesque costumes, equipped themselves with their pistols, flasks and torches and set out on foot.

To cross the intervening piece of land in darkness would have proved impossible, as more than half of it consisted of salt marsh and treacherous stretches of muddy ground that, when trodden on, sucked evilly at their boots. But, shortly after the sun had disappeared behind the great range of now distant peaks in the west, the stars came out. In that crystal-clear, rarefied atmosphere, myriads of them could be seen sparkling in the great dome of blue-black sky, and they gave ample light by which to distinguish firm from dangerous ground.

Nevertheless, it took them well over an hour and a half to cover the four miles. Outside the settlement nothing was stirring, but there were lights in most of the windows and there was a loud murmur of activity. In view of the complete isolation of the place, the possibility of sentries being posted round it could be ruled out; so the three friends went boldly forward and entered the end of the nearest street. The buildings were all of one storey, of uniform design and apparently constructed from standard parts which had been flown in. This side street, or rather passage-way, for it had no road surface or pavements and was no more than a hard-trodden earth path between the lines of hutments, was almost deserted, and the few people they encountered took no notice of them.

As they advanced, they saw through the lighted windows that some of the buildings were long dormitories for either men or women, and others were divided into sections for couples. One was a bath house and another a communal laundry. The lighting was electric, inclined to be dim and, at times to flicker slightly.

Having walked some two hundred yards, they entered the main street. It was much broader than the others, but also unpaved. In it there were many more people. There was no traffic of any kind, and no street lighting, but all the buildings were lit up. Many of them were offices in which a few people were still working; one contained a printing press, another was a library, a third a clothes store. Further along, they caught the sound of drumming and a band. On both sides in the centre of the long street there were two mess rooms, crowded with people eating their evening meal, and between them a large kitchen. Beyond these were recreation rooms, with billiard and ping-pong tables, a cinema, a card room and a gymnasium. The sound of the band had been coming from one in which couples were dancing, out with no sign of abandon.

The men and women inside these rooms could be seen clearly. They were mainly blacks and half-breeds, with only a sprinkling of whites. Some were sitting quietly by themselves, but the majority were talking and laughing. There did not appear to be anything abnormal about any of them. The features of those outside in the street were more difficult to see, for not only was it semi-dark there, but a mist was rising from the not-far-distant marshes, having the effect of a light fog. It slightly muted all sound, and gave the people moving in it a curiously mysterious quality. But, singly or in chatting couples, they passed up and down, intent on their own business.

On reaching the far end of the main street, the Duke said, 'There is nothing for us here. Things are as Nella Nathan told you. This is a colony of innocent do-gooders who are being made use of. Like citizens of any town run on communal lines, they work in the offices or do other jobs during the day and amuse themselves according to their fancy in the evenings. There is not even the faintest suggestion that the Black Art is practised here. On the contrary, as you may have noticed, two of the huts we passed held rows of chairs and had altars at one end with crosses on. They are probably Baptist and Methodist chapels. Anyway, those who follow the Christian religion are catered for and another hutment contained a lectern carved with Moslem symbols, so was obviously a mosque. No doubt there are also a synagogue and a Hindu temple; although I didn't notice them. They were probably in darkness or, perhaps, in one of the side streets.'

143

'Where do we go from here?' asked Richard.

'To the building on the rise, just outside the town. The odds are that it contains the quarters of the people who run the place. We may learn something there.'

They retraced their steps for some distance, again mingling with the passing crowd, then turned down a side street that led in the direction of the rise. On the way they crossed the landing strip, and Richard was able to get a close-up look at the aircraft on it. They were one medium large and two small passenger 'planes, and two transports.

As they approached the building on the rise, they went forward cautiously, peering through the mist before and on either side of them, as they thought it possible that a look-out might be patrolling somewhere in the vicinity, to prevent any-one from the town, impelled by curiosity, sneaking up to see what was going on in what seemed probable was the adminis-tration centre of the settlement.

The place was constructed in the same way as the others, but was larger. Light came from only two windows and, like those in the town, neither of them was screened by blinds or curtains. To avoid making more noise than was necessary, the Duke sent Richard forward on his own. He tiptoed up to first one then the other lighted window and, crouching down, peered in over the sills.

The first room was a kitchen in which two Negro women were working; the second was a dining room. Seated eating at a large table were four men; one was a very tall Negro who had a fine forehead and was dressed in expensive clothes. Richard thought he was the man who, at the barbecue, had offered up the ape to the goat; but, having seen him only from the distance, could not be certain. It occurred to him that, should that be so, the man was probably Lincoln B. Glasshill. Opposite him was a round-faced man in a turban. The third had his back to the window but, from his lank, black hair, was possibly an Andean Indian. The fourth man was von Thumm.

Richard crept back. Having rejoined the others, he told them what he had seen. He then went on excitedly, 'As there are no guards, we've got them where we want them. We are armed, they don't appear to be. Anyway, we can take them by sur-prise. A couple of shots through that window, then we'll hold the swine up and threaten to shoot them unless they tell us what they've done with Rex.'

'No good,' de Richleau murmured. 'You forget that they

are Adepts. Of what degree I do not yet know, but if von Thumm acted as Grand Master at a combined Sabbat, he would certainly have enough power to deflect bullets. He would defy us and, with the others all merging their wills with his, probably overcome us.'

It had become very cold, and Simon asked with a shiver, 'What can we do, then?'

'We shall have to wait until they go to sleep. Then I will try my strength against von Thumm on the astral.'

'It will be hours yet before they go to bed. We'll freeze to death.'

The Duke took him by the arm and turned him towards the airstrip. 'Don't worry. I will attend to that. We will wait in one of the hangars.'

Through the mist they made their way down the slight slope to the deserted airfield. Entering one of the hangars, Richard flashed his torch round. It lit up a small pile of empty packing cases. Rearranging the cases, they sat down and took a pull at their flasks. After a moment, de Richleau said:

'Our enemies are not yet aware we are here, and the cold we are feeling is not that of evil. It is the altitude and this accursed mist. If you each give me one of your hands I can overcome it.' Soon after they had obeyed him, the cold seemed to become less intense as he threw an aura of warm air round them. After a while they both fell into an uneasy sleep.

Three hours later, de Richleau roused them by saying, The time has come, and I have made a plan. If von Thumm is now asleep and I can overcome him on the astral, I will compel him to return to his body and leave the house. We will then kidnap him, hold him to ransom and compel him to have Rex delivered up to us as the price of his life.'

The others agreed this to be an excellent scheme. Having stretched their stiff limbs, they left the hangar and started to make their way back to the house. When they had first crossed the airstrip, the lights of the settlement could be seen behind them through the mist, as a rosy glow. Now all was dark in that direction; but the murk was a ground mist and, as they breasted the slight rise, they could again see the myriad of stars twinkling in the sky. There was no moon, as it was now in the dark quarter, but enough light by which to see their way.

The house was in darkness. De Richleau led the way round to the left side of it, halted opposite a window and said, 'This is von Thumm's room. Give me your hands again and concentrate with all your might on sending your spiritual energy into me. I am about to leave my body and challenge him. I need all the support I can get.'

Standing between them, he gradually became rigid so that they had to lean against and support him. For what seemed a long time nothing happened, then he gave a shudder and relaxed. Drawing in a deep breath, he murmured, 'That was very unpleasant, but I got the better of him. He is coming.'

A few minutes later an ungainly figure which Richard and Simon immediately recognised as that of the Baron, appeared round the corner of the house. As he limped up to them, the Duke said to him harshly:

'You have surrendered your soul to the demon Abaddon, but he has raised you only to an Adaptus Major with six circles and four squares. So I am your master. Do you acknowledge that?'

'*Jawohl, Sohn vom Heiligen Michael,*' muttered the Baron in his native German.

'Then you will come with us. Should you attempt to escape, we will deprive you of your present body by shooting you down. Should you call on your associates with Dark Power to come to your assistance, I will blast you on the astral.'

'*Zu Befehl, Meister,*' came the cowed reply.

The party then moved down the slope, de Richleau leading and von Thumm between Simon and Richard, the latter holding his pistol ready in his hand.

The trek back to the coppice close to which they had left their aircraft put a great strain upon them. Had it not been for the Duke's supernatural powers, they would have become hopelessly lost and ended up in one of the many quagmires. He could at least lead them in the right direction. But even so and given the aid of their torches, it was very difficult to find their way through the salt marshes and between clumps of five-foot-high pampas grass. Several times they had to turn back and search in the gently-moving mist that limited their range of vision, for another causeway of firm ground on which they could advance for a few hundred yards.

It was past two o'clock in the morning before they at last reached the slightly higher ground with its semi-circle of trees. After their long day and the ordeal of flying through the mountains, they were almost dead on their feet with exhaustion. Shining their torches before them they stumbled up the slope to the aircraft. As they reached it, there was a sudden movement near both the head and tail. From both sides a group of dimly-seen figures came rushing out to converge upon them.

De Richleau was still leading. He barely had time to raise his torch to defend his face from one attacker before another had struck him on the head with a cudgel and felled him to the ground. Richard swung round on the Baron and squeezed the trigger of his automatic; but von Thumm had thrown himself backward. As he fell, the bullets passed over him. There was a gasping grunt as one of the men behind him was hit. Next moment both Richard and Simon were seized and disarmed. Panting, they ceased their struggles and stood with their arms held behind them.

Von Thumm picked himself up, gave a guttural laugh and sneered: 'You poor fools! With the trial for murder you get away, *ja*. But haf you not sense to anticipate that we you overlooked from then? We haf expect you here to come, and make preparation. When you land, we know it. For you to come spying in our town we wait. Then send our men to make ambush for your return. Interfering *englische Schweine*! For you very soon now it is curtains, and a death very painful.'

12

At the Mercy of a Fiend

There was nothing Richard or Simon could do, or the Duke either, when he came to a few minutes later. To have brought occult power to bear on von Thumm would have required concentration and, at the moment, his head seemed to be splitting.

The ambush had consisted of eight men. One was a powerful Arab and another a yellow-faced mulatto with a crop of tight curls. The others were all big Negroes. One of the latter had been shot by Richard in the fleshy part of the arm; but the seven uninjured men were more than sufficient to keep the captives under control. None of them had uttered a word. The Baron was now holding one of the torches, and as its beam swept over the faces of two of the Negroes, de Richleau caught sight of their gaping mouths and lacklustre, fixed stare. It confirmed the impression he had already formed from the jerky movement of their limbs as two of them had pulled him to his feet. Turning his head, he said to von Thumm:

'Do not be too certain that you have triumphed. Had you sent men with all their faculties to ambush us, they would have reacted promptly to any unexpected situation. But Zombies are incapable of doing so. When the pain in my head has lessened, I may spring an unexpected surprise on you. Then these poor wretches will only gape and look on while I again force you into submission.'

As the Duke spoke, he was well aware that several hours must elapse before he again became capable of using his occult powers; so his only object had been to undermine von Thumm's confidence in himself. The Baron replied harshly:

'Should you anything attempt, with you on the "down here" level I will deal as you threatened to do to me. A bullet in the guts you will get. But the Undead haf their uses. No tales can they tell. As you will haf guessed, we of the hierarchy take much precaution against those morons in the settlement our secret activities getting to know. Times are when one of them too inquisitive becomes. For such situation, these six Undead at headquarters we keep. No talk, no packdrill, as you English haf saying. *Ach*, I haf good new thought. To cheat me try and I will shoot only to wound. Then into the marsh I will haf you thrown, to choke out your lives in mud.'

After a moment he added, 'Also with aid I now haf, on the Astral I am also your master.' Then he jerked his head in the direction of the Arab and the mulatto. 'El Aziz is son to Baal, and Benito to Baron Samedi. United we haf power to your astral bind. March now, all of you.'

As they moved off, both Simon and Richard glanced at the two men with quick interest, as it was Benito who had brought Nella to the Sabbat and El Aziz who had raped her.

For what seemed an endless time, mud became a nightmare to the prisoners. As they were forced on by their captors, they staggered from one piece of solid ground to another, through intervening stretches of spongy, oozing soil that threatened to suck their shoes from their feet. The march back to the settlement proved incredibly laborious, and the fear grew on all of them that they would never make it. With incredible fortitude, the elderly Duke trudged on, and Richard, the fittest of the three, managed to keep going, in spite of the laboured breathing that racked his lungs. But, on the final mile, poor Simon's legs gave way with increasing frequency and he slid to his knees in the mire. Silently the two Zombies who were holding his arms dragged him to his feet and, eventually, had practically to carry him.

At long last they reached the building outside the settlement. Von Thumm led the way in. The prisoners were taken down a flight of concrete steps to the basement and pushed into an unfurnished room. A steel door clanged to behind them. The key was turned in the lock, and the light was switched off. Utterly exhausted and caring no more what happened to them, they lowered themselves to the bare floor and, very soon, fell asleep.

When they woke, still in darkness, they had no idea for how long they had been unconscious. De Richleau was convinced that they had slept the clock round nearly twice, as they had flown up to the Sala on February 1st and the 2nd was Candlemas, one of the four great Satanic feasts of the year; the others being Walpurgis Night, St. John's Eve and Hallowe'en. It was certain that von Thumm, El Aziz and Harry Benito, together

149

with the other Satanists who lived in the house, would all have flown off to a Sabbat; and that would account for their being left to have their sleep out, instead of being roughly awakened a few hours after being pushed into the cell.

Miserably they exchanged a few words on the events leading up to their capture. The Duke exhorted his companions to have faith that the Lords of Light would come to their assistance. His friends endeavoured to believe that, but were so unutterably depressed that they responded only half-heartedly. Then, for a period of several hours, they remained almost silent.

Suddenly the light was switched on. They were still blinking when the steel door of the room was unlocked and swung open. Framed in it was the big negro Richard had seen at dinner with the Baron. Without bothering to close the door behind him, he advanced into the room, glared down at Richard and said:

'I am Lincoln B. Glasshill. I've a score to settle with you and your little friend. By instigating police inquiries, you have rendered it no longer safe for us to hold Sabbats at my house in Santiago, and forced me to abandon my practice there. Stand up.'

Richard got to his feet. The big Negro's fist shot out, caught him on the jaw and hurled him back against the wall. Before he could recover and get his fists into a position to defend himself, Glasshill struck again, this time at Richard's stomach. The savage blow drove the breath from his body. He lurched forward, endeavouring to cover his face. But in vain. With cold malice, his attacker smashed down his guard and slammed his clenched fists again and again into Richard's eyes, nose, mouth and chin. Dazed and bleeding, Richard sank to the floor.

Turning to Simon, who had got up with the futile thought of coming to Richard's assistance, Glasshill seized him by the collar, shook him as a terrier shakes a rat and, towering over him, cried:

'You miserable little whitey. You are not worthy of being chastised by a proper man. I'll not stoop to skin my knuckles on your face. Instead, I'll send the fire-imps to you.'

With a great heave, he sent Simon sprawling in a corner, turned on his heel and marched from the room, slamming the door behind him.

De Richleau's immediate concern had been to get as much sleep as possible, in order to recharge with energy his physical body; so, some while before Glasshill had entered the cell, he had induced sleep to come to him again. At the sound of the shouts and scuffle as the Negro beat Richard up the Duke's ego returned down the silver cord that attached it to his body during unconsciousness; but his physical senses were too freshly aroused for him to be capable of any attempt to protect his friend.

Now he stood up, laid his hands gently on Richard's battered face, drew out the pain and soothed him. But soon afterwards he had to turn his attention to Simon. He was still lying in the corner where Glasshill had thrown him, and tiny lights had begun to flicker up and down his body. A smell of burning cloth drifted across the room, then Simon started to cry out in distress as the fire-imps settled on his face and hands, inflicting burns on him that were more painful than mosquito bites. Frantically he endeavoured to destroy the imps by smacking at them; but, with incredible swiftness, they evaded his attempts and settled on him in other places.

'Be patient for a few minutes, Simon,' de Richleau urged him swiftly. 'I have now regained enough power to deal with this at least.' Sitting down cross-legged on the floor, he bowed his head and extended his arms as high as they would go above his shoulders. Simon could not stop himself from continuing to swot about and exclaim in pain and anger; but gradually the little flames that were tormenting him went out with a faint, hissing noise, as though they were being doused with invisible water.

There followed another long period, during which they sat or lay in the darkness, changing their positions every few minutes, to ease the soreness of their flesh from pressure on the hard floor. They reckoned that they had been put in the cell at about five o'clock in the morning, and from their wrist-watches they knew that Glasshill's visit had taken place at about three o'clock, so they reckoned that they had been in the cell for at least thirty-four hours; and, as no food or drink had been brought to them, they were all now both hungry and very thirsty.

Shortly before five o'clock, the light came on again, the door opened and von Thumm limped into the room. Behind him stood a little group of his Zombies. For a moment he regarded his prisoners with his crooked smile, then his face took on a discontented look, as he snarled:

'English swine! *Ach*, to haf had you in my hands in the old days, how goot it would haf been. I was then *Gruppenführer*

151

S.S. For English spy-swine, dirty Jews and such, we ha. the ice-water bath, the steel rod to beat and the electric apparatus for attaching to genitals. These we haf not here. I haf ideas, though. *Ja*, plenty to make you for mercy scream. But for the present, no. Orders haf come that I to another place take you. *So!* Perhaps I am fortunate and you returned to me for disposal are. If not make no merriment. Others will with you deal and you curse the day when into our business your big noses you stick.'

De Richleau made no attempt to subdue the Baron mentally, because he thought it certain that he would be able to call on help to resist, and felt that, in any case, wherever they were being sent, they would not fare worse than they would in the hands of this Nazi sadist.

The Zombies hustled them up the stairs to a wash-room, where they were allowed to relieve themselves; then out on to the airstrip. Von Thumm led the way over to one of the smaller aircraft. It was already ticking over. They climbed into it and saw that the long-haired man, whose back view Richard had seen through the dining room window two evenings before, was sitting in the back seat. He had the hook nose of an Andean Indian and the thick lips of a Negro. In his right hand he held a two-foot-long blade, with a very sharp point; a more practical weapon for keeping prisoners under control in an aircraft than a pistol, a bullet from which might have damaged the structure. The Baron awkwardly levered himself up into the pilot's seat, and tested the controls; then they took off.

From the direction of the sinking sun the prisoners knew that they were flying slightly east of north. For about fifty miles the dreary Sala, with its endless marshes and stretches of reddish earth passed smoothly beneath them, then they entered mountainous country and the going became very rough. The 'plane bucked, swerved and dropped alarmingly as it struck air pockets; but von Thumm was a good pilot and evidently knew well the route he was taking. Their discomfort lasted only twenty minutes, then they came round a high peak to see, melting into the misty distance ahead, the fifty-mile long Lago de Poopo. The blueness of its waters was in startling contrast with the yellow of the heights surrounding it. But they had little time to take in the full grandeur of the scene, for the Baron had put the aircraft into a steep dive to bring it down.

Another few minutes, and it became clear that he was heading for an island about ten miles from the southern edge of the great lake. As they approached, it could be seen that to have landed on it from the water would have been next to impossible, as sheer cliffs dropped to the beaches. The southern two-thirds of it was flat, and largely covered with forest, but towards its northern end there were hills, mounting to a lofty eminence of rock, crowning which there stood an irregular building of grey stone, that looked like a ruined fortress.

The foothills at the far end of the island were broken by a half-mile-long, oval plateau. It had been developed into a landing strip, and had two small aircraft parked in bays clear of the runway. Von Thumm brought the 'plane down with practised ease. It was met by two men, both short, but of formidable appearance. They had the hook noses and lank, black hair of Andeans, and were wearing gaudy clothes, with bandoliers across their chests, pistol holsters on their hips and knives thrust through their waistbands.

The Baron signed to the prisoners to get out of the 'plane, but did not follow. With no more than a gesture, he handed them over to the two Andeans and, having thrown a malevolent glance at them, slammed shut the door of his aircraft. Two minutes later it was again in the air, and heading back towards the Sala de Uyuni. Meanwhile, one of the Indians had signed to the prisoners to follow him and the other took up the rear.

For twenty minutes they made their way laboriously up a series of steep stairways cut in the rock, until they reached the partially-ruined stronghold. Its towering walls were composed of great blocks of stone which had been cunningly dovetailed together. How man could possibly have constructed such a building without cranes and modern engineering machinery posed a fascinating problem, as do the similar pre-Hellenic palaces at Mycene and Tirens in Greece. From many photographs the prisoners had seen, they knew this one to have been built by the Incas, probably in the fifteenth century A.D., which would have made it nearly three thousand years later than those the pre-Hellenes had built with similar huge blocks of stone.

Their escort led them through a flat-topped arch, the transom of which was a monolith twelve feet in length and four in depth, into a courtyard, then through a much lower arch and down a long, narrow passage. At the far end there was a modern door of heavy wood. One of the men pressed a bell-push. They waited for a while and the door was opened by another Andean Indian, dressed in a green, scalloped jerkin

153

and trunks that were reminiscent of the clothes worn by Robin Hood's men. Behind him stood a Negro with a wall eye, who beckoned them in.

Incongruously, after the courtyard of great stones, there was a carpeted stairway, with walls of pale, natural wood, and lit by electric light. Mounting the stairs, they reached a wide landing which might have been that of a large private house. It was furnished with a Louis XV settee and chairs of the same period. On the walls there were prints after Bouchard and Fragonard. Two passages led off it. They were taken along the one leading to the right. To one side, some way down it, there was an open arch. Through it the prisoners could see a bar, in front of which several men were sitting drinking. Among them there was an immensely fat Babu, together with a Negro with a face like a skull, an almost white Caribbean octoroon and an apparently Spanish half-cast.

The wall-eyed Negro who had met the captives signed to the green-liveried servitor and gestured for him to take them on down the corridor; then walked through the archway to join his companions in the bar. The servitor led them along the passage for another eighty feet, then halted and knocked on a door. A voice bade him enter. He opened the door and signed to the prisoners to go into the room.

It was a boudoir, again furnished in the style of Louis XV, with a beautiful Aubusson carpet. Seated near the window was Silvia Sinegiest. She had been reading a book. As she laid it down, her little shaggy-haired dog jumped from her lap, barking furiously and bounded towards her visitors, racing round their legs giving them an excited welcome. Standing up, Silvia cried, 'Down, Booboo, down! You bad boy! Stop it!' But she was smiling and, turning her smile on Richard, she said in her low, musical voice:

'Hello! How nice to see you again, and Mr Aron. Your friend, of course, must be the Duke de Richleau.'

The Duke made an inclination of his head. 'You are right, Madame. By hearsay you are equally well known to me, and I recall with pleasure seeing two films that you made some years ago. I only regret that we should meet under such far from happy circumstances.'

Her bright glance ran swiftly over them. Their clothing was creased and mud-stained, their hair awry, and they all had bristly stubble on their chins.

She sighed and shook her head, with its aureole of strawberry blonde hair. 'We owe you an apology. Unfortunately, so many Germans are still barbarians at heart, and von Thumm is one of them. But I suppose one must allow for the malice he feels at the destruction of his Nazi ideals and the humiliation of his country.'

'One could forgive him a lot,' Richard burst out, his speech now thick from the thirst that had been tormenting them for several hours past. 'But not for denying us water ever since we were caught.'

'Oh, you poor things!' she exclaimed; then, in a few swift steps she crossed to a drinks table and asked, 'What will you have—whisky, gin, brandy?'

'For me, water please,' replied de Richleau. 'Later we may accept your invitation to partake of something more potent.' The others nodded agreement. Quickly she poured three glasses from a carafe, popped a lump of ice into each and carried them over.

'As the Baron refused you drink, I suppose he denied you food, too,' Silvia remarked. 'If you are very hungry, I'll send for something at once, but we shall be dining in about an hour, and I can promise you a very good dinner.'

Their enforced fast had given them all excellent appetites, but they were not afflicted by hunger to the same degree as they had been by thirst; so they thanked her for her offer to send for food, but refused it.

Looking at Richard, she said, 'Your face is in a shocking state. Is that the result of your having gotten into a fight, or did von Thumm beat you up?'

'No, it was not the Baron,' he replied tartly, 'but another of your friends: that great brute of a Negro, Lincoln Glasshill.'

'They are not my friends, only my associates,' she told him with a quick lift of her chin. 'I will do my best to make amends by patching you up.'

Turning away, she tinkled a glass bell that stood on an ornate, buhl writing table. In under a minute her summons was answered by Pedro, the Spanish manservant who had been with her down in Punta Arenas. She said to him, 'Take these gentlemen to their rooms. See to it that they have everything they want.' Glancing at Richard, she added, 'When you have shaved and had a bath, say in half an hour, I'll come to you and do what I can to your face.'

Pedro led them away down the long corridor to the landing, then down the other corridor to three rooms near its end. Their original stone ceilings and floors had been left untouched, but the walls had been plastered and painted with evidently modern murals of Inca scenes, and there were colourful handwoven mats on the floors. The beds looked comfortable, and there were fitted cupboards. Adjacent to each room was a small, well-equipped bathroom, with all they would need to make themselves presentable.

Wearily they struggled out of their filthy clothes, shaved and luxuriated for a while in hot baths. When, considerably revived, they returned to the bedrooms, they found that Pedro had removed the gaudy garments they had been wearing and, instead, laid out for them the type of suit that up-country white men wore in that part of the world. Richard had just put his on, and found that it fitted not too badly, when there came a knock at his door. He called 'Come in', and Silvia entered, carrying a tray on which were numerous items for first aid.

His lips were swollen, his chin and cheek cut, but his worst injury was to his left eye. It was already half closed, and promised to become a glorious 'shiner'. Having remarked it, Silvia had brought with her a piece of raw meat which she proceeded to lay on it and securely bandage in place. She smeared a healing salve on his mouth and the cuts, then lightly powdered over the latter.

Standing back, she said with a laugh, 'Poor Mr Eaton, you do look a guy. How very distressing for such a handsome fellow. But, never mind. In a day or two you will again be an Adonis.'

Regarding her coldly with his remaining eye, he said sullenly, 'Not if your so-called "associates" get at me again. And why you should think me good-looking, I've no idea. Apart from my wife, no-one else tells me so.'

'But you are,' she insisted. 'You're the perfect type of the well-born English gentleman, whom I have always admired. How old is your wife?'

'I should say she is the best part of ten years younger than you.'

Silvia laughed again. 'But a man is as old as he feels, and a woman as old as she looks; so if she is forty or so I'll bet she couldn't compete with me. It is part of my reward for doing what I do that I keep my face and figure so that I look not more than thirty.'

'I see. So you really are a witch?'

'Indeed I am. I can raise a wind, cast spells and make love potions.'

'I'll bet you couldn't make one that would affect me,' remarked Richard aggressively.

'I could, given the right ingredients. I'd need a lapwing, bull's gall, the fat of a white hen, ants' eggs, the eyes of a black cat, musk, myrrh, frankincense, red storax, mestic, olibenum, saffron, benzoin and valerian.'

'God, what a brew! It would stink to high heaven. No man in his senses could be persuaded to swallow it.'

'A horrid mess, I agree,' she laughed, 'and I've never resorted to it. You'd be surprised, though, what I could do with a few of your nail-parings, let alone a neat little clipping of your pubic hair. But, in my case, such aids are not really necessary. I've never failed to get a man I wanted with my own resources.'

Richard gave her a half-admiring, half-surly look. 'I've rarely seen a woman better equipped with what it takes. But, if you have designs on me, you'd better indent for the cat's eyes and bull's gall.'

'Don't worry, darling,' she laughed again. 'I just couldn't bear to wake up in the morning and see your face on my pillow, as it looks at present. But in a few days you will be your handsome self once more. Then we'll see.'

'I don't think we will. But, while we are on the subject, I'd like you to tell me something. As you know, Aron and I were onlookers at that so-called "barbecue" which took place out at Glasshill's house. After the feast, everyone let themselves go with a vengeance. But you remained sitting up on the table. As you are so keen on that sort of thing, why didn't you join in?'

'Because I am the "Maiden".'

'Oh come! With two or three marriages and what all behind you, you can hardly claim to be a virgin.'

'The Maiden does not have to be. It is a rank in the hierarchy of the true priesthood. Joan of Arc held that rank and openly acknowledged it.'

Richard frowned. 'I know that we English burnt Joan of Arc as a witch, but all the world knows that she was a saint.'

'She was a prisoner of the English, but it was not they who condemned her to be burned at the stake. It was a tribunal of the Christian Inquisition, presided over by the Bishop of Beauvais. From the account of her trial, it emerges quite clearly that she was not a Christian. Her religious instruction was given to her by her godmother, who was known to consort

157

with the "little people". They were, of course, the descendants of a race older than the Franks, who had never wavered in the True Faith, and were steeped in the lore of magic. The wife of her first protector, the Sieur de Bourlemont, was one of them.

'In those days, early in the fifteenth century, the Christian heresy had a hold only on the upper strata of society. The great majority of the ordinary people still believed in the True God. That is why the soldiers were willing and even eager to give their lives for Joan in battle. They looked on her as a minor deity. She herself stated that she could not be killed, but would be of value to the Dauphin for one year only. That was because she had made a pact with Satan for twelve months of power. Even in prison, when there was no longer any practical point in it, she insisted on wearing men's clothes, so there could hardly be a less suitable title to give her than "The Maid", unless a special reason lay behind it. And there did. All the Grand Covens have their Queen Witch, known as "The Maiden", and she ranks next in power to the Grand Master. When Joan was first put forward by her sponsors and accepted by the Dauphin, she ranked only as "The Maid of Orleans". But later she was elevated to the highest honours as "*La Pucelle de France*".'

Richard shrugged. 'I don't know enough about the matter to argue with you; but the fact remains that millions of people venerate Joan of Arc as a saint today.'

'Of course.' Silvia showed her lovely teeth in a smile. 'The Christian priesthood is not quite so stupid as to let people continue to make a heroine of someone they condemned as a pagan. They are experts at applying whitewash to their own victims, when it suits their purpose, and in persuading people to accept new explanations for the origins of ancient festivals. As, for example, converting the Roman Saturnalia into Christmas; in spite of the fact that Jesus Christ was actually born in March. But I must go and tidy myself for dinner.'

A few minutes later Pedro came to collect the three prisoners, and led them down a flight of stairs to a long room divided by partly-drawn, heavy curtains. The part the door led into was a lounge, furnished with armchairs, tables beside them and, on one side, a cocktail bar. Through the gap between the curtains, they could see a dining table. Silvia was standing near the bar; as they came she asked them, 'What can I make you? I seem to remember, though, that you like champagne. It's here if you prefer it.'

Simon nodded. Richard said he would like a Planter's Punch if that was not too much trouble. To the surprise of his friends, de Richleau declared himself to be a tee-totaller, and said he would have only a glass of water.

Deftly Silvia produced the drinks, then she said: 'I've been given a rough idea of your recent doings, and you must all be rather tired; so perhaps it would be better if we put off talking of why you have been brought here and all that sort of thing, until you've had a chance to relax and fortify yourselves with a meal.'

De Richleau inclined his white head. 'As we are in your hands, Madame, that is considerate of you. We arrived here in very poor shape, but our baths have freshened us up and, as we slept for twenty-four hours between the time of our capture and this morning, none of us is in urgent need of sleep. Naturally we are anxious to know the intentions of your . . . your associates towards us. But that can quite well wait until after we have dined.'

Silvia smiled. 'How wise of you not to press for an immediate explanation. But, of course, we have found out a great deal about you and, as an Adept, you will have trained yourself to patience.'

A quarter of an hour later they were enjoying an excellent dinner and Silvia succeeded in temporarily banishing from their minds the fact that they were prisoners. As they were waiting for the second course to be served, she asked the Duke, 'How did you enjoy your stay in Chile?'

He replied that he had been there only long enough to see the capital, which he had found very pleasant, but Simon and Richard held forth on the extraordinary variety of the climate and the scenery and how enjoyable they had found Santiago until they had been thrown into prison. De Richleau then asked their hostess if she knew anything about the history of the fortress.

She shook her head, 'Nothing, except that it formed part of the defence complex centred on the Inca city of Potosi, which lay just across the lake and was the southernmost centre of their civilisation. But I have recently read quite a lot about them and found it fascinating. The extraordinary thing is that they should not only have created their vast Empire but brought the whole of it under complete control in so short a time. Although they are known to have been established in the Cuzco valley as early as about 1100, theirs was quite a small

159

territory until they began their conquests in 1350. In little over a hundred years, the Lord Inca wielded absolute authority from Quito in Ecuador right down to Maule in central Chile: a territory of over three thousand, two hundred and fifty miles.'

'The secret of their power was road building,' remarked the Duke. 'Until the recent creation of the Pan-American highway, their trunk road down the Andes was the longest in the world. They had another nearly as long down the coast and shorter, lateral ones running down every valley. And, although they were mountain roads, their standard width was twenty-four feet. By means of them they could, by forced marches, rush troops in a matter of days to any part of their Empire that was threatened.'

'I know, and the Lord Inca was always warned of trouble with incredible swiftness. Their relay runners could transmit messages at the rate of two hundred and forty miles in twenty-four hours. What they achieved was fantastic when one remembers that they had no wheeled vehicles and no horses. Llamas were their only means of transport, and the blocks of stone in all their great fortresses had to be carried many miles up those steep mountains by men. But what I admire most about them is the orderly way in which they administered their Empire. Records were kept of the numbers of each age group in every village; what crops could be expected from it, and the amount of work on roads and bridges of which its people were capable; and the land was shared out among the villagers afresh each year, according to how many men there were in each family able to cultivate it.'

'I remember reading Thornton Wilder's book, *The Bridge of San Luis Rey*,' put in Richard. 'It was an incredible feat to have made a bridge a hundred and fifty feet long, with only twisted rope, and to have got it up across a deep gorge between two precipitous mountains. It was no gimcrack affair, either. It was still in use up to 1890, after five hundred and forty years.'

'The only people comparable to them were the Romans,' said the Duke, 'both as road builders and administrators. Moreover, the Romans had the enormous advantage of being able to read and write, whereas the Incas could do neither. They had to send their messages and keep their records by means of bunches of coloured strings, in which they tied knots at varying intervals.'

Silvia stubbed out her cigarette and lit another, then she asked, 'Did you know that more than half the foods the world eats today were first developed by the Inca agriculturalists? They irrigated great areas which had previously been desert, and grew an amazing variety of vegetables. They had two hundred and forty varieties of potatoes and twenty of maize. We owe to them many kinds of beans, tapioca, peanuts, squash, cashews, pineapples, chocolate, avocados, tomatoes and paw-paws. And, may I remind you, this wonderful civilisation was utterly destroyed by the zealots of the Christian Church.'

When they had done full justice to a meal ending with a savoury of flamingo tongues, Silvia asked them to make themselves comfortable in the lounge end of the room, and left them for ten minutes. On her return, she settled herself in a low armchair, crossed her peerless legs so that they were displayed to the best advantage, and said:

'You must be aware that your investigation into Rex's disappearance has aroused against you a most powerful enemy, and brought you into great danger. About the reason for Rex's leaving Buenos Aires I, of course, lied to you. I was ordered to, as it was hoped that, believing my story that he had committed murder, you would call off your hunt for fear that you might lead the police to him. However, I now give you my word that he is well, cheerful and has no regrets about what he has done. More than that, for the time being I am forbidden to tell you. Most unfortunately, I failed to stall you off, with the result that you have found out many things that we regard as most important to keep secret. In consequence, you now have only one way in which you can escape paying for that with your lives.'

They had all been mellowed by an excellent dinner. Only the Duke had refused all alcohol, but he had special resources upon which he could draw to restore his vitality and, with the dessert, Silvia had served to Richard and Simon as a liqueur an elixir that had counteracted the fatigue they would normally have felt after such a very tiring day. So Richard asked quite amiably:

'Tell us what it is.'

'You must reassess your spiritual values.'

'How d'you mean?'

'By accepting and worshipping the True God.'

'Meaning the Devil,' Simon put in, and gave a slight shudder. 'No, thank you. Few years ago I got in pretty deep with a Master of the Left-Hand Path. But de Richleau saved me, thank God. Never again.'

She smiled at him. 'Then your friend did you a great disservice. And you are wrong to refer to the True God as "the Devil". That is only the name bestowed upon him in hatred and fear by his enemies, the Christians who denied him. It was invented by them as late as the Middle Ages.' Glancing at the Duke, she added, 'Am I not right?'

He nodded. 'Yes, there are many mentions of demons and evil spirits from the earliest times, but none of the Devil until the Christian Church began to get the upper hand in its war against paganism in the fifteenth and sixteenth centuries.'

Richard gave him a doubting look. 'Oh come! Nearly all the monarchs in Europe were Christians the best part of a thousand years before that.'

'It is true that many kings, queens and nobles were converted by missionaries sent from Rome during what we term the Dark Ages. But it is reasonable to believe that they accepted the new faith only on the old principle that it was bad policy to refuse to acknowledge any god, in case he took offence and did you a mischief. That belief was prevalent in the Roman world, and they had inherited it. Christianity did not secure a serious hold in Britain until well after the Norman conquest. There were, of course, many priests and priestesses of the old religion, and everybody knew who they were, but very few were brought to trial as witches until early Stuart times. In fact, the first witch trial ever to be held in England did not occur until the reign of King John, and then it was brought against a Jew who, in spite of the wave of anti-Jewish feeling at that time, was found not guilty.'

'Thank you, Duke,' Silvia said. 'And one can add that, even during Norman and Plantagenet times, Christians were in the minority. Only the upper classes endowed monasteries and were in favour of the Crusades. The great majority of the people still followed the true religion. That was recognised by those who tried to put an end to it. And, even when its votaries were driven to hold their ceremonies in secret, they were still a great power in the land. One has only to recall the origin of the Order of the Garter.'

'What has that to do with it?' Richard asked.

'The account of how it happened is well known. At a ball, the Countess of Salisbury's jewelled garter fell off. She was the mistress of King Edward III, and was dancing with him. He snatched it up and founded a new Order of twenty-six knights, including himself and the Prince of Wales. Covens always

162

consist of thirteen members, so he had created two new covens, with himself and the Prince as their Grand Masters.'

'I don't see why you believe them to be covens, or what seizing the lady's garter has to do with paganism.'

'From the earliest times the insignia of the Chief of a coven has always been a string worn round the left leg, below the knee. There is a prehistoric painting in the caves at Cogul, showing a dance in which a figure is wearing one. The Countess was the "Maiden" or, as you would put it, the Queen Witch of England, and the King knew it. By securing her garter, he supplanted her. It gave him power over the many thousands of people in his kingdom who still followed the Old Faith. And he did not look on them as evil people, because he held the garter aloft and cried *"Honi soit qui mal y pense"*—"Evil be to him who evil thinks"—and took that for the motto of the new Order. What I tell you is confirmed by the regalia worn by the Sovereign. It embodies one hundred and sixty-eight garters, and the one round the leg makes the one hundred and sixty-ninth—that is thirteen thirteens, symbolising an all-powerful combination of thirteen covens.'

Richard remarked with a slight sneer, 'You'll be telling us next that, just because Jesus Christ and His disciples numbered thirteen, they, too, were a coven.'

'They were,' she retorted swiftly. 'Jesus spent many years in the wilderness, training Himself to become a Magister Templar, the highest of all grades of occultists. That is why He was able to draw down the power to perform many miracles, and they were all what you would term white magic—for the benefit, not of Himself, but others. It was only later that the message He brought was distorted. When He spoke of God the Father, He was referring to the True God—the God of Love.'

'Ner,' Simon shook his head stubbornly. 'He was speaking of Jehovah. Plenty of evidence of that.'

'Only from people who were writing many years after Christ's death, the men who, for their own evil ends, perverted His teachings. Jehovah was the God of Hate; the terrible primitive entity whose jealousy had to be appeased by burnt offerings—and this horror still, today, remains the supreme deity of the Christian religion.'

'Nobody really believes that any more.'

Silvia gave a little laugh. 'Of course they don't. But that does not alter the fact that, through St Paul and other masochistic fanatics, Jehovah succeeded in inflicting incalculable frustra-

tion and suffering on many millions of people. His priests—
the priests of the Christian Church—made a virtue of suffering.
They preached self-denial; that all enjoyment was wicked. They
urged the people to fast and scourge themselves, and live in dirt
and squalor. They coerced them into confessing their so-called
sins and, as a penalty for having succumbed to pleasure,
ordered them to wear hair shirts. They stigmatised the divinely-
given urge of men and women to give physical expression to
their lives, as lust. Contrary to nature, they decreed that a man
and woman could choose only one partner for life and, even
then, cohabit only for the purpose of begetting children. These
were "God the Father's" servants. But what a Father! Can
you wonder that, right up to Tudor times and even later, a
great part of the people doggedly refused to submit to this horrible tyranny and, in secret, continued to worship the True
God? It was He who had created them in the beginning and
given them their instinct to crave for all the pleasant things in
life that He had provided for them. To eat, drink and be merry
and to make love without fear.'

Silvia paused to light a cigarette, then went on. 'In ancient
times, the True God was accepted and revered in all the great
civilisations. Often, a special devotion was shown by sects to
various aspects of His power and personified in the many minor
gods that made up the Pantheons of Chaldea, Egypt, India,
Greece and Rome; but all acknowledged the supreme entity.
It is only in recent centuries that the evil heresies of the Dark
Power have gained a formidable foothold in many nations.

'That is why I am urging you to readjust your spiritual
values. Because, in a great part of the world those who realised
the truth have been forced to conduct their ceremonies in
secret, you have been brought up to believe that they worship
the powers of Darkness. But that is not so. It is they who continue to carry the torch that they know in their hearts to have
been ignited from the source of Eternal Light.'

De Richleau smiled. 'Madame, I congratulate you on having
presented an excellent case. I grant you that the early Christians
perverted the teachings of Christ, and that the priests of His
Church have inflicted untold misery on millions of people. But
you have neglected to mention that the Old religion has also
been perverted by its priests. Time was when they served the
True God well. They were the doctors who healed the sick, the
confidants who advised people wisely when in trouble, and they
presided over those ceremonies at which the masses could for

get the drudgery of every-day life, in feasting, revelry and in giving full licence to their sexual urges. Such Saturnalia were an admirable outlet for the frustrations of mankind. Were they permitted today, addiction to drugs would be almost unknown and one in every seven of the population of the United States would not have to go into homes for the cure of alcoholism or mental instability. But times have changed.

'The power of a faith increases or wanes in accordance with the number of people who believe in it. As the Old religion was gradually suppressed, the number of its true priests dwindled. At length they lost their authority, and by the Middle Ages, had been supplanted by evil persons who promised their followers gratifications they had not earned. That is contrary to the Logos. The cult became one of Darkness, instead of Light.

'It was used by the unscrupulous to inflict pain and loss on their enemies. To gain their ends, people trafficked with demons: the emissaries of Satan the Destroyer who, from the beginning, has waged war against the Powers of Light.

'They served him in a thousand ways to sow dissension and substitute chaos for law and order. In many cases their activities brought about wide-spread misery. To give you one example. It is known to initiates that, on the night before Worcester fight, Cromwell made a pact with the Devil. He bartered his soul for victory and seven years of power. He triumphed and seven years after to the day, the Devil's emissary came to fetch his soul. He died in the midst of the most terrible thunderstorm that had been known in England for a generation. And during his seven years the Devil ruled through him. Never have the people of Britain and Ireland lived through such periods of misery. The proof of that is the frenzied, unalloyed rejoicing with which the whole nation welcomed the return from exile of King Charles. So, you see, misguided as the clergy of the Christian Churches may have been in many matters, they were right in stigmatising this evil power by naming it the Devil.'

For a moment Silvia was silent, then she replied, 'Yet today your Christian clergy are so abysmally ignorant of spiritual matters that they do not even recognise when they see them the signs their predecessors created to represent Good and Evil. You will recall that during the war the whole centre of your city of Coventry in the English Midlands was destroyed by a great German air-raid, and that the ancient cathedral was reduced to a heap of rubble. It is now being rebuilt but on a revolutionary plan. Church architecture always decreed that the high altar should face the East, towards Jerusalem. In the new cathedral, the high altar faces very nearly south. The windows in its sides, instead of throwing light upon the body of the building, are in bays, and so slanted that they leave the altar in darkness. In the great tapestry over the altar, the figure of Jesus Christ has round it, not, as you might suppose, figures of the four Evangelists or Christian Saints, but those of four demons. Upon the spire there is a witches' broomstick and, believe it or not, upon the high altar reposes Satan's crooked cross.'

De Richleau shook his head. 'I have been told so. It seems incredible that such sacrilege should ever have been permitted by the Committee of Bishops, or whoever are responsible for passing such plans; but I have not sought to deny the decadence of the Christian Church.' On a lighter note, he added, 'Supposing that the Devil, as we term the Principle of Evil, really was a person, it would be insulting to assume that so high an intelligence has no sense of humour; so how he would be laughing at Christians bowing down before his cross.'

Giving a little laugh, Silvia said, 'You're right about that. But what is being done at Coventry is only symbolic of the Age of Unbelief. As you have admitted, Christianity is a heresy; and the True God is indestructible. He has withdrawn His countenance from mankind only because of the abuses committed in His name. If His votaries were purged of the evil priests among them, a new and happier era would dawn.'

'It could,' the Duke agreed, 'but such a hope is to build castles in Spain. Everything goes to show that, since the coming of the so-called Age of Reason, the power of Satan had steadily increased. And now the greatest blow of all against peace, prosperity and happiness is being prepared, here in this very place. It is planned to divide the world into two warring camps, so that in every country and city there will be strife and bloodshed between men and women, solely because they have different coloured skins. That must be the inevitable result of inciting the underprivileged races to attempt to impose Black Power.'

'It is clear to me that you need further instruction,' said a firm, male voice.

Amazed that anyone could have entered the room in complete silence, the three friends automatically turned their heads

166

to look over their shoulders. Yet there was no-one there, and the voice seemed to have come from behind Silvia's chair. Swivelling their heads back, they stared at her.

As they did so, a bright light appeared above and beyond her crown of hair. A mauve mist began to swirl round the light as though it was the vortex of a miniature cyclone. The mist thickened and took form, coalescing so that it had the outline of a man. Another moment and it had solidified, so that they found themselves gaping at a tall, slim, handsome human. as much flesh and blood as themselves.

Richard instantly recognised this apparition which had so startlingly materialised. It was the man who, in Buenos Aires had introduced him to von Thumm—Don Salvador Marino.

13

Black Power

Silvia had come to her feet, swung round and made a low curtsy. Don Salvador touched her on the shoulder and, as she rose, said: 'My dear, you did well. Your arguments were cogent and, of course, based on the truth. But the understanding of our friends is still obscured by the beliefs of a lifetime. That they should hold them so stubbornly is regrettable. But I do not despair of bringing them to see reason.'

The three friends had all instantly stood up. Richard, hardly able to believe that he was not dreaming, gasped, 'We met you in Buenos Aires. You . . . you are . . .'

'Yes.' The tall man gave his enchanting smile. 'You knew me there as Don Salvador Marino. But I take precautions against it becoming suspected that I am in any way associated with what goes on here. It was clear to me that you, and your friend Aron, would prove not only persistent in your enquiries about Van Ryn, but were also highly intelligent; so you might possibly have got on his trail. That was why I used von Thumm as an intermediary and had him send you to my charming associate, the "Maiden". Here I am known as the "Prince".'

'Prince of Evil,' Simon burst out, belligerently for him.

'You are mistaken,' came the quiet reply. 'A Prince in the hierarchy of the Outer Circle, yes; but not of evil. Of that I hope to convince you, and . . .' he made a slight bow '. . . your knowledgeable and partially enlightened friend, *Monseigneur le Duc*.'

De Richleau returned the bow and said, 'It would be discourteous to refuse to listen to your argument, Prince. But my own beliefs are based on the Eternal Verities; so are unshakable.'

'About that we shall see. But you have had a long day and, to my regret, suffered severely at the hands of my over-zealous associate, von Thumm. That you must attribute to his "down here" personality, in which he cherishes an abiding hatred for the English. Now it is my will that you enjoy sweet repose. Be good enough to go to your rooms. We will talk of shaping the future of the world tomorrow.'

As he finished speaking, his figure began to shimmer, then dissolved into mauve mist, leaving only the bright light. Then that, too, went out.

Awed into silence by this miraculous spectacle, they said good night to Silvia and went quietly to their rooms. During the day, making so many calls on his fortitude had drained the Duke of energy, and the effect of the vitalising elixir that Silvia had given Simon and Richard had now worn off. Too weary to hold an inquest on the situation in which they found themselves, they undressed, flopped into their beds and were asleep almost immediately.

When they awoke in the morning, they found that it was past ten o'clock. It seemed probable that, from time to time, the green-clad servitors had looked in on them; as, shortly after they had roused, they were brought trays of coffee, cream, hot rolls, butter, honey and fresh fruit. When Richard and Simon had finished eating, they joined de Richleau in his room, and Simon said jerkily:

'Seems we're in a muddle. What are we going to do?'

'Nothing,' replied the Duke quietly. 'You may be sure that we stand no chance of escaping from this place and, even if we could, that would mean abandoning our search for Rex. I have a very strong feeling that he is about here somewhere. All we can do for the time being is to play along with the Prince. Incidentally, his ability to materialise and dematerialise at will is proof that he has a right to his title. His exact rank in the hierarchy I do not yet know. But it must be higher than mine; and that makes me very far from optimistic about our chances of rescuing Rex from his clutches.'

Unhurriedly they shaved, bathed and dressed; then, at midday, walked down the long corridor to the room in which they had spent the previous evening with Silvia. She was sitting there on a sofa, with her little dog Booboo beside her. As they entered, he jumped down, began to bark furiously and raced round them. Ignoring her smiling admonishments, he continued to spring about like a Jack-in-the-box for some minutes. Then, when order was restored, they saw that she had been working on a piece of tapestry. Knowing what he now did about her, it struck Richard as incongruous that she should be employing her leisure in the same way as did many ladies of his acquaintance who lived normal lives; and, after they had all exchanged greetings, he asked to see her work.

She spread it out for him on a nearby stool. It was a large piece, nearing completion. The stitches were fine and even, and she told him it was to cover the back of a sofa at her house in Buenos Aires. The subject was a forest scene, with a blue sky above. In the foreground there was a large figure wearing an ass's head, with many small figures dancing round it, so it was obviously a portrayal of Bottom and the fairies in Shakespeare's *A Midsummer Night's Dream*. But there was one curious thing about it. The fairies had no wings. When he remarked on this anomaly, she looked up at him and laughed:

'That is because fairies never did have wings and, to be strictly accurate, I should have had them drawn very much larger. They were not really "little people", but only somewhat smaller than other races. I mentioned them to you yesterday when we were talking of Joan of Arc. It was her proved connection with the fairies—or "little people" as they were called—that sent her to the stake. The legend that they were minute beings who drank from acorn cups and flew about astride butterflies had its origin in Shakespeare's play.'

He smiled down at her. 'Are you seriously suggesting that there ever were such things as fairies,'

'Indeed I am: They inhabited the British Isles and many areas on the Continent in very early times. When England was conquered by the Romans, those who had lived there migrated to Wales, but many of them came back when the Romans withdrew. They were a race of pigmies with brown skins. That is why they were sometimes called "Brownies". Small communities of them lived in big, round huts, the floors of which were several feet below the level of the earth, and which were roofed with boughs Their settlements were always on desolate moorland, and they were very secretive and cunning. It was so that they could easily conceal themselves when strangers were about that they always wore green. The ordinary people in the villages went in fear of them, because they could be very malicious and they were deeply steeped in primitive magic. At times they used their powers for good. But for the most part they were hated and dreaded. When the great witch-hunts of early Stuart times were taking place, it was enough for a woman to have been seen begging a favour of the fairies for her to be condemned as a witch, and burned.'

170

'Presumably they bred like other races, so what became of them?'

'No-one knows for certain. Each group lived only on a few cattle and odds and ends of food that they could steal or blackmail the villagers into giving them. Perhaps their cattle were stricken with some disease and, not being numerous enough to raid the villages for supplies, they died out.'

Putting aside her work, Silvia got drinks for them. As she handed the Duke a glass of water, he said, 'Tell me, what led you to become one of the people whose headquarters this is? I accept that you now believe in all that you said last night, but it does not square with your normal personality. I see no aura of evil about you; yet you are obviously collaborating with others who are evil.'

'You only think them evil because you have not yet seen the Light,' she replied. 'But I am a witch, as you would call it, and a very potent one. If you must know, it was the Prince who first intrigued me with the mysteries of the occult. By then I had played every game worth playing, and found life unutterably boring; so I took up the study of the supernatural. That was the real reason why I leased that house in Punta Arenas. There, if I wanted to, I could remain undisturbed for days on end, and I spent many hours in contemplation, learning how to leave my body at will. I practised minor magics, and endured long fasts.' She gave a little laugh. 'That was excellent for my figure, so I killed two birds with one stone.'

'And then you met Rex?' asked the Duke softly.

'Yes, but that was comparatively recently.'

'Now that we are your prisoners will you not tell us what has become of him?'

She shook her head. 'No. That is not my secret. But I can assure you that he had a good reason for disappearing as he did.'

'Perhaps; but why did he make off with all that money from his bank?'

'He needed it to carry out his plans. That is all I mean to tell you, so now let us talk of something else.'

In due course they moved to the far end of the big room, where the table was set for lunch. It had been dark when they had sat round it the previous evening, and the curtains of the big bay window had been drawn. Now they could see the magnificent vista spread below them.

The Inca stronghold was three hundred feet above the lake

and, from the window, there was a sheer drop to it. The view was to the north, and the great lake stretched away into the distance, the placid blue waters unruffled by wind or the passage of any craft. On either side rose the lofty mountains, equally innocent of any sign of human activity. The sun glared down, bringing out the stark colours of the earth and water, but within the big room the temperature was no more than pleasantly warm.

After the meal they again talked for a while over coffee and liqueurs, then Silvia said, 'If you wish to stay here, you are welcome; but it is possible that it may be very late tonight before we get to bed, so I am going to rest, and it might be as well if you do, too.'

Accepting her advice, they walked to the end of the long corridor but, instead of separating, they all went into the Duke's room.

As soon as the door was shut behind them, Richard asked, 'What are we going to do? Do you think there is any chance of our escaping from this place?'

'Ner. Not an earthly,' Simon volunteered.

'I agree,' de Richleau concurred. 'And, even if we could, would we want to? It is here that lies the answer to the riddle of Rex's disappearance. I don't think any of us would be willing to throw in his hand until we have solved it. If we do succeed in that, it will then be time enough to plan our next move.'

Simon gave him an uneasy glance. ' 'Fraid we're in a muddle, whether we learn what's become of Rex or not. Don Salvador —or the Prince, as he calls himself—struck me as a pretty high-powered performer. Think you could get the better of him if it comes to a showdown?'

The Duke spread out his long-fingered, beautifully-shaped hands. 'How can one say? I certainly would not invite a confrontation. The fact that he can materialise shows that his powers are greater than mine. I could only hope that the Lords of Light would come to my assistance. But it may be that, in their wisdom, they have decreed that this evil man should be permitted to continue in his course unchecked for a while yet, until the time appointed for his destruction.'

Separating, they lay down on their beds. De Richleau slept, recharging his body with the electricity without which it would inevitably break down. The others dozed, their minds going back and forth like squirrels in a cage; at one moment conscious that they were actually in an ancient Inca fortress and the prisoners of Satanists; at others believing the whole series of events into which they had been drawn no more than a nerve-racking dream.

By six o'clock they were fully awake. They refreshed themselves with a wash and dressed ready to face whatever the evening might bring. Shortly afterwards Pedro came to summon them; but he did not take them to the room in which they had talked and eaten two meals with Silvia. Instead, he led them down a flight of stairs and ushered them into a room that was evidently the Prince's sanctum.

As in the other rooms, the ceiling consisted of irregular, perfectly dovetailed blocks of stone. But it had a carpet so thick that the feet sank into it. All four walls were lined with books, mostly in old, calf bindings. There was a fireplace, in which logs were burning, and several big arm-chairs. Although there was no ceiling light, wall brackets or standard lamps, the room was pervaded by a warm, soft glow.

The room was empty. While the others sat down and helped themselves to cigarettes from a low table of highly-polished malachite, de Richleau browsed among the books. There were several copies of the *Mallus Maleficarum* and of comparatively modern works, such as Aleister Crowley's *Magick* and *The Doctrine and Ritual of Magic* by Eliphas Levi. But the Duke was much more interested to see books traditionally famous, yet no copies of which were believed still to exist. There were a *Clavicule of Solomon*, a *Sword of Moses* by Abraham the Jew, *The Red Book of Appin*, a *Safer YeSua*—the oldest known Kabalistic work, an *Almagest of Ptolemy*, and a *Grimoire of Pope Honorius*.

He was still studying them when the door opened and the Prince, followed by Silvia, came in. He was carrying a beautiful blue Persian cat. Silvia, as usual, had Booboo under her arm and, sitting down with him in her lap, she lit a cigarette. The Prince, with a gesture that was in part courteous, but had just a suspicion of haughty command, signed to de Richleau to settle himself in another of the armchairs; then, putting down the cat, he took up a position in front of the fire, with his hands clasped behind his back.

Anyone entering the room without knowledge of the place and its occupants, would have taken it for a cheerful domestic scene—perhaps in a French château, or a modernised English castle.

As Richard looked at the Prince, he again thought how

173

extraordinarily handsome he was. His thin, bronzed face, under the slightly wavy black hair, portrayed health and purpose. His large, dark eyes radiated vitality. His beautifully-modelled mouth, with its very red lips, would have made most women long for his kisses. The tilt of his head, his prominent nose and high, arched eyebrows conveyed his arrogance and assumption that any command he issued would be instantly obeyed.

Having looked steadily at each of them in turn, he said: 'The Maiden put the case for worshipping the True God to you very ably last night. That Mr Eaton and Mr Aron should have rejected it does not particularly surprise me, because they have no long-time memory and their knowledge of the great truths is elementary. But you, my dear Duke, are in a very different category. You have only to elevate your ego to the astral and, from your Vase of Memory, you can recall your past lives. Among them was that during which you were a priest of Ra in Egypt, another in which as a Roman Pro-Consul you were initiated into the mysteries, and many others in which you never questioned the true faith. Last night you even admitted to Silvia that, in so-called pagan times, the people were very much happier and mentally healthier before they fell under the domination of the Christian Church. Why, then, do you now reject the beliefs you held through so many centuries?'

'I thought I made that plain,' de Richleau replied quietly. 'It is because, just as the teachings of Jesus Christ were distorted and used by ambitious, ignorant men as a vehicle to acquire worldly power, so the old faith was distorted and used by evil men as a vehicle to acquire worldly power.'

The Prince shrugged. 'With regard to the Old Faith you are wrong. Of that I hope to convince you. About the future of your companions I am indifferent; but you have acquired both power and wisdom, so would prove a great asset to the cause I serve. However, for the moment I will do no more than point out to you the obvious. In every priesthood, there have always been good and bad men. Many hundred witches were sent to the stake unjustly, but some abused their power to do harm. That does not affect the fact that those of high rank have always adhered to the fundamental principle of serving the best interests of mankind.

'My present purpose is to disabuse you of the belief that the movement to achieve Black Power has for its object the permanent destruction of law and order. The world is sick, and every year becoming sicker. You have only to look into the future, as I have done, to become aware that, unless some drastic measure is taken to prevent it, in the sixties and the seventies civilisation will begin to disintegrate. Money will lose its value. Famine will come to India, Africa and South America. The young—discontented, rudderless and fearing that, at any moment, their lives will be cut short by the use of nuclear bombs—will rise in despair and wrath against the older generation whom it holds responsible for having brought about a state of things in which they can see no security or hope of lasting happiness. Ultimately they will rise in rebellion and overturn the feeble, fumbling Governments. But they will prove incapable of replacing them, so chaos will ensue.

'The age-old remedy for discontent among a people is for their rulers to pick a quarrel with a neighbour and start a war. Personal frustrations are then forgotten in a surge of patriotism that unites all classes in a country. But the whole world is sick, so nothing short of another world war could have the desired effect. And a third world war we dare not risk. The danger of the whole earth becoming uninhabitable owing to nuclear missiles is too great.

'Our problem can be solved, though. Raising the flag for Black Power will do it. You are, of course, quite right in that it will mean street-fighting, murder, arson and looting in every city. But the resulting death, destruction and suffering caused will be incomparably less than would result from another world war. Even one in which only conventional weapons were used.

' "Out of Evil cometh Good". I repeat "Out of Evil cometh Good". We must inflict the ills of bloodshed, terror and loss upon the people, in order to arrest the decline of civilisation and bring them back to a healthy, progressive way of life. You may liken this operation to an inoculation for yellow fever. For a day or two it makes one wretchedly ill, but it can save one from a terrible death.

'One of your fears, no doubt, is that the movement will succeed so completely that the white races will be overwhelmed and those members of them who survive will be made slaves by the black races, in revenge for what they themselves have suffered in the past. Dismiss that thought. There is not the least danger of such a situation developing. It is, of course, the hope of those poor, deluded wretches of whom we are making use down in the settlement. But they are fanatics who cherish an idle dream. It is certain that the whites, with their machine-

175

guns, tear gas and tanks, will triumph everywhere. The actual fighting will be very brief; very extensive damage and loss of property is bound to take place, but the loss of life will be no greater than would occur in a minor war, and that is acceptable in view of the final outcome at which we aim.

'That final outcome is Equal Rights. Not Equal Rights as mouthed by hypocritical politicians to win votes, but a genuine equality in which men of all colours will regard one another with respect and with open-hearted friendship. As I have said, the riots will soon be put down. It is through the events to follow that we shall reach our goal. Black Power will have organised world-wide underground. There will be secret sabotage squads in every city. Fires will be started to burn down many of the finest buildings; bombs will be placed in air-liners and oil-tankers; leading statesmen will be assassinated; trains will be wrecked; the wives and daughters of important people kidnapped. No-one will be safe, and everyone will walk in fear during this reign of terror.

'The white governments will take reprisals. Hostages will be taken and later shot in batches. They will set up huge concentration camps to confine hundreds of suspects. In desperation they may wipe out whole Negro communities. But they cannot possibly imprison all the millions of people who have coloured skins.

'The acts of violence will continue. Every day the situation will deteriorate. People will no longer dare to travel. Communications will have been cut, trade will have been brought to a standstill, factories will lie idle, cities will be threatened with starvation. In the end the white governments will be forced to capitulate. In the meantime, as in a war, the younger generation will have been purged of its degenerate tendencies. Wise leaders will emerge and insist that the only way to save civilisation is to agree to the just demands of the coloured races. Thus we shall bring about a new era, and the real Brotherhood of Man.'

All the time the Prince had been speaking, his dark eyes had never left the Duke's face; but de Richleau knew that the eyes of such a man could send out most powerful hypnotic suggestion; so, to avoid the danger of falling under it, he had kept his own eyes cast down. He lifted them only when the Prince put the question to him:

'Now do you see the error into which you have fallen, in believing that we, who serve the Old God, have entered into a

176

conspiracy for evil? The explanation I have given will, I trust, cause you to re-orient your beliefs, and join us.'

For a full moment there was silence, then de Richleau replied, 'I have been fascinated by your dissertation, Prince, and there is much truth in what you have said. Two world wars within a quarter of a century have destroyed the foundations of society. Those who returned from them have acquired a new, and not altogether desirable freedom. Instead of pursuing a normal course of marrying and rearing a family, a high proportion of girls and men had become promiscuous. Although great numbers of them were scarcely out of their teens, they refused to submit again to parental control, or take advice from people older than themselves. They had become used to danger and excitement, and continued to crave the latter. But their new independence gets them nowhere. Owing to their frustration, crime has increased to a degree never before known; addiction to drugs, almost unheard of before the first world war has, in both Europe and the United States, become a menace; a gap is developing between the generations which, in the future, could bring about violence.

'Yes, the world is sick. But many a patient has been killed by a bad doctor. Sometimes it is better to let nature run its course, and the body works the poison out of the system. The medicine you propose would, in my view, eat away the tissues to a degree that would give the patient no hope of recovery.'

For a moment the Prince's handsome face was contorted by a spasm of anger. Then he regained control of himself and said, 'Then you persist in your blindness? You refuse to give us your aid?'

The Duke nodded. 'I do so because, all else apart, there is a great fallacy in your predictions. Even given that dozens of acts of sabotage, carried out day after day, would eventually force the white governments to accept the terms of the coloured leaders, that could bring about no genuine rapprochement. Their cities half-ruined, their trade destroyed, innumerable cases in which loved ones had been killed or injured through the activities of your saboteurs, would leave the white populations harbouring an unquenchable bitterness against the coloured. The coloureds, too, having for year after year to see the bravest among them become victims of the whites' furious reprisals, would be equally unlikely to forgive and forget.

'There would ensue no Brotherhood of Man. But you would

have done the work of your master, Satan, well. Yes, I said Satan the Lord of Misrule. The Destroyer, whose objective it has always been to bring about disruption to such a degree that mankind will be plunged into darkness and misery.'

Again the Prince revealed his seething rage. His hands trembled and his mouth worked, until he rasped out:

'I can use your help, and I mean to have it. Since you refuse to give it willingly, I must make you. I have already said that I am indifferent to the fate of your friends. Either you will agree to serve me, or I will send them back to von Thumm, to vent his sadistic hate on.'

Simon drew in a sharp breath. Richard's hands were clasped and he clenched them until the knuckles stood out white, while waiting for the Duke's answer. It seemed an age in coming, then he said:

'I dearly love my friends. If you carry out your threat, thinking of them in that man's hands will cause me greater mental torture than they will suffer physically. But this issue is far too great to allow the fate of individuals to weigh in the scale. And, if it is decreed that they should forfeit their present lives, both they and I will be fortified by the knowledge that their martyrdom will be rewarded in lives to come.'

The Prince's dark eyes narrowed as he stared at the Duke. A silence ensued, so tense that it could be felt. At length he said. 'Where I have failed, perhaps another may succeed.' Then. raising his left hand aloft, he snapped his first finger and thumb together.

For perhaps three minutes none of them moved or uttered a word. Then the door opened, and framed in it stood Rex Van Ryn.

14

The Horrors that came by Night

Rex's friends had expected that, if they did find him at the Sala de Uyuni, it would have been as a prisoner, held there against his will for some reason they could not guess, by the Satanists into whose hands he had fallen; a prey to great distress and, perhaps, dreadful thought, even mentally deranged after being exposed to the horrors that his captors could bring from the Outer Circle.

But here he was, a splendid figure of a man, wearing the easy but expensive clothes that rich Americans favour when they are at leisure, his slightly curly hair neatly brushed, exuding as ever abundant health and bonhomie. He gave them a delighted smile and said:

'Well now, it's certainly good to see you folks again.'

They had all come to their feet. Simon's jaw had dropped and his short-sighted eyes were open to their maximum extent. Richard stared at his old friend with a puzzled frown. De Richleau said:

'We have spent quite some time and considerable exertion in endeavouring to find you, Rex. Now that we have, I am much relieved to see you do not appear to have suffered from your recent experiences.'

Rex beamed at him. 'No, I'm as fit as they make 'em, and haven't a worry in the world. I'm only sorry that you three should have been so concerned about me, and have come all this way to satisfy yourselves that I hadn't got out of orbit without good reason.'

'That we have yet to see,' the Duke returned sharply.

The Prince smiled and said, 'Rex will soon set your minds at rest about that. Since you would not accept the truth from me whom, I admit, you have no reason to trust, I felt that you might alter your views when you had talked with Rex, knowing as you must his complete integrity.'

'If he can tell us that he has freely subscribed to your views, I shall be amazed.'

'I take it you are referring to the Black Power movement?' Rex said, sitting down in an armchair and stretching out his long legs.

'Yes,' the Prince told him. 'I have explained to your friends how important it is to cure the people of the sickness that has resulted from two world wars and in that, they . . . or at least the Duke who, I assume, speaks for them . . . agrees with me. Where we are still at issue is whether Black Power would prove a remedy which would not only stop the rot but, ultimately, bring about the Brotherhood of Man.'

Rex turned to the Duke. 'I know that on many questions you're a real old-fashioned die-hard. You'd like to see Britishers still running a third of the world, and playing polo in their off-time, with a Two-Power Navy to back them up. But you've liberal views where human relations are concerned. Surely, if it lay with you, you'd not deny coloured folk equal rights?'

'My dear Rex,' de Richleau gave a sad little smile, 'amazed as I am to find you here, being used as a cat's paw by our, er, host, I have no objection to discussing these matters with you. As you say, my views in many ways are old-fashioned. With regard to the colour question, they were well expressed by a character in Maurice Edelman's excellent book: "I welcome the black man as my brother, but not as my brother-in-law". In other words, I am against mixed marriages, because the children resulting from them are saddled with a terrible handicap; but I do not regard coloured people as inferior to whites, and would like to see them enjoy a true equality with us.'

'It's not for you or me to adjudicate on mixed marriages. That's for the individuals concerned. But you've admitted my point in principle.'

'I have, but I am unshakably opposed to the Prince's plan for bringing it about.'

'Why?'

'Because it would cause immense suffering to millions of people and, in the end, fail to achieve its object.'

'Sure it will entail suffering. Riots, street-fighting, arson, murder, the lot. But you can't make omelettes without breaking eggs and, when our omelette's cooked, it'll be a better world.'

'I disagree. After your movement has brought about the deaths of thousands of people and ruined the lives of countless

180

others, no permanent reconciliation between whites and blacks will be possible. Only a world in ruins will be left, with its inhabitants scraping a bare existence; each side blaming the other for its fate and obsessed with bitterness and hatred.'

'Oh come!' Rex gave a laugh. 'You can think that only because you haven't gotten the full picture. For a time the whites will naturally show resentment. That's to be expected. But they'll come round when the coloureds get going with their stuff.'

'Stuff? What do you mean by "stuff"?'

'Why, making good the damage that they've done. The white governments will be stunned, nearly bankrupt and incapable of clearing up the mess. But the coloureds will have both money and organised labour. They'll move in, rebuild the gutted buildings, erect refugee camps for the homeless, and become the source from which all blessings flow. Once the whites realise that and that the coloureds are really on the level, prejudice will disappear. They'll let bygones be bygones, and genuine friendship all over will result.'

'You are talking through your hat,' said Richard sharply. 'Even if you could succeed in organising hundreds of thousands of blacks into labour corps to restore the *status quo*, where is the money coming from to feed them, let along purchase the materials needed for a world-wide rebuilding programme?'

Rex laughed again. 'We'll have it, old chap. Not a doubt about that. Remember, we don't intend to blow the works for fifteen or maybe twenty years. We have already started our fund and have over a hundred thousand contributors who are each anti-ing up a few dimes a week. Nearly half the workers down on the Sala are employed in increasing the number of subscribers. In a few years' time, we'll number them by the million.'

'Was it to support this fund that you stole a million from your bank?' asked the Duke.

'Well . . .' Rex hesitated a second. 'Yes. But we're not relying only on contributions. Maybe you know how the Bolsheviks raised the money to organise the Russian Revolution? They made armed raids on the banks. Stalin began his career as one of the bank robbers for the Party. We've started that already in a small way. But our big time for that will come after the blow-up, when our sabotage campaign is in full swing. With law and order gone for six, there'll be any number of opportunities to lift cash from the banks and hold up vans carrying pay-rolls for big factories. Don't you worry. We'll have plenty of money to replace everything we have destroyed, and lots over to distribute to white people who have been rendered homeless by the upheaval.'

De Richleau shook his head. 'Rex, my dear friend, I can only suppose that you have fallen completely under the influence of these evil people. Not consciously, of course, but by their exerting their dark power to distort your mind. They are using you as their mouthpiece. Otherwise you would never countenance this terrible plot to bring wholesale anarchy into the world. It is totally against your nature and everything you have ever stood for.'

Suddenly the Prince spoke. His handsome face had become contorted with rage. In a spate of berserk fury, he stormed at de Richleau:

'So you refuse to be persuaded! You have the impudence to defy me! To thwart my will! I have been patient with you. Given you an opportunity to play an important role in our great crusade. To use the powers you have to further the intentions of the Old God—the True God. And you have spurned it. Very well, then. I will show you who is master here. I will break your stubborn spirit and force you to obey me. You shall spend a night that you will never forget, and in the morning you will be chastened.'

Rex had come to his feet. 'No, Prince,' he pleaded. 'Have a heart. These are old friends of mine. What you have in mind might send them off their rockers. Let them have a night's sleep and, maybe, tomorrow they'll see how wrong they are.'

'Silence!' stormed the Prince. 'They need a lesson. If they survive it, they will be eager to do my bidding for fear of the power I wield. If they have gone mad by morning, no matter. I can do without them.' As he spoke he raised his hand and snapped his fingers twice.

In less than a minute the door was opened by an immensely fat Babu. Behind him stood two of the silent, green-clad servitors. With a sweeping gesture, the Prince indicated the Duke, Richard and Simon, as he snapped:

'Kaputa, take these people down to the Hall of Divination and leave them to face what I shall send them there.'

De Richleau knew it would be futile to resist. Without a glance at the Prince or Rex, he walked towards the door, Simon and Richard followed. The Babu squeezed past them and led the way along several corridors, down two flights of stone stairs and into a dimly lit, empty, circular room some forty feet in diameter.

The ceiling was low, not more than eight feet high, and the floor was an elaborate mosaic of an eight-pointed star within two circles that contained many strange hieroglyphics. The walls were of smooth, dead-black stone, undecorated except at the four corners. At these, standing out boldly in white were the reversed swastika which Hitler had taken for his emblem, the Star of David upside down, the Mohammedan Crescent with its horns pointing at the floor, and the crooked Cross. The place was dimly lit. As soon as they were inside it, Kaputa closed the door behind them.

The Duke gave a heavy sigh. 'My friends, I am afraid we are in for a very bad time. All we can do is to pray for fortitude and hope that we may survive.' Standing between them, he put his arms about their shoulders and drew them to him, then he went on:

'We shall not kneel. Only slaves make supplication in that attitude of humility. In each of us resides a tiny spark of the Eternal Light, which makes us the little brothers of the Lords of Light; so we address them as children who hope one day to become their equals. After me, repeat in silence the words I am about to say.'

For the next few minutes he spoke quietly and clearly, sending his winged words out into the silent night.

When he had finished his appeal for succour, he said, 'We must now prepare to face the evil entities the Prince will send against us. I would give half my remaining years to have here the holy water, horse-shoes, candles and other things that I collected while in Santiago and which we had to leave in the aircraft on the Sala. Then we could have made a pentacle. But at least the mosaics on which we are standing do not make a Satanic diagram. It is an Inca calendar and the two circles, together with what I have here, will at least protect us from lesser horrors endowed with little intelligence.'

As he spoke, he took from his pocket a handkerchief in which were wrapped two cone-shaped objects, an inch and a half thick and three inches in height. 'These,' he said, 'are salt containers. Fearing that we might have to face some such ordeal as this, I managed to get away unobserved with one at dinner last night and another off my breakfast tray. Salt being essential to the well-being of man, is anathema to all entities sent by Satan to do men harm. We shall have to use it very

183

sparingly; but I think there is just enough to sprinkle round the inner of the two circles on the floor here. A circle in itself is some protection, and this inner one must be about nine or ten feet in diameter, so there will be ample room for the three of us inside it.'

Exercising great care, he spread very thinly the grains of salt along the line that formed the circle; then, although he had nothing with which to write the letters, he traced just inside the circle, with the forefinger of his right hand, the words: IESUS + NAZARENUS + REX + IUDAEORUM +.

He had hardly completed this preparation when the dim light became still dimmer, until it had faded completely and they were plunged into total darkness. Drawing the two others to him, the Duke sat down with them in the centre of the circle and said:

'Now, there is nothing we can do but wait. I need hardly remind you that, in no circumstances, should you allow yourselves to be lured out of the circle, or even move more than a foot or so in any direction, in case, inadvertently, your foot makes a breach in the ring of salt.'

For a while they sat in silence, back to back, their legs stretched out in front of them. The stone floor was very hard and uncomfortable. Every now and then they shifted their position to ease one buttock or the other. All of them were conscious that it was gradually getting colder. From previous experience they knew that it was not a natural drop in the temperature, but that the place was becoming pervaded with the chill of evil which always precedes a Satanic manifestation.

The cold increased until their teeth began to chatter. A faint glow appeared near the place on the wall where they had seen the upside-down crescent. Its radiance increased until it lit the room with a reddish light. Their hearts began to beat faster as they watched it, expecting that it would take the form of a demon conjured up from Hell. Instead, black bars appeared across it. The light coalesced into flickering flames above them, and they saw that it was a glowing brazier heaped with red-hot coals. But no heat from it penetrated to the ice-cold circle.

As they stared at it, they yearned to warm their hands and limbs at its tempting glow, but they knew it to be a device to lure them outside their frail defences. Rigidly they kept their places and the fire in the iron brazier began to burn down until the big room was again in semi-darkness.

They still had their eyes on the brazier when, behind them,

there came a slithering sound. Swivelling their heads, they peered in that direction. A creature was squatting outside the circle. It was as large as a medium-sized turtle, and had a body of that shape; but, instead of a shell, its bumped back was covered with rough, pink skin which gave out a pale light. The thing was sitting still, but the skin on its back slowly pulsated so that little ridges rippled along it. Low down in front, it had a long slit that was obviously a mouth; from it there drooled a yellow liquid. Above the mouth there rose what, at first glance, appeared to be two nine-inch-long horns; but, when looked at again, could be seen to have beady eyes at the extremities. Slowly they swayed from side to side, obviously examining the inmates of the circle.

Suddenly the creature hunched itself and jumped. It came down with a plop, leaving at the place where it had been a horrid oval of phosphorescent slime. Slowly it began to advance towards the circle, with the undulating movement of a worm. As the pendulant underlip of its mouth came in contact with the salt, it gave a loud hiss, began rapidly to expand until it was twice its former size, then burst into a thousand writhing fragments, leaving behind a stench like that of a charnel house.

For a time, nothing happened. The three friends continued to shiver in the pentacle, now and again glancing apprehensively from side to side. The brazier still glowed, giving them just sufficient light to make out vaguely the perverted symbols of Christianity, Islam, Judaism and the Oldest Faith painted on the walls.

It was Richard who was the first to see a thickening of the shadows under the swastika. Quickly he drew the attention of the others to it. Straining their eyes, they saw a long patch, stretching a good twelve feet along the floor. Slowly, it materialised into a great snake. Suddenly it began to move, circling the pentacle. Every few yards it jerked to a halt, swerved its head inwards and darted out its long, forked tongue.

Instinctively the three friends came to their feet. Shuffling round they faced each attempt by the serpent to penetrate their defence. Seven times it made the circle. They were no longer conscious of the cold. Fear had caused the sweat to break out on their foreheads. Shifting round and round to keep the great beast in full view had begun to make them giddy. Simon tripped and fell to his knees. At that moment the snake reared up on

185

its tail. so that its head was a foot above them. Its jaws were wide open, its poison fangs glinted in the light from the brazier. Richard dragged Simon back on to his feet. As he did so, de Richleau cried in a loud voice, 'Avaunt thee, Satan!' The head of the snake recoiled as though it had been smashed by a giant, unseen hand. It fell writhing to the floor, and dissolved into a cloud of evil-smelling smoke.

After that they were not troubled for a long time. In spite of the cold they began to feel drowsy. At length, a slight snore from Simon told the others that he had fallen asleep. De Richleau gave him a quick shake and said:

'Simon, you should know better than to let yourself drop off. Unless we remain alert, you may be certain that they will make some new move that will take us by surprise and we shall fall into a trap.'

'Sorry,' Simon muttered. 'Seems as though we've been here for hours. What's the time?'

The Duke glared at the luminous dial of his watch. 'It is only half past eleven, so there is still a long time to go until dawn. And, as it is eternal night down here, they may not cease their attacks on us even then.'

'Half past eleven,' muttered Richard. 'And we've had no dinner. Although we had a good lunch, I'm so hungry I could eat a horse.'

As he spoke, the door of the room opened and a table loaded with food rolled in. On it there were smoked salmon and lobsters, jellied eggs, a tongue, a York ham, trays of hors-d'œuvres, avocados, globe artichokes, snipe, pheasants, a duck, a baron of beef, steak and kidney and chicken pies, and a fine variety of puddings.

At this sight, the hunger they felt far exceeded anything that could normally have resulted from the fact that they had not eaten for ten hours. As they craned forward, eagerly eyeing these good things, the saliva ran hot in their mouths. Beside the table there materialised a tall, thin figure clad in impeccable evening clothes. All three of them recognised him instantly as a friend of many years. It was Vachelli, who had looked after them in the twenties at the Berkely, and long since moved to become the maître d'hôtel at the Savoy Grill. Smiling at them he said:

'Good-evening, gentlemen. What can I order for you? Paté, or *melone con prosciutto* perhaps, to start with. Then, for His Grace, *Canard Montmorencey*, for Mr Eaton two *becca-*

sine flown lightly through the flames, and for Mr Aron his favourate *Omelette Arnold Bennett*. To follow, some wood strawberries brought in by air from France this morning, with marraschino ice.'

Richard had risen unsteadily to his feet. Simon was about to follow. De Richleau said sharply, 'You fools! Do you not realise that all this is illusion? And in this they have over-reached themselves. To tempt us with real food would have been possible; but not to produce Vachelli. That is no more than a likeness of him. He is ten thousand miles away in London.'

Almost sobbing with frustration, the others covered their eyes with their hands and sank back on to the hard floor.

Again, for what seemed a long time, they sat back to back, staring into the semi-darkness, wondering with trepidation what new horror or temptation they would next be called on to face. It came in the form of a multitude of small spiders. To the alarm of the inmates of the circle, the insects did not attempt to cross the thin barrier of salt, but fell inside it from the roof. Within a few minutes they were crawling with them, and the little brutes had a most powerful bite.

Jumping up they slapped at their hands and faces, ran their fingers through their hair and brushed down arms and legs, in an endeavour to kill or throw off their small tormentors. The floor inside the pentacle was soon swarming with them. They ran across their victims' shoes, up their socks and bit into their calves. Cursing, Richard stamped about, trying to shake them down. Inadvertently, he put one foot outside the pentacle.

With incredible swiftness, a monster materialised beside him. It had claws and wings like a dragon. Where its head should have been there sprouted tentacles like those of an octopus. One of them whipped round Richard's ankle. He gave a shout of terror.

The Duke swung round. In case the circle became breached, he had kept handy the handkerchief in which he had wrapped the salt containers. It still had in it a little salt which had spilled. Pulling this handkerchief from his pocket, he threw it at the tentacles of the beast. They flared up in a sheet of blue flame. It scorched Richard's face, but his leg was free. Simon pulled him back to safety. Almost weeping with relief, he slid to his knees, while the monster continued to burn, the smoke from it giving off the filthy smell of a cesspit. Meanwhile, the

187

little spiders, having performed the task for which they had been sent, had vanished.

From this crisis it took them some while to recover. They were now very tired and knew that their resistance was being worn down. Now and again de Richleau looked up at the roof, fearing that some evil entity far more dangerous than the spiders might emerge from it. But the next visitation to which they were subjected was a very different one. The light increased until they could see the whole big room quite clearly. Then the door swung open and framed in it stood Miranda.

She was dressed in the black lace dress she had worn on the night that Simon had taken her out to dinner in Buenos Aires. But there was something different about her blue eyes. They no longer had the fixed, unseeing stare due to near-blindness. Instead they were clear, bright and beamed with happiness. In one hand she held a tray with three glasses, in the other she was carrying a large jug that was full of what looked like a delicious wine cup.

De Richleau drew a sharp breath. Richard gaped, and Simon cried, 'Miranda! Your eyes! You're no longer blind. You can see.'

She smiled. 'Yes, darling. They flew me up here from Santiago yesterday and the Prince has restored my sight. Isn't it wonderful? He has sent me to tell you that, as you have resisted all the horrors of the past few hours, he won't torment you any more, but give you another chance to think things over. And I know how thirsty you must be, so I've brought you a lovely drink.'

During the past hour thirst had plagued them even more than hunger. Their throats were parched. Their thickened tongues felt like lumps of leather in their mouths. Beaming with delight, Simon took a step forward. The Duke grabbed him by the arm and pulled him back, gasping hoarsely:

'No, Simon. No! That is not Miranda. It is a fiend who has taken her form. This is another trap. One step outside the pentacle and you will perish.'

Tears started to Simon's eyes. Overcome with bitter disappointment, he collapsed. At the sight of him crouching with bowed head on the floor, Miranda's lovely face became transformed with hate and rage. Slowly her figure faded, and once more the room dimmed to semi-darkness.

Hungry, thirsty and again shivering with cold, they huddled together in the circle, now feeling that this night of terror would never end. Filled with dread that, long before morning they must succumb, they waited for their next ordeal.

They were roused from their semi-torpor by a distant scream. It came again, this time louder. The screams continued. Suddenly the door flew open. A woman hurled herself through it. Although the light was still dim, all three of them recognised her immediately. No-one who had seen Richard's wife, that pocket Venus, Marie-Lou, could easily forget her small but perfect figure and lovely, heart-shaped face. It now portrayed stark fear, and the reason was at once apparent. A huge, naked Negro was in swift pursuit of her. Him, too, they recognised. It was Lincoln B. Glasshill.

The shock of his wife's sudden appearance and the peril she was in caused Richard to forget time, place and the danger of his own situation. Giving a loud cry, he sprang forward to intercept the Negro. Simon was still crouching on the floor; but, at the sound of the screams, he had raised his head. His mind still filled with the vision of Miranda and the snare into which he had so nearly fallen, he threw his arms round Richard's legs and brought him crashing to the ground.

By then Glasshill had caught up with Marie-Lou. Seizing her, he swung her round and began to tear the clothes from her body. As she strove to fight him off, she began to scream again:

'Richard! Richard! Save me! Save me!'

Still struggling with Simon, Richard gasped, 'Let me go! Damn you, let me go!' Kicking himself free, he staggered to his feet. But now the Duke came into action. Drawing back his fist, he hit Richard hard beneath the jaw. Richard gave a gulp, sagged at the knees and rolled over, unconscious. An instant later, the figures of Marie-Lou and the powerful Negro had vanished.

After a few minutes Richard began to moan, then came to. Once more the three friends huddled together, their nerves taut almost to breaking point, and all but exhausted. The big room was again silent, except for the sound of their heavy breathing. Many minutes passed while they knelt there, looking constantly from side to side, in grim anticipation of the next attack.

At length, the door swung open. This time they did not stir, but gazed with fear in their eyes at the tall figure that stepped through into the room. It was Rex Van Ryn.

Putting his finger to his lips, he said in a low voice, 'Not a word. Come on. Follow me, and I'll get you out of here.'

The Duke managed a laugh that held a sneer. 'Is it likely? Surely your Prince must realise by now the stupidity of repeating this game since we have shown so clearly that we are not to be trapped by it.'

Rex frowned. 'I don't know what he's been up to. Looks like you've been given a mighty bad time. But not to worry. It's over now. Come on.'

'You filth, get out!' Richard shouted. 'Get back to Hell where you belong.'

Rex swiftly raised a hand. 'Quiet, for God's sake, or you'll wake some of those bloody Satanists. Then I'll never be able to get you away.'

Simon's words came thickly from his dried-up mouth. 'Get us out of this circle, you mean, so your Infernal Master can set his ghouls upon us. No thanks.'

The light was just strong enough for the white, thinly-spaced grains of salt which made a trail round the inner circle of the Inca calendar to be seen. Looking down, Rex grasped their significance, and said, 'If this wasn't so darn serious, it 'ud be a laugh. I guess he's been sending ab-humans to lure you out of your fortress, and you think I'm one.'

'You are,' croaked the Duke, making the sign of the Cross, 'Avaunt thee, Satan.'

To the amazement of the three, instead of wilting and disappearing under the anathema, Rex burst out, 'You bloody fools! Can't you tell a live man from an apparition?' Then he stepped over the barrier of salt into the circle.

15

The Raising of the Whirlwind

Simon and Richard cowered back. Nearly exhausted from the horrors they had faced earlier in the night, they now felt that the end had come. It could only be that the Prince had exerted his powers to the utmost to enable this manifestation in the form of their friend to cross the barrier. They expected that, within a moment, the smiling face would become distorted with malevolence and hatred, that the form would suddenly turn into some monstrous creature that would seize upon and destroy them. Sweating with fear, they shrank away, their arms extended to fend off this menace that the Prince had called up from Hell.

But de Richleau stood his ground. The figure before them had not only ignored the sign of the Cross and his abjuration. It had actually stepped on the line of salt spread round the circle. For him that could mean only one thing.

With a gasp he thrust out his hand, grasped Rex by the arm and cried. Then it's really you!'

Next moment he laughed and hurried on, 'After the apparitions we've seen tonight, I just couldn't believe it. Oh, thank God, you've come to us! We couldn't have held out much longer. But from the way you behaved this evening, I thought . . .'

'No time to talk of that now.' Rex cut in. 'We're not out of the wood yet, by a long sight. And we've not a moment to lose. If anyone is awake and challenges us, leave everything to me. Come on now.'

Hardly able to take in the fact that they had survived the night's terrible ordeal, and now stood a good chance of escaping. they followed Rex as quietly as they could out of the circular room and along a succession of corridors until they came through a doorway to a courtyard. Eagerly they breathed in the fresh, cold air and looked upwards to see the myriad of stars above.

On the further side of the courtyard a flight of over a hundred steps led downward. They were very steep, broken in places, and had no handrail alongside them. One false step and anyone could have hurtled head over heels to the bottom. With Rex still leading and the others, each with a hand on the shoulder of the one preceding him, they made the perilous descent in safety.

A walk of two hundred yards brought them to the airstrip. It was in darkness, and no-one was about. Telling the others to wait where they were, Rex boarded one of the two smaller passenger 'planes and flashed a torch on the instrument board in the cockpit. A moment later, he was back on the ground and said in a low voice:

'No good. She's practically out of gas. And we daren't refuel her. The noise would rouse those lousy Andeans. Several of them sleep in that hut near the pump. I'll take a look at the other. If she's dry too, we're scuppered.'

Anxious moments passed while he clambered into the other aircraft and made a swift survey of her fitness for flight. Then he leaned out and beckoned to them. When they had scrambled aboard, and settled themselves in the bucket seats, he said:

'She's nearly full, thank God. Ample gas to take us to the coast. But I dare not attempt a night flight through the mountains. We'd sure end up as deaders. But I can fly us across to Potosi, the old Inca city south-east of the lake. I went over there out of curiosity not long ago. It's now an area of ruins, with only a handful of peasants squatting in some of the courtyards, where they've put up shacks and lean-tos. Plenty of places there where we can lie up for the rest of the night. Then, come dawn, we'll fly down to Iquique.'

The others caught his last words only indistinctly, as he was already revving up the engine. It vibrated for two minutes, then the aircraft took off smoothly. The moon was now in its first quarter. Its light silvered the placid water of the lake and, as they flew over the land on the far bank, was sufficient to throw up groups of trees here and there in a flattish landscape. They had been in the air for barely a quarter of an hour when Rex brought the 'plane down with the expertise of long practice. For a couple of hundred yards it tore through low scrub, then came to a halt.

As they were about to climb out, Richard said huskily, 'My throat's like a lime-kiln. I'd give fifty quid for a drink—even a glass of water.'

192

'Me, too,' agreed Simon. 'So dry I can hardly swallow.'

'Soon put that right,' Rex replied cheerfully. 'These aircraft are always furnished with supplies for several days, in case they have to make a forced landing in this bloody wilderness. Look in the tail; and you'll find lots of liquor.'

Without losing a moment, Richard and Simon opened up the several small hampers containing emergency stores of tinned food and drink. Hastily pushing aside bottles of Pisco and Brandy, they seized on some Coca-Cola and, together with the Duke, avidly quenched their thirst.

Rex had left the aircraft. When they joined him on the ground, he pointed to a low rise about half a mile away. On it there was a patch of black, one end of which made a sharp angle which stood out against the sky line. As they looked in that direction, he said:

'We're in luck. I doubted whether at night I'd be able to locate that place so as to land fairly near it. But it's sure the building I had in mind for us to lie low in. Let's get going to it.'

Richard turned back to the 'plane. 'O.K. But I'm still as hungry as a hunter. We'll take some of those emergency stores with us, so that we can have a meal when we get there.' Simon followed him back to the aircraft, and together they repacked one of the hampers with their choice of things to eat and drink.

When they emerged, carrying the hamper between them, the four friends set off through the low scrub. It proved hard going; but, twenty minutes later, they reached the rise, and saw that the ruined building on it had been a church.

'There must have been an Inca temple here once,' the Duke remarked. 'Wherever the Spaniards found pagan temples, both here and in Mexico, they pulled them down and built a church on the ruins.'

'So I've heard,' Rex nodded. 'There was probably an Inca village here, too, once. This place is two miles or more from the ruins of the city. That's why I chose it. The Andean peons are harmless enough, but we don't want them nosing around.'

As they entered the roofless church, they saw by the moonlight that the greater part of the floor was covered with rubble; but the altar was intact and, carved in the stone above it, there was a tall cross. Beckoning to the others to follow him, the Duke scrambled over the debris to the altar and, for some minutes, they stood silently before it, rendering thanks for their preservation.

Simon and Richard then opened up some of the tins of food they had brought sliced up chicken and ham on to cardboard plates and poured drinks into the cups. As Rex watched them, he said with a grin, 'Guess the eyes of you boys are going to prove larger than your tummies.'

Richard laughed. 'Maybe we've overdone it, but what we don't eat we can take back to the aircraft when it's daylight.'

As soon as they had satisfied their first hunger, de Richleau said, 'Now, Rex, we're all anxious to know what you've been up to. I confess that you fooled me last night. I simply could not believe that you were really in favour of this Black Power movement. I could only conclude that you were yourself no longer, and that these Satanists had caused a devil to take possession of your mind. But the fact that we owe our escape from that hellish place to you shows that I was right off the mark. What is the explanation of this mystery?'

Rex shrugged his great shoulders. 'It's simple enough. As Silvia's told you, she was my girl-friend. A couple of years before I met her, Don Salvador—or the Prince, as he calls himself in these parts, had interested her in the occult. She told me about it, and tried to get me to play, too. With the memories I have about Simon, Tanith and that devil Mocata, I naturally declined and did my best to make her understand what a hellishly dangerous game she was playing.

'Mark you, she'd not let on that Don Salvador was an Adept following the Left-Hand Path, so I wasn't particularly worried when she persisted in continuing to attend his "seances", as she called them. Then one night, when I was waiting for her in her apartment, she returned a bit potted. She talked a lot of what I took at the time to be nonsense, about how in fifteen or twenty years' time, there would be world-wide revolution, out of which would arise a new state of things. There would be one supreme government, that would control everything and, if I liked, she felt sure she could get me made a member of it.

'Naturally, I laughed and said that would be O.K. by me. At that point she seemed to sober up, and refused to say any more for the time being. I assumed that she'd gotten this pipe dream at one of Don Salvador's occult sessions, so I thought no more about it. But the next night we spent together she brought up the subject again. Evidently, in the meantime, she'd had a talk with Don Salvador and he'd O.K.d her approaching me seriously. She said they needed someone like me, with wide experience of banking, to take charge of their financial interests. Then she swore me to secrecy and told me about their Black Power movement. According to her it was simply a means to an end, a way to bring about Peace on Earth, and a good time for all.

'By then, the penny had dropped. I'd tumbled to it that Don Salvador was a real topline Black, and that he aimed to serve his Infernal Master by letting loose all hell. The idea of his pulling off this ghastly coup properly scared the pants off me. But I realised that it was up to me to get in on this thing, and somehow scotch it. I played hard to get for a bit, putting up various snags to the scheme that I knew she could find answers to. Then, when she spoke about the power I would have, I agreed to play.

'The next time I saw her, she was a bit worried. It emerged that Don Salvador was not altogether happy about taking me on. He needed a guarantee that I wouldn't rat on them. They could only be sure I wouldn't if I agreed to cut myself off entirely from the life I was then leading, and perform some act that would prevent my returning to it.'

'I see,' murmured the Duke. 'That is why you stole a million from your bank.'

'You've hit it, Greyeyes. Of course the thing they didn't realise, when they put up the idea, was that I'd not become a wanted criminal. I knew that my family would move heaven and earth to keep quiet what I had done, and anti-up the million I'd made off with from their private funds. All I have to do when I reappear is to repay the bank by selling a big block of my own shares, and everyone I know will be glad to see me back. But the fact that I did commit the crime and was apparently willing to throw up everything for the cause, convinced Don Salvador that I was on the level.'

'Have you now got the low-down on the whole organisation?' Richard enquired.

'Yes, more or less. The Prince is the Chief of a Coven, probably the most powerful in the world, as each of its twelve members are in turn the Chiefs of other Covens which dominate the whole Satanic set-up in great areas.

'Von Thumm is his number two, and responsible for the settlement down at the Sala. Under him it's run by the Moor El Aliz, Harry Benito, a Jamaican, and an Andean Indian whose name is Pucara. They have a batch of Zombies who act as their servants and, if need be, could be called on to help keep order. But, so far, that hasn't proved necessary. All the workers down there are sweet innocents. They haven't an idea that they're being used as the tools of Satanism. Their heads are in the clouds, with visions of securing for the coloureds real and permanent equality with whites.

'Lincoln B. Glasshill is number three in the hierarchy but, like von Thumm, he comes up here only occasionally, to take his orders from the Prince. The others, too, all have quarters in one city or another where they spend a part of their time. There are two other Negroes: a tall, wall-eyed fellow called Ebolite, and Mazambi, who's head was like a skull.

'Pierre Dubecq is a white. He is the Prince's top pilot, and with the assistance of a Spanish half-caste, Miguel Cervantes, runs the aircraft. The men who service them are Andeans. They are quite good mechanics, but in other ways are ignorant types and they are not allowed inside the fortress. The green-clad chaps who fetch and carry inside are Andeans, too. But they know nothing of what goes on behind the scenes, because they are always kept under light hypnosis.

'Kaputa, a fat Babu, is in charge of them. He is an ace-high hypnotist, and the only one who lives up here permanently. Singra, a Pakistani, and Ben Yussuf, an Egyptian, make up this diabolical thirteen.

'For most of the time since mid-December, I've been up here. Radio brings me quotations for all currencies on the principal markets daily, and I have a transmitter by which I can send code messages to the Prince's agents in Geneva, New York, London, Paris and the rest, instructing them to buy or sell. Before I arrived, the Babu used to handle their foreign exchange, but now he's become more or less my assistant.

'Down at the Sala, half a dozen of the innocents are employed as accountants and clerks. They keep the ledgers, showing all expenses connected with the settlement, and revenue from outside sources. Once a week I go down there and check up on the increase in the subscription lists, and transfer the surpluses from the collecting centres in scores of cities to the central funds. After that, no-one except the Babu and myself knows what happens to the money. But, having taken on this job as their foreign exchange expert has enabled me to secure particulars of all their own agents and collecting centres. So, when it comes to a show-down, we'll be in a position, by fair means or foul, to close in on the lot.'

De Richleau smiled. 'You've done a fine job, Rex.'

Rex grinned back. 'Not too bad, though it's been a tough

assignment living with this hellish crew and pretending to go along with them. I'd have liked a few weeks longer before I blew the gaff. But you boys arriving on the scene with the best intentions have put paid to that; and I've got enough dope now to kill this Black Power movement in its cradle.'

Simon swallowed the last chunk of pineapple from his plate and asked, 'How d'you plan to do that?'

'No problem there,' Rex smiled. 'Way back home I know plenty of folks who're near the President. I'll get a private interview and lay out the deck. The old man's no fool. He'll jump to it that this is real dynamite. The settlement on the Sala de Uyuni and the Inca fortress being so remote from the outside world cuts two ways. It enabled the Satanists to keep their operations secret, but C.I.A. or Marines could be flown in with equal secrecy. The Bolivian Government would never hear a word of it. I'll take it on myself to see to it that the fortress and everyone in it are blown to hell. All the papers at the settlement would be seized, and that would enable us to deal with the stooges there. They'd be given a choice. Either to face a charge of conspiracy and inciting to riot, which would land them in the cooler for a term of years, or to sign a confession and receive a thousand dollars each, to tide them over until they could start a new life. Three hundred thousand dollars, or say half a million for the whole job, is only peanuts to Uncle Sam; and we'd have put paid to the most dangerous conspiracy the Devil has hatched since he made use of Hitler to wreck ten million lives.'

Rex broke off to light a cigarette, then asked, 'Now tell me your end of the story. The Prince put me wise to it that you boys had started a hunt for me, and mighty good of you it was. But he told me only the bare facts, then that you'd been caught and were being flown up here. I want to hear the details.'

Between them, Richard and Simon gave an account of their doings in Buenos Aires, Punta Arenas and Santiago, of the barbecue, Nella's murder, their imprisonment and Simon's engagement to Miranda. When Rex heard this last piece of news, he slapped his thigh and cried:

'Oh boy! Isn't that just great I'm crazy with delight. That poor kid has had one hell of a life. And she's a real sweetie. Just think, too, of old Simon being hooked at last. But you won't regret it, Simon. Blind or not, Miranda's a girl in a million. Come now. We must have a drink on this.' And, taking a bottle of Three Star Brandy from the hamper, he filled four of the paper cups to the brim.

It was very cold there, although not with the cold of evil; and the neat brandy was welcome as a means of warming them up. As they sipped it, the Duke took over, recounted how he fooled the police by forging the statement by Nella that had got his friends off, then how they had flown up to the Sala and been captured by von Thumm.

'That Nazi swine!' Rex exclaimed. 'What wouldn't I give to get my hands round his throat. When I'd agreed to join Don Salvador's outfit, he turned me over to the Baron for instruction. We were supposed to be running a poker school on Saturday nights, but the thought of what we actually did makes me want to vomit. It was all I could do to take it; but it was that or throwing in my hand, so I just had to grin and pretend I was enjoying the fun.'

They had made their escape shortly after one o'clock. It had taken them half an hour to reach the ruined church, and they had been talking for over an hour; so it was now close on a quarter to three, and Rex said, 'Guess we'd better get a few hours' shut-eye, as I'd like to take off soon after dawn.'

'Ner, not all of us,' Simon shook his head. 'Best take turns, so that one of us is always awake. At any time the Prince may find out that we got away. He can overlook us, so he'll know where we are. He might start something, and we mustn't be caught napping.'

'You would be right, Simon, if we were in most places,' said the Duke. 'But not here. We are now under the protection of the Cross. So all of us can sleep without fear.'

They stood up and faced the altar, praying silently for continued protection, then lay down and huddled together for warmth. Soon they were all sound asleep.

Shortly after first light they were woken by a whistling and rising and falling keening sound. Inside the ruin it was perfectly still; but when they got up and went over to the broken-down doorway, they realised the reason for this eerie noise. Outside, it was blowing a hurricane.

'Hell's bells!' exclaimed Rex. 'He's raised the wind against us.'

'You are right,' agreed de Richleau grimly. 'This is no ordinary storm. The wind would be rushing through this ruin at a hundred miles an hour; but it's as still as a mill-pond. Look at the way those trees are bent over almost double.

There! One of them has been uprooted and is being carried away like a matchstick.'

Incautiously, Richard stepped out through the open doorway. A fierce gust caught him and would have swept him off his feet had not Rex grabbed his arm and yanked him back to safety.

Gloomily they stumbled back over the rubble to the clear space near the centre of the nave, where they had slept.

'We're stymied,' said Simon bitterly. 'Not a hope of our flying down to the coast while this lasts.'

'He won't be able to keep it up indefinitely,' the Duke sought to comfort them. 'With luck we may be able to get away this afternoon.'

Rex grunted. 'I doubt it. The odds are that the aircraft will have been caught up and smashed to fragments.'

'I don't think so. It is half a mile away. And look at those two women.' De Richleau pointed at two distant figures with bundles strapped to their backs, and wearing the bowler-like hats favoured by the Andean peasants. They were trudging along unaffected by the wind.

'I'm certain that this is purely local. The wind is not blowing in one direction, but surging round and round the building. It is as though we were in the centre of a cyclone. Until it drops, we are as much prisoners as though we were in a big, circular cage; but there is at least one consolation.' De Richleau turned and glanced at the hamper. 'We have plenty of food and drink left to see us through the day.'

Unhappily, they set about opening two more tins and sat down to breakfast. For a while they speculated on what the Prince's next move would be, but it was impossible to do more than make guesses. They endeavoured to cheer themselves with the knowledge that, as long as they remained in the church under the protection of the Cross, they would be safe. But they could not remain there indefinitely.

During the morning they tried to forget their anxiety about the future by talking of the past: the desperate situations they had won their way out of, and the happy days of idleness and laughter they had spent together.

While they talked, the wind never ceased to howl and whine round the building. Neither did it stop as they ate a meagre lunch, nor during the long hours of the afternoon. When evening came, its force had not lessened, and it was clear that there was no longer any hope of their getting away that day.

At about eight o'clock, they ate what remained of the food they had brought from the aircraft and, an hour later, with the sound of the hurricane still at full blast, settled down to get what sleep they could.

In the early hours of the morning they had been captured, they had all been so tired out that, in spite of the fact that they were lying on cold, hard stone, they had dropped off almost at once. But now they twisted and turned for a long time, until, one by one, they fell into an uneasy sleep.

Rex was the first to wake. The pale light of dawn lit the ruin. Suddenly he was struck by the complete silence. The wind had stopped blowing. With a cry of excitement, he grasped the Duke by the shoulder and shook him. De Richleau opened his eyes and stared up at Rex for a moment, as though he did not see him, then he slowly sat up. Rex's cry had roused the others. Like him, they realised that the hurricane had ceased, and were exclaiming joyfully that they were now free to fly down to the coast.

But the Duke showed no sign of sharing their relief and excitement. His eyes were fixed on Simon and his gaze was filled with sorrow. In a low voice, he said:

'My dear son. I have bad news for you. How to break it to you I hardly know. But I have just returned from the astral. What I am about to tell you is no figment of the imagination induced by sorcery, such as we saw down in that dungeon the night before last. When I was on the astral I was confronted by the Prince. He said that we must return to him, or pay a forfeit. He is holding someone to ransom. Yesterday, while he kept us captive here, they kidnapped a young woman in Santiago, and flew her up to the fortress. She is now there, a prisoner at their mercy. Need I . . . need I name her?'

The blood had drained from Simon's face. His mouth hung open, and his eyes were staring.

De Richleau nodded. 'Yes; Miranda.'

16

The Agony of Simon Aron

'It can't be true!' Simon's voice was almost a wail.

The Duke stood up and laid a hand on his shoulder. 'Alas, it is, my son. In this my heart bleeds for you, but there is no escaping the truth. On the Astral personalities never lie. They may like or dislike one another, but they are incapable of disguising their true feelings. It is the Law, and cannot be evaded. The Prince made the situation clear to me beyond all misunderstanding. It proved very easy to trick Miranda. Within an hour of learning of our escape, he had a wax image made, cut upon it the name Pinney, performed his conjuration, then stuck a thorn into the leg of the puppet.

'Yesterday morning, when Pinney went to have her bath, she slipped, fell heavily and broke her leg. The next move took place a few hours later. A young Frenchman, who is one of the Prince's pilots, arrived at the Hilton. He told Miranda that you had sent him to fetch her. When asked why, he said that he had no idea; that he had received his orders through a third party, but it had been impressed upon him that you needed her urgently.

'Naturally, Miranda was torn between two loyalties. Should she remain with the unfortunate Pinney, or respond to your appeal? As anyone could have foreseen, love won. Fearing that you were ill or in serious trouble, she agreed to be flown up here. She is in no immediate danger, and believes herself to be among friends. Silvia Sinegiest is looking after her, and she has been told that we are on our way to the fortress; that we shall be there for lunch.'

Simon groaned. 'What . . . what does that fiend mean to do with her?'

'Nothing, provided we surrender to him.'

'And if we don't?'

De Richleau did not reply, but looked away.

'I know! I know!' Simon almost screamed. 'You don't have

to tell me. When she was trapped in that fire on her cousin's ranch, she was only nineteen and a virgin. She's still a virgin. They'll use her in their unholy rites. They'll rape and murder her. They'll offer her up as a sacrifice at a Black Mass.'

There were tears in the Duke's eyes as he gave a slight nod. 'That is what the Prince threatened unless we agree his terms. But they are not unreasonably harsh. His anxiety now is to keep secret his Black Power movement. I made it plain that, in no circumstances, would I use such powers as I have to further his plans, and he accepts that. He would, though, require all of us and, of course, Miranda, to remain up here indefinitely. We should be given one of the hutments in the settlement at Sala, and be free to enjoy such amenities as there are there.'

'Good God, what a prospect!' Richard burst out.

Simon turned to him. 'It'd mean you'd never see Marie-Lou again. I couldn't ask it of you.'

'We might persuade him to agree to a compromise,' the Duke suggested. 'I've had a wonderful life and I cannot expect to live for many years longer. If I remained here as a hostage for you keeping your word, he might accept your oath that you would never mention what is going on here, and let you go.'

'Greyeyes, be yourself,' Rex cut in abruptly. 'I'd go a long way to save Miranda, so would we all. But not that far. What is the martyrdom of one woman and ourselves when set against the appalling suffering that Black Power will inflict on the world? As long as we have the slightest chance of killing this thing, we've just got to keep on trying. And you know it.'

'Ummm,' Simon nodded. 'You're right, Rex. Greyeyes made that offer without considering its implications. Not like him; but he was thinking only of me. Tell you what, though. I'll chuck in my hand. Go on my own to the Prince. Have to . . . have to take a chance on what happens to Miranda and me. Pretend that I've been sent to try to negotiate a new deal. Keep him busy for a few hours while you three get away.'

'No dice,' said Rex. 'He's much too wily a bird to fall for that. But he might if I went, because I'm the only one of you who knows the whole set-up and it's more important to him to keep his claws on me than all three of you together.'

'I won't allow that.' De Richleau's voice was sharp. 'His resentment against you for having betrayed him will be far stronger than against any of us. His power is greater than mine when we are pitted against each other; but he must have many

202

things besides ourselves to occupy his mind. If he takes it off us for even a short time I could subdue any of his lieutenants, protect you and, with luck, we might get away. So I shall go with you.'

'I must go,' said Simon. 'Couldn't clear out as long as they've got Miranda.'

Richard gave a little laugh. 'That settles it then. You can't possibly think I'm going to quit and leave the rest of you up to your necks in this?' "One for all and all for one", as the great Dumas put it. We'll see this hellish business through together.'

'If we do, it is certain that our chances will be better,' de Richleau told them. 'Everyone has in him a divine spark and, united in purpose, a number of ignorant but good people can defeat a warlock who has considerable power for evil. For example, powerful as he is, the Prince could not overcome the congregation of a small Christian parish church if they had faith and the will to resist him. All of us are well advanced on the path of understanding, so together, we are a force to be reckoned with. Unfortunately, we are not pitted against the Prince alone. He will have the support of his lieutenants: but, if the opportunity to confront them separately occurs—as I did the Baron down at the Sala—we may win through.'

Simon picked up the carving knife with which they had cut up the tinned meat, and thrust its point through the bottom of the pocket inside his jacket, then buttoned the jacket so that the knife could not be seen. Casting a gloomy glance at the others, he said, 'Taking no chances. If that bastard is planning to sacrifice Miranda at a Black Mass, I'll kill her first and myself afterwards.'

'How dare you contemplate suicide?' de Richleau rebuked him sharply. 'In certain circumstances one is justified in taking the life of another. When one's country is at war, for example, or to put someone one loves out of pain. But never must one take one's own life. The length of each of our incarnations is decreed to the split second and by no possible means can we lengthen it. As you all know, during these incarnations we are set certain lessons to learn and given certain trials to bear, so that we may increase our knowledge and fortitude. To cut short an incarnation is to turn back the page, and results in having to face an even greater affliction in the next. Few Christians realise it, but to commit suicide is the Sin against the Holy Ghost, for the Holy Ghost is our own spirit.'

For a moment there was silence, then Richard said, 'Come on, chaps, let's get going.'

Gathering up their few belongings, they scrambled over the rubble and out of the ruin, then crossed the intervening low scrub to the aircraft. As the Duke had felt certain, it had been outside the area of the hurricane and was just as they had left it, anchored only by two light ropes.

They had not eaten since their meagre meal the previous evening, so they opened up some more tins of meat and fruit. Then they settled in their places and, with Rex at the controls, the little 'plane took off. A half of an hour later he brought her down on the island airstrip.

Ebolite, the wall-eyed Negro and the Babu, Kaputa, had come down from the fortress to meet them. Neither uttered any sneering remarks about their Master having forced his prisoners to return. On the contrary, they might have been two officials receiving V.I.P.s. After greeting the four friends courteously, they escorted them up the steep stairway and between the towering massive walls of stone blocks, into the modernised part of the stronghold. There the Duke, Simon and Richard were shown into the rooms they had previously occupied, and Kaputa accompanied Rex to his own quarters.

Clean clothes had been laid out for them and, when they had shaved, bathed and changed, Richard and Simon joined de Richleau in his room. Less than three hours had elapsed since they had left the ruined church, so it was still only mid-morning. Simon could not contain his impatience to see Miranda and, thinking she might be in the big room at the end of the passage, he opened the door with the intention of going along there. But he found his way barred by one of the servitors, who abruptly signed to him to go back. It was a sharp reminder that, in spite of their friendly reception, they were still prisoners.

For the best part of two hours they sat in the Duke's room, talking in a desultory fashion while endeavouring to forget their equivocal situation. At length the servitor opened the door and beckoned them to follow him. He led them to the big room and ushered them in.

Miranda was sitting there alone. As Simon came through the door, she jumped to her feet and, without a second's hesitation, ran to him with outstretched arms. Previously, at the distance she had been from the door, she could have made him out only as a blur; but, as he moved to meet her, he saw how her eyes had changed. They were now clear, bright and shining.

For a moment he was utterly aghast, believing that the Prince had tricked them—that this was the same figment of his imagination conjured up from Hell as that which had tempted him with a drink two nights before, and that the real Miranda was still in Santiago. But, before he could check his forward movement, her arms were round him. They were warm flesh and blood, and she was crying:

'Oh, darling! Isn't it wonderful that you should have found this marvellous Prince and had me flown up to him? Bless you and bless him a thousand times. I can hardly believe it yet. But it's true. He's restored my sight.'

Her joy was so infectious, for the moment, they did not even wonder what their enemy's object could be in having performed this miracle. Sharing her happiness, they crowded round kissing and congratulating her.

When the first excitement had subsided and they had sat down in the easy chairs, she said, 'By now, like me you must have realised that we were all wrong about the people up here. Silvia Sinegiest explained everything to me last night. They are not Satanists at all, and they had nothing to do with the murder of Nella Nathan. It is simply that they don't believe in Christianity, as it is taught in our churches. They hold that the Church taboos make people miserable and frustrated, whereas the Old God wanted everyone to be carefree and happy. Of course, parties like that barbecue you told me about are going a bit far. But some people like that sort of thing, and one doesn't have to take part in it if one doesn't want to. As Silvia said, the only commandment they have is, "*Do what thou wilt is the whole of the Law*".'

De Richleau shook his head, 'My child, you have been grievously misled. That one and only Satanist commandment, "*Do what thou wilt shall be the whole of the Law*" frees those who subscribe to it from all responsibility. In effect, it is a decree that everyone should give way to every temptation and use any means he can think of to secure for himself anything he desires without the least consideration of the unhappiness it would bring upon others. Just consider the sort of thing that would lead to. I will give you a few examples:

'Let us say that two pretty girls are in love with the same man. One does what she wills. She slashes her rival's face to pieces with a razor, in order to put her out of the running.

'A young man has just become aware of the joys of sex. One night he picks up a street girl and contracts from her a

205

venereal disease. His sex urge is not lessened by it. Instead of waiting until he is cured, he light-heartedly goes with other girls, passing the disease on to them.

'There are two brothers. The elder is his father's heir, but a weak character. The younger deliberately leads him into evil ways: drink, dope, laziness and theft, until the father is so disgusted that he disinherits him in favour of the younger son.

'A woman is ambitious to achieve a high position. A man stands in her way. She invites him to her flat to discuss matters, then attempts to seduce him. Whether she succeeds or not, she raises the house and accuses him of raping her. The scandal ruins both his public life and his marriage, while she achieves her object.

'A convict, anxious to have his sentence reduced, initiates a plan to escape with several others. At the eleventh hour he betrays them to the Governor. They are severely punished, while he has earned remission.

'A man desires a beautiful young girl. His attempts to seduce her fail. He succeeds in getting her alone, rapes her and makes her pregnant.

'A woman is tired of her husband and has a lover whom she wishes to marry. So she either poisons her husband or arranges some accident that will cause his death.

'A head of State is inordinately ambitious. Solely to make himself a greater figure in the world and with no thought for his people, he picks a quarrel with a smaller State and plunges his country into war.'

The Duke paused for a moment, then went on, 'Surely you see, my child, how the acceptance of this terrible doctrine "*Do what thou wilt shall be the whole of the Law*" would bring unbelievable misery on the world? No. There is only one way by which universal happiness can be achieved. That is by everyone practising the way of life urged on His followers by Jesus Christ; and that, at least, the Christian churches have continued to preach: '*Do unto thy neighbour as thou wouldst be done by.*"'

Miranda stared at him, wide-eyed with consternation at the thought that she had failed to realise the universal duplicity, fear and grief that would result if a great number of people became Satanists. She was just about to express her feelings when the Prince and Silvia came in, both carrying their familiars.

In spite of the recent conversation, Miranda had developed such a liking for Silvia, that she jumped up, ran to her and kissed her as though she was a much-loved sister. As Simon saw them embrace, he gave an inward shudder. Apart from deceiving them down at Punta Arenas, Silvia had done them no ill; but she held the high office of 'The Maiden', so was steeped to her beautiful eyebrows in the Satanic faith.

Meanwhile, with his warmest smile, the Prince was saying to de Richleau:

'My dear Duke, I am so happy that you and your friends have decided to stay on with us. When that wicked fellow Rex took you off in one of my aircraft, without even letting me know his intentions, I was really quite worried. I gather now that you only wished to see those interesting ruins at Potosi. But I am annoyed with him, very annoyed.'

There was nothing to be gained at the moment by forcing a show-down and, for Miranda's sake, de Richleau even returned the smile. 'I am sorry that you were concerned about us, Prince. And it was good of you to provide such a pleasant surprise for us on our return. We are naturally delighted that you should have restored Miss Van Ryn's sight.'

The Prince shrugged. 'It was nothing. Just a minor magic, and an expression of goodwill. I felt it would compensate the three of you, particularly Mr Aron, for the discomfort you suffered while guests of von Thumm.'

'How is the Herr Baron?' asked the Duke smoothly.

'In excellent health. You will see him this evening. He is flying up from the Sala. Glasshill, El Aziz and Harry Benito are coming with him, as I have bidden them to a party.'

Richard's eyes narrowed, and his chin stuck out aggressively. Noticing his expression, the Prince laughed and chided him, 'Now, now, Mr Eaton. You must remember that Lincoln had good cause for resentment because you made it necessary for him to abandon his profitable practice in Santiago. Now that we are all to be friends, you must let bygones be bygones.'

At that moment luncheon was announced and they all walked between the curtains to the table in the window that had such a superb view. During the meal the Prince exercised his magnetism to make them feel as though they were enjoying a normal social occasion. He kept the conversation going on a variety of subjects, none of which had any bearing on the occult. De Richleau, knowing the nervous tension that his friends must be feeling, ably seconded him.

When they had finished luncheon, the Prince said, 'And now I have an unpleasant duty to perform. I trust that you, especially, Miss Van Ryn, will not be too upset, as it concerns your uncle. I maintain a strict discipline here and, by taking one of my aircraft without permission, he has deliberately broken a rule of which he was well aware. For that he must be punished.'

Taking up a dessert knife, he tapped an empty glass with it, so that it gave out a little ping. Rising from the table, he added, 'That will bring him to us.' Then he led the way to the far end of the room.

Now acutely anxious about what form the unfortunate Rex's punishment was to take, the others sat down, but the Prince remained standing. After a few minutes Rex came in and the Prince addressed him:

'I have been greatly shocked by your conduct. For a moment it even occurred to me that you intended to play the traitor. Be that as it may, you used one of my aircraft to take my guests away without my consent. I have been considering what form your punishment should take. There came to my mind the truth about the events which occurred in the Garden of Eden at the time of the Fall.

'The second chapter of the book of Genesis has been misinterpreted. There was not one enchanted three, but two. The Tree of Knowledge of Good and Evil *and* the Tree of Life, which is mentioned both in verse nine and in chapter three, verse twenty-two. God the Creator, the One indivisible and eternal, having created Man in His own image, was so pleased with His work that he decided to make him immortal. He therefore sent His messenger, the Serpent who, at that time, was an angel with wings and limbs, to tell Man that he should eat the fruit of the Tree of Life.

'But the Serpent was vain, ambitious and had Evil in his heart. He perverted the message, beguiled Eve into eating the fruit of the Tree of Knowledge of Good and Evil, and himself ate the fruit of the Tree of Life.

'As a result, symbolically, the Serpent sheds its skin, but never dies; whilst Adam and Eve and all their descendents unto this present generation were condemned to age and die, to strife, sorrow and the pains of childbirth, then driven out of Eden. But the Serpent did not escape without punishment. The Lord God said to him:

' "Because thou hast done this, thou art cursed above all cattle and above every beast of the field; upon thy belly shalt thou go and dust shalt thou eat all the days of thy life." '

The Prince paused to glance at his gold wrist-watch, then went on, his large, limpid eyes beneath half-closed eyelids, riveted on Rex, 'This morning I cast a spell on you. In three minutes' time it will take effect.'

Rex had listened to him, pale but defiant. He made no reply and continued to stand there. The others watched him, a prey to the most awful apprehension. They felt as though they had been made rigid by being encased in invisible armour. None of them moved a hand or foot, and they were terribly aware that there was nothing they could do. Even the beautiful cat and the bouncy little dog remained completely still. An utter silence had fallen. The three minutes seemed interminable.

Suddenly Rex's legs gave beneath him. With a loud cry he fell to the floor.

For a moment the Prince's handsome features were transformed into a mask portraying sadism and hatred. In a loud voice he said: 'Even as the Lord God struck down the treacherous Serpent, I have struck you down. You shall crawl on your knees and feed on the floor like a dog until it is my pleasure to release you.'

His words broke the spell that had held them rigid. Cursing him, Richard jumped forward and grasped Rex's arm to help him to his feet. Seconds later, Simon was at his other side. But Rex was sixteen stone of splendid manhood. It was all they could do to drag him up between them, and that only for a moment. His weight proved too much for them. He sagged back on to his knees.

With an imperious gesture, the Prince waved them aside and said harshly to Rex, 'You may go now. Crawl to your quarters and remain there until I summon you again.'

Silvia had remained pale but self-contained throughout this frightful scene. Miranda had sat frozen with horror, her big, blue eyes starting from her head. Now, with a despairing cry of 'Oh, God, Uncle Rex!' she sprang out of her chair, cast herself down beside him and kissed him on the cheek. But Rex, his eyes moist with unshed tears, put her gently from him and, obeying the command he had been given, crawled out of the room.

Miranda burst into tears, rounded on the Prince and cried: 'How could you? Oh, how could you?'

He shrugged, shook his head and gave her his most charming smile. 'Please spare me your reproaches. I warned you that

I must punish your uncle. But, just as I gave you back your sight, I can restore the use of his legs to him whenever I wish. For how long or how short a time he will have to suffer depends, to some extent, on the behaviour of you and your friends. I might even relent soon enough to enable him to stand up and give you away when you are married.'

'Married!' she repeated. 'But . . .'

With a sharp gesture he silenced her and went on, 'Yes. I can hardly suppose that either you or Mr Aron wish for a long engagement. So why should you deny yourselves longer than necessary the joy of being united? I have arranged for you to be married tonight.'

'But . . .' she stammered. 'But, how can we be married here?'

He smiled again. 'We have a temple, and the ceremony will take place there. The rites will be performed as they were in the beginning and you will receive the blessing of the True God.'

'No!' de Richleau came to his feet. 'I forbid it! I forbid it!'

The Prince turned and gave him a mildly contemptuous look. 'In my presence you have not the power to forbid anything. And you know it. If you and your friends prove troublesome, I will deal with you as I have dealt with Van Ryn. Then all of you shall witness the ceremony, *and* the consummation of the marriage on your knees.'

'The consummation!' cried Simon. 'Ner, ner! Damned if . . .'

Miranda's cheeks had gone scarlet and she gasped, 'You don't mean . . . ? You can't!'

The Prince's voice was silky. 'My dear young lady. True marriage does not consist only of exchanging oaths and, perhaps, the giving to the woman of some symbol, such as a ring. As it is said that justice should not only be done, but be seen to be done, so with marriage. The two principals, the Yang and the Yin, must be brought together before witnesses. Then the offspring of this mating, should the woman be so blessed as to conceive, is vowed to the service of the True God.'

'What! Sold to Satan before it is even born?' Richard snapped. 'You bastard!'

'Mr Eaton, you are still comparatively young in time, or you would know that the word Satan, which you regard as a designation of Evil, is only a name used by the ignorant for the Deity from whom all blessings flow. As for your abuse of myself, I will let it pass. But it distresses me that a man of your breeding should permit himself to display such ill manners.'

Since the Prince had silenced de Richleau, the latter had stood with bowed shoulders and downcast eyes. Now, making a gesture towards Miranda who, with Simon's arm about her, was weeping hysterically, he looked up again and said:

'You tell us that the God of the Christian churches demands that His followers should deny themselves the joys of life; whereas your god is ever anxious to foster people's happiness. How can you possibly maintain that assertion when your proposals have brought such shock, distress and horror to these two?'

'Their reaction is due only to the false beliefs in which they have been reared. It is understandable that Miss Van Ryn should shrink from exposing herself naked and being possessed by others in addition to her husband. But you will find that she will swiftly overcome this reluctance. There has never yet been born a woman endowed with a good figure who, however prudishly brought up, in her secret heart would not delight in displaying her beauty.

'But that is not all I am, of course, aware that she is a virgin. That being so, her bridegroom is unfortunate, for a first penetration rarely brings much pleasure to the man and, for the woman, is usually painful. The result in Christian marriages very often is a most unhappy period, during which the woman is unwilling to repeat the act, and the man suffers an infuriating frustration. Indeed, not infrequently, it leads to the couple never developing a satisfactory sex life.

'In his wisdom, the True God devised a means by which this sad state of affairs would be overcome. He decreed that, on her wedding night, the bride should be possessed by seven men. After the second or third has had her, she feels no more pain; with those who do so later, she experiences an ecstasy of passion. Tomorrow, when Miss Van Ryn has recovered from her exhaustion, she will be beseeching her husband to embrace her.'

So horrified had those about the Prince been by his revelation of the procedure at a Satanic wedding that they had heard him out in silence. As he ceased speaking, they gave vent to a chorus of protest.

Miranda had fainted. Simon lowered her to a chair and stood trembling, his mouth agape. Richard, his eyes glaring, was half crouched, his fists clenched and about to launch himself on their tormentor. Just in time the Duke grabbed his arm, held him back and said hoarsely:

'Young women indoctrinated into your evil cult might accept the ceremony willingly and, perhaps, enjoy it. But that could not possibly be the case with one brought up to be chaste and who, above all, is not only physically attracted to one man but has also given him her spiritual love. To be defiled by a succession of men would so revolt her that it might well drive her out of her mind. This marriage must not take place. I know well that we are in your power. But is there not some alternative, some inducement we can offer you to refrain from forcing Miss Van Ryn to submit to this hideous ordeal?'

The red lips of the Prince's beautifully-modelled mouth parted in a smile, revealing his gleaming white teeth. 'Ah, now we are talking. Yes. Since you are so bigoted and anxious to deny this charming couple entering in the true joy of life, there is an alternative. You have only to agree, as I urged you to when you first arrived here, to acknowledge the True God as your Master, and give me your aid in my undertakings.'

'No,' the Duke replied at once. 'That I cannot do. And my friends would not ask it of me.'

The Prince shrugged. 'Then there is no more to be said. Silvia will take charge of Miss Van Ryn and later prepare her for her wedding. You others will now go to your rooms. You will not communicate with one another, as I have no intention of giving you the chance to hatch some plot which might cause a temporary hitch in my arrangements. In due course, you will be sent for.'

Fixing his large dark eyes for a few moments on each of them in turn, he pointed to the door. Dominated by his will their urge to resist crumbled. Silently, with bowed heads, they filed out of the room.

Simon spent the greater part of the hours that followed alternately sitting on the edge of his bed hunched in despair and imploring the help of the God of his fathers. Richard, as an old soldier, knew how important it was to get as much sleep as possible before a battle. Feeling certain that the Duke would put up a fight, he was anxious to be in a state to give him as much support as he could. It took him a long time to clear his mind of the heart-rending scene in which he had participated, but eventually he dropped off. De Richleau deliberately left his body for the astral. There he sought out as many of his long-time friends who were out of incarnation as he could, and asked them to spend the coming night thinking

212

of him and supplicating the Lords of Light to come to his assistance.

In due course a meal on a tray was brought by the servitors to each of them. The Duke neither ate or drank anything. Simon, feeling that he ought to recruit his strength, attempted to eat a wing of chicken *chaud-froid*, but he was in so grievous a state that, after having swallowed a few mouthfuls with difficulty, he was sick. Richard, true to form, made a good meal and drank three-quarters of the bottle of champagne that had been brought him with the food.

In vain he had searched his bedroom early in the afternoon for something he could use as a weapon. The bottle, he decided, was the answer. It made the perfect club. But it would be missed when the servant came to collect the tray. Moreover, it was too big to be easily concealed about his person. Emptying the remaining contents on the floor, he took the empty bottle into the bathroom and smashed it on one of the bath taps. The punt fell off and several other pieces, leaving in his hand the neck of the bottle and, projecting from it, a six-inch-long sliver of glass.

Folding a light hand-towel into a narrow strip, he tied the centre twice round the lip of the bottle, thus making a handle for this improvised dagger, then wrapped the ends round the blade, so that he should not cut himself on it but, being loose, the ends would fly apart when he pulled the dagger from the side of his trousers belt where he intended to hide it. Collecting the other pieces of shattered bottle, he took them into the bedroom and threw them into the wastepaper basket.

When the silent servitor came for the tray, Richard pointed first to the wet patch where the wine had stained the carpet, then to the pieces of glass in the basket and made a grimace to indicate that he had had an accident, dropped the bottle and it had broken. The servant only shrugged and took the tray away.

Quite a long time later, he came back again, carrying a white robe with gold cabalistic signs on it, and laid it on the bed for Richard to change into. Richard ignored it as, in due course, he found had the Duke and Simon, who had had similar robes brought to them.

It was half an hour before midnight when, having been summoned by Pedro, they met Kaputa in the corridor. The grossly-fat Babu signed to them to follow him down the stairs to the basement.

They did so, knowing that the vital hour had come.

213

17

The Satanic Marriage

The three friends were taken to the big, circular, underground room where, protected only by a circle of salt, they had faced the horrors that the Prince had sent against them. It was no longer cold down there, but there was a strange smell of burning herbs.

Waiting for them were von Thumm and the long-haired Andean Indian. Both of them were wearing wizard's robes of different colours, embroidered with various designs in gold and silver. The Duke recognised those on the Baron's robe as the symbols of Earth, those on the Indian's as symbols of Fire, and those on the robe the Babu was wearing as symbols of Air.

As the door of the chamber closed, leaving the two servitors outside, von Thumm limped forward to meet the prisoners. Having eyed them for a few moments with grim satisfaction, he said in his guttural voice:

'*Mein Führer*, the Prince, of your submission haf told me. After the ceremony with me to the Sala you will all come, there under me to live. My orders you take; *ja*, and no questions ask. Do so and it will be no worse for you than prison camp. But make for me trouble and much pleasure I haf in teaching you good lesson. So! It is understood?'

They made no reply to this, so he went on, 'Now, for what we make tonight. As you people Christians are, we hold service appropriate. For Muslims, Buddhists and others we haf different ritual. All amended are, so as to the True God to be acceptable. Tonight then we haf wedding Mass. Follow me now. Attempt interference and you are struck blind. Stay silent. One word and you are struck dumb.'

Walking to the wall that had the crooked Cross on it, he pressed a hidden spring and a large panel slid smoothly back, revealing a Satanic temple. The source of the smell was now evident. The atmosphere in the temple was slightly misty and

214

two young boys, both naked, one white with golden hair and the other a coal-black Negro, were swinging censers.

There were no pews or *prie-dieux* in the temple. The furniture consisted only of an altar raised up on a step, and so forming two stages; but the walls glowed with the colour of several beautiful mosaics. They portrayed the Seven Deadly Sins and under each in large lettering was the Satanic creed, '*Do what thou wilt shall be the whole of the Law*'.

The broad upper stage of the altar consisted of a single sheet of rough-hewn stone and had clearly been designed for sacrifices. About a foot from the left end of it, a groove had been cut, on the step below which reposed an onyx bowl, to catch the blood of the victim so that none of it should be lost. But now, upon the stone of this lower shelf, there had been laid out a shallow mattress about three inches thick, of quilted satin, the reason for which was obvious.

Upon the upper shelf were two seven-branched, gold candelabra, in which black candles were burning. Between them rose a hideous, bearded figure, which de Richleau at once recognised as Baphomet, the idol before which, in the Middle Ages, the heretical Knights Templar had been initiated into revolting rites.

The idol had the head of a goat with two great horns between which stood a black candle that burned with a steady blue flame, and gave off a stench of sulphur. On its forehead there glittered a pentagon, one angle of which pointed downwards towards its beaked nose that had monstrous, gaping nostrils. It had human hands, held up so that they pointed to two white crescents, above and below them were two black crescents. Its sexual organs were those of a hermaphrodite. Its belly was green and covered with scales like those of a fish or reptile. Its naked breasts were blue, and as full as those of a pregnant woman's. Its lower limbs were covered in shaggy hair and ended in cloven hooves. It was seated on a cube, the symbol of four, the square and foundation of all things. Its hooves rested on a sphere, representing the world. Its eyes were large, oblong and yellow. They gleamed with a malevolence which gave the impression that, utterly still though the creature was, it was conscious of what it saw, and was endowed with life.

As de Richleau recognised the figure of Baphomet, he recalled the fate that had overtaken the Knights Templar. Their Order had originally been founded to protect the Holy Sepulchre. They had been a cosmopolitan body, each of their companies being termed a 'Tongue', according to the Christian nation from which its members had been recruited. Their principal bases had been Rhodes and Malta. In both, and in many other places, they had built huge castles. They had become rich and powerful and, during the centuries of the Crusades, had protected pilgrims to the Holy Land by keeping at bay the Barbary pirates.

But their contact with the Saracens had led to their becoming Gnostic heretics. It was said that they uttered terrible blasphemies and conducted revolting rites in front of a Satanic idol. These rumours reached the Pope, who drew the attention of Philippe le Bel, King of France, to them. Philippe was in financial difficulties. He coveted the great wealth of the Templars, a considerable part of which they kept in their Paris headquarters, a fortress called the Temple.

At that time, early in the fourteenth century, Jaques de Morlay was the Grand Master of the Templars. The King invited him and his principal lieutenants to a banquet at the Louvre. There he had them arrested. They were thrown into prison, terribly tortured, then burned at the stake.

Nevertheless, the Templars had the last word. As the funeral pyre that was to burn them alive was ignited, Jacques de Morlay put a solemn curse on the Royal House of France. He called on his Infernal Master to bring about its ruin and, nearly five hundred years later, the monarchy was brought to an end by the imprisonment of King Louis XVI and Queen Mary Antoinette in the tower of the Temple.

This recollection of the power of Satan, exerted in support of the cult of Baphomet, ran through the Duke's mind in less than a minute, while he and his friends followed von Thumm until he halted in front of the altar, and made obeisance to the figure of Baphomet. The other two Satanic priests, who had brought up the rear, also bowed themselves down until their heads nearly touched the floor.

A silence of several minutes ensued, then came the sound of footsteps. Turning, they saw that the bride had entered the Temple. Her hand rested lightly on Rex's arm, so it was evident that the Prince had given him back the use of his legs in order that he could stand while giving her away. Behind them came Silvia and Glasshill. She was wearing the pleated white linen dress trimmed with gold of an Egyptian priestess; he had on a wizard's robe embroidered with the symbols of the fourth element—Water.

Miranda was wearing a bridal costume, but it was very different from the conventional white dress, tulle veil and wreath of orange blossom. Anyone who had seen illustrated books portraying ancient civilisations would have identified it at once. It had a very full skirt that came right down to the ground, a tight waist and was almost topless, so that the whole of her beautiful round breasts were revealed. The priestesses of ancient Crete, who had worn such costumes, are always shown holding a serpent in each hand. Instead, Miranda's mauve satin skirt was embroidered with gold snakes, and a gold snake was entwined in her dark hair.

To the great surprise of Simón and his friends her expression was serene and she displayed no reluctance to approach the altar. They were even more surprised that she showed neither fear nor revulsion when von Thumm announced the form the ceremony would take. With an air of relish, he said:

'The Prince, our *Führer*, has been called away on a matter important. His place as celebrant I take. First we make prayer to our Father, the True and Only God. Next we perform Mass and urinate on Holy wafer taken from La Paz Cathedral. Bride and bridegroom then clothes remove and copulate on altar. Virgin blood most potent is. With it I anoint you all. Last, six of us in turn complete the work of in the bride passion arousing. The Lord God will determine the semen of which of us her pregnant makes. We are here eight males. After the bridegroom, our three other guests will possess her. Myself next and of my assistant priests two. There is, though, possibility that age has the Duke impotent made. If so, my third priest will his place take.'

Simon, Rex and Richard were all staring at Miranda. They were astounded that, on hearing this account of the ordeal before her, not a muscle of her face had changed. She was looking intently at the crooked Baron, and her lips were parted in a slight smile. The only possible explanation occurred to all three of them, that she must have been doped to prevent her from putting up any resistance or understanding what was going on.

The Duke's thoughts were not on Miranda. His heart had leapt at the announcement that the Prince had been called away, because some other evil business required his immediate attention. De Richleau knew himself to be a more advanced adept than von Thumm, and had, down at the Sala, used his power to overcome him temporarily. It was just possible that

217

he might be able to do so again. But it had been the united strength of Glasshill, El Aziz, and Benito, added to that of the Baron, which had reversed the position when the prisoners were in the cellar.

Here the Baron had three Satanists to support him and all of them Adepts, whereas Richard, Rex and Simon were not. The odds were, therefore, against the Duke; but there was one possibility, the thought of which gave him a gleam of hope. His friends on the astral were aware of his situation, and their intercession with the Lords of Light might yet lead to his winning the uneven battle. But he was far from sanguine, for he knew that, as a general principle, those on earth were expected to fight their own battles, and that their Mightiness of Eternity rarely allowed themselves to be distracted from their own great work and brought from the remote Seventh Astral Plane, which they alone occupied, to intervene in matters on earth.

While he was ruminating on these hopes and fears, von Thumm, his head—as was frequently the case—tilted towards his left shoulder, began to intone. He now spoke in Latin and recited the Lord's Prayer backwards. The Mass proceeded in that language, the assistant priests uttering the responses. In due course, the Baron produced a Holy wafer from a gold, jewel-studded casket on the altar. Crying out, 'This is the body of the impostor, Jesus Christ,' he spat upon it, threw it down, then urinated on it. His assistants followed suit. Crushing it under his heel, he said to Simon and Miranda:

'Now we consummation of your marriage make. Take off your clothes.'

Simon swung round towards Miranda. Before anyone could lay a hand on him he had whipped out the carving knife with which they had cut up the tinned food in the ruined church. At his movement, Miranda turned to face him. His arm flew up to bring the blade slashing down between her breasts.

De Richleau, having impressed on Simon how great a sin it would be to kill himself, had thought no more of the matter. But he had also said that, given certain circumstances, the killing of another could be justified and, evidently, Simon had decided that, rather than allow Miranda to be defiled, he would kill her.

She was within an ace of death when the Duke acted. It was as though those long-time friends of his on the astral had shouted in one great chorus:

218

'Now! Now is your chance! If you can kill von Thumm, you will be the master down there.'

His right arm shot out from the shoulder. The first and second finger of his hand pointed at Simon. The Duke spoke no word. Simon was so placed that he did not even see the gesture. But, as though struck a violent blow from behind, his body turned in a quarter-circle. Caught by the light of the candle on the goat's head, the steel blade flashed for a second, then it streaked down and half its length was buried in von Thumm's chest.

The assistant priests uttered wild cries of rage. Glasshill had been the nearest of them to von Thumm. As the Baron, his eyes glaring, his mouth agape, collapsed on to the altar steps, the big Negro sprang forward. He raised his fist to strike Simon to the ground. That gave Richard the chance for which he had been waiting. Jerking his home-made knife from beneath his coat, he drove the big sliver of glass with all its force into Glasshill's liver. The Negro gave one awful scream and pitched forward on to the dying Baron.

The shouts and cries had brought Miranda out of her trance. She cast one horrified look at the figure of Baphomet and the two men choking out their life blood on the altar step below it, then let out a terrified cry. Next moment she realised that she was half naked, made as if to put her hands up to cover her breasts, and fainted.

The two young, naked acolytes dropped the censers they had been swinging and made a dash for the door. Silvia had turned and was also heading for it as fast as her long legs would carry her.

The Duke did not even glance in her direction. There still remained to be dealt with the two fat priests of Satan: the long-haired Andean and the grossly-fat Babu. The Duke was praying desperately that, together, they would not rank in circles and squares a magical degree higher than his own. The Babu had already raised his left hand and opened his mouth to pronounce a conjuration. Instantly, de Richleau lifted his right hand, so that it pointed at him, and shouted:

'Be silent!'

The Babu's thick lips wobbled uncertainly for a few seconds, then closed, and his arm fell to his side.

Richard had turned his glass dagger in the fatal wound he had inflicted on Glasshill, and drawn it out. As he straightened himself, he could see over the Duke's shoulder. The Andean was behind him. He had drawn a knife and was just about to stab de Richleau in the back. Richard gave a cry of warning. It came too late. The Duke heard it in time to make a sideways movement that saved his life, but the point of the knife pierced his left shoulder with such force that he was thrown forward on his face.

The fat Babu's face suddenly broke into a smile of triumph. He lifted his left arm again and opened his mouth to hurl a binding spell on the Duke's companions. But Rex was within a yard of him. Raising his 'leg of mutton' fist, he struck the Babu a terrific blow on the side of his flabby jaw. His head snapped back and he went down like a pole-axed ox.

With the agility of a panther, the Andean had gone down on one knee and raised his knife again, to finish off de Richleau. Richard flung himself forward bodily. His chest thudded into the kneeling man's shoulder, deflecting the blow and sending him over sideways. Richard came sprawling on top of him. Like an eel, the Andean wriggled from beneath the body of his attacker, and came to his knees. Again his knife went up, this time to slash at Richard.

Simon had caught Miranda as she fainted and lowered her to the altar steps a few feet from where von Thumm was gasping out his life in agony. With one arm round Miranda's shoulders, Simon was stroking her cheek and kissing her forehead, in an endeavour to bring her out of her faint. On hearing Richard's cry, he looked up. A second later he heard de Richleau crash to the floor behind him. Swinging round he pulled himself away from Miranda to go to the Duke's assistance. By then Richard had acted and the Duke was out of danger but he himself was in imminent peril.

Jumping across de Richleau's prone body, Simon landed a kick on the side of the Andean's cheek. He dropped his knife and heeled over. A second kick from Simon and the Andean fell sideways, his head hitting the floor. With a ferocity utterly alien to his nature, Simon continued to kick and kick and kick until the evil priest's face was reduced to a mass of blood and pulp.

For a few minutes nothing was to be heard in the temple but the sound of their panting, as they strove to get back their breath. Rex was kneeling by the unconscious Duke, anxiously examining his wound. As soon as he could speak, he gasped:

'Thank God! . . . It's only a flesh wound . . . and not deep. The point of the knife struck his . . . shoulder blade. It was

ither hitting his head when he fell, or loss of blood that
aused him to faint.'

'All the same. I don't like it,' Richard said anxiously. 'He's
leeding badly, and at his age he can't afford to lose a lot of
lood.' As he spoke, he ripped off his jacket, then began to
nbutton his shirt. Pulling it off he handed it to Rex, and
dded, 'Here, take this. Staunch the blood with it and we'll
ind the wound up.'

Rex already had the Duke's coat off. As he began to tear
ie coat-tail of Richard's shirt into strips, Miranda gave a moan
nd opened her eyes. Simon bent over her again, took her
ands in his and, sobbing with relief, murmured, 'Oh, my
arling! Are you all right? Can you see me and hear me?
efore, you acted so strangely. As though your mind wasn't
orking.'

'It wasn't,' she murmured. 'But I'm all right now. I . . . I
nly became fully conscious of what was going on round me
hen you stabbed that awful priest. Oh, Simon darling! How
in I thank you for saving me from these beasts?'

Smiling down at her, he confessed, 'Nearly killed you instead,
iy precious. Had made up my mind to, rather than . . . well,
een you driven out of your mind. But we're not out of the
ood yet. That hell-cat Silvia got away. May be other priests
p above. If so, she'll be raising them against us by now.'

Miranda shook her head. 'Silvia's not a hell-cat. It was she
ho hypnotised me, so that I wouldn't know what was being
one to me. Even if she is a witch, I'm sure she's not deliber-
ely evil. She's in this thing for kicks.'

As she was speaking, Miranda had got to her feet. Slipping
it of his jacket, Simon helped her into it so that she could
iver her breasts. Then he turned to look down at the Duke.
There was a lot of blood on the floor that had run from the
ound in his shoulder, and some of it had stained red the white
iir on one side of his head. But Rex had managed to staunch
e flow and, with Richard's help, got a tight bandage round
s shoulder and under his armpit. As they sat him up to get
m back into his torn jacket, he came to. His grey eyes were
ill half-closed as he looked about him, and his head wobbled
steadily. After a minute or so, he said in a husky whisper:

'So help was sent us. Praise be, and . . . and we got the better
them. But . . . but I'm out of the game for the moment. I
el as weak as a kitten.'

'Your wound's not too bad,' Richard told him, 'but you've

lost a lot of blood. Silvia disappeared while we were all fighting. By now she's probably got some of the retainers together, so we mustn't lose a moment in getting away. Think you can manage to walk with the help of Rex and me?'

Between them they got de Richleau on his feet, and with his arms round the shoulders of both of them. Resolutely he began to walk forward, but they had to bear most of his weight. Simon and Miranda, their arms round each other, followed them out of the temple, across the circular ante-room beyond it and into the dimly-lit passage.

They were reluctant to go upstairs, as to do so meant that they would be taking a big risk of running into Silvia and some of the Prince's minions. But they knew that there were several ways out of the ancient fortress. To find one was far from easy, as the stone-walled passages formed a veritable maze, with many chambers on either side evidently once doorless store-rooms, opening off them. Several times they entered cul-de-sacs, that ended in a barrier of roughly-cut rock. At last they found a door which, when wrenched open, brought in a sudden cold draught and gave them a view of the star-spangled sky.

Outside was a small stone terrace, from which a flight of worn steps led down. As they went towards them they could see the airstrip below, because it was lit up. That it should be lit in the middle of the night alarmed them, for it suggested that the Prince had left in an aircraft and was shortly expected back.

The stairs were too narrow for three people abreast, so Richard led the way down, while Rex picked up the Duke in his strong arms and carried him. As they descended, they saw that there was now only one aircraft on the strip, which confirmed their supposition that the Prince had flown off in the other.

They were about halfway between the bottom of the stair-case and the 'plane when a figure emerged from a nearby hut. In the glare of the arc lights they could be seen as clearly as though they were upon a brightly-lit stage. The squat figure was a man in Andean costume. He halted abruptly and gave a loud shout. His words were Chiquito, the language of the Bolivian Indian, so they did not understand them; but, obviously, he was calling on them to halt. His voice had barely ceased to echo in the still night air before he had pulled a pistol from its holster and was pointing it at them.

Simon still had the carving knife with which he had killed

222

von Thumm, and Richard his glass dagger. But the man who was holding them up was a good twenty paces away—much too far off for them to attempt to rush him. Inwardly they groaned. In two minutes they could have been in the 'plane and in another five, in the air. To have come so near to escaping and now to be marched back and locked up until the Prince returned was a most bitter pill to have to swallow.

Through their minds raced sickening thoughts of what now lay before them. When he learned that four of his principal henchmen had been slain, the Prince's fury and malice would know no bounds. They would pray in vain for an easy death, but they knew him to be merciless. He would extract the last quiver of agony from their mutilated bodies before they slid into the peace of death.

It was only a matter of seconds after the challenge rang out when de Richleau cried, 'Rex! Put me down.'

Rex did as he was bidden, but kept a hold on the Duke, in order to support him. For the second time that night de Richleau extended his right arm, with the first and little fingers of his hand thrust out; but this time the movement was slower and cost him a big effort.

The effect of his gesture made them catch their breath. Invisible power streaked from his pointing hand at the man who was holding them up. There came a burst of flame, followed by a loud report. De Richleau had exploded the bullets in the magazine of the pistol. What remained of the weapon dropped from the man's shattered hand. With a shriek, he reeled away, blinded and bleeding, to fall backward on the ground.

But the effort had taken the Duke's last remnant of will power and physical strength. He suddenly sagged in Rex's arms. His bloodstained head fell forward, and he again became unconscious.

Now fearful that the sound of the explosion would bring other retainers of the Prince on the scene, Rex, carrying the Duke, ran towards the little aircraft. Richard raced him to it and yanked the door open. Between them they got de Richleau into it and sat him on one of the rear seats. Miranda and Simon scrambled after them and the latter closed the door.

Rex switched on the light and looked down at the instrument panel. With a curse, he announced, 'Nothing like enough gas to get us to the coast. What'll we do?'

'Couldn't fly through the mountains during the night, anyhow,' Simon said quickly. 'Take us down to that church near Potosi. We'll be safe there.'

'What then?' Rex snapped. 'No gas to be got there. We'll be stranded, and at any time that bloody Prince will be after us.'

'Fly us to the Sala,' Richard suggested swiftly. 'Von Thumm and his chums came up here for the wedding; so it's unlikely we shall meet with any opposition. We can refuel on the airstrip and take off again at first light.'

'Good for you,' Rex threw back, and switched on the engine.

'Get her off! Get her off quickly!' Simon shouted. Glancing through the window he had seen three men who had just come out of the hut, running across the tarmac towards the 'plane, and one of them had a Sten gun. 'They're after us!' he cried. 'Get her off, or we'll all be riddled with bullets.'

Rex revved up the engine for a moment, then the 'plane ran forward. As it lifted there came a burst of fire. A spate of bullets ripped into the tail of the aircraft. It shuddered, dipped steeply, then lifted again. They were off.

The flight down to the settlement in the Sala entailed an agonisingly anxious twenty minutes' flight through the moonlit mountains; but, in all, took only three-quarters of an hour. During this time de Richleau came round, but he was very weak, and his friends were very anxious about him. At the Sala airstrip the lights were on and, as usual, Rex brought the 'plane down in a perfect landing. Four aircraft were parked on the strip, but no-one was about. Richard and Simon climbed out and lowered de Richleau to them. Two minutes later, all five of them were on the ground.

Suddenly they caught sight of a solitary figure walking towards them. 'Not to worry,' Richard said in a low voice. 'We'll tell him that the Prince sent us down here, and take a meal off them in the house. That will kill time till we can fly off again.'

He had hardly finished speaking when the face of the man who was approaching was lit up by a beam from one of the pylon lights. The hearts of all of them jumped, then sank. It was the Prince.

His voice was sharp with anger, he cried, 'So you thought you would cheat me, eh?' Then he raised both his hands above his head. 'Down on your knees, all of you. Get down!'

For an agonising moment the muscles of their calves were seized with cramp, then the strength drained from them, and they sank to their knees.

224

18

Caught in the Toils

Unprotesting, humiliated, despairing, they knelt in a little group beside the aircraft. The Prince had halted ten feet away from them. Through Simon's quick mind, then through Richard's slower one, there drifted the thought that they had weapons. As had been clearly demonstrated less than an hour ago by de Richleau, when he had caused the gunman's pistol to blow up in his face, anyone possessing enough occult power could protect himself from physical harm if he knew he was going to be attacked. But taken by surprise, as von Thumm and Glasshill had been, they were just as vulnerable as other people. If then the Prince came close enough, there was a possibility that he could be knifed before he had a chance to defend himself.

Alas for their embryo hopes. The Prince caught the vibration made by their thoughts and said sharply, 'Mr Aron, Mr Eaton. You are armed. Throw your weapons at my feet.'

Reluctantly they took out their knives and threw them on to the tarmac within a yard of him. He looked down at them and frowned. 'A carving knife and a spearhead of glass partly wrapped in a bloodstained towel. What is the meaning of this blood?'

No-one answered him, so he snapped, 'Come! Tell me everything, and quickly. I was too occupied to overlook you earlier tonight. It was not until a quarter of an hour ago that my sixth sense suddenly told me that you were on your way here. What happened? The wedding! The girl, Miranda, is with you; so it could not have taken place. How did you escape? Whom have you killed? Van Ryn, I make you spokesman for your party. Speak now! A full account! Attempt to hide nothing, or I will send fire to consume your testicles.'

The horrible threat was redundant. Rex needed no telling that they were at the Prince's mercy and that by no means could he be prevented from learning very shortly all that had taken place that night in the Satanic temple. As briefly as he could, he related the events which had led up to their escape.

The Prince heard him out in silence, but even in the artificial light they could see that his face was going livid. When silence fell again, he glared at them for a moment, then screamed, 'Von Thumm, Glasshill, Kaputa and Pucara. All dead! Four of my best lieutenants. By Lucifer, you shall pay for this. By Ashtaroth, Memon, Theutus and Nebiros, oh! how you shall pay.'

His fury was such that he was shaking and had clearly lost control of himself. De Richleau watched him with lack-lustre eyes, sadly registering the fact that this was a moment when, had he been his normal self, he could have overcome their enemy. But the wound in his shoulder was throbbing madly, and that made it impossible for him to concentrate.

They heard the sound of swift footsteps, then caught sight of a figure pounding down the slope from the headquarters house. A minute later the curly-headed Benito came to a halt beside the Prince. He made a swift obeisance, then panted:

'My Prince. I hears yo' shout; so I come runnin'.'

The Prince ran his tongue over his now pale lips, then replied hoarsely, 'These heretics have taken advantage of my absence from the fortress to strike us a savage blow. But the Lord of Eternity is not mocked. He has cast them back into my hands. For their crime they shall spend an hour in torment for every hair on their heads. I have subdued them. They are now powerless. Take them to the house and put them in the cellar with those others.'

With a sudden gesture he removed the spell that he had put on the group. The calves of their legs began to tingle, the muscles flexed and they came slowly to their feet. Benito beckoned to them and, with the Duke again supported by Rex and Richard, they followed him up the slope.

On entering the house they were met by two of the Zombies, to whom Benito handed them over. Realising that resistance would be hopeless, they allowed themselves to be led down to the cellar. It was in darkness but, as the door was opened, the light in the passage outside showed them that two men were already there. One was a full-blooded Negro, the other a quadroon with a pale skin, thick lips and crinkly hair.

The first concern of the newcomers was the Duke. Before the door was shut on them, while there was still light enough to see, Miranda sat down in a corner and de Richleau was

226

then lowered to the floor so that his head rested in her lap. With a sigh, he murmured:

'Thank you. Now that I am lying still, I will be able to help myself. My Yoga breathing will counteract the pain so that I can sleep. Please don't wake me until you have to.'

By then the door had been slammed and locked, and it was pitch dark. One of the other prisoners who they thought was probably the Negro, asked, 'Say, folks, what you bin thrown in de can for?'

'Getting up against the big-shot,' Rex replied succinctly.

'Same wid us, man. Leastways, that Jamaican sod didn't approve none of a talk we give the folks this evenin', an' he sent fer his boss.'

'What was the talk about?' asked Richard.

'Well, man, my buddy here an' me, we's bin doin' a lot of thinkin' dese pas' few weeks. Dis bid to bring de world under Black Power seemed jus' fine to us when we was indoctrinated. But we's bin gettin' doubts. You whites got all der guns, tear gas an' that. Reckon we don' stan' no chance. You'll sure come out on top. Slaughter'll be bad as a first-class war; an' we poor bastards'll end up wors' off than we was before.'

The other man added in a thin, piping voice, 'It's not only that. It's against the teachin' of Our Lord. He preached Peace an' Goodwill. Turn the other cheek, He said. Well, we coloured folk have done that for generations. But things are better than they were. I figure Dr Luther King has the right of it. Patience an' peaceful protest is the answer. Plenty decent white folk are on our side. It'll take a bit o' time; but given a few more years an' the good Lord Jesus will lead His coloured children out of darkness.'

'I'm sure you're right,' Richard agreed. 'But what exactly did you do?'

'First we talked o' makin' a break an' tryin' to get away from heah. But reckon that's near impossible. Fer hundreds o' miles round there's nought but marsh, scrub and them awful mountains. Guess we couldn't make it. Seemed to us then we'd best let on to some of the others 'bout our feelin's. Quite a few agreed that up heah we wasn't doin' the Lord's work arter all. No, sir; far from it. We planned ter stir up real trouble fer the badmen who run this outfit. What we were arter was to grab the aircraft, so as we could get away in them. Only chance o' that was a mass defiance of the bosses. Tonight we laid on a meetin'. Where we slipped up was to hold it arter usual time fer

227

lights out. The bosses got on to us. They didn't interfere. Just waited till the folk had dispersed, then picked up the speakers. That was me and Malli heah. The Jamaican, the Moor and a couple o' those dumb bastards who do the chores fer the bosses come fetch us wiv' guns. That's how it happen we're thrown in the can.'

To his listeners this explained why the Prince had left the fortress at such short notice. Evidently when the threat of a revolt had been reported to him by Benito, he had thought it so grave a menace to his plans that he had decided to fly down and deal with the matter himself. To the man who had been speaking Rex said:

'That certainly was hard luck. But you're one hundred per cent right. This Black Power movement is inspired by the Devil. It could lead to bloodshed in hundreds of cities, and there's not a hope of coloured people bettering their lot through it.'

'What you think they'll do wiv' us?' the man asked anxiously.

Neither Rex nor Richard could bring himself to make a truthful reply. It was a certainty that the Prince would never let the two men return to the outer world, where they would tell others of the settlement in the Sala and about what was going on there. Neither would he allow them to go back among their fellow workers and risk their causing others to question the wisdom of the movement. And he was not the man to keep and feed two useless prisoners indefinitely; so the odds were that, within a few hours, he would have them quietly done away with.

Simon was of that opinion, too. But he could not bring himself to refrain from trying to comfort the two poor wretches. So he said, 'Can't do more than guess. Still, they wouldn't want to keep workers who're unwilling. Expect they'll have you flown back to the States, or wherever you come from.'

'Oh, man! I does hope you'se right,' the Negro said miserably. 'I's mighty scared. May the good Lord ha' mercy on His lil' chillen.'

Silence fell. De Richleau slept. The others lay or sat in great discomfort and dozed uneasily through the remaining hours of the night.

It was about six o'clock in the morning when the Zombies opened the door. Covering the Negro and the quadroon with their pistols, they stared at them with glazed eyes then, with jerky gestures, signed to them to get up and leave the cell-like room. Cowed, the two men offered no resistance and disappeared up the stairs. The door was shut on the others and they were again in darkness.

The Duke was in such a deep sleep that he had not woken. Time drifted on. The rest of them were not actually suffering from hunger and thirst, but they would have welcomed a good breakfast, or even a cup of water and some biscuits. But nothing was brought to them. They could only sit there in misery, wondering what form the Prince's vengeance would take for their having killed four of his henchmen.

At a little after eleven o'clock, Benito came to them. He had them wake de Richleau; then, with two patient Zombies as escort, they were taken upstairs and led into the washroom. The Duke's sleep had greatly improved his condition. He told them that, although he was still weak from loss of blood, he now felt only a dull ache in his shoulder.

When they had freshened themselves up, they were taken out to the airstrip. The Prince was at the controls of his 'plane, and the engine was already revving over. In a back seat sat the Moor, El Aziz. Across his knees lay a long, slender sword, the blade of which was only slightly curved.

As soon as they had settled themselves, the Prince said to Benito, 'If there is any more trouble, deal with it promptly, then report to me.' The door was shut and they took off. Three-quarters of an hour later they landed on the island in the Lago de Poopo. During the journey the Prince had not addressed a word to them. When they had all disembarked, he threw a haughty, contemptuous look at them and said to El Aziz:

'As we have no cells here, take them down to the swimming pool. In any case, to lock them up would be unnecessary, as I shall put a spell on them which will prevent them from leaving the fortress.'

Evidently having some further urgent business, he turned away and ran up the hundred and more steps to the fortress with a swiftness which put into the minds of the onlookers that he must be supported by invisible wings.

As de Richleau looked about him, he saw several of the airstrip men glaring balefully at his party. Their attitude showed that they must be aware that he or one of his friends had killed their companion during the previous night. It meant that if, in spite of the Prince, they could get down to the air-field again, the Andeans would probably open fire on them at sight. With Rex's assistance he slowly climbed the long flight of steps and they entered the stronghold.

El Aziz took them down to the big, circular Hall of Divination that served as an ante-room to the temple. As before, it was lit by a rosy glow and was empty. Crossing to the segment of the circular wall that had the panel bearing the reversed crescent upon it, El Aziz pressed a spring and a section slid smoothly back, revealing a long, low chamber.

It was dimly lit and they could see that the walls and ceiling were formed of the big, stone blocks used by the Incas; but an oblong pool filled the centre, and round it was a broad walkway of modern tiles. At the far end the tiled space was wider and there they could make out some low tables and several lounge chairs.

Halting by the entrance, El Aziz signed for them to go ahead. Rex ignored the gesture and asked that a bed should be provided for the wounded Duke. From the expression on the Moor's face it was clear that it delighted him to refuse this request, but he did not even bother to reply. Turning his back, he left them, crossed the Hall of Divination and closed behind him the section of wall leading to the passage.

Rex then led the way along one side of the pool and said, 'In the old days this was the Incas' Treasure chamber. Occasionally the Prince enjoys a swim, so he had it converted to hold water and fitted with all the gadgets that go with a luxury pool. I've swum down here with Silvia and some of the others several times. Lord alone knows what His Satanic Highness means to do with us, but at least we'll be better off here than in that cellar down at the Sala.'

At the far end of the pool there was a bar, holding a good selection of bottles, and several tins of cocktail biscuits and nuts. As Rex went behind the bar, for the first time in days he laughed. Picking up the shaker, he said, 'Sorry there's no ice, but never mind,' and started to pour gin into it. Then he uttered his old crack, 'Come on, folks. Make 'em small but drink 'em quick. It takes a fourth to make an appetite.'

Regretfully de Richleau doused their temporary elation by saying, 'Nothing for me, Rex. I have denied myself alcohol for over a week now. That is important for an Adept who wishes to exert his powers to the full. For you others it does not matter so much, because you are not initiates. All the same, I think you should limit yourselves to two drinks each, because it could be dangerous to slow up your reactions in an emergency.'

Accordingly the Duke drank limejuice and water, and the others had only one snifter to brace them up, followed by a

230

long drink to quench their thirst. As they had had no food that day they made swift inroads into the biscuits, except for the Duke who was determined to continue the semi-fast he had maintained ever since their arrival and, when they had made him as comfortable as possible on one of the lounge chairs, he refused all but a few small handfuls of nuts.

After the grim hours they had been through, this interlude greatly lightened their spirits; but they had had little sleep during the past night, so they soon fell silent and dozed for the greater part of the afternoon.

When they roused, their minds were again filled with thoughts of the dire peril they were in, and they began to speculate gloomily on what horrors the Prince might send against them during the coming night. Richard remarked despondently on there being nothing available with which they might form a pentacle to give them some protection, upon which the Duke said:

'The Prince must have had his mind on other things when he ordered us to be brought down here. The pool will serve us as well, if not better, than a makeshift pentacle. If an attack does come, we can take to the water.'

Looking down at the calm, unruffled sheet, Miranda asked, 'How will that help us?'

'Water, far more than bread, is the staff of life,' the Duke replied. 'One can exist without food for forty days and more; but not without liquid. For that reason most evil manifestations are highly allergic to water. For example, it is one of the few things that hamper the activities of vampires. No vampire can cross running water, not even a little stream.'

Simon asked, 'What do we do then? Stand in the shallow end fully clad, or strip and swim round in circles?'

'It would be best for us to stand in a ring, holding hands. Our vibrations are so well attuned that, when united, there is still a chance that we may be able to fight off anything that is sent against us.'

'Any idea what form the attack will take?' Richard enquired.

'None. He won't try to send us out of our minds by producing thought-forms of people we love in heart-rending situations. Having tried that, he knows it won't work. But he may send more of those revolting elementals. They are terrifying to look at, but a very low form of occult entity; so, if you all keep your nerve, we should be able to resist them. My real fear

231

is that he may summon up one of the mighty forces from the Outer Circle. If he does that, we can only pray that the Lords of Light will take pity on us. Should that happen, though, we'll be saved only at the price of our lives. The whole fortress will be destroyed by an eruption and our present bodies with it.'

After a moment, Rex said, 'Say we do pull through. What then? It's impossible for us to escape because the Prince has put a spell on us.'

'Not through our own efforts,' the Duke agreed. 'The spell will nullify any attempt we might make to break out. But if, by a miracle, someone here took pity on us, he could get us away as though we were so many Zombies.'

'What a hope!' Richard exclaimed bitterly.

'I don't know,' Miranda said hesitantly. 'Remember Silvia put me under hypnosis last night before that awful ceremony. If she hadn't, I think I'd have died of horror and disgust. But she did, and that was quite contrary to the delight in sadism that everyone else here displays. They would have enjoyed seeing me suffer the most frightful agonies of apprehension. She saved me from that, so she can't be altogether bad.'

De Richleau smiled. 'You're right, my dear. As the Maiden of the Grand Coven of South America, she must be a powerful witch and fully approve the object that her companions are working for. Yet, unless I am much mistaken, a spark of light remains within her.'

Turning to Rex, he went on, 'Would you mind telling us exactly what your relations with Silvia are—or rather were? That might prove helpful.'

Rex spread out his hands. 'From you folks I've nothing to hide about my affair with her. If we hadn't been either too much up against it, or so tired out these past few days, I'd have given you the full story before now.

'It was this way. I met her in B.A. about eighteen months ago. I fell for her, and she didn't hide the fact that she took a good view of me. That is one of her attractions. She never seeks to disguise her feelings and calls a spade a spade. You can either like her or do the other thing, and she doesn't play hard to get. Anyhow, we made a date and, after we'd dined, she gave me that dazzling smile of hers and said, "You know, one of us may fall under a bus tomorrow, so why should we wait? Let's go back to my apartment."

'There was nothing of the whirlwind courtship about it. We were just two sophisticated people who, during our lives, had

232

had quite a lot of fun with the opposite sex, and we liked each other. It was as simple as that. In the circumstances, it would have been a pretty queer thing if we hadn't enjoyed our roll in the hay. And you bet we did. That's how Silvia became my mistress.

'You know her record. She's slept around more than most women, and she doesn't give a cuss what people think of her. But she's got at least one good principle. I know she did her best to lead you up the garden path down at Punta Arenas; but, in the ordinary way, she never tells a lie. In view of her past, during our first few months I more or less took it for granted that when I had to go off on business to other capitals in South America, she would amuse herself with other guys. That didn't worry me over-much, because I've never really been in love with her. We had some wonderful times and were always happy when we were together, but I wasn't in love to the extent that I would have chucked everything and followed her to the other end of the world.

'I've a hunch that she felt the same way about me, but liked me enough not to tangle with anyone else when, now and then, I had to leave her for a week or so. That was the conclusion I came to after a while, because she was always so frank about everything—except in one particular. I used to spend two or three nights a week with her. Other nights we'd entertain or go out independently, and after such occasions she would always tell me how she had spent her evening. But once a month she would keep some date and clam up tight on what she'd been up to.

'Being fairly regular but so far apart, it didn't seem plausible that these dates were with some other guy. But naturally I was curious, so one night about six months ago I went to her apartment and waited for her to return. When she did get back, in the early hours of the morning, she was pretty potted. It was then that she spilled the beans to me that on these dates she attended seances.

'I've told you how things developed from there on, how she induced me to take an interest in the game, and how, when I learned about this Black Power movement, I felt that it was up to me to play along with them so that I could find out enough about this god-awful conspiracy to take steps which would bust it wide open.

'As you know, after I quit B.A., Silvia put in her annual few weeks at Punta Arenas, then came up to Santiago and on here.

When she arrived we enjoyed the happy sort of reunion that we used to have after one of my trips to Rio or Lima. Since then, up till the day before yesterday, we've carried on just as we used to. Now you know how things stand between us.'

'Ner.' Simon shook his bird-like head. 'Since then situation's changed. She knows now that you ratted on them. Never even made a protest when the Prince deprived you of the use of your legs.'

'For her to have done so would have been useless. And she knew it.'

'Do you think,' asked the Duke, 'that, in spite of your having betrayed them, she still has tender feelings for you?'

'I wouldn't know. After all we've been to each other, she'd not be natural if she wasn't sorry to see me in the jam I'm in now. But it could be that she's too far committed to Satan to do more than stand on the side-lines and let matters take their course. Your guess is as good as mine.'

'I appreciate that. But you're probably right that her attitude depends on how deep she has got herself in. She is a witch, of course, but there are witches and witches. The majority of the poor old women who were burnt at the stake after the great persecution that started in the time of James I were innocent, and seized upon only because they lived alone, were ugly and kept a white mouse in a cage, or some other pet. Most of the others were capable of no more than blighting the crops of neighbours who had behaved badly towards them, or putting a murrain on their cattle, or causing their wives to miscarry. But there were a number who acted as midwives. They stole foetuses, resulting from premature births and unbaptised infants, then ate parts of them and used others as ingredients in revolting brews that could have a most potent effect on those who partook of them. They aided gangs of wreckers by raising hurricanes that drove ships on to the rocks, could influence people at a distance and brought death to their victims by melting wax images before a slow fire. How far do you suppose that Silvia has gone, in her desire for excitement, along this path of evil?'

Rex sighed. 'It's hard to say. Maybe she didn't take me into her full confidence because she has cast spells she knew I wouldn't approve of. But I've known her perform magics that you could class as bringing punishment on those who deserved it.

'One time a young maid of hers was driven out into the

234

country and raped. Silvia managed to get hold of a pair of the man's socks and did her stuff on them. A few days later he contracted galloping syphilis and, within six weeks, his genitals rotted away.

'Another time a woman friend came to her and told her in tears how her husband used to whip her every night, and showed her her bottom, which was criss-crossed with bloody weals. Silvia had the girl bring her the whip, then returned it to her with instructions that next time she was in for a beating, she should complain to her husband that it still had dried blood on it and that he must wash it before he used it again. He took it into the bathroom and put it under the tap. What Silvia had done to it Heaven alone knows, but I imagine she had somehow charged it with electricity. Anyway, when this guy held it under the water, it earthed. The shock darn' near killed him and he got a most ghastly burn across the palm of his hand. It's clenched now, like a claw, and he'll never again be able to use it.'

'Those are certainly not the type of enchantments one would expect from a woman associated with the Prince and the Baron,' de Richleau commented. 'Either would have regarded the raping of the maid and the whipping of the wife as deeds inspired by an elemental, and approved of them. I think we can take it as proof that Silvia has not yet crossed the Abyss and become fully committed to the Left-Hand Path.'

'She has always said that she went into the game because it offered a new form of interest and excitement. She has much too happy a nature to be evil, and I doubt if she has ever seriously considered what the Black Power movement may ultimately lead to. But she enjoys the power that being a witch gives her.'

' "Power corrupts and absolute power corrupts absolutely",' de Richleau quoted. 'It seems to me that she is now standing on the brink. Since she enjoys power, they will give it to her—at a price. It is always so with those who dabble in the Black Art. It can be only a matter of time before she becomes corrupted, and as evil as the rest of them. In my opinion it is only because they have found her very useful in other ways that they have not so far lured her into taking the fatal step.'

'I guess you're right. Same as with myself. They thought me to be too valuable to them as a foreign exchange expert to press me to do things they knew I wouldn't do willingly.'

'How far have your own studies of the occult brought you?'

'Oh, I'm still only a neophyte, just coming up for the second

235

grade. I'm capable of only small-time stuff. In secret, I concentrated on a friend of mine and succeeded in curing him of arthritis. For fun, one day I caused that old stick-in-the-mud, Harold Haag, the manager of our bank in Buenos Aires, to make a hopeless mess of his accounts. I can make cold water become tepid, but not to boil as yet. I'm getting on well as a clairvoyant, and I've made a beginning at thought transference with Silvia.'

'Ah!' exclaimed the Duke. 'There we have something. Could you manage to get into touch with her, and find out how she is disposed towards us?'

'No, I don't think I could do that. I can send thoughts out, but not receive them. At least, only now and then in a garbled version, and sometimes I have put quite a wrong interpretation on them.'

'To send her a message is the more important. Let her know that we have great cause to fear what may become of us. Ask her to aid us if she possibly can. Tell her that if she knows of any way in which we might escape we should be forever grateful if she would give us guidance to it.'

'O.K. I'll do that.' Rex got down on the floor and arranged himself in the traditional cross-legged position, then bowed his head. The Duke looked round at the others and said:

'There is no need to leave your seats, but all of you must remain silent and pray for Rex's success.'

For the best part of an hour they sat there. Rex appeared to have gone to sleep, but at last he raised his head and shook it. 'Maybe she got the message, maybe not. There was no response at all, so it's impossible to say.'

Soon afterwards two of the green-clad servitors appeared and brought them a meal, but it consisted only of a peasant fare, coarse bread and a basin each of maize mush, which made it clear that the Prince did not intend them to derive any enjoyment from their nourishment.

By the time they had finished the evening was well advanced, so they began to make preparations for the night. After they had visited the washrooms, the Duke had them arrange all the cushions from the easy chairs in one group on the pavement near the edge of the pool. The five of them then sat down on the cushions back to back, and he said:

'None of us must leave the others in any circumstance. Not only is union strength, but anyone who failed to remain in physical contact with the rest would be overcome much more easily. If an attack develops, whatever form it takes we must get up, form a line with clasped hands as quickly as we can; then, when I give the word, scramble into the shallow end of the pool here.'

Suddenly, to their consternation, the radiance that lit the swimming pool was switched off. The only light now came through the open panel of the Hall of Divination. They watched it anxiously, fearing that it, too, would go out. It remained on, but as it was over eighty feet away, it was no more than a bright patch faintly illuminating the gloom between it and them.

Looking uneasily about them, they began to imagine that the shadows thrown by pillars and buttresses were solidifying into strange forms and gruesome shapes that menaced them. The eerie half-light played havoc with their nerves and strung them up nearly to breaking point.

For a long while they hoped that Silvia would come to them, but at length they reconciled themselves to the belief that either she had not received Rex's message, or was in the enemy camp and had no intention of aiding them even if it was possible for her to do so.

At about eleven o'clock, they all jerked erect. They had caught the sound of footsteps on stone. Anxiously they peered in the direction of the ante-room, hoping that, after all, Silvia was coming to them. Holding their breath, they craned forward, only to release it in bitter disappointment a moment later. It was Singra, the Pakistani. He did not even glance through the opening into the almost dark swimming pool, but turned in the opposite direction and went into the temple. Having presumably performed some duty there after some ten minutes he came out again, recrossed the circular ante-chamber and disappeared.

Utter silence fell again. Another hour dragged by. Nothing happened. Suddenly Richard burst out, 'I can't stand this much longer. Let's have a sing-song.'

'Excellent idea,' agreed the Duke. 'I ought to have thought of that myself.' Spontaneously Rex started 'Rock of Ages', and they all joined in. 'Onward, Christian Soldiers' followed; but none of them was sure of the words of even these best-known hymns, so they fell back on old popular numbers: 'Roll out the Barrel', 'If you were the only girl in the world', 'Keep the home fires burning', 'Land of Hope and Glory', and so on.

As they sang, they never ceased to keep an uneasy watch for

some evil thing to materialise out of the shadows. But still the attack they expected failed to develop. After singing for two hours, they were so hoarse that the sound of their voices made a travesty of the tunes. At about two o'clock in the morning they fell silent. All of them felt utterly played out. By then they had ceased, except occasionally, even to throw apprehensive glances into the shadows. Still leaning back to back, their heads dropped on their chests. All of them except de Richleau fell asleep.

Without warning the dim lights of the swimming pool went on. As they roused, the Duke glanced at his watch and saw that it was morning. He told the others that while they had slept there had been no disturbances, and they felt that, for the time being, the danger was past.

They breakfasted off the remaining biscuits and nuts, then settled themselves again in the lounge chairs. De Richleau dropped off into a doze, while the others again speculated fruitlessly on what the Prince intended to do with them. As they had killed four of his principal lieutenants, they had no illusions that he would show them mercy, and could only suppose that his having left them in peace during the night meant that he intended to play a cat and mouse game with them.

Soon after they had eaten, the white pilot Dubecq and the half-caste Cervantes, both of whom they had glimpsed in the bar on their first arrival at the fortress, came down for a swim. Neither of them took any notice of the prisoners, so it could be assumed that the Prince had given orders that they were not to be interfered with.

After that nothing happened until about half past ten. Their attention was then caught by a new sound: that of high heels tapping on the stone floor of the ante-room. A moment later Silvia appeared. She was wearing a white Grecian robe, with gold embroidery at the neck and wrists. They all sat forward eagerly but, without giving them a glance, she let the robe fall to her feet, kicked off her mules and, naked, dived into the pool.

'By Jove! She's a dish, isn't she?' Richard murmured. 'I've never seen a girl with such splendid shoulders and so slim a waist.'

'Woman,' the Duke corrected him. 'We know her to be close on fifty. Obviously she's taken great care of herself; but latterly, I don't doubt, she has used her occult powers to renew her youth. The old beldames of whom we were talking last night were not in a class that knew the spells needed to make

238

themselves physically attractive. But really potent witches always appear young and beautiful.'

Meanwhile Rex had stood up and was stripping off his clothes. It had been his custom to swim nude with Silvia, and he did not want her to think that he had suddenly become prudish; so, ignoring Miranda's presence, he dived in without a stitch on.

The onlookers watched them eagerly, but Rex and Silvia did not greet each other. At times they crossed each other's path, but anyone observing them would have taken them for complete strangers. After about ten minutes Silvia climbed out of the pool, dried herself on a towel she had brought with her and, without any indication that she was aware of the presence of the prisoners, walked away through the ante-room.

Standing in the shallow end of the pool, Rex said to his friends in a low voice, 'The Prince may be overlooking us, so we didn't dare exchange more than a few sentences, and those only because we were in the water. I did get through to her last night. She had no excuse to come down here then; but nearly every morning when she's here she has a swim, and the Prince hasn't said that while we are being kept prisoner she is not to.

'He is so furious about our having killed von Thumm and the others that he can't make up his mind what would be the most painful death to inflict on us. As we hoped might be the case, she would help us to get away if she could. You see, she's got it on her conscience that it is her fault that we have all been drawn into this. But there's nix that she can do. If the Prince even suspected that she had qualms about us, he'd blast her where she stood. So she can only play along with him.'

Their hope that Silvia would be able to aid them had been a very slender one, so they were not unduly cast down to learn that she was powerless to do so. But they were pleased, particularly Rex, to know that her mind was not entirely dominated by the Prince.

Later in the morning the skull-headed Negro, Mazambi, came down to bathe. Then, at midday, the prisoners were brought the same unappetising meal that they had been given the previous evening.

During the afternoon they dozed for a while; then, to keep their minds free from thinking of the most unpleasant forms of death and wondering which the Prince would decide on for them, they told stories, held a spelling bee and reminisced

239

about their past adventures. Somehow they got through the dragging hours until, late in the evening, another ration of bread and mush was brought to them. Afterwards they held another sing-song; then, no longer fearful now that the Prince would send occult forces to attack them, settled down for the night.

Early next morning they all refreshed themselves by going in for a swim. In due course, Dubecq, Cervantes, and the Egyptian, Ben Yussuf, came down and swam. Then Silvia again arrived, so Rex went in to exchange a few words with her each time they passed one another in the water.

When she had gone he had the most exciting news for his friends. With a wide grin he said, 'There's more trouble down at the settlement. Seems those two poor guys who were in the cellar with us started something. The speeches they made at the meeting they called met with pretty wide agreement. Everyone down there is now debating whether this Black Power movement would pay off in the long run, and there is to be another meeting tonight. It's quite on the cards that a lot of them will decide to down tools unless they are sent back to their home towns.'

'By Jove! That really is something,' Richard exclaimed. 'It might wreck the whole movement.'

Rex nodded. 'There's still better to come. It seems there's a limit to even the Prince's powers. Silvia says that the binding spell he has put on us to keep us here is not operative at a distance. If he goes down to the settlement to quell this meeting tonight, as she thinks he means to, she should be able to get us out.'

'Oh, how wonderful!' Miranda cried. 'I knew she was good at heart. But when he comes back and finds out what she's done, won't he punish her most terribly?'

'I thought of that, and you're right. She told me she wouldn't dare remain here. If she did, it would cost her her life; so she will come with us.'

'Surely the Prince would not go off leaving her in charge here?' remarked the Duke. 'What about Mazambie, Dubecq, Singra and the rest? How would she deal with them?'

'She said that if von Thumm or Glasshill were still alive, that would have stymied her, because they were capable of reading her thoughts. But the rest of the bunch are not; so she'll offer to make them a *bouillabaisse* for dinner from the fish and what-have-you from the lake. It's quite a thing of

240

hers, and very strongly flavoured, so they won't notice the drug she means to put in it, and that will knock them all for six. About the retainers she says we don't need to worry. Mentally they're pretty low material, and it just wouldn't occur to them to question anything she does.'

'May the Lords of Light be praised for having brought her back on to the Right-Hand Path,' murmured the Duke. But a moment later, he said anxiously, 'We shall still have one big hurdle to get over, though. As far as we know there are still two 'planes on the airstrip. The Prince will take one to fly himself down to the Sala; but how are we to get hold of the other? The Andean mechanics down there will jump at the chance of avenging their comrade, and I can subdue only one of them at a time. Unless Silvia has some way of dealing with them, the odds are that several of us may be shot down before we can reach the aircraft.'

Rex made a grimace. 'I hadn't thought of that, and it's a nasty one. Maybe Silvia could get us weapons. If so, and we could take them by surprise, we'd be able to put them out of the game before they had a chance to shoot us up.'

The best part of two nights and a day had passed since they had been caught. During those long hours they had slept little and had been in constant fear of the unguessable, but certainly agonising, death the Prince would inflict upon them. In consequence, this sudden prospect that Silvia might save them dispelled their utter despair and cheered them all enormously. Compared with the unknown horror that had filled them with such awful foreboding, they were inclined to take lightly the physical hazard of dealing with the Andean mechanics.

Now, buoyed up with optimism, they passed the rest of the morning in an almost happy frame of mind. With midday there arrived another unappetising meal, then in the afternoon they dozed. When, in the evening, food was brought to them again, as soon as the servitors had gone Richard said:

'Unless everything goes wrong, as soon as we get in that 'plane, we'll break open its stores and enjoy some decent food, so I'm not eating any more of this muck.'

De Richleau's spells of Yoga-induced sleep had done wonders for him. His wound was healing well and his voice was perceptibly more vigorous, as he said, 'Let's not count our chickens yet. You may need all your strength before morning. Think of yourself as back in the nursery and eat up your porridge like a good little boy.'

In due course the lights went out and the big chamber was plunged in darkness except at the far end, where the faint glow from the ante-room of the temple still showed.

Despite their new-found optimism, at the back of all their minds there nagged the disturbing thought that the Prince might decide to begin the torment with which he had threatened them before he flew down to the Sala; so, in order to offer the maximum resistance, they again arranged themselves sitting back to back on the cushions.

Knowing that Silvia would not be free to act until her associates had fallen into a heavy, drug-induced sleep, they thought it very unlikely that she would come to them before midnight, so they whiled away the late evening hours with such patience as they could muster.

At last midnight came and they all roused to a new alertness, listening eagerly for the least sound that might break the stillness. As time drifted by, their tension grew, but nothing occurred to relieve it. At ever more frequent intervals Rex gave a quick, nervous glance at the luminous dial of his wrist watch. One o'clock came, then two o'clock. Their suspense became almost unbearable. At last, a little before three o'clock de Richleau broke a long silence to voice the thought that, for an hour or more, had been tormenting them all and renewing their fears about their future.

'My friends,' he said softly. 'I fear we must face it. Something has gone wrong, or Silvia would have come to us by now.'

With heavy sighs they agreed, but sat on, still hoping desperately, through what seemed the never-ending hours until, at last, morning came and the light went on.

Weary and miserable, they got up and helped themselves to drinks at the bar. Now sleepy from their long vigil, they settled down in the lounge chairs where, still half awake, they mused with fresh apprehension on what fate might hold in store for them, and what might have happened to Silvia.

Her failure to appear might be owing to the Prince's having decided not to go down to the Sala after all. On the other hand it might be because the drug she had intended to give his lieutenants had failed to work on one or more of them. Still worse, her intention to help them escape might have been found out and she was now a prisoner who would share with them her Master's vengeance.

At about half past eight Dubecq and Cervantes came down

to swim. As they splashed about and shouted to each other in the water, they showed no sign at all of having just come out of a heavy sleep, which seemed to indicate that they had not partaken of Silvia's drugged *bouillabaisse*.

Then, no more than five minutes after they had left, to the immense relief of Rex and his friends Silvia emerged from the ante-room, threw off her robe and, without a glance in their direction, dived into the water.

Within a couple of minutes Rex had pulled off his clothes and was swimming towards her. For nearly a quarter of an hour they passed and repassed each other without, apparently, exchanging a word; then Silvia climbed out at the far end. While she was drying herself, Rex stood only waist deep in the water and, in a low voice, said to his friends:

'She was stymied last night by the Prince's not going down to the Sala after all. Seems the trouble there has reached such proportions that he, with a few of his lieutenants and half a dozen Zombies, would be incapable of controlling such numbers by ordinary means; so he's taken a new decision. He means to turn the people there from volunteers into slaves.'

'How does he propose to do that?' Richard asked.

'By occult means. I gather that there's an exceptional source of power that they term "The Pit". He plans to open it, call up a host of elementals and send them down to the settlement.'

'The Pit!' exclaimed de Richleau in horror. 'Heavens alive! Can he really mean to open the gates of Hell?'

Rex nodded. 'That's what Silvia said. The elementals he conjures up from it will scare those poor do-gooders out of their wits for a few nights. Then they will be placed at the disposal of Benito and his pals, and anybody who refuses to do his job will wake up to find a demon sitting on his chest. It is going to be a horrible business, but it will give us a break. The Pit is somewhere in the rain forests of Brazil, and the Prince means to fly down to it tomorrow evening. With luck, while he's absent Silvia will be able to get us away.'

'Provided we're still alive to be got away,' Simon remarked gloomily.

'You've gotten a point there. It's still on the cards that he'll give us ours before he goes down to this hell-spot. But, at the moment, he's too concerned about the rebellion down at the settlement to think of much else. I gather that a good half of the stooges would have quit the place by now if they'd had transport; but it's so utterly cut off that they're scared of dying in the salt marshes or the arid mountains. Anyhow, Silvia says the Prince has hardly mentioned us since he sent us down here. This "opening of the Pit" business is going to be an all-time high Satanic jamboree. He is summoning the whole of the thirteen senior covens that operate in South America to attend it, and it's making the arrangements that is keeping him so fully occupied now.'

'What are elementals?' Miranda asked the Duke.

'They are quasi-intelligent thought creations,' he replied. 'Every thought we have produces an invisible form, and beautiful thoughts beget auras of good about the thinker. But evil thoughts are the product of evil habits and, if persisted in, they build up an elemental. Unless called up by a Black magician for some malevolent purpose, they are rarely seen. But alcoholics see them as green rats and other horrors. There are, of course, far worse ones created by murder, brutality, rape and all the vices. Drug addicts are sometimes driven to suicide by being haunted by them. The forms they take are hideous. Perhaps you have seen paintings by Breugel the Elder? In some of the most famous ones elementals are admirably portrayed.'

Miranda shuddered. 'Yes, when I was "finishing" in Paris, before I lost my sight, I was taken to the Louvre and saw some Breugels there. How awful for those poor people whom they are being sent to terrify. Are they only evil spirits or have they some sort of life?'

'They certainly have life of a kind, because to keep in being they have to feed. They batten on every sort of unpleasant substance: offal, faeces, urine, sexual secretions, menstrual blood, the pus from sores, drunkard's vomit and corpses. Some of them are termed Incubi and Succubi. The former visit women and the latter men in their beds at night. Except when deliberately summoned up by witches and wizards, they remain invisible, but copulate with their victims, drawing the vitality out of them. Their need for sustenance keeps them constantly on the prowl, seeking out vicious men and women who will provide them with regular nourishment.'

'Why, then, should they be down in the Pit?' asked Richard.

'Those would be elementals whose original creators are dead, so at the moment they are only the lowest sort of spirit. They are eagerly waiting to be despatched to someone whose vices would re-create them, or upon some mission that would gratify their Infernal Creator.'

244

During this second day that the friends had spent beside the swimming pool, their routine had not varied. The meals brought them continued to be prison fare. They twice went in for a swim and passed the time playing games which needed neither cards nor dice. As evening came, apprehension grew in them that the Prince would come to, or send for them that night, and despatch them, most painfully, to eternity. But somehow they managed to get through the long hours until morning came again and Silvia came down for her daily bathe.

After talking with her Rex reported that the Prince was still fully engaged on the preparations for the great occult ceremony that was to take place that night. He had been on communication with Adepts of the Left-Hand Path far and near; and appointed new Chiefs to the covens previously led by von Thumm, Glasshill, Kaputa and Pucara. He also intended to take with him the majority of his remaining lieutenants, of whom he had six there in the fortress and two down at the settlement.

In spite of the turmoil and partial stoppage of work there, he was confident that, for some time to come, his dupes would make no attempt to march out in a body. Any bid to cross the hundreds of miles of wilderness that separated the Sala from civilisation needed organisation and, as was to be expected, so far no-one among those woolly-minded people had emerged as a leader.

Moreover, the intelligence of elementals was very low; so, when they were launched against the do-gooders they could not be expected to discriminate. The Prince's lieutenants, although capable of driving them off, would be seriously plagued by them, and the Zombies would be scared out of what wits they had left.

In consequence, the Prince had decided to withdraw his own people from the settlement for three days, thus enabling them to attend the ceremony. Meanwhile, the dupes down there would be subjected to a reign of terror. After the three days their Satanic overlords would return. Using the threat of causing further terrifying manifestations, they would restore order and get the people back to work.

Silvia had not dared ask the Prince's intentions towards the prisoners, as it might have proved fatal to draw his attention to them. But the previous evening he had volunteered the information that he meant to continue to keep them on ice; so that when he returned from having opened the Pit, he could relish

245

inflicting a long and painful death on them. It was his intention to leave El Aziz in charge of the fortress, and with him he would have the Zombies who were to be brought up from the settlement.

That had not given Silvia grounds for worry, since she felt confident that, with the aid of de Richleau, who was rapidly recovering from his wound, she could overcome El Aziz. What had worried her was the Prince's having made it clear that he took it for granted that she would accompany him to the ceremony. For her to do so would lay all their plans in ruins. But she had thought of a valid excuse to remain behind. When she went up from her swim, she intended to tell him that she had been called to the astral and go into a trance. It was certain that he would be furious, but such a summons from a powerful Master temporarily out of incarnation could not be ignored.

On the previous day Rex had put to her the hazard they would have to face from the enmity of the Andean mechanics, before they could get hold of an aircraft. But about that she had now reassured him. The odds were that all the aircraft would be used, so she was not counting on one being left behind. But below the almost sheer cliff on the far side of the stronghold there was a small harbour, which could be reached by steps cut in the rock, and in it there was a powerful motor boat. It would easily carry them the thirty miles to the north-east corner of the lake. There lay the little town of Poopo, which gave the lake its name and, only a mile or so beyond it, ran one of the greatest arterial roads in the world: the Pan-American Highway.

Learning of her plan cheered them immensely. Instead of the risks entailed by a flight through the mountains, or having to march, ill-equipped and with scant provisions, for several days through uninhabited areas, it meant that within a couple of hours of leaving the fortress they would be in direct touch with civilisation. Cars and long-distance lorries were constantly passing along the broad highway; so there should be little difficulty in getting a lift which would carry them right out of the area in which, during the past twelve days, they had miraculously survived so much suffering and danger.

But all of them needed no telling that 'there is many a slip 'twixt the cup and the lip'. Would the Prince sense that Silvia was deceiving him? Would she succeed in evading El Aziz or, failing that, would they be able to overcome him? De Richleau

246

had assessed the Moor's psychic powers as only a little less than those von Thumm had possessed. Silvia, not having passed the Abyss, certainly could not contend with him, and the Duke had lost so much blood from his wound that his powers were far from fully restored. Worst hazard of all, would the Prince, while flying across to Brazil, spare a moment to overlook them, learn that they were escaping and promptly take measures to stop them?

As the day wore on, the elation they had felt on learning of Silvia's plan to get them speedily to the Pan-American Highway gradually evaporated. Fears that some hitch would occur, or that the Prince would again alter his arrangements at the last moment, took its place. Should their attempt to escape fail, they realised only too well what the consequences would be for them. The Duke had forbidden them the possibility of endeavouring to abbreviate their sufferings by suicide. With flayed nerves they would have to stick out their torment until unconsciousness brought them merciful oblivion.

All through the morning they sat nearly silent, exchanging a remark only now and again. Their midday meal of maize gruel and coarse bread was brought to them. This fare, unappetising at any time, now made them feel sick at the sight of it. Somehow they got most of it down. They then endeavoured to settle to their afternoon doze, but found it impossible to put out of their minds the alternative possibilities of freedom or death that the night would bring.

At about three o'clock they were roused by the sound of footsteps in the ante-chamber. Looking swiftly across the pool, they saw that it was El Aziz, accompanied by two Zombies. Purposefully the powerful Moor strode along the side of the pool towards them. Coming to a halt, he said tersely:

'His Highness the Prince desires speech with you. Follow me.'

Getting up from their chairs, they obeyed. Without a glance behind him, he led them through the Hall of Divination, along the stone-walled passages and up to the library. The Prince was alone in the room, except for his familiar, the beautiful Blue Persian cat, and standing in front of a blazing log fire. Having surveyed them for a moment, he smiled and said:

'The stubble on your chins does not improve your appearance, and the lady's hair looks like a bird's nest. But no matter. These physical imperfections will shortly be burned away. For a purpose which is no concern of yours, tonight I intend to

247

open the Pit. Apart from a comparatively small circle of Adepts, only the entities on the higher planes know of its existence; but, deep in the rain forests of Brazil, there are the ruins of an ancient temple—probably the oldest in the world. It is one of the few gateways by which man can physically contact that part of the Great God's domain which is termed the Underworld. I have decided that there could be no more fitting end for you than to enter it while still alive. So I am taking you to Brazil with me.'

19

The Opening of the Pit

The Prince's words came as a most shattering blow. Frequently as their hopes of escape had been eroded by fears that, for a dozen reasons, they would be prevented from getting away, hope *does* 'spring eternal in the human breast'. After seven days of terrible uncertainty they had, that morning, felt incredibly keyed up but confident that, before dawn came again, they would be safe and free. Now, at the eleventh hour, they were to be dragged off to die in a manner the horror of which they could not even imagine.

Like invisible armour, the aura of power round the evil Prince protected him from attack. To argue or plead they knew to be equally futile. When he summoned El Aziz and two of his Zombies to take them away, there was no alternative but to submit and allow themselves to be escorted out of the stronghold, down to the airstrip.

The only aircraft there was a twenty-seater passenger 'plane. Pierre Dubecq already sat at the controls. Near it stood Benito, the Pakistani, the Egyptian and the two Negroes. Presumably the Spanish half-caste, Miguel Cervantes, had flown off one of the other 'planes as, now that the prisoners were to be taken down to the rendezvous, it was no longer necessary to leave anyone in the fortress other than the hypnotised servitors. The Prince came down the steps, followed by the remaining Zombies that Benito had brought up from the settlement, and took his seat beside the pilot. All the others followed him into the 'plane. The prisoners were seated together about halfway along the aircraft. De Richleau glanced round and gave a sigh. Against such a formidable array of black vibrations, even had the Prince not been present it would not have been possible for him to do anything at all.

The door was slammed shut, the engine revved up. Suddenly there was a shout from near the front of the 'plane, an arm pointed upwards. Rex and Richard, who were sitting on the same side of the aircraft, looked in that direction. They saw a woman descending the steps. One glance at her halo of strawberry blonde hair was enough to tell them that it was Silvia. She was coming down the steep steps two and three at a time. They marvelled that she succeeded in keeping her balance. Had she stumbled, she would have pitched forward, bounced down the rest of the flight and ended up a crumpled heap of broken bones and blood at the bottom.

By a miracle she reached the tarmac safely and, her long legs flying, came racing towards the aircraft. The Prince had put his hand on the arm of the pilot. The engine died. Someone opened the door of the 'plane. White-faced and panting Silvia was hauled into it. While watching her make her dash to join them, everyone had fallen silent, so the friends heard her gasp out to the Prince:

'I persuaded the Master to allow me to leave the astral. I . . . I couldn't miss this.'

He gave her a smile of approbation and she collapsed into a vacant seat a few rows behind him. The engine revved up again. The 'plane made a smooth take-off.

The route the aircraft took was north-east across the lake. It had been in the air only a few minutes when the friends saw below them the small, straggling town of Poopo, where they had hoped to land in freedom that night. Twenty minutes later they had crossed the eastern Andes, leaving La Paz on their left. The pilot found the Rio Beni and followed its course up to its junction with the Memora river. From that point he took a more easterly course, keeping in sight the mighty Madeira river for about a hundred miles, then he turned north towards the upper waters of the Amazon. Another hundred or more miles, and he began to come down.

They had been in the air for the best part of four hours and, after leaving the mountains behind, had been flying all the time over dense areas of jungle, broken here and there by patches of waste land. The only villages were situated many miles apart along the rivers. Otherwise there was no sign of human habitation.

Twilight had fallen, but as they descended they approached two clearings in the forest, both lit by a number of bonfires. On the larger, for which they were heading, they could make out a dozen or more aircraft of varying sizes, which had evidently brought the senior covens of witches and wizards from other parts of South America to this Grand Sabbat.

Slowly the 'plane sank to earth, bumped three times on the uneven ground, then slowed to a halt. A crowd of some hundred and fifty people ran towards it. As the Prince emerged from the cockpit, he was greeted with a great ovation. Men and women of every shade of colour pressed forward to kiss his hands.

After a while the greater part of the multitude withdrew, leaving in the Prince's company only his lieutenants, several men, who were evidently the chiefs of other covens he had summoned, and Silvia. As she had alighted from the 'plane, Rex had heard the Prince say to her, 'I am so pleased that you managed to return to earth and accompany me. I have quite enough on my hands tonight without having to choose another woman to take the role of the "Maiden".'

The prisoners stood a little apart, with El Aziz keeping an eye on them, and his armed Zombies close at hand. De Richleau assumed that the Prince and the group about him were discussing the form the ceremonial should take, or it might be that they were killing time while waiting for the completion of the assembly for, nearly half an hour after they had landed, another belated aircraft came in.

The conference seemed to go on interminably, and this period of waiting put a great strain on the prisoners. They had now accepted that there was no escape, and that before morning they would certainly be dead. Having keyed themselves up to face whatever fate might be inflicted on them, their one thought was now to get it over.

Simon stood with his arm about Miranda's waist. Her head rested on his shoulder. From time to time he murmured endearments and strove to comfort her. The Duke had been with his three friends in too many tight corners to feel the need to urge them to have fortitude. But he did for a while speak of the fact that no-one is ever subjected to more pain than he can bear—to ensure that is one of the duties of each person's Guardian Angel—and that, although they were about to leave their physical bodies, they would not be separated. They would ascend together to the astral, and there would be many long-time friends there to welcome them.

At last the conference ended, torches were lit from the bonfires and a procession was formed. Half a dozen torch-bearers led the way, followed by the Prince and Silvia. After them came the chiefs of nine covens and deputies for the other four of which von Thumm, Glasshill, Kaputa and Pucara had been the chiefs representing in all the one hundred and sixty-nine witches and warlocks who had assembled to take part in this Grand thirteen-coven Sabbat. Behind the chiefs came the rank

251

and file. The prisoners brought up the rear, escorted by the Zombies.

Leaving the big, open space where the aircraft had landed, they entered what amounted to a tunnel that had been cut through the dark forest. In the light of the torches the boles of gigantic trees, some of them as much as thirty feet in circumference, loomed upon either side. Above, only occasionally could a few stars be seen; for, in most places, the topmost branches met overhead. They were an immense height. From them trailed the green ropes of lianas and other creepers, making the sides of this long lane so dense that they could not be penetrated except at a dozen feet an hour by the arduous use of a machete.

The only sounds that broke the stillness of the night were the steady padding of the many marching feet and an occasional swift rustle in the undergrowth. Although little of it was visible, the forest teemed with life. Occasionally they glimpsed a boa-constrictor hanging head down from a low branch and, along others, a jaguar or wild cat crouched, its yellow eyes fixed and glowing as they caught the light from the torches.

The tunnel was over a mile in length, then it debouched into the other clearing lit by bonfires they had seen from the aircraft. In the centre stood the ruin of what had evidently once been a large temple. Broad flights of steps led up to a pillared portico that was cracked and broken. The roof was gone, but there was no debris on the floor, and urns holding masses of orchids lined the walls.

It had no resemblance to an Inca building and, indeed, it was several hundred miles outside the territory the Incas had occupied even when their Empire was at its maximum extent; but there was a definite suggestion of Egyptian architecture about it, and the Duke thought that it had probably been built by Atlanteans who had survived the deluge that had submerged their great island about 9600 B.C.

The Prince and the chiefs of covens entered the temple while the mass of the people remained outside. At its far end there were two low doorways. Passing through one of them, the Prince and his entourage disappeared, except for El Aziz, who waited until the prisoners were brought forward then led them in and lined them up at right angles to one side of what had been the altar. In front of it lay a strange phenomenon. Instead of ancient stone covering the whole floor, there was an area about twelve feet square, formed of some other substance.

252

It looked like a thick, leprous skin, with some form of life beneath it, for it slowly pulsed and undulated.

While the prisoners were still looking at it with repulsion and dread, the multitude had been taking off their clothes outside the temple. Now they began to trickle in: tall and short, fat and thin, their naked bodies forming a motley mass ranging in colour from pink to coal black. There was no wind, and the humid atmosphere was so hot that many of them were still sweating from the march.

When they had all assembled in the body of the temple, a trumpet sounded. It was the signal for the Prince, and those who had accompanied him to the rooms behind the altar, to return and take their places. He was now clad in flowing robes of white satin, on which were embroidered in black the signs of the Zodiac. Upon his proud head he wore a triple crown that resembled the tiara of a Pope. The other Satanic dignitaries had robes of varying colours, emblazoned with dragons, serpents, toads and other beasts associated with the Satanic cult. The Prince took up a central position in front of the altar, his assistants lined up on the far side from the prisoners of the square of crepitating skin. Silvia, now sheathed in skin-tight gold and wearing a black crown on her strawberry-blonde hair, placed herself facing the Prince, on the nave side of the sinister square.

Silence fell. Suddenly the Prince lifted both his arms. A tremendous shout went up from the congregation. When its echoes had subsided, in a loud, clear voice he proceeded to intone a litany in Latin. The responses from a hundred and sixty-nine throats rolled through the ruin like thunder.

The service went on and on. The prisoners thought it would never end. But, as it proceeded, the square of leprous skin became more and more agitated. It began to heave. Big, oily bubbles appeared on the surface. As they burst, a horrid stench filled the air. Gradually the repulsive crust broke up into scores of smaller pieces. From between them steam began to rise. Soon even the pieces were obscured by it. The whole square had become a Pit from which clouds of smoke were billowing upward.

The Prince shrieked a last conjuration. *Zazas, Zazas, Nasatanada, Zazas!* The congregation repeated it three times. Then silence fell. Now, in the smoky mist, forms were perceptible. They were not solid, but transparent, yet their appearance was terrifying. Among them were human faces supported by bats' wings, snakes with arms and claws, rats with eyes on stalks and two tails, toads with eyes as large as the rest of their bodies, mosquitoes as big as pheasants, winged swine that had only hind legs, grossly fat, undulating slugs that were armed with claws, three-foot-long phalli, women's genitals in proportion on four legs, a griffin with webbed feet and a spiked tail, a lynx with two heads and a curved horn between them.

These horrors, the prisoners knew, were the demons and demiurges that the Prince was raising out of Hell, to batten on all that was unclean down in the settlement, and drive the people there half crazy with fear.

As they surged upward through the smoke and out through the open roof, an awed silence had grasped the whole community. Rex swung round on the Duke and cried:

'Can we do nothing? Is there no way to stop it?'

The Duke's reply came clearly. 'Only one way. The Pit could be closed by a voluntary sacrifice. Someone who does not fear Satan must throw himself down into Hell.' Drawing a quick breath, he added, 'That could also save all of you.' Next moment he had taken a quick step forward.

'No!' cried Richard. 'No!' and grasped one of his arms to pull him back, while Rex grabbed the other.

Silvia was standing only a few feet away and had heard de Richleau's words. Her face chalk white, she gave one swift glance at the prisoners, and shouted, 'I brought you into this. I renounce Satan and all his works.' Throwing up her arms, she hurled herself forward and through the smoke into the Pit.

Instantly, there came an ear-splitting crash of thunder. Forked lightning streaked down from the sky. The walls of the temple began to rock. Simon grasped Miranda. He pulled her to him, so that her face should be buried in his chest and she should be spared the sight of the terrible things that were happening about them. Screams and curses rent the air. The scores of naked black, white and brown bodies of the congregation now formed a writhing mass. The lightning played among them, causing terrible havoc. Struck down or reeling about with terrible burns, they endeavoured in vain to escape. Some were crushed under falling masonry, others fell fainting to the floor. The twelve chiefs of covens on the far side of the Pit from the prisoners fared no better. Their robes on fire, their faces scorched, they fled screaming, only to trip and crash into the heaps of dead and dying that now filled the body of the temple.

The Duke's eyes were on the Prince. His features were handsome no longer. In seconds he had aged fifty years. His